The Destruction

of Convoy PQ.17

DAVID IRVING

Simon and Schuster : New York

INTRODUCTION

ALL BOOKS have something which their authors most wish to bring to their readers' attention. Some authors are successful in this, and their readers remain prejudiced to the authors' points of view for the rest of their reading lives; some authors are not, and when the last page, the last appendix and wearisome footnote have been scanned the reader asks himself: what was it all about?

I fear that I fall into the latter category, and lest this book be misunderstood its readers should know before they enter into the narrative proper that the guiding light in deciding which incidents in this canvas of tragedy to dwell upon, and which to suppress, has been a conviction that gallantry is best portrayed in its real setting; the ships should be shown to be crewed by normal men with normal fears and feelings. Too often one has read histories of individual acts of heroism, and one's appreciation has been dulled by the picture's lack of relationship to normal human character. So *The Destruction of Convoy PQ.17* is primarily a book peopled with ordinary people: we see how men reacted when confronted with a grim situation which meant certain disaster and probably death. But against this sombre background we shall find that the individual jewels of gallantry sparkle most, emerging unexpectedly to dazzle us by their now unaccustomed shine.

Nor can there be any doubt but that in PQ.17 it *is* a sombre background; crews mutiny, and are confined in chains below decks; their Masters haul down the Allied flags and display signals reading 'Unconditional Surrender'; they deliberately run aground and abandon their vessels; nine merchant ships are deserted by their crews even though still seaworthy, some of them before they have even been attacked; and American captains volunteer to scuttle their ships so that they can finish their voyage in safety. But it is this background which allows one fully to savour the heroism of the few brave men, faced with identical perils, who single-handed bring their ships and cargoes into port, often against the wishes of their crews, with officers like the British lieutenant who urged the Americans to drop their plan to scuttle their ships, like the Welsh rescue-ship captain whose gallantry was such that he was one of the first three Merchant Navy officers to win the military Distinguished Service Order.

In the story of PQ.17 we find that there are indeed *two* kinds of courage in war—both the single and outstanding acts of reckless gallantry with which we have come to associate the individual units of the Royal Navy, and a quiet moral courage which alone can sustain an officer in acting against his every human instinct, when he understands from the orders given him that this is the only way in which he can serve the higher plan. The dogged manner in which Captain E. D. W. Lawford of the anti-aircraft ship *Pozarica* (afterwards awarded a D.S.O. for his rôle in this operation) carried out the instructions which had been given him in spite of the entreaties of the merchant ships, is an example of moral courage as worthy of our admiration as the more spectacular feats of the smaller vessels' skippers.

These are, I hope, more convincing brands of heroism than the synthetic deeds of valour of which the war's propaganda media were so monotonously full.

✳

Because so much that is wrong has been published about this tragic convoy operation, PQ.17, partly in an attempt to depict all the participants as heroes and partly in an endeavour to lay the blame for the disaster on officers who were least at fault, I have felt compelled to weary the reader with extensive indications of my sources, so that the reader may rest assured that even the least credible part of the narrative is securely footed in contemporary war records.

The original research for this book was done in 1962 and 1963 in the commission of Neuer Verlag, Cologne, and I am grateful to Herr Egon Fein for permission to make use in this work of all the material then collected, to which considerable further material has since been added, notably the diary and personal records written at the time by one of the RN lieutenants, Mr James Caradus, of New Zealand, and a detailed chronicle of the operations of the cruiser covering force, written by Mr Douglas E.

Fairbanks, Jr, at the time a lieutenant USNR. I wish to express my thanks to Miss Jean and Captain Henry Hamilton, who gave me permission to use the papers of the late Rear-Admiral Sir Louis Hamilton, one of this book's central figures; and to the Custodian of Manuscripts at the National Maritime Museum for the same reason. Mr Leo Gradwell, Commander Peter Kemp, Mr F. H. Petter, Doctor Jürgen Rohwer and Commander M. G. Saunders all afforded me special assistance, and I am grateful to Rear-Admiral E. M. Eller, Captain F. Kent Loomis, Mr J. Allard and Miss M. D. Mayeux of the US Navy Historical Division for supplying me with copies of German files and the various American war diaries and voyage reports to which reference is made in the notes. Further assistance was rendered by the owners of the convoy's ships—in Britain Chapman and Willan Ltd, the Clyde Shipping Co. Ltd, General Steam Navigation Co. Ltd, J. & C. Harrison Ltd, Hunting and Son Ltd and Royal Mail Lines Ltd; in America Isthmian Lines Inc., Matson Navigation Co., States Steamship Co., United States Lines and Waterman Steamship Corporation; in Norway Wilh. Wilhelmsen of Oslo. The Bundesarchiv in Koblenz provided me with specific documents, and many newspapers in this country and America, including local newspapers, and the American National Maritime Union and National Marine Engineers' Beneficial Association aided me in my search for eye-witnesses and survivors. I found in all over three hundred, British, American and German. Those to whom I am most grateful are: Mr James E. Akins, the late Rt. Hon. Earl Alexander of Hillsborough, Captain G. R. G. Allen, Captain I. J. Andersen, Captain Humphrey Archdale, Mr William Arnell-Smith, Mr Ronald G. Baxter, Mr Philip J. Beard, Mr Patrick Beesley, Mr P. R. B. Bennett, Mr Hawtry Benson, Rear-Admiral Sir R. H. L. Bevan, Mr George R. Bissilf, Herr Otto Bork, Mr S. J. Bowden, the late Admiral Sir E. J. P. Brind, Mr James Bruce, Mr David Burroughs, Mr J. F. Carter, Captain Harold W. Charlton, Mr John Chvostal, Mr John J. Collins, Mr William O. Connolly, Mr J. B. Corlett, Rear-Admiral J. H. F. Crombie, Mr Richard Crossley, Herr Hugo Deiring, Vice-Admiral Sir Norman Denning, Herr Günter Döschner, the late Commodore J. C. K. Dowding, Mr W. A. Dunk, Admiral Sir John Eccles, Mr Hugh Edwards, Captain John Evans, Mr R. B. Fearnside, Mr Eric R.

Fiske, Captain J. R. G. Findley, Mr N. E. Forth, Mr John F. Geisse, Admiral J. H. Godfrey, Mr Thomas Goodwin, Captain Stanley Gordon, Mr Albert Gray, Captain J. Haines, Mr William Harper, Mr Alan L. Harvie, Lieutenant-Commander H. R. A. Higgens, Admiral H. W. Hill, Captain Archibald Hobson, Lieutenant-Colonel Karl-Otto Hoffmann, Captain Rupert F. Hull, Dr Hümmelchen, Mr Richard Keating, Vice-Admiral E. L. S. King, Commander W. E. B. Klinefeld, Mr Iain Laing, Captain C. T. G. Lennard, Mr Frank Lewin, Mr E. A. Leycock, Captain John Litchfield, MP, Dr Norman McCallum, Mr Norman McMahel, Mr Shaun Maloney, Mr Norman McCorison, Captain Guy Maund, Mr J. Mickelburgh, Admiral Sir Geoffrey Miles, Mr E. C. Miller, Mr T. J. Mooney, Admiral Sir H. R. Moore, Captain Owen C. Morris, Mr K. Morton, Mr Ted Narovas, Captain C. A. G. Nichols, Mr T. D. Nield, Commander P. E. Newstead, Mr L. H. Norgate, Dr Arthur J. O'Friell, Captain John Pascoe, Herr Emil Plambeck, Mr William H. Porter, Mr N. E. Platt, Captain E. Rainbird, Lieutenant-Commander J. G. Rankin, Commander Reinhard Reche, Mr Robert P. Rucker, Herr Admiral a. D. Hubert Schmundt, Herr Hermann Schwabe, Vice-Admiral R. M. Servaes, Mr Leslie F. Smith, Mr E. G. Soliman, Commander S. S. Stammwitz, Captain Mervyn C. Stone, Mr D. D. Summers, Mr H. C. Summers, Mr W. G. Taylor, Mr Lloyd Thomas, Mr H. B. Tours, Mr P. Vance, Mr J. Waterhouse, Mr S. Webster, Captain J. Wharton, Mr Alexander Williams, and Mr Jack Wright.

I am also deeply indebted to my Father, the late Commander John Irving, R.N. Retired, who made valuable contributions to the manuscript at every stage, but died a few months before it could be published.

CONTENTS

ILLUSTRATIONS

Photograph Sections

General-Admiral Carls
Rear-Admiral von Puttkamer

Tirpitz
Imperial War Museum

Lützow
Imperial War Museum

Admiral Hipper
Imperial War Museum

Admiral Scheer
Imperial War Museum

Tirpitz in Foetten Fiord
Official photograph: Crown Copyright reserved. Courtesy: Admiral Denning

The German air-raid on Murmansk, 1 July 1942
Benno Wundshammer

Commander Reinhard Reche
Gunter Döschner

Lieutenant-Commander Heinz Bielfeld
Herman Schwabe

FOLLOWING PAGE 194

KG.30's Ju.88s attack PQ. 17, 4 July
Both: Benno Wundshammer

The Heinkels of *KG. 26* attack PQ. 17 on 4 July
Both: Associated Press

The British freighter *Navarino* is hit
US Navy Department

A torpedo hits the Russian tanker *Azerbaijan*
Associated Press

The rescue ship *Zamalek*
Associated Press

Paymaster-Commander N. E. Denning
Courtesy: Admiral Denning

HMS *Keppel*
  Imperial War Museum

Lieutenant Gradwell
  Courtesy: Leo Gradwell

Ju.88 bomber crews being briefed, 5 July
  Benno Wundshammer

Ayrshire
  US Navy Department

Two lone merchant ships of PQ. 17 after the convoy had been scattered
  Both: Benno Wundshammer

The sinking of *Bolton Castle*
  Both: Benno Wundshammer

Carlton's happy survivors, by *Signal*
  Benno Wundshammer

Paulus Potter, abandoned
  Benno Wundshammer

Captain O. C. Morris and the crew of *Zamalek*
  Both: Courtesy Captain Morris

Earlston's barrage balloon
  Otto Bork

Survivors from *Earlston* approaching U-334
  Otto Bork

FOLLOWING PAGE 290

Lieutenant James Caradus
  Courtesy: James Caradus

Captain F. W. Harvey
  Imperial War Museum

Pozarica and *Poppy* in Matochkin Strait
  Courtesy: James Caradus

Pan Atlantic, hit by a bomb

Olopana breaks in two
  Courtesy: Hugo Deiring

HMS *Britomart*
    Imperial War Museum

Commander Friedrich-Karl Marks

The *coup de grâce* for *Hoosier*

HMS *Dianella*
    Imperial War Museum

Ironclad aground in Matochkin Strait
    US Navy Department

The sinking of *Paulus Potter*
    Courtesy: Hugo Deiring

Colonel-General Stumpff awards decorations to his pilots
    Benno Wundshammer

The crew of *U-334* receive their commendations
    Otto Bork

Maps and Diagrams

Facsimiles

THE DESTRUCTION OF CONVOY PQ. 17

THE REGULAR MILLSTONE

1942

These Russian convoys are becoming a regular millstone round our necks. . . .—Admiral Sir Dudley Pound to Admiral King, USN, 18 May 1942

THE SUMMER OF 1942 saw German military accomplishment at its zenith. Waves of grey men and armour were storming eastwards across the Soviet Union, and thrusting deep into Egypt, extending the domain of German rule over the greatest area it ever had been, or ever would be. All but a fraction of British armour in the Middle Eastern desert had been crushed; Tobruk had fallen with over thirty thousand men, and the British Eighth Army was on the retreat. The evacuation of the great port of Alexandria had begun; by the first days of July 1942, Cairo was in panic and the British embassy and military headquarters were already destroying their files, while unseemly crowds of refugees packed the city's railway station.

At the beginning of the fourth week of June, the Germans had unleashed their major summer offensive in the Soviet Union too, crashing through the Russian lines and beginning that summer's extraordinary advance on the Volga and the Caucasus. It was at this time that a Conservative member of the British Parliament placed on the Order Book a motion that the House had lost confidence in Mr Winston Churchill's direction of the war. During the debate which followed on 1 July, Sir Archibald Southby, Conservative MP for Epsom, raised his voice in protest at the continuing slaughter of Allied ships running the Arctic convoy routes to North Russia: 'It is true to say that upon the merchant navies of the Allies rests our hope of victory, and the hope of salvation of all those who are now enslaved under the Axis. The world will never be able to repay the debt it owes to the officers and men of the Merchant Navy.' He continued by warning:

If then, by foolish strategy, we suffer reverse after reverse which not only involve us in military defeats but dissipate the sea power upon which the whole of our war effort is built, we render impossible the fulfilment of the task of guarding those merchant ships upon which we all depend.[1]*

Three days after he had uttered this warning, the British Admiralty took a certain decision, and issued orders to an Allied convoy bound for Russia, which resulted in the loss of two-thirds of its ships. It is true that the convoy, PQ.17, would never have been sailed had it not been for the Prime Minister's personal directive: but it took more than 'foolish strategy' for the disaster to assume the proportions which it did.[2]

✳ 2 ✳

'The Russian convoy', said Rear-Admiral Hamilton, 'is and always has been an unsound operation of war.'[3] The first convoy from Great Britain to Russia had sailed in August 1941, two months after the German armed forces had invaded the Soviet Union. By the spring of 1942 only one ship out of the 103 that had made the passage had been lost; twelve convoys had been sailed to north Russia. The one casualty was a merchant ship lost to a German submarine as the new year began, the first appearance of U-boats in the Arctic. The presence of enemy submarines brought a new threat to the escorting cruisers, as it was no longer safe for them to cruise at the 8 knots the average convoy made; the cruisers were ordered in future to leave the convoy between 14° East and 26° East—the most likely zone of U-boat operations—and hurry through it at increased speed, to rejoin the convoy emerging from the other side of this zone. At that time it was considered unlikely that the Germans would risk their surface units in waters infested with their own submarines, so the cruisers could be dispensed with temporarily in that zone.

The next convoy, PQ.8,† was also attacked by submarines,

---

* Throughout this book, superior figures refer to sources, which are listed chapter by chapter, commencing on page 307.

† The officer in the Admiralty's Director of Operations Division originally charged with planning the north Russian convoys was one Commander P. Q. Edwards: the eastbound convoys were soon popularly known as 'P.Q.'s' convoys, while the westbound convoys logically became 'QP' convoys.[4]

north-east of the Kola Inlet, the entrance to the port of Murmansk, and on 18 January one of the two escorting destroyers—the *Matabele*—was sunk with nearly all hands. The British authorities were particularly disturbed by the increasing effort being devoted to attacks on these convoys now, as the early spring was approaching: the ice-barrier would not have receded far enough to the north to permit the convoys to give northern Norway, with the German air bases, a wide berth; while the combination of fair weather and short hours of darkness would give the enemy the greatest advantage.

It became one of the chief commitments of Admiral Sir John C. Tovey, the Commander-in-Chief of the British Home Fleet, to ensure the safe passage of these convoys. He pointed out to the Admiralty that attacks on the convoys might well reach a scale beyond the escorting resources of the Home Fleet. He suggested that the Russians should be pressed to patrol the Kola Inlet and make it uninhabitable to the German submarines; they should also provide fighter aircraft to protect the convoys, as it was foolhardy for British cruisers to accompany the convoys through hazardous submarine zones solely to provide additional anti-aircraft defence for the convoys. For some time his appeal remained unheeded.

For Germany, the triumphant summer of 1942 had been preceded by the disappointments of the winter campaign in Russia, the bitter months when the Germans had been checked at the very gates of Moscow, and their forces in North Africa had been on the defensive too. It was a winter that had brought renewed pressure on their exposed northern flank in the Arctic, where the newly belligerent United States had completed their occupation of Iceland.[5] On Christmas Day 1941, the German High Command (*OKW*) cited information which indicated that Great Britain and the United States were planning a major operation in the Scandinavian area, and ordered an immediate investigation of the prospects of defeating an Allied invasion attempt in Norway; the conclusions were not encouraging.[6]

By chance, two days later the Royal Navy staged a seaborne raid on the Lofoten Islands, off the north-western coast of Norway, and this undertaking—although unconnected with any Allied invasion plan—gave a sharp stimulus to the German fears:

all eyes in the German higher commands turned to the northern theatre of operations, and the Führer's own stubborn belief in an impending Allied invasion of those shores once again guided the Germans in their immediate strategic dispositions. To meet the danger to this exposed northern flank, Adolf Hitler ordained that the Norwegian coastal defences should be reinforced, and that Germany's most powerful naval forces should be concentrated in Norwegian waters. In connection with Norway's air defence, he rated torpedo-carrying aircraft very highly.

> The German fleet must therefore use all its forces for the defence of Norway [the Führer was reported as deciding on 29 December]. It would be expedient to transfer all battleships there for this purpose. The latter could be used for attacking convoys in the north, for instance.[7]

The Commander-in-Chief of the German Navy and Chief of Naval Staff, Grand-Admiral Erich Raeder, expressed himself unconvinced of their suitability for such an active rôle. Despite his objections, the middle of January 1942 saw the new battleship *Tirpitz* transferred to Trondheim, a move the German Naval Staff had in fact been planning since November primarily for the effect it would have in tying down British heavy naval units.[8] The battleship berthed at Trondheim on 16 January 1942. Commanded by Captain Topp, she was the most formidable warship afloat. The Admiralty Intelligence officer most concerned with the German surface vessels later declared that '*Tirpitz* and *Bismarck* were in my opinion two of the finest battleships ever built.'[9] With a displacement of 42,000 tons and eight 15-inch guns as her main armament, *Tirpitz* would have been a match for any vessel the Allies could confront her with. The strategic effect of her move to Norway was great. Mr Churchill estimated at the time that the entire naval situation throughout the whole world would be altered by the battleship's successful destruction; in particular, it would enable the Allies to regain naval supremacy in the Pacific.[10]

Some weeks after *Tirpitz*'s move, the Germans transferred still further heavy warships to Norway. Hitler realized that the time was past for sweeping Atlantic sorties by the battle group at Brest, consisting of the 31,000-ton battleships *Scharnhorst* and *Gneisenau*, sometimes called 'battle-cruisers', and the 14,000-ton heavy cruiser *Prinz Eugen*. Brest was now the sole Atlantic base available to the Germans, and if the warships were to stay bottled up indefinitely there, well within range of RAF Bomber Command, the Germans would sooner or later have to reckon with their warships being crippled in air attacks. On Hitler's orders, the battle group was withdrawn eastwards through the English Channel in the second week of February 1942. The immediate value of the break-out was lessened by the mine damage sustained by both battleships during the dash and by subsequent further air-raid damage to *Gneisenau* while lying in dock at Kiel. Only *Prinz Eugen* was fit to sail for Trondheim, with the 11,000-ton heavy cruiser *Admiral Scheer* (sometimes called a 'pocket-battleship') in attendance, on 20 February. Bad luck still dogged the German Navy's movements: off the Norwegian coast *Prinz Eugen*'s rudder was blown off by a British submarine's torpedo, and she had to return to Germany from Norway for repairs. While the German plan to form a squadron composed of *Tirpitz*, *Admiral Scheer* and *Prinz Eugen* 'to conduct offensive and defensive operations from Trondheim in northern waters' had gone awry, they could still mount a formidable striking force from Norway.

The dual rôle now expected of the Home Fleet increased the anxieties of Admiral Tovey: how could he guard against a break-out by this powerful German squadron through the northern passages into the Atlantic, while at the same time covering the passage of the Allied convoys to north Russia? He warned that no disposition of the Home Fleet could adequately protect both the convoys and the northern passages.[11] With the present concentration of German heavy warships in Norway, Tovey expected any or all of them to attack the convoys to the west of Bear Island while the eastern part of the convoy route would be subjected exclusively to submarine and air attacks. Plans were accordingly laid for the western part of the next Russian convoy's route to be covered by movements of the Home Fleet.

At the same time, the German Naval Staff had decided that the mere presence of their naval forces in Norway was not sufficient to bind Allied heavy warships in northern waters, and they decided to send out *Tirpitz* to attack the Allies' next eastbound convoy. The sequel to this operation was of the greatest importance for an

understanding of the German battle fleet's behaviour during its
later operations against PQ.17.

✳ 3 ✳

The British convoy PQ.12 sailed in the first week of March at
the same time as the westbound convoy QP.8 left the Russian end.
The battleship *Tirpitz*, wearing the flag of Vice-Admiral Ciliax
(Flag Officer Battleships), put out with three destroyers of the 5th
Destroyer Flotilla, to attack it.[12] According to their operation
order, they were to 'avoid becoming embroiled with superior
enemy forces', while they were to accept battle with equal or
inferior forces in so far as this did not prevent them from dis-
charging their main function, destroying the convoy. Lone
merchantmen were *not* to be attacked, to preserve the element of
surprise.

Admiral Ciliax did not think highly of accepting battle with
'equal forces', as a duel with a battleship like *King George V* would
result in *Tirpitz* being badly damaged at least; for the possible loss
or damaging of one of many enemy battleships, it was not worth
it. The German Naval Staff in Berlin subsequently endorsed
Ciliax's view.

So much for the best laid plans: on the outward run, the German destroyers found a lone Russian merchantman straggling far
behind the westbound convoy, and despite their clear orders to
the contrary opened fire on her; before the luckless Russian sank,
she transmitted a wireless signal reporting the attack and her
position. Soon after, *Tirpitz*'s wireless room picked up an acknow-
ledgment of the distress signal from the wireless station at
Cleethorpes.

After three days' cruising, and having failed to find the eastbound PQ convoy which had by then been diverted by the
Admiralty, the German warships were ordered to return. The
weather closed in, but early on the morning of 9 March it began
to clear, and at eight o'clock *Tirpitz* saw through the breaks in the
cloud layer several aircraft, apparently shadowing her. The gravity
of the position was at once apparent: the aircraft were Albacores,
which meant that somewhere within striking range there was an
Allied aircraft-carrier. Admiral Ciliax radioed an urgent appeal for

fighter aircraft from nearby Bodö airfield, but the naval radio
station there was out of order and the fighters never came. Too
late, the Germans realized their exposed position—uncomfortably
similar to the situation which had sealed *Bismarck*'s fate in May
1941, and that of *Prince of Wales* and *Repulse* seven months later.
As Ciliax looked about himself he saw *Tirpitz* accompanied by
only one destroyer—the other two having been detached for
refuelling—and this one remaining destroyer was unserviceable
because of ice formation and the heavy seas; the battleship had no
air cover, and there was an enemy aircraft-carrier within striking
range. Why had his wireless room picked up no nearby Allied
wireless traffic? He knew that an Allied carrier would not have
ventured so far into Norwegian waters without an adequate
battle fleet to protect her. The *Tirpitz* was trapped.

Ciliax turned to make a dash for the shelter of the Lofoten
Islands, and catapulted an aircraft to drive off his shadowers; but
his aircraft met a cloud of Albacores coming in to attack the
German battleship. Twenty-five torpedo aircraft attacked *Tirpitz*
in a nine-minute battle which none of the German sailors was
ever likely to forget, the British aircraft racing in three and six at
a time from every angle, heedless of the defences, forcing the
battleship to dodge, yaw and weave in a way that she cannot have
been designed to do. This time, as the Germans afterwards wryly
commented, the luck was on their side: *Tirpitz* was able to comb
the torpedo tracks and they all missed, every one of them. The
only German casualties were three officers on the battleship's
bridge, injured by machine-gun fire from the planes.

At the time, the Allies did not realize the fright which the sudden encounter with carrier aircraft had given the Germans; but
from this traumatic experience the Germans derived an 'aircraft-
carrier complex' which was to beset all the remaining operations
of the German capital ships.

The muffing of this opportunity to engage *Tirpitz* was the
object of some recrimination among the Royal Naval officers who
had participated in the action. Rear-Admiral L. H. K. Hamilton,
newly appointed commander of the First Cruiser Squadron, called
particular attention to the Fleet's difficulties in situations where
the Commander-in-Chief, Admiral Tovey, was at sea and unable

to break wireless silence, even in an operation so basically simple as this.[13] Stressing that the enemy would take every possible precaution to avoid *Tirpitz*'s being brought into action, and was 'believed to have adequate arrangements for direction-finding', Hamilton pointed out that it was unrealistic to expect a Commander-in-Chief if at sea to maintain wireless silence during vital operations lasting over a period of several days: the fact was that the movement of a single W/T key in a capital ship in a position to intercept *Tirpitz* would be sufficient to drive her back forthwith to the shelter of the fiords.

The corollary of the British Commander-in-Chief's having been at sea during the last operation, with the consequent need for him to maintain strict wireless silence, had been that at one stage Tovey was controlling the movements of his battle fleet and aircraft-carrier, while the Admiralty was controlling his cruisers and destroyers; at 5.22 p.m. on 8 March, Tovey had eventually been obliged to wireless the Admiralty, stating his position and intentions, and asking them to operate his cruisers and destroyers for him. This, commented Hamilton, was hardly the most effective way of conducting operations. Notwithstanding these criticisms, the Commander-in-Chief persisted in accompanying the Home Fleet to sea during convoy operations up to PQ.17; after which, as will be seen, he desisted. For the time being, also, the Admiralty continued to intervene in the fleet's operations, to Tovey's 'serious embarrassment'.[14]

The British were not alone in drawing important conclusions from the attack on *Tirpitz* by aircraft from a British carrier on 9 March. For the character of the operations of the German battle fleet against PQ.17, and for Hitler's own attitude to such operations, the conclusions reached by Raeder and the German Naval Staff from this first sortie by *Tirpitz* were eloquent:

> The course of events shows our own naval weakness in these northern waters. The enemy responds to every German sortie by sending out strong battle groups, particularly *aircraft-carriers*, which must be recognized as *the most dangerous opponents* of our heavy ships!
>
> It is an indication of our own extremely exposed position that the enemy dares to advance into our own northern coastal waters with-

out being annihilated by the German Air Force. Our own escort
forces (destroyers, torpedo-boats) are numerically so weak that our
capital ships are inevitably under the utmost pressure during air
attacks and enemy engagements.[15]

Reporting on this to the Führer three days after *Tirpitz*'s escape,
Raeder insisted that as long as Germany had no aircraft-carriers,
the German Air Force must provide the closest land-based support for any planned naval operations from Norway. Raeder's
own belief was that as there could be no major naval operations
in the Arctic without committing the whole German battle fleet
based on Norway, it would be better for them to stay at anchor,
as a fleet-in-being able to deter the Allies from undertaking invasion operations. They must be risked in Arctic operations only
when the German Air Force could establish beyond doubt exactly
where the enemy was, and was strong enough to neutralize any
enemy aircraft-carriers in the vicinity.

The final conclusion the Germans drew from *Tirpitz*'s adventure was not capable of early implementation: the Germans must
proceed with all haste with the construction of their own aircraft-
carriers, and the provision of suitable aircraft. Hitler agreed that
he believed now that an aircraft-carrier was urgently needed.
Work on the only carrier under construction, the *Graf Zeppelin*,
had in fact been shut down earlier because of the steel shortage.*
Now Hitler realized that the sooner a battle group comprising,
say, *Tirpitz*, *Scharnhorst*, an aircraft-carrier, two heavy cruisers
and some twelve or fourteen destroyers could be formed, the
better: that would change the character of the German naval
position in northern waters—and indeed elsewhere—more
decisively than any other action.

Two days after his evening discussion with Grand-Admiral
Raeder at the 'Wolf's Lair', Hitler issued the first order for inten-
sive operations against the Allied convoy traffic to Murmansk,
'which so far has hardly been touched.'[17] The Navy was to concentrate more submarines in the north for this purpose, and the

* On 13 April 1942, Raeder had to report to Hitler that for technical
reasons the *Graf Zeppelin* would not be completed before the end of
1943; and a month later Hitler began to plan in terms of converting
four other ships into auxiliary aircraft-carriers, 'even at this late date'.[16]

Air Force was to strengthen its long-range reconnaissance and bomber forces in that region, and to move up torpedo-bombers from other theatres of war; the Air Force was instructed to keep Murmansk under constant air attack, to survey the waters between Bear Island and the Murman coast, to interdict the convoy traffic itself and to attack the escorting warships.

Five days later, the new 14,000-ton heavy cruiser *Admiral Hipper* also left Germany for Norway, where she anchored near the *Tirpitz* at Trondheim. As the build-up for the major surface attack on north Russian convoys continued, the Germans began attacks with light forces. On 28 March three destroyers of the 8th Flotilla sailed to attack PQ.13, then passing North Cape barely one hundred miles off the coast. Because of inadequate air reconnaissance, the destroyers failed to locate the convoy, which had become widely scattered; they did locate and sink a Panamanian vessel, whose survivors disclosed to them the composition and movements of the erstwhile convoy's escort. The destroyers altered to engage these vessels, and in appalling conditions that evening fought a series of confused actions against the cruiser *Trinidad* and two British destroyers. During the actions, *Trinidad* was damaged by a torpedo (one of her own) and two guns of the destroyer *Eclipse* were knocked out. The convoy itself lost one-quarter of its merchantmen during German air and submarine attacks. The Germans claimed 'a notable success'.

Looking back on the history of the north Russian convoy operations up to this point, Admiral Tovey called attention to the importance which the enemy now clearly attached to stopping convoy traffic.[2] There was evidence enough for this in the continued northward movement of enemy warships and of submarines and aircraft reinforcements: clearly every north Russian convoy would now involve the Allies in a major fleet operation. Tovey was promised a number of destroyers and corvettes from Western Approaches for the next convoys; and early in April he received sufficient to increase each convoy's anti-submarine escort to ten vessels. The Russians were also pressed—and agreed—to receive an RAF Coastal Command mission to assist them in organizing their own over-seas reconnaissance and fighter-escort services, particularly at the eastern end of the convoys' 2,000-mile journeys from Iceland. They were also asked to bomb the

German airfields in northern Norway. 'The result was disappointing', commented Tovey later.*

Early in April the First Sea Lord, Admiral Sir Dudley Pound, warned the Cabinet's Defence Committee that geographic conditions in the Arctic were so heavily in the enemy's favour that losses to the convoys might well reach a point where their running became an uneconomical proposition; but political pressure for their continuance was mounting in both London and Washington.[19] Alarmed by the increasing scale of enemy attack, Admiral Tovey proposed during the third week of April that if the convoys could not be postponed until the ice receded farther north, they should at least be limited in size; but on the 27th, President Roosevelt cabled Mr Churchill a reminder that the USA had made such a 'tremendous effort' to get its supplies moving to Russia that it seemed to him it would be a serious mistake to have them blocked, 'except for most compelling reasons'.[20] At this level, the objections advanced by Tovey were not considered 'compelling': the convoys were not restricted in size, but expanded successively as each one sailed, far beyond the prudent limits ascertained by the Admiralty's operational research.

President Roosevelt informed Mr Churchill soon afterwards that there were at the end of April 107 ships loaded or being loaded in Britain and America; he wanted to see them being moved within the next month. On 2 May, Churchill replied: 'With very great respect, what you suggest is beyond our power to fulfil.' He could not, he said, press the Admiralty any further. Four days later Marshal Stalin was also approaching Churchill with a request to 'take all possible measures' to ensure that the supplies reached Russia during May: 'This is extremely important for our front.'

In that same month, Admiral Tovey went so far as to advocate a reduction in the number of convoys during the coming months: the improvement in the condition of the German bomber airfields and in their aerial reconnaissance service would greatly facilitate the enemy's operations, while the ice barrier would still not have receded far enough to the north to allow the convoys to evade

---

* The Russians did bomb Banak airfield in the first two days of July, destroying three of *KG.30*'s Junkers 88s on the ground.[18]

them. Three bombing attacks had now been delivered on the anchored *Tirpitz* within a space of thirty days by RAF Bomber Command, but these costly operations had resulted in no hits at all. And still the United States was insisting on first priority for the convoys. It seemed there was little prospect of their reduction.

✳ 4 ✳

There is no doubt that by now Adolf Hitler believed that Germany's ultimate victory could depend on her destroying the greatest possible weight of Allied shipping tonnage: if they could achieve a steady attrition of the merchant fleets, they could slow down all the Allies' offensive operations or even choke them off altogether. In this connection he reaffirmed in mid-April[21] that 'attacks on the Murmansk convoys are most important at the moment'.*

Grand-Admiral Raeder did not see the tactical conditions for a full-scale German fleet attack on the PQ convoys met as yet; but on 1 May a German naval operation was mounted with the objective of finishing off the British cruiser *Edinburgh*—crippled by a U-boat while proceeding about fifteen miles ahead of the eastbound PQ.15 on the day before. Admiral Hubert Schmundt, the German 'Admiral Commanding, Arctic' (*Admiral Nordmeer*), sent out three destroyers, including the large destroyer *Hermann Schoemann* (Captain Schulze-Hinrichs) to finish off the British cruiser, lying disabled, her guns in studied disarray. After a skirmish with four destroyers escorting the homeward convoy QP.11, the Germans found *Edinburgh* next day with four smaller vessels fussing round her. They closed in for the kill. Against their expectations, the cruiser's main armament was not out of action, and as they manœuvred into position to launch their torpedoes, *Edinburgh*'s main batteries suddenly tracked round on them and opened fire. The cruiser's second salvo straddled the German flotilla leader *Hermann Schoemann*, stopped both her engines and smashed her funnel. The disabled destroyer had to be abandoned under heavy fire and scuttled by her crew. The sur-

* It is clear how he had come upon this strategy: 'Time and again, Churchill speaks of shipping tonnage as his greatest worry.' Führer Naval Conference, 13 February 1942.

vivors were picked up by another German destroyer and the submarine *U-88* (Lieutenant-Commander Heino Bohmann). The British attempt at salvaging *Edinburgh*, which had been hit by another torpedo, was given up soon after, and her flood valves were opened to sink her.[22]

In the meantime, the cruiser *Trinidad* had had her self-inflicted torpedo wound temporarily repaired at Murmansk. She left on 13 May *en route* for the United States for a more permanent refit. She was sighted by German aircraft next day, bombed and abandoned.

The loss of *Edinburgh* and *Trinidad* underlined to the British Commander-in-Chief the grave risk to which heavy naval vessels of convoy-covering forces were constantly exposed in the waters east of Bear Island, not only from German submarines but from German aircraft. For a great part of the route there were up to eight submarines operating against them, and the necessity for conserving fuel did not permit protracted anti-submarine chases; the submarines could be put down and harassed, but seldom destroyed. So although it was adequately recognized that the cruiser forces could provide effective cover only if in the immediate vicinity of the convoy, it was here that the cruisers were most endangered by enemy submarines.

The inevitable result was that just as the Germans were plagued by their 'aircraft-carrier complex', so the British—smarting from the loss of their two cruisers—were now equally troubled by fears for their cruisers in the face of attacks by German submarines and bombers. Admiral Tovey went so far as to recommend that unless the enemy airfields in northern Norway could be neutralized, or until the months of darkness returned, the convoys should be stopped altogether. 'If they must continue for political reasons,' he warned, 'very serious and heavy losses must be expected.'[23] The political reasons were very formidable, however. On 17 May the Prime Minister minuted the Chiefs of Staff Committee:

> Not only Premier Stalin but President Roosevelt will object very much to our desisting from running the convoys now. The Russians are in heavy action, and will expect us to run the risk and pay the price entailed by our contribution. The United States ships are queueing up. My own feeling, mingled with much anxiety, is that the

convoy [PQ. 16] ought to sail on the 18th. The operation is justified if a half gets through.[24]

It was in his view that to fail to make the attempt would weaken Britain's influence with both her major Allies, while on the other hand the vagaries of the Arctic weather or—failing that—good fortune might work on the British side. The Admiralty did not share Mr Churchill's callous sentiment. 'These Russian convoys are becoming a regular millstone round our necks,' Sir Dudley Pound told Admiral E. J. King, the American chief of naval operations, on 18 May; and again: 'The whole thing is a most unsound operation, with the dice loaded against us in every direction.'[25] Pound's sentiments were echoed by every officer engaged on the north Russian convoy movements. But they were overruled—the convoy operations were pressed to the inevitable climax which forms the central subject of this book.

✳ 5 ✳

The clear conclusion drawn by the Germans from their light forces' sorties into the Barents Sea (on 23 March and 2 May) was that destroyer flotillas could not be matched against Allied convoys covered by cruisers if the Germans were not to suffer such casualties as to make these operations unprofitable.

The German Navy's heavy warships had been offered no opportunity to strike at Russian convoy traffic since the first alarming sortie of *Tirpitz* in March; as the Germans themselves admitted, their own aerial reconnaissance was still inadequate to permit major surface operations. *Tirpitz's* one brief March sweep with three destroyers had alone cost the German Navy some 7,500 tons of fuel oil and the consequent critical logistic situation of the naval forces in Norway ruled out any extended fleet operation where the enemy had not been clearly identified and located first.[26] This did not affect the submarines; they operated on diesel oil, of which there was as yet no real shortage.

By the beginning of May, the offensive build-up ordered by the Führer two months before was taking effect: the Navy now had one battleship of no mean capabilities, two heavy cruisers, eight destroyers and twenty submarines stationed along the Norwegian coast at Trondheim, Narvik, and Kirkenes. Of the twenty sub-marines, twelve had been allocated to the anti-convoy operations, the remainder being defensively deployed. The German Air Force had also taken immediate action to implement Hitler's order: German airmen subsequently captured during the battle of PQ.17 described to British Intelligence officers how they had been on conversion courses for torpedo-bombers at Grosseto in Italy when 'at about the end of March they were suddenly hurried through the remainder of the course' and sent up to Norway; by the beginning of May the first twelve torpedo-bombers—newly converted from standard Heinkel 111 medium bombers—had been delivered to their units in northern Norway.[27] Nine of the torpedo-bombers of their squadron, the first squadron of *KG.26*, had attacked Convoy PQ.15 on their first-ever sortie into the Arctic on 2 May; they claimed three sinkings.

By the second half of the month the German build-up was complete. The 11,000-ton heavy cruiser ('pocket-battleship') *Lützow* had also arrived in Norway. All the German fleet units available were thus assembled there, waiting for the order from their Commander-in-Chief to mount the first all-out attack on an Allied eastbound convoy.

Despite the fact that this was the least favourable period of the year for convoys in the Arctic, PQ.16, which sailed with thirty-five merchant ships from Iceland on 20 May, was the largest convoy yet to leave for north Russia. A contemporary description by one of the American seamen sailing in this convoy gives the full flavour of the hazards of northern convoy duties: his ship was the elderly American freighter *Carlton*, laden with a cargo of explosives, tanks and tank ammunition and bound for Murmansk with a crew of forty-five seamen. The 5,217-ton vessel had left Philadelphia in March, on the day before Hitler had signed the order for an intensification of attacks on Murmansk convoy traffic. To add to the freighter's trials, it had sailed from Philadelphia on a Friday the Thirteenth: even the novices among the freighter's crew knew that this was cocking a snook at implacable Fate. The name *Carlton* was to hover over the disaster of PQ.17 like some bird of ill-omen: everywhere it went, trouble and dislocation was churned up in her wake; and even when the rusty tramp was finally sent down, the curse still did not desert her unhappy crew.

One of her seamen was James E. Akins, who wrote a contemporary record of the ship's last voyage.[28] He had signed on in Philadelphia just before they sailed, and had learned only afterwards that the *Carlton* was destined for Murmansk. Akins was a cynic: 'We were loaded with war materials including 450 tons of high explosive, loaded fore, aft and amidships: they were not taking any chances on our getting through to Russia. . . .'

The *Carlton* proceeded alone to Halifax, Nova Scotia, her seamen gaining a grim forewarning of the hazards of their calling as they passed the steel ribs and skeletons of several ships claimed by prowling German submarines. One ship was a 'Gulf' tanker. Her bows reared a hundred feet out of the sea like some ugly sentinel, marking the start of the 6,000-mile voyage to Russia. Off Halifax the *Carlton* lay idle for seven days. Then she left as part of an Atlantic convoy of sixty-five ships, some heading for Iceland and some for English ports.

On 20 May, the *Carlton* sailed as part of PQ.16, the convoy bound for Murmansk.[29] The Germans planned to deliver their first major assault on this convoy, but because of the fuel shortage the surface warships were not included in the operation. The convoy was given a large escort—five destroyers, four corvettes, four trawlers, one minesweeper and an anti-aircraft ship, and there was a Sea Hurricane fighter-plane waiting on the CAM ship.* As the days passed, the seamen also saw a plane circling the convoy all day long; it was only two days later, when a destroyer opened fire on it, that the Americans realized it was a German shadower. The plane departed to the horizon and kept on circling there, unimpressed by the convoy's escort's fire. 'I began to wonder', said Akins, 'how anyone got medals if this was what they called war.'

Three days later, on the 25th, he had his answer: a flight of eight bombers was seen approaching at low level on the horizon, while high overhead about twenty Junkers 88 dive-bombers appeared; one by one the latter peeled off and dived on the merchantmen. One plane flew close to *Carlton* and her gunners

* Catapult Aircraft Merchantman.

[16]

opened fire with their machine-guns, putting about five hundred rounds into the aircraft before it caught fire. A man baled out, and the plane—the CAM ship's Sea Hurricane—crashed into the sea.

The attack was hardly over before 'eight bells' sounded and Akins went on watch as a lookout on the foc's'le-head, directly above most of the ship's explosive cargo in No. 1 hatch. He confessed that he would have given his right arm to have got out of that watch: 'Another plane dived on us and gave us the works. There were three or four bombs within three feet of us, one by the poop deck, one by No. 4 and two amidships. They sank about fifty feet and then went off one at a time.' The ship was picked up 'like an egg-shell' and Akins heard the Master shouting to the crew to stand by the lifeboats. He admitted breaking all speed records himself in reaching his lifeboat station. When he arrived there, everything was blanketed in steam issuing from the engine-room. The *Carlton*'s Norwegian captain, Hansen, refused to abandon ship, but asked the chief engineer to see what damage had been done. 'The chief engineer did not know, and looked like he didn't care either; so Captain Hansen asked me to go and take a look around and find out about the damage. I said I was willing, but that as I was a sailor I wouldn't know what damage there was when I saw it.'

Finally two seamen, one of them an oiler destined not to survive the German attack on PQ.17, went below. They reported that all the steam pipes were broken. Now Akins and the boatswain were sent below to take soundings in the shaft-alley, about as far below decks as human beings could penetrate: 'We went all right, but not cheerfully.' They had taken the soundings when two more bombs detonated in close succession right next to the *Carlton*. Akins claimed to have beaten the boatswain back on to deck by thirty feet.

Two British destroyers came alongside the disabled freighter and regretted that they had orders to sink the vessel as she was holding up the escort. Captain Hansen asked the chief engineer whether the damage could be repaired; the engineer replied that given about two hours he felt it could be done. Hansen requested an escort to stay with him, as the convoy proper had now vanished. The escort commander gave him a trawler, *Northern Spray*, to tow them back to Iceland. 'All this time the black gang [the engine-room crew] was on deck, refusing to go below until the chief engineer went too, as is customary in any emergency. Well, Captain Hansen gave them all quite a *spiel* and they all went below, leaving the chief engineer on deck "to watch for planes".'

Even then the *Carlton* was not left unmolested: after twelve laborious hours in tow of the tiny trawler, the nervous Americans —whose natural thirst for coffee was unfortunately unrequitable as the drinking-water had been polluted by a leaking oil line— spotted a second plane coming in to attack. The trawler opened fire at the German aircraft and the *Carlton* fired eighteen rounds from her 4-inch gun. The bomber dived too soon and its bombs fell some way short. As the aircraft flew over the freighter, it strafed them with machine-gun fire; the Americans claimed to have hit the plane.

As usual Akins was again on watch when a new threat arose: 'The fourth mate, Franks, was giving us stuff about what we would do if anything bothered us now, when someone reported ships astern of us.' The Americans were understandably jumpy, and began visualizing the whole German fleet closing in. Soon after, one of the warships sent off a plane, and the seamen saw to their relief that it had British roundels. The ships were the carrier *Victorious* with a screen of three destroyers. 'They signalled, "Congratulations on your lucky escape".'

The American freighter limped back into Iceland on 30 May, and her seamen swarmed ashore 'with visions of getting good and drunk', but the strongest beverage they could buy in Iceland was coffee. Akins expressed some dissatisfaction at the almost indecent haste with which the ship was patched up and cleared for the next convoy's sailing: 'I guess they figured, if we stayed any longer we would sink in the harbour.' Their spirits somewhat impaired, the American seamen settled down for the long wait before the next convoy, PQ.17, was due to sail.

While the *Carlton* had still been on its way back to Iceland, the main air attacks on PQ.16 had begun, continuing almost without pause until 30 May; the Germans directed 245 bomber and torpedo-bomber sorties against the convoy, sinking five more ships and damaging three. The Germans believed they had sunk nine, a success which suggested to them that simultaneous attacks by high-level conventional bombers and low-level torpedo-bombers would present the Allied convoy defences with the maximum distraction.[30]

By the time PQ.17 eventually sailed, towards the end of June, the German Air Force had amassed a mighty attacking force of aircraft in the vicinity of North Cape, under the commanding general of the Fifth Air Force, Colonel-General Stumpff: the armada included 103 twin-engined Junkers 88 bombers, fifteen Heinkel 115 torpedo-bombers on floats, thirty Junkers 87 dive-bombers and seventy-four reconnaissance aircraft including the four-engined Focke-Wulf 200—the 'Condor'—the Junkers 88 and the Blohm & Voss 138; all forty-two of *I./KG.26*'s Heinkel 111 torpedo-bombers had also been concentrated at Bardufoss, their training complete. Stumpff thus disposed of 264 operational combat aircraft for the strike.[31]

It should not be thought that the whole German Air Force organization in Norway was of an offensive nature: there was also an Air Force unit engaged solely on Intelligence work of the greatest importance. One company of the Air Force's 5th Signals Regiment had been established at Kirkenes with the primary duty of monitoring and intercepting enemy radio transmissions, whether they originated from the western Allies or from the Russians; particularly important was the interception of wireless signals from aircraft.[32] The German cryptographical service was by that time at the high peak of its efficiency, and we know now from German naval records that at the time Admiralty signals were regularly being intercepted and decoded up to a certain level. The service as a whole was so efficient that they were greatly alarmed lest the Allies realize the extent to which their wireless traffic was being overheard; reports originating from the Kirkenes unit were forwarded without details of how they had been obtained, in order not to compromise their method.

All the main German heavy vessels were now concentrated in Norwegian waters. The battleship *Tirpitz* was at Trondheim, together with the heavy cruiser *Admiral Hipper* and the 5th and 6th Destroyer Flotillas; and the rather slower 'pocket-battleships' *Lützow* and *Scheer* together with the 8th Destroyer Flotilla and the German 'Leader of Flotillas' were farther north at Narvik. This disposition of the surface forces was dictated by the task that lay ahead of them. The units based on Trondheim were to form a 'First Battle Group'—to term them a 'squadron' implies too inflexible a grouping—under the tactical command of Admiral Schniewind, the Fleet Commander, wearing his Flag in *Tirpitz*; while the Narvik units would form a 'Second Battle Group' under Vice-Admiral Kummetz, Flag Officer Cruisers. (Schniewind had temporarily replaced Vice-Admiral Ciliax as Flag Officer Battleships during the latter's illness.)[33]

At first Naval Group North, Schniewind's operational superiors, were uneasy about the idea of committing their heavy warships to an attack on PQ.17: late in May, they pointed out that by the following month the ice edge would have receded sufficiently far for the Air Force to have some difficulty in guaranteeing to locate the enemy's heavy units—a prerequisite for any sortie of the German battle fleet. To preserve some element of surprise, therefore, the group's commanding admiral, General-Admiral Carls, recommended that the Trondheim group should delay its move northwards until *after* the next convoy, PQ.17, had been sighted, and then sail simultaneously with the pocket battleships while U-boats shadowed the convoy.[34]

Admiral Schniewind was more emphatically in favour of a major fleet operation, and when Grand-Admiral Raeder visited Trondheim on 30 May, the Fleet Commander took the opportunity to hand to his Commander-in-Chief his own fifteen-page appreciation of the naval situation in the Arctic. He stated that he was inclined to discount the frequent Intelligence reports warning of imminent Allied landings in Norway; on the other hand, he believed that the Allies would do all in their power to aid the Russians now that the German spring offensive had opened on the Eastern Front. Schniewind suggested a lightning demonstration of German naval superiority against the next Russian convoy; for this the ideal time would be June, when twenty-four hours of daylight would permit continuous aerial reconnaissance, and his own fleet had been strengthened in both destroyers and torpedoboats. Above all, Naval Group North had been allocated some 15,500 tons of fuel oil for its operations in June, a considerable improvement on the May position. In short, Admiral Schniewind recommended a 'simultaneous attack by all naval units in northern waters, including *Tirpitz* and *Hipper*'; he believed that the total destruction of a PQ convoy would have immense consequences on the development of the war at sea.[35]

The Naval Staff was in principle in favour of this proposal, and on 1 June Vice-Admiral Krancke, Raeder's permanent representative at the Führer's headquarters, was asked to inform Hitler that a plan was being weighed which would involve *Tirpitz* putting to sea.[36] June certainly seemed to be the most favourable month for such an operation: the period of spring storms would be over, and the calmer seas would enable the destroyers to exploit their great speeds to the full. Sea fog was less prevalent in June— with an average of only nine days of fog in that month compared with nineteen in July. Against that, the ice barrier would still stand so far to the south that any convoys were bound to pass within 220 or 240 miles* of the German naval and air bases in northern Norway. If the German battle fleet were to lie low in these northernmost fiords, it could be up to the convoy within eight hours of weighing anchor; it could strike at the convoy and be away before the distant cover force of the Allied battle fleet could arrive to offer battle. Past experience strongly suggested that the Allies would contain this force in an area to the west of Jan Mayen Island until then, so that it could equally keep one eye on the northern passages, to guard against a break-out by one of the pocket-battleships into the Atlantic Ocean.

On 4 June, Naval Group North drafted an operational directive for the attack on PQ.17, and General-Admiral Rolf Carls outlined the plan verbally to Admiral Schniewind, Admiral Schmundt (Admiral Commanding, Arctic) and the Fifth Air Force soon after. The written orders were marked Top Secret, and endorsed: 'Number of those in the know is to be restricted to very minimum.' Carls planned that at a given codeword, both battle groups would sail from their advanced bases at speeds and times adjusted so that they would arrive together at a rendezvous off North Cape, from which they would advance on, and destroy, the convoy. 'Above all, the enemy's dispositions demand a swift assault and a brief operation. The primary object of the attack is the rapid destruction

---

* All 'miles' in this book are nautical miles.

of enemy shipping space. To this end it will suffice for ships
to cripple the freighters with gunfire. . . . The taking of prizes,
especially tankers, is important.'³⁷ The operation was to be code-
named 'The Knight's Move'.

The Naval Staff in Berlin formally approved the group's recom-
mendations and the detailed suggestions put forward by Admiral
Schniewind, but learned soon after that Adolf Hitler was still
reluctant to commit his heavy warships. Krancke informed them
that the Führer was not wholeheartedly in agreement; on the
other hand, he had not rejected the plan altogether. This was a
disappointment for the Naval Staff, but they directed Krancke to
reassure Hitler that no kind of 'gamble' was involved, and that
they thought the operation of the highest importance. Hitler was
also to be instructed that the operation's total success would be
in no small measure dependent on the degree of co-operation
provided by the Air Force.³⁸ One suspects that in making this
latter point the German Naval Staff were already preparing a
possible excuse for failure later on.

At first the Air Force ran true to form. Its operations staff
advised the Navy that while the Fifth Air Force would of course
perform a reconnaissance function for the Navy, there could be
no question of doing so at the expense of their bombing effort,
which had been so dramatically demonstrated against PQ.16.
This suggestion that only the Air Force was of any consequence
in the campaign against the Murmansk convoys greatly angered
the Naval Staff, and they pointed out that impressive though the
Air Force's success against PQ.16 had been, it seemed that
twenty-five ships had in fact reached Russia: 'But an operation
like The Knight's Move promises the opportunity, given moderately favourable conditions, of *completely destroying a convoy down to
its very last ship.*'³⁹ In this vein, a detailed scheme was prepared for
Admiral Krancke or—if he should see the Führer first—Grand-
Admiral Raeder himself to put to Hitler, to persuade him to give
his blessing to the operation.⁴⁰

In the meantime, German photographic reconnaissance of
Scapa Flow on the last day of May had shown a formidable collection of British and American warships lying at anchor there,
including three battleships, three heavy cruisers, four light
cruisers and twenty-two destroyers; agents' reports and aerial

reconnaissance showed that there were further Allied warships gathering at Iceland—including aircraft-carriers.

Early in June, German agents reported convoy PQ.17 forming off the south-west coast of Iceland. On 11 June Admiral Schmundt ordered his first three U-boats (*U-251*, *U-376* and *U-408*) to take up patrol positions in the Denmark Strait, watching for the first signs of PQ.17. These U-boats were grouped into the 'Ice Devil' pack. To these and the several U-boats that Schmundt ordered to sea in the next few days, the following instructions were issued:

> During joint operations with our surface forces the following special orders will come into force on reception of codeword *Concord*:
>
> (*a*) positive shadowing of the convoy takes predominance over attacking it;
>
> (*b*) surface forces from destroyers upwards in size may be attacked only when positively identified as hostile. In thick weather or uncertain situations, all attacks on warships are prohibited;
>
> (*c*) our surface forces have orders not to attack submarines, but otherwise to act as though submarines they meet are hostile.[41]

On 14 June, Admiral Schniewind completed his own operation order for *The Knight's Move*.[42] It was outlined by Raeder to Hitler at Berchtesgaden next day.

2

'THE KNIGHT'S MOVE'

Saturday 15 June — Wednesday 1 July

When the chances on both sides are equal, it is intelligence that makes one able to look down on one's opponent, and which proceeds not by hoping for the best (a method only valuable in desperate situations) but by estimating what the facts are, and thus obtaining a clearer vision of what to expect. —Pericles to the Athenians, in Thucydides: *The Peloponnesian War*, Book Two

THE BRIEF LEAVE which Hitler had planned for himself in his private home, the Berghof, at Berchtesgaden during early May had been interrupted by an unseasonal fall of snow; Hitler disliked snow, and he had curtailed his holiday. On 11 June, he left Munich in his special train to resume his leave at Berchtesgaden.[1]

Four evenings later, Grand-Admiral Raeder, his Chief of Naval Staff, hurried to Berchtesgaden from Berlin to broach to the Führer the plan for the battle fleet's attack on Convoy PQ.17. He described to Hitler in detail how their naval forces, including the German capital ships, planned to execute *The Knight's Move*, and drew particular attention to the favourable weather to be expected during June.[2] He assured Hitler that the operation would be executed only if air reconnaissance had established with certainty that the fleet ran no risk of becoming embroiled with superior enemy forces. Hitler showed that one aspect of the operation was still causing him anxiety, and Raeder afterwards wrote:

> The Führer considers aircraft-carriers a great threat to the large vessels. The aircraft-carriers must be located *before* the attack and they must be rendered harmless by our aircraft (Junkers 88s) beforehand.

The only acceptable alternative to this would be if the carrier forces were found to be so distant as to rule out any possibility of their intervening against the German battle fleet before it had broken off its operations and withdrawn. Raeder stressed to Hitler that the Navy was dependent on the Air Force for adequate aerial reconnaissance; he suggested that the Air Force should concentrate on this even at the expense of participating in the attack on the convoy. Given the Navy's prospects of obtaining a total victory with their warships alone, this seemed a not unreasonable request. (In the event, air reconnaissance was to prove the operation's weakest link.) To all this Hitler agreed, and he approved Raeder's plan for the two battle groups to transfer to advanced bases in the far north as soon as the convoy was sighted.

Raeder specifically minuted that the actual order to sail would be 'subject to the Führer's approval'.

The operation order issued for *The Knight's Move* by Admiral Schniewind from his flagship *Tirpitz* on the day before this Berchtesgaden conference had dealt with every likely contingency. The objective was 'the annihilation of the PQ convoy in collaboration with U-boats and the Air Force.'[3] The strategic purpose of the attack was the destruction of the enemy's shipping capacity; the sinking of the actual cargoes carried was of secondary importance. Enemy escort vessels were to be neutralized only in so far as necessary for the achievement of this objective. According to the German Intelligence service, the convoy was due off Jan Mayen Island on about 20 June. Previous convoys had steamed hard up against the ice-barrier in a broad pattern of four or five columns, escorted by one or two cruisers and several submarines; PQ.16 in particular had also been screened by about five destroyers proceeding three to ten miles ahead of the convoy and a number of destroyers on either flank and bringing up the rear. It was believed to have been met by an escort of Russian destroyers and submarines from about 35° East onwards. A force consisting of one or two battleships, an aircraft-carrier, cruisers and destroyers had stood in its usual covering position between Iceland and Jan Mayen Island, while a cruiser covering force, of two heavy and two light cruisers and a destroyer screen, had accompanied PQ.16 to about 10° East, at which meridian it had turned back. On that occasion, the Allies had flown continuous reconnaissance sorties over Trondheim and Narvik both before and during the convoy's passage, to watch for German fleet movements.

The command structure for *The Knight's Move* was complex and confused, and Schniewind saw in this a source of possible embarrassment later. While he himself would retain tactical control of the sortie from his flagship, operational control was vested in General-Admiral Carls at Naval Group North headquarters in Kiel; Carls would assume command of all naval forces—both surface and submarine—during the actual sortie. The movements and operations of the U-boats would be the immediate responsibility of the Admiral Commanding, Arctic, Hubert Schmundt, who would remain at Narvik aboard his command vessel *Tanga*. His office would repeat all submarine signals, sighting reports, and the like to the fleet commander, Schniewind, in *Tirpitz*. Schmundt's communications with the Air Force units were even less direct, and on several occasions during the coming operation Intelligence derived by Air Force units was to take an inordinate time reaching his headquarters at Narvik.[4] The reason was that the Oslo-based Fifth Air Force, in overall charge of the air operations, had established a forward headquarters at Kemi, and as wireless traffic between the two headquarters could be intercepted by the enemy all communication had to be conducted by time-wasting coded teleprinter signals over a thousand miles of landline, which—the Germans believed—could not be monitored by unfriendly ears.[4] The links between Oslo and Narvik, and between the various naval headquarters, were of a similar nature.

The German Navy's entire available strength in Norway was to become concentrated on the convoy: the First Battle Group, comprising *Tirpitz*, *Hipper*, five destroyers of the 5th and 6th Flotillas and two torpedo-boats, all currently at Trondheim; and the Second Battle Group, consisting of *Lützow*—flagship of the Flag Officer Cruisers, Vice-Admiral Kummetz—and *Admiral Scheer*, and five destroyers of the 8th Flotilla, all stationed at Narvik. The potency of this battle fleet cannot be over-emphasized: the formidable armament of the new battleship *Tirpitz*, mounting eight 15-inch guns, has already been referred to; *Hipper* mounted the more conventional 8-inch guns, but both *Scheer* and *Lützow* had 11-inch guns as their main armament.[5]

As soon as the preparative order had been issued, all the warships would transfer northwards to advanced bases: the First Battle Group would transfer from Trondheim Fiord to the Gimsöy Narrows, in Vestfiord, while the somewhat slower Second Battle Group would transfer from Narvik right up to the northern reaches of Altenfiord, the Leads at Soröy being suggested for their wait. There the destroyers would complete with fuel oil from oilers awaiting them.* Both battle groups were to be ready to sail within twenty-four hours of leaving for these advanced bases.

As soon as aerial reconnaissance had detected the approach of the Allied convoy, and the codeword had been issued for the attack by Naval Group North in Kiel, both battle groups would sail at their respective maximum speeds, which would enable them to join up about a hundred miles to the north-west of North Cape, having by then covered about half the run to the chosen battleground east of Bear Island. *East* of Bear Island! It was to the west of this dreary, uninhabited hummock in the middle of the Arctic that Admiral Sir John Tovey had anticipated that the German fleet's attack would develop. But Schniewind was quite plain about this:

> The most favourable conditions for the attack are at present met in the sea area to the east of Bear Island and between about 20 and 30 degrees East.

At least four hours before action was joined, Schniewind was to pass details of the probable timing, location and direction of the German attack to the command authorities ashore by means of a message flown off by one of his ship's aircraft—*not* by wireless telegraphy, which might be intercepted by the enemy. The two torpedo-boats were to await the return of the battle fleet to the Leads off North Cape.

In the meantime, the German Air Force was expected to carry out continuous sweeps reconnoitring the sea routes along which the warships planned to advance on the convoy, beginning some five hours before the battle fleet weighed anchor, and extending two hundred miles out from the coast in an arc subtended by the latitude of 68° North and the meridian of 25° East. The Fifth Air Force had also been requested to lay on fighter cover for the fleet, both as it lay in wait at its northern bases and during its outward and inward movements, for as far as fighter endurance would permit.

Schniewind realized that it was imperative for the battle fleet to

---

* The destroyers of the First Battle Group to oil from *Nordmark*, *Tiger*, and—if necessary—from *Tirpitz* herself; those of the Second Battle Group from *Dithmarschen*.

attack and wipe out the convoy in one rapid, concentrated strike before the Allied fleet could rush down to intervene; hence the need for reliable air reconnaissance all the time. He intended, if the convoy should prove to be escorted by several heavier naval units, to attack with both battle groups in concert from one side of the convoy. The elimination of any cruiser covering force would fall to the First Battle Group—*Tirpitz* and *Hipper*—while the remaining warships would deal with the light forces and merchant vessels. Action with superior or equal forces was to be avoided at all costs. The German battle fleet would circle round to surprise the enemy from ahead, where they would be least expected. If on the other hand he had reliable information that the convoy's cover consisted only of one or two cruisers, then he would order an enveloping attack, the battle groups attacking from both sides of the convoy right from the start, which would ensure even swifter destruction.

Should the convoy be hugging the ice-barrier, he would open the action by circling right round to the north to force the ships away from the ice, and thus enable his destroyers to deliver their attacks unhampered by ice floes. There was one other possibility for which Schniewind had to prepare, the unlikely event that the Allies should accompany the convoy for part of its voyage with a heavy covering force including one or more battleships. He would then continue to press his attack, but only so long as the balance of strength allowed any prospect of neutralizing the Allied strength. It was no part of German naval strategy to engage superior enemy forces.

Admiral Schniewind envisaged the fleet action against convoy PQ.17 taking the following course: the first battle group to sight the convoy would alarm the other by signal lamp. The enemy's warships would probably at once come out to offer battle, while the convoy escaped under a smokescreen. The enemy would probably send in their destroyers first to launch a torpedo attack; then they would endeavour to lure the German battle fleet over the waiting Allied submarines that would have accompanied the convoy. The counter-measure would be to keep on the move, while each ship's guns opened fire on several targets from the start, as the battle fleet—and primarily *Tirpitz* and *Hipper*—set about annihilating the cruisers accompanying the convoy. The

German destroyer flotillas were to engage the enemy destroyers and prevent them from manœuvring for torpedo attacks, while they themselves were to seize every opportunity of launching torpedo attacks on the enemy's cruisers—and if the range were to close so far—on the enemy's destroyers and merchant ships as well. But these diversions were not to jeopardize their main rôle, screening the heavy German warships. The German battle fleet might open fire on any merchant ships coming within range as soon as opportunities presented themselves, even during the preliminary action with the covering forces; but once this action was over, and the convoy's covering forces were on the run, the real massacre would begin.

For the attack on the convoy it would be sufficient to cripple the merchant ships. There was neither time for nor sense in waiting to finish off each one; the disabled freighters could be sunk afterwards by the following U-boats and bomber aircraft. If possible, prizes were to be taken by the destroyers, particularly any tankers in the convoy, but only if there was no likelihood of new enemy forces arriving on the scene and turning the tables. They might also attempt to force enemy freighters from the convoy to steer for German-occupied ports, without attempting to set a prize-crew aboard each one. Destroyers might attempt to take some prisoners for Intelligence purposes, but their primary rôle was unchanged: screening the capital ships.

Visibility on the field of battle would be poor, with fires, fumes, smokescreens, and possibly fog. German warships were enjoined to exercise especial care not to engage their own ships; their attention was called to their radar device enabling them to distinguish friend from foe. The German U-boats were for their part directed not to fire torpedoes during the battle unless their targets had been identified beyond all doubt as Allied; any submarines encountered, on the other hand, were to be treated as hostile to the extent of forcing them to dive, without actually sinking them. The German bomber crews were reminded that the roofs and sides of gun turrets on German ships were painted luminous yellow, while large red-white-and-black swastikas were painted on the fore- and afterdecks, should there still be any doubt in their minds.

The task of the German Air Force would be to locate and

shadow PQ.17 and its covering force, the latter particularly as it passed through the area between 15° and 30° East, paying special attention to the number—if any—of battleships and cruisers; to the convoy's distance from the ice-barrier; to the composition and deployment of the convoy's close escorts, and to whether there were any submarines or fighter aircraft among its defences; and to obtaining general meteorological information just prior to the battle's commencement. The Allied naval bases were to be kept under constant surveillance too. Once the battle had begun, the Air Force was to provide spotter planes as well. Finally, the Fifth Air Force was asked to arrange a mass bombing attack on the convoy just before the arrival of the German battle fleet, so that the latter could exploit any confusion and disarray to the full. After the action was over, all destroyers were to keep at least three torpedoes in reserve for possible actions on the homeward run. Admiral Schniewind ended with a sober provision for disaster: 'The tugs *Atlantik* and *Pelworm* are to stand by at instant readiness at Narvik, as soon as the First Battle Group has put to sea from its advanced base.'

On 16 June, Admiral Schmundt ordered *U-657* to sea with *U-88*. *U-355* was already putting out from Narvik, and *U-334* had left Trondheim on the previous day. On the 17th, he ordered *U-457* to sail from Trondheim next day, and on the 23rd he ordered *U-255* and *U-456* to put out of Narvik and Bergen respectively. All these U-boats received the same orders, and all were to join the 'Ice Devil' pack being formed to fight Convoy PQ.17.[6] * But the middle of June, which the 'rhythm' of previous convoy sailings had suggested would be the time for the sailing of PQ.17, had come and gone and still the convoy had not been sighted.

The German Air Force had completely reversed its former attitude towards the Navy and now promised to carry out total air reconnaissance up to a radius of 300 miles off North Cape, with fresh reconnaissance available at four hours' notice. This far

---

* Nine U-boats were now at sea: *U-88* (Bohmann); *U-251* (Timm); *U-255* (Reche); *U-334* (Siemon); *U-355* (La Baume); *U-376* (Marks); *U-408* (von Hymmen); *U-456* (Teichert); *U-457* (Brandenburg). Two more U-boats, *U-657* (Göllnitz) and *U-703* (Bielfeld) were later attached to the 'Ice Devil' pack for the attack on PQ.17.

exceeded the Navy's wildest expectations, and made success for
The Knight's Move a virtual certainty. Word was passed to Captain
von Puttkamer, Hitler's naval adjutant, about this development
at once.[7]

Despite the lack of hard information on the convoy's departure,
the German Naval Staff judged by the end of June that the time
had come to throw a spanner into the works of any Allied plan
for a battleship force to cover PQ.17 so far east as to make it impossible for *Tirpitz* safely to attack. On 29 June, arrangements
were made for 'reliable' information to be channelled into the
British Intelligence network to the effect that the pocket-
battleships *Admiral Scheer* and *Lützow* were fully provisioned and
ready to break out together into the Atlantic 'through the Denmark Strait', as soon as weather permitted. The ships were to be
correctly described as lying at Narvik.[8]

At last the nerve-eroding inactivity of the ten U-boats sent out
by Admiral Schmundt to patrol south of Jan Mayen Island seemed
to be over: at 4.40 p.m. on 30 June air reconnaissance glimpsed a
large westbound convoy, QP.13, only 180 miles north of North
Cape.[9] Now Naval Group North knew that PQ.17 must also have
sailed. Somewhere, *The Knight's Move*'s victim was at sea.

✳ 2 ✳

During June, the backlog of shipping in Icelandic ports had
assumed considerable proportions. In Reykjavik there were
dozens of ships awaiting the formation of convoys. The protracted delays and the waiting at anchor among the steep and icy
cliffs led to increasing unrest among the Allied merchant crews,
already taxed to the utmost by the unwelcome prospect of the
hazardous duty that lay ahead. The crews of earlier convoys had
run amok in Iceland, enraging the local populace by starting
costly battles using the precious eider eggs as missiles, and by
'fraternizing' with the women. All shore-leave had been cancelled.

Two-thirds of PQ.17's ships were American, and the United
States had been at war only six months: their merchant ships were
still crewed by an unhappy mixture of extravagantly paid ($500
a month, plus danger-money) professional seamen, mercenaries
and an international mob of cut-throat nomads. Each had been

provided with an 'armed guard' of American servicemen to man the guns. Typical of the ships was the *Troubadour*, a 5,808-ton tramp built twenty-two years before by an English firm and already a veteran of both the Belgian and the Italian merchant marines; now she was American-owned, but flew the Panamanian flag—a rusting steamer that had been scuttled by her truculent crew at Jacksonville when America entered the war, and now boasted a seventeen-nation crew of ex-convicts and the rakings of the U.S. deportation camps. While at anchor in New York harbour one month before, the ship's ammunition magazine had been deliberately flooded 'by a person or persons unknown'. Eight Colt automatic pistols had been issued to the naval Armed Guard officers shortly before sailing: 'This was considered necessary in view of the conduct of the ship's crew.'

In Iceland on 20 June, twenty members of *Troubadour*'s crew mutinied, having been told their ship was now bound for Russia; they sent a deputation up to their Master, the Norwegian Captain George Salvesen, and told him they refused to take the ship any farther. The Reykjavik port director ordered Salvesen to use his ship's Armed Guard to quell the mutiny. The American naval gunners rounded up the seamen and barred a dozen of them into a stinking hold in the forepeak area, in 'very crowded, foul conditions'. The seamen held out in there under armed guard for fifty hours and then surrendered. 'We didn't have any more appreciable trouble until the convoy reached Russia,' reported the Armed Guard officer, Ensign Howard E. Carraway, to his superiors.* [10]

The days rolled by and still the merchant ships lay at anchor there. Early in June, the Chief of Naval Operations in Washington had been advised that the British Admiralty had postponed PQ.17's departure until the 24th, but that the number of ships in this and the following convoys was to remain unchanged. A week later Washington had again been advised that PQ.17 was to depart on 24 June, but that date came and went, and still the

---

* In Archangel, following trouble over women, the ship's crew was again imprisoned in a tiny hold, for 2½ weeks this time. They were eventually turned over to the Russian penal authorities. The ship's Master, two officers and Carraway were cleared at a Court of Inquiry subsequently held by the War Shipping Administration. [10]

convoy had not sailed. At about the same time, the American naval authorities learned that the normal rule, that there must be sufficient lifeboat capacity *on each side* of a ship to accommodate all its crew, had been waived by the British Ministry of War Transport, provided that the ship had enough rafts and floats; this relaxation of the rules would not in itself be dangerous—provided that the ship remained in convoy with other vessels, of course.[11]

In Iceland, the American seamen were not allowed to listen to the wireless, so they built their own illicit sets and even tuned in to the broadcasts of Mr William Joyce (Lord Haw-Haw) beamed from Germany. Joyce's warning, shortly before PQ.17 sailed, to American seamen to stay out of the Barents Sea caused them great amusement; the seamen naturally preferred the BBC's more palliatory bulletins on the shipping war. 'We were to learn later to our disgust the loose manner in which the BBC handled the truth,' an officer of the American *Bellingham* said.[12]

During June, Allied Intelligence had appreciated that the Germans intended to employ their heavy surface ships to attack the next eastbound convoy, PQ.17, east of Bear Island.[13] This was a reversal of the tactics previously expected of the enemy, and one might have expected that the Admiralty would persuade the British Government to postpone the operation until the conditions were less favourable to the enemy; as it was, the political pressure was the stronger, and the decision was taken to sail the convoy, even though the Cabinet knew that their naval forces could not protect it in the area where the German battle fleet planned to attack it. This was the point of error; but apparently PQ.17, like its predecessor, would be considered 'justified' even if only half got through.

The Cabinet had given the British Admiralty a task which it could not possibly perform: if *Tirpitz* were to attack east of Bear Island, circumstances would be wholly in her favour; she would be fighting close to friendly shores, under a powerful air 'umbrella', with the maximum co-operation of the German reconnaissance and bomber forces assembled at North Cape. The Allied naval forces would have no shore-based air support in these waters; they would be a thousand miles from base, and their destroyers would have insufficient fuel to escort a damaged ship to harbour.

There seemed to Admiral Tovey, Commander-in-Chief of the Home Fleet, only two ways of successfully challenging a German surface attack on PQ.17: the Allied submarines stationed off the Norwegian coast could attempt to stop the German battle fleet—at best a meagre chance; or alternatively, by a ruse, the enemy heavy ships could be lured farther westward than they had bargained for, lured westward on to the guns of Tovey's distant battle fleet. This latter could be achieved, as Tovey suggested to the Admiralty, by turning the convoy back as it reached about 10° East at which juncture the German battle fleet would probably have been sailed; the convoy would retrace its path for twelve to eighteen hours, in the hope that the German battle fleet would either be tempted to search westwards for the reported convoy—bringing them within range of the cruising Home Fleet—or would at least be obliged to move for an extended period in the waters off North Cape, where the Allied submarines were waiting for them. Tovey's proposal, which later study of German intentions suggests would not have met with success, was soon after disapproved by the Admiralty.

Admiral Tovey's distant covering force would consist of the battleships *Duke of York* (his flagship) and *Washington* (the latter wearing the flag of Rear-Admiral R. C. Giffen, USN, commanding the American Task Force 99); three cruisers, the aircraft-carrier *Victorious* and fourteen destroyers were also included in the force, which would stand to the north-east of Jan Mayen Island. PQ.17 was the first such operation for which a substantial American force had been subordinated to British command. Tovey issued orders according to which the British cruiser *London* (wearing the flag of Rear-Admiral L. H. K. Hamilton, commanding the First Cruiser Squadron), together with the cruisers HMS *Norfolk*, USS *Wichita* and USS *Tuscaloosa*, would form a 'cruiser covering force' for PQ.17, screened by three destroyers—USS *Wainwright* (Captain D. P. Moon, USN, 'ComDesRon 8'), USS *Rowan* and HMS *Somali* (6th Destroyer Flotilla leader).[14] A signal was accordingly made to *Wichita*, on patrol in the Denmark Strait, ordering her to depart forthwith for Hvalfiord in Iceland. On the same day Admiral Tovey instructed the cruiser covering force to be prepared to reach the vicinity of PQ.17 on 2 July, and to remain in a covering position until 4 July, 'or as circumstances dictate'.[15]

The convoy would, as before, be provided with a close escort, with Commander J. E. Broome, RN, as Senior Officer Escort; Broome's force would consist of no fewer than six destroyers, four corvettes, three minesweepers, two anti-aircraft ships and four trawlers as a measure of protection against German submarines and aircraft throughout the whole of the convoy's passage. There were also two submarines in the convoy, which would remain concealed from the enemy as far as possible; should a German surface attack develop they were to endeavour to attack the German heavy vessels.

Rear-Admiral L. H. K. Hamilton had been appointed to the command of the First Cruiser Squadron four months before; known as 'Turtle' Hamilton not only to his family but throughout the Royal Navy, he had been one of the original Osborne cadets in 1903; after going on to Dartmouth he had passed out of the training cruiser *Cumberland* with the King's Gold Medal for the 'most gentlemanlike bearing', and for his good influence on his fellow cadets.

The Royal Navy was his life's career, and he viewed its detractors with proud disdain. In 1915 he had been awarded his first DSO for an expedition several hundred miles inland in an Army support operation in West Africa. After commanding both *Norfolk* and *Delhi*, he was given command of *Aurora* in January 1940, winning a bar to his DSO during the ill-fated Norwegian campaign. Hamilton was universally popular with all ranks, in a service noted for its rivalry. He was a humane officer and a chivalrous warrior, a man who wrote a weekly letter to his mother ('My Dear Mum . . .') in London, a regular correspondence which paused momentarily only for the black week surrounding the events depicted in this book.

When he was promoted to Rear-Admiral in the spring of 1941, he had been one of the first to disapprove: it represented a first departure from a naval tradition of two centuries whereby promotion to flag rank went by seniority alone. He had been given command of the First Cruiser Squadron only in February 1942. In many respects, he was old-fashioned in his service outlook:

he took the cruiser *London* as his flagship, as *Norfolk* had the Senior Captain in the squadron and he preferred a junior Flag Captain.

Like other senior officers in the Navy, he did not worship Mr Churchill, nor could he stomach the 'Winnie's back!' idolatry surrounding the man who had twice been First Lord of the Admiralty at hours of deep disgrace for the Navy. He regarded Churchill as 'the complete dictator', with an unbridled lust for power—unable to brook opposition from any quarter. Hamilton's letters home were an interesting reflection on how feeling was running in the fleet. In particular, he saw in Churchill the man who was deliberately starving the Navy of vital air-power, in order to wage a ruthless and immoral campaign against the civilians of his enemy; since all senior officers who were to participate in the tragedy of convoy PQ.17 were later to agree that the provision of long-range reconnaissance and submarine-hunting aircraft in adequate numbers, not to mention long-range fighter escort and bomber support operations, would have averted the disaster, Hamilton's views were of some significance. He wrote that he hoped that the recent loss of *Prince of Wales* and *Repulse* to Japanese torpedo-bombers and the escape of the German battleships from Brest would bring the Cabinet to its senses. Hamilton realized that the loss of *Prince of Wales* would lead to the loss of Singapore and probably Rangoon and the Dutch East Indies as well, but he hoped that the loss of command of the sea in the East was only temporary: that once it was won back, all those places would quite easily be recaptured too. 'The side of the war that really interests me at the moment,' wrote Hamilton, 'is how strongly Winston is going to deal with the RAF after the *Prince of Wales*, followed by the escape of the German ships. The whole question has, of course, been blatantly obvious to the naval officer since the beginning of the war, and now it must be obvious even to Winston in spite of his prejudice against the Navy. We are a hopelessly unmilitary nation to imagine that we could win the war by bombing German women and children instead of defeating their Army and Navy.'[16]

Mr Churchill he compared unfavourably with Sir Frederick Richards, the terror of politicians at the turn of the century, a 'first naval lord' of stubborn will and impervious to argument when the interests of the Navy were at stake: 'We should be better off now if more of our First Lords before the war had been more like him!'* Was not the aeroplane as much a naval weapon now as a submarine or a destroyer? 'As you know,' he wrote again to his mother on 11 April, 'I have always maintained that the lack of a proper Naval Air Service was the greatest handicap we fought under. It has now become an urgent requirement if we are going to win the war. It makes me mad to see the air strength of the country being devoted to killing a few women and children in Germany, whilst our fleet and Empire are being lost to the Japanese daily. . . .'

To say that the advent of air-power had 'done away' with battleships was nonsense: 'It has done away with *our* battleships, because we have been starved of fighter protection.'[17]

While Tovey seriously considered the sinking of *Tirpitz* to be 'of incomparably greater importance to the conduct of the war than the safety of any convoy', Hamilton expressed it as his view that no other single event could have so profound an effect on the course of the war. Five days after *Victorious*'s carrier-aircraft attack on *Tirpitz* in March, Hamilton had written, 'That ship is an infernal nuisance and the most important business of the war at the present time is to cripple or destroy her. It would just make the whole difference in the way of freeing ships for other theatres.' And again, 'I still think that the most pressing requirement of the war is to dispose of the *Tirpitz*, then things would begin to straighten out a bit.'[18]

On the morning of 25 June, two days out from Scapa Flow, Hamilton's flagship *London* anchored in Hvalfiord, Iceland, where the American battleship *Washington* and the American cruisers *Wichita* and *Tuscaloosa* already lay.[19] Some hours later, Lieutenant Douglas Fairbanks Jr, USNR, Admiral Giffen's Flag Lieutenant, reported aboard the *Wichita* for 'temporary additional duty';

---

* Sir Frederick Richards (1833–1912) was one of the leading administrators in the history of the Royal Navy. In carrying through his 1895 naval reconstruction programme with Lord Spencer they overcame the most formidable opposition from Mr Gladstone, which eventually was one of the causes of the latter's retirement from office. Cf. *British Naval Policy 1880–1905*.

during the operation that was to follow, Fairbanks wrote an hour-by-hour chronicle of the events in the cruiser force for his admiral's personal files.[20] This diary captures better than any other contemporary record the mood and feelings of the American sailors throughout the operation. Fairbanks was immediately taken before *Wichita*'s Executive Officer, Commander Orem, and the need for utmost secrecy about the coming operation was impressed on him. 'Other than Captain Hill and Commander Orem no one aboard knows where we are going or what our mission is to be,' wrote Fairbanks. 'That the whole ship's company "smells something is in the wind" is certain. A seaman's intuition is very strong and his common sense is stronger. He can, for instance, see that about three dozen heavily laden merchant ships are riding at anchor in the narrow harbour of Hvalfiordur. He sees HMS *Kent* and HMS *London* put into port while their captains accompany their admiral about their ship for a dinner, which seems to be as much for business as for pleasure.'

The visiting officers vanished from the curious gaze of the American bluejackets, and the luncheon party began. Admiral Burrough, Hamilton's predecessor, once described this for-gathering as 'a picking of each other's brains'. Admiral Giffen, Admiral Hamilton and the latter's Flag Captain, R. M. Servaes, RN, were joined round the table by Rear-Admiral 'Freddie' Dalrymple-Hamilton, the Admiral Commanding Iceland, and the captains of all the other heavy warships and their destroyer screen. The captains of *Kent* and *London* described the experiences they had had during previous north Russian convoy operations, and then Hamilton outlined the Admiralty's plans for the operation that lay ahead of them. The convoy itself would be escorted by the strongest force of destroyers, corvettes and anti-submarine vessels ever employed, and the four cruisers of the cruiser covering force would be covering the convoy from a position out of sight, over the horizon, with the primary duty of engaging any enemy surface forces which might come out. At the moment, it was known that *Lützow* and *Admiral Scheer* were at Narvik, ready to attack when word was given. Once the convoy had safely passed what Hamilton decided was the danger zone, as far as surface attack was concerned, the cruisers were to return. Should the convoy sustain serious casualties, the three rescue ships sailing with it were to proceed straight to Archangel and discharge their wounded at a hospital there.

Some way to the south, the main forces of the Home Fleet would be on patrol, ready to intervene should the Germans decide to operate *Tirpitz* against the convoy. More than one of the officers present hoped that they were on the eve of a historic naval engagement; none doubted what its outcome would be.

Admiral Giffen, who had previously flown his flag from *Wichita*, took leave of his old friends aboard her and returned to the battleship *Washington*. At 5 p.m. *Washington* sailed, bearing Giffen to Scapa Flow to join the main body of the Home Fleet. Commander Orem sent a farewell signal to Giffen and his staff, containing a private joke, but ending: 'Happy cruising'. As the battleship, accompanied by four destroyers, steamed slowly out of Hvalfiord, Giffen signalled back, 'The best of luck, and remember science and skill cannot but prevail over ignorance and superstition.' Giffen's former Flag Captain, Captain Hill of *Wichita*, replied with a further traditional pleasantry: 'Many thanks. Will try to call signals just as if the Old Master were in the center of the huddle.'[21] Then the ships were no longer in sight of each other, and the clattering signal lanterns fell silent.

Rear-Admiral Hamilton returned to *London* and wrote out his operational orders to the cruisers. 'The primary object', he stressed, 'is still to get PQ.17 to Russia, but an object only slightly subsidiary is to provide an opportunity for the enemy's heavy ships to be brought to action by our battle fleet and cruiser covering force.' To increase the chance of bringing the German heavy ships to action, it was proposed to turn PQ.17 back on to its tracks for a while on reaching the meridian of 10° East.

It is thus hoped to lure the enemy further from his bases or keep him longer at sea in our submarine zones.

In effect, the convoy operation was to be a trap set to catch *Tirpitz*, with over thirty heavy-laden ships, mostly American, as bait. The goat would have been tied to the tree: everything would depend on the hunter's getting to his place before the tiger reached the goat; it would also depend on the hunter keeping his nerve, but this was only to be realized afterwards.

Hamilton correctly guessed that *Tirpitz* and *Hipper* would probably operate as one battle group, because of their comparable speeds, while the pocket-battleships *Scheer* and *Lützow* would form a second battle group. British submarines had been stationed off north-western Norway, and until the eighth day of the convoy's passage (4 July) the Home Fleet would occupy its distant covering position, from which it could fly off torpedo aircraft to reach the convoy in time should the German battle fleet suddenly appear. (Hitler had shown considerable prudence in warning Raeder to find out what the Allied aircraft-carriers were up to before allowing the battle fleet to sail.)

The four cruisers would remain in the convoy's immediate vicinity until about the eighth day or 'longer if circumstances dictate'. It was not Hamilton's intention to allow his cruiser force to come within range of German aircraft or enemy submarine concentrations; he was not there to provide anti-aircraft fire during air attacks on the convoy, but to protect it from surface force attack. This was a significant departure from the practice of his predecessor during PQ.16. For tactical reasons, Hamilton's force would remain out of sight of the convoy to the north for the greater part of the voyage.

Having talked with the other commanding officers, he also knew what he intended to do should a German surface attack develop: he would close the enemy rapidly to about 14,000 yards, having flown off his cruisers' spotting aircraft beforehand if possible (his force disposed of eleven aircraft altogether). If there should prove to be only one German raider, the cruisers would move out to engage it from well-separated bearings while the destroyers would lay smokescreens or carry out torpedo attacks; if there were two enemy warships, his two divisions would each engage one, on well-separated bearings, using flank-marking procedure. But if—as the Germans planned—the *Tirpitz* were to be included in the raiding force, then the cruiser squadron's orders were primarily to scout and decoy:

> It is not my intention to engage any enemy unit which includes *Tirpitz*, who must be shadowed at long range and led to a position at which interception can be achieved by the Commander-in-Chief.[22]

On the following morning Hamilton ordered complete wireless

silence at the Icelandic naval bases where the forces covering the convoy were assembling. At noon, he summoned a formal conference of the American commanding officers and went over every aspect of his operational orders, and the tactics likely to be employed against the two German pocket-battleships if they should make a showing. The American cruiser captains were confident that their effective range on opening fire could be as great as 21,000 yards, and said so. They seemed puzzled by the British tactics. Hamilton recorded that 'although they might still find our methods strange', the Americans could not have displayed more enthusiasm to co-operate with the British.

During the afternoon, units of the convoy's close escort—destroyers, corvettes and minesweepers—began to arrive at Hvalfiord. Among them were the destroyer escort leader *Keppel* (Commander J. E. Broome, RN) and the two submarines *P-614* and *P-615*, who were to accompany the convoy to Archangel. Hamilton met all their commanding officers and explained his intentions to each of them, in so far as they were affected. In the meantime, however, the Admiralty was itself intervening to reshape the convoy operation in one aspect: early on 27 June, the Admiralty issued instructions to Admirals Tovey and Hamilton in which the former's suggested tactic of turning the convoy back on its track for twelve to eighteen hours was rejected, while they introduced the possibility that they might themselves turn the convoy back, without necessarily timing this manœuvre to achieve what Tovey had had in mind. The Admiralty also stressed that the safety of the convoy against German surface attack while west of Bear Island was primarily the responsibility of the Allied surface forces, but that any German surface attack east of that meridian—about 19° East—would have to be countered by the Allied submarines patrolling off Norway.

Hamilton's cruiser force was forbidden to proceed east of Bear Island unless the convoy was threatened by an enemy force that his 8-inch gun-cruisers could fight—which meant to all intents and purposes any German force not including *Tirpitz*. In any case, his force was not to proceed beyond the meridian of 25° East.[23] This left less latitude for personal interpretation than Tovey's own directive to the cruisers: Hamilton could no longer continue to cover the convoy 'as circumstances dictated'. As a general principle the Admiralty added: 'Our primary object is to get as much of this convoy through as possible, and the best way to do this is to keep it moving to the eastward even though it is suffering damage.' Finally, the Admiralty foresaw that once the convoy was to the east of Bear Island, circumstances might arise whereby the convoy's ships would have to be 'dispersed' with orders to proceed to Russian ports singly and alone.*

✳ 3 ✳

For the cruisers, this Saturday, 27 June 1942, was a routine day: not so for the merchantmen, for today was their 'zero day' after months of waiting. During the morning, *Wichita* held captain's inspection; her ship's band was out in all its glory. A baseball team went ashore in full uniform to play a team from another ship, but launches were already going around from freighter to freighter, collecting their Masters and Chief Officers for the main convoy conference at 1 p.m.

The conference was held in a large new YMCA hall in a camp being built by Royal Marine engineers at Hvalfiord. It was a muddy and inconvenient site, but well guarded by marines and far from prying eyes. When the ships' Masters trooped in, they found the Admiral Commanding Iceland there, with the commanding officers of the cruisers and destroyers of Hamilton's force and those of Commander Broome's close escort force as well (Hamilton considered it to be in both parties' interests for the Senior Officer of the Escort to meet the ships' Masters before sailing). 'The long hut was soon smoke-stuffed through the combined efforts of some two hundred pipes and cigarettes,' wrote Lieutenant Fairbanks afterwards. 'There was not much excitement —talking was of the low, constant hum variety. There was a good deal of just milling about or sitting on the long benches or tables that spaced the length of the hut.' At the far end, naval officers were sorting out large envelopes, imprinted ON HIS MAJESTY'S SERVICE, containing the secret convoy instructions and codes for each ship.[24]

---

* The full text of these Admiralty instructions is reproduced as an Appendix, page 303.

The British ships' Masters were bowler-hatted and wore dark suits, and diligently took notes throughout the conference. The Americans were less formally attired in shapeless denims and sweaters and bright tartan shirts. After the assembly had been addressed by the convoy's Commodore, J. C. K. Dowding, RNR, ('you will near no news of the outside world until you get the best news of all—"safely arrived in port" ') and by Commander Broome, who assured them of his destroyers' intentions to lend all possible assistance, Rear-Admiral Hamilton rose and talked briefly about the operations planned on their behalf.

He began by warning them all that the convoy would be 'no joy-ride', but he promised that there would be a very strong close escort force, including two anti-aircraft ships and one catapult-aircraft merchantman.[25] The conference was not informed of the Intelligence finding that the enemy really was intending to bring out his main units to attack this convoy; but the sight of so much brass and braid at the top table must have disheartened as many of the ships' Masters as it encouraged: Why was this convoy to be afforded such special protection? Nor were they eased to identify the Masters of no fewer than *three* 'rescue ships'—Captains Mc-Gowan, Morris and Banning—among their number. The ships of the last two named, *Zamalek* and *Rathlin*, had been ordered to Iceland at such short notice three days before that the fitting of their additional armament for the voyage had not been completed, and *Zamalek* had put to sea with the dockyard workers still hammering and riveting aboard her, installing new heavy anti-aircraft guns, four Oerlikon guns, 'pig-trough' rocket-launchers and paravanes. The two rescue ships had been cleared down the Clyde with Number One priority all the way, *en route* for Hvalfiord.[26] Clearly the Admiralty expected this to be no ordinary convoy.

Hamilton reassured the ships' Masters that in addition to Broome's close escort, there would be strong covering forces consisting of British and American cruisers, and an additional distant cover provided by a battle fleet of British and American battleships and other heavy vessels. 'You may not see a lot of these ships during the passage,' he explained. 'But they will be in close support of you throughout.' He added that there were British and Russian submarines suitably disposed to intercept enemy surface forces, and the RAF would be busy over the enemy's Norwegian airfields. Taking it all round, he thought there was every chance of getting the convoy through 'practically intact'. Hamilton's remarks were greeted with evident enthusiasm by the ships' Masters. As he observed a few days later, this made the part he had to play on the evening of 4 July 'all the more distasteful'.*

Hamilton explained to the conference that the greatest annoyance the convoy would encounter would be German air attacks, so it was important not to waste ammunition: 'Impress on your men the necessity for strict fire discipline. All experience goes to show that it is no use continuing to fire at an aeroplane once it has dropped its bombs or torpedo.' Further, a favourite German tactic seemed to be to operate the Junkers 88s first, circling high over the convoy just before the low-level torpedo-bombers attacked to distract attention from the latter. 'Keep a look out for torpedo-bombers—and be careful not to fire into other ships in excitement.'

After the conference, Hamilton had a brief parley with the Commodore and Vice-Commodore and with the Master of the CAM *Empire Tide*. With the pilot of the latter's Sea Hurricane he discussed whether it was preferable to succumb to the temptation of attacking the shadowing aircraft when they began to circle the convoy, or to wait for the mass attacks by the more cumbersome torpedo-bombers before catapulting the plane. He reached the conclusion that downing the one shadower would be only a momentary annoyance to the Germans, while if the Hurricane were to be catapulted during air attacks the chances were much higher. He suggested that the plane should be catapulted only east of Bear Island, when the danger of air attack was highest; he also ordered a wooden dummy plane to be made for the ship, to replace the Hurricane as soon as it had been shot off.

Of his address to the main conference, one off-the-cuff remark

---

* Of this conference, one of the American freighter captains reported: 'Convoy conference held 27th June at 1.00 p.m. Hvalfiord. . . . At the conference, attended by the highest ranking naval officers, Iceland, it was stressed that PQ.17 would have the strongest screen force yet employed in the protection of Arctic convoys. Action was expected, but plans had been laid which promised discomfiture to the enemy.'[27]

he made has remained in the memories of those who were there. Hamilton said: 'You may well be the cause of another general fleet action—perhaps even another Jutland.'

Perhaps another Jutland! With these words ringing in their ears, the Masters of the merchant ships trooped out of the YMCA hall into the pouring rain and made their way down to the jetty, where motor-launches were waiting to ferry them out to their vessels, looming grey and ugly across the fiord. The Masters silently watched the high-ranking naval officers depart; then, as the skippers of the Asdic trawler *Ayrshire* and the two fleet oilers stepped into the waiting launch, Captain Gansden of the oiler *Gray Ranger* turned to the trawler skipper and said, 'What did you make of the Admiral's speech?' Lieutenant Gradwell replied, 'For myself, I don't think much about fleet actions. I just want to get this convoy through.' Three hours later, Hamilton's flagship weighed anchor and sailed with three destroyers for Seidisfiord, to see to the sailing of the convoy's ocean escort, the First Escort Group under Commander 'Jack' Broome, RN.

Broome, a broad-shouldered, Rabelaisian Royal Navy career officer, was famous throughout the service for his ribald humour and his ability to express it in cartoons. Officers secretly treasured his saucy postcards, few of which would have passed the portcullis of the most liberal Watch Committee ashore. One of them depicted an admiral—instantly identifiable by all the postcard's acquirers—improbably sharing a bath with an equally recognizable Wren; the admiral was explaining, 'This is how the torpedo goes, Miss Snodgrass'. The admiral concerned had learned about this cartoon and taken offence to it; but Broome had subsequently regained some of his former favour by designing a masterly poster, which had adorned the walls of the YMCA hall used for the PQ.17 convoy conference. The poster was said to be one of Mr Churchill's favourites—Churchill probably had a weak spot for any naval officer reminding him of his earlier hero, Beatty. Entitled '*How to Join the Stragglers' Club*', it showed a solitary merchant-ship dawdling far behind an Allied convoy, while German aircraft and submarines closed in. The poster bore the ominous sub-title: '*Subscriptions in advance, please*'.

After lunch, Captain Hill and Commander Orem of *Wichita* inspected some of the merchant ships at anchor. After chatting to

the two Hurricane pilots—one of them almost blind—carried by
the British *Empire Tide*, they boarded the brand-new American
William Hooper, the fourth of the 'ninety-day wonder' Liberty
ships. She was on her maiden voyage from North Carolina, and
although her decks were well scuffed up she was still spanking
new inside. She had left the United States early in April, with a
cargo of ammunition and tanks: 'Already the rubber on the tanks
was beginning to rot from exposure to the salt air,' wrote Lieutenant Fairbanks. 'We had a talk with the young Ensign in charge of
the naval armed guard of 15 men. His main worry was that the
men under him were inexperienced. They were all merely appren-
tice seamen, who were more than willing but less than able. He
was shockingly short of ammunition, and had but 90 rounds for
his four-inch gun. . . .' With only two hours to go before sailing
time, *William Hooper* was still without some important spares for
her guns. Captain Hill did what he could to encourage the ship's
crew.[28]

✳ 4 ✳

At four o'clock that afternoon, 27 June, the ships of convoy
PQ.17, the war's worst disaster convoy, slipped in single file out
of Hvalfiord: 'like so many dirty ducks', wrote Fairbanks, 'they
waddled out past the nets and out to sea. No honors or salutes
were paid to them as they passed, such as there are for naval
vessels. But every one who was watching paid them a silent tribute
and offered them some half-thought prayer'. Thirty-five heavy-
laden ships, their holds packed with the paraphernalia of war,
their decks groaning under the weight of tanks, guns and crated
bombers destined for our Russian allies; three gallant rescue
ships, one of which would never return, and two fleet oilers
brimming with fuel for the thirsty destroyers of the escort. What
a cargo for the Russians; what a prize for the enemy! Seven
hundred million dollars' worth of armaments—297 aircraft, 594
tanks, 4,246 lorries and gun carriers, and over 156,000 tons of
general cargo besides—enough to equip an army of fifty thousand
men if it ever arrived in Russian ports.[29]

In low visibility the ships were shepherded in double column
northabout round Iceland, and past the minefields of the Denmark

Strait. Of the thirty-five ships, all but eight were bound for Archangel; these eight—all Americans—were to split up into a separate convoy at the end of the voyage and with the Liberty ship *Christopher Newport* as Commodore ship head off early into Murmansk.[30] Of the two oilers accompanying the convoy, one, RFA *Gray Ranger*, was to accompany the convoy all the way, while the other, RFA *Aldersdale*, was to be detached on 2 July with an elderly destroyer as 'Force Q' to await the westbound convoy QP.13 off Jan Mayen Island.

Soon after the convoy had formed up in double column, it 'lost' its first ship: in dense fog, the Liberty ship *Richard Bland* ran aground on the Iceland rocks, and was badly holed; she had to be returned to port, but not before she had transmitted an ill-considered distress signal. Off Stromness Point, the ships were formed up in the broad cruising formation—nine columns wide, with four ships in each column—in which they continued north-eastwards towards Jan Mayen Island. For this first part of the voyage, the ships had been given the temporary protection of three minesweepers and four anti-submarine trawlers, with *Halcyon* as Senior Officer. Their long-range escort under Commander Broome would put out from Seidisfiord and rendezvous with the convoy on the afternoon of the 30th.

No contact had been made with the enemy yet, but more than one freighter was aware of its own weakness should a major battle ensue. So long as the convoy remained intact, its fire-power was immense; but individual ships were poorly armed, and there was a grave shortage of ammunition, particularly of the heavier calibre. The executive officer of the USS *Melville*, the depot ship at Hvalfiord, had privately shown American Armed Guard officers a despatch authorizing them to broach the ships' cargoes and use the ammunition and guns they found, if necessary for the defence of their ships. On 28 June, Ensign Carraway discussed *Troubadour*'s lack of ammunition with her Master and Chief Officer, and they decided to break the seals on one of the three American M-3 tanks on their deck, to see if the tank's 37-millimetre gun could be used. A quantity of armour-piercing and tracer shell was broken out of the below-decks cargo, and two men were trained to man the tank's gun. On the following day, a second tank was broken open, and its gun prepared for use. All this was

[47]

highly illegal, of course; but the officers may reasonably have deemed the arrival of a broached cargo was more use to the Russians than the arrival of no cargo at all.[31]

At 5 a.m.* on the morning of the 29th, with the convoy edging forward at 8 knots in a fog which brought visibility down to less than fifty yards, the ships ran into a field of heavy floating ice; four of the merchant ships suffered serious damage. The American SS *Exford* wirelessed that she could not continue, and the Commodore passed permission to her to return to port. With a bad hole in her bows, *Gray Ranger* was reduced to 8 knots and eventually had to take up the waiting position assigned to the oiler *Aldersdale*; the latter vessel proceeded with the convoy, following the course which was to confront her with disaster five days later.

At 8 a.m., the two slow-moving British submarines ordered to accompany the convoy left Iceland in company with their 'mother' ship, the Flower-class corvette *Dianella*. Commander Broome called a final escort conference two hours later on board Hamilton's flagship *London* at Seidisfiord, attended by the commanding officers of all the long-range escort vessels. It should be commented that PQ.17's 'scratch' ocean escort was as makeshift as it was large: as Commander Broome himself complained, none of the escorts' commanding officers had the chance to meet before sailing, which was an awkward departure from the 'escort group' practise so successful in Western Approaches Command. Officers who tried to approach Broome independently at the PQ.17 conferences were waved away. The escort force was also ill-assorted: there was even a 'Free French' corvette with a 100 per cent British crew, flying the French tricolour side by side with the White Ensign; two anti-aircraft 'cruisers'—converted MacAndrews banana-boats—had also been attached to the convoy, their armoured decks bristling with every calibre of anti-aircraft gun.

At Broome's conference, Rear-Admiral Hamilton told the officers the more confidential details of the general plan, including the likely movements of the battle fleet and the cruiser covering force; it was on this occasion, it seems, that the escort officers

---

* Unless otherwise stated, all times throughout this book are Zone–2, two hours later than GMT.

first learned that the Admiralty believed that the enemy's main units would come out to attack this convoy.*

After the escort destroyers had completed their complex fuelling programme from the one oiler at Seidisfiord, Broome's whole escort force had sailed by 3.30 p.m. on the 29th.

As they headed out towards their rendezvous with the convoy, the Commander-in-Chief of the Home Fleet was engaged in what was to prove a crucially important telephone call from Scapa Flow to the First Sea Lord in London: Tovey was discussing with Pound the disadvantages of sending heavy cruisers to cover the convoy into the Barents Sea east of Bear Island, where they would be prey to attack by U-boats and aircraft. The Admiralty considered close cruiser support essential for the convoy—the Germans had at the last count ten destroyers stationed in Norway; but Tovey assessed the risks to the cruisers more gravely than did the Admiralty. Moreover, large though the convoy's close escort under Broome was, he considered it inadequate for a convoy as large as PQ.17 in conditions so favourable to the enemy. Pound was adamant that the convoy should not be cancelled.[33]

It was at this juncture, according to Tovey's recollection of their conversation, that the First Sea Lord first mentioned the possibility that the Admiralty might order the *scattering* of the convoy if it appeared to be in imminent danger, presumably meaning the danger of attack by enemy ships. In itself this was an accepted tenet of convoy strategy, and it would not be the first time a convoy had been scattered; the procedure for scattering was laid down in the MERSIGS code books. But Tovey later professed himself aghast at Pound's gloomy suggestion, even though Pound was clearly only planning for a contingency which now seemed increasingly likely to occur.

At five o'clock on the afternoon of his disturbing telephone conversation with Admiral Pound, Admiral Tovey's battle fleet left Scapa Flow: the battleships *Duke of York* and *Washington*, the

---

* From the Diary of Lieutenant Caradus, *La Malouine*'s Asdic officer, 29 June: 'Captain attends conference . . . [details of warships in covering forces] . . . must be very important convoy to have this escort. Possibility of German fleet attacking.' He added: '3 p.m. Started [out] to rendezvous with convoy. *Lotus* did not have a chance to return *La Malouine*'s set of football boots. Seamen upset about this.'[32]

same aircraft-carrier *Victorious* as had nearly provoked *Tirpitz*'s nemesis four months earlier, two cruisers and eight destroyers sailed out into the North Sea; they steered an easterly course in the latitude of the Faroes, so shaped as to give the impression that it was covering 'Force X', a dummy convoy that had left Scapa Flow that same day, designed to simulate a raiding force heading for southern Norway.[34] There was no German reconnaissance of either force for two days, and they were not sighted; it is unlikely that the Germans, long forewarned of the imminent PQ convoy operation, would have been much misled in any case.

The American half of the cruiser force, transferring from Hvalfiord to Seidisfiord that day, picked up a signal from the Senior British Naval Officer at Murmansk reporting that QP.13 had been sighted by German aircraft when only one day out, so the Germans would know that something was now afoot.* A little before noon on the following day, 30 June, the two cruisers and three destroyers wound round and up the narrow channel to Seidisfiord, surrounded on all sides by the cold, gaunt mountains towering up into the clouds. The American sailors were awed by this spectacle of giant bleakness: 'The whole town looks like it might have slid down the hundreds of tiny waterfalls from the cloud-crowned mountaintops and then bumped to a stop when it came to the water,' was how Fairbanks described the port. The American warships passed and exchanged honours with HMS *Norfolk* and Hamilton's Flagship *London*. Bugles sounded their long, steady blasts, the windlasses started whirring, and by two o'clock the cruiser force was riding at anchor, while naval tankers pumped thick oil into their hungry bellies. Liberty boats ran between ship and shore—not that there was much to see: some inhospitable Icelanders had painted black Swastikas on some of the walls and houses, but that was all.

All the commanding officers assembled aboard *London* for luncheon with Rear-Admiral Hamilton, and he held a last conference to brief them on his planned action manœuvring signals and the like. In *Wichita*, the Executive Officer addressed the entire crew in the hangar deck aft, and told them of the operation that lay ahead. The crew listened with 'solemn, tense faces'.

---

* In fact, the full convoy was not sighted until 30 June, as will be seen.

After dinner, Captain Hill ordered all his officers to assemble in the cruiser's wardroom. A chart of the Barents Sea had been hung in the place where the cinema screen normally went. He announced that they were to sail at 2 a.m., and cover the convoy as far as the meridian of 25° East—the farthest point yet reached by a cruiser covering force. He reminded his officers of the military importance of PQ.17: 'Its cargo is valued at over $700 millions.' Finally, he dealt with the likelihood that there would be a naval action: seldom had a ship been able to know in advance approximately where and when such action would come; this was Intelligence of which he felt sure his officers would take full advantage. Perfect discipline was vital at all times, he stressed. As the outgoing convoy, PQ. 17, had still not been sighted by the Germans, things were going well so far. Just before he concluded, he slipped off his impersonal manner as commanding officer. Fairbanks, sitting not far away, noted that Captain Hill leaned on the table and smiled: 'Do you realize, I've been in the Navy since before many of you were born?' His eyes glistened visibly as he went on, 'All my life I've been studying, training and waiting for this one moment—and now it's come!' He sighed, wagged his head, and with a wave added,'Good luck to you all!'[35]

All evening the ships' padres were hearing confessions, and again there was a long quiet line of young sailors waiting with prayerbooks in their hands outside the chaplain's office doors. At 2 a.m., Hamilton's cruiser squadron, screened by the destroyers *Wainwright*, *Somali* and *Rowan*, sailed from Seidisfiord and proceeded north-eastwards at 18 knots to take up its covering position with the convoy.

All the Allied naval forces were now at sea.

3

'THE VICTIM IS PQ.17'

Tuesday 30 June — Saturday 4 July

The Russian convoy is and always has been an unsound operation of war.—Rear Admiral L. H. K. Hamilton, 30 September 1942

IN THE WAR CABINET's subterranean map room, in the First Sea Lord's room at the Admiralty and on the great square table dominating the Submarine Tracking Room in the Citadel behind Whitehall, the naval war charts now began to show the first traces of six tracks starting out from several shores fringing the Arctic ocean. There was the huge 8-knot convoy PQ.17 which had sailed four days before from Hvalfiord; there were the tracks of Broome's escort force and of Hamilton's cruiser squadron, hastening to the convoy's vicinity; there was the Home Fleet's heavy covering force under Admiral Sir John Tovey, and the abruptly curtailed track of the dummy convoy that had tried in vain to distract the attention of the enemy; finally, far to the east, there was the track of the QP convoy plodding from its Russian ports towards the western world.

If there were such charts in the German operational headquarters at Kiel, Narvik, Kemi and Berlin, then they were still bare, save for the cluster of flags around Jan Mayen Island—the cruising submarines of Admiral Schmundt's 'Ice Devil' pack. The Germans had detected nothing of the Allied movements yet.

Early on the afternoon of Monday, 30 June, some of the tracks had joined and merged, as the central characters in the developing tragedy took their place on stage. At 3.15 p.m., as the overcast and hazy horizon cleared, Commander Broome's escort force caught sight of the convoy and within half an hour he had stationed his vessels round the perimeter of the tight formation of merchant ships, still keeping excellent station despite intermittent low visibility. It was already very cold indeed.

The Germans had begun to suspect that convoy PQ.17 had left Iceland, for some days before sudden wireless silence had descended on the Icelandic anchorages, while at the same time there had been a sharp increase in radio traffic at Murmansk. Again, the RAF's aerial surveillance of the Trondheim fiord where *Tirpitz* lay had been intensified, and British reconnaissance activity over the more northerly of the Norwegian fiords had increased as well; finally, the German Air Force had reported both on the afternoon of the 28th and early on the following morning that British naval forces had been sighted off Iceland. Bad weather had prevented German reconnaissance either of the waters between Iceland and Jan Mayen Island, or of the ports of Murmansk and Kola Bay until the end of June, and it was not until 30 June that the Germans had located the full westbound convoy QP.13, and by that time it had already reached Bear Island, some 180 miles north of North Cape. The Germans decided to give their Air Force a free hand with this westbound convoy, while their battle fleet stood fast, lying in wait for the more precious PQ convoy which was now certain to have left Iceland for Russia: past experience suggested that the convoys would pass each other just to the east of Jan Mayen Island, a point known to British convoy veterans as 'suicide junction'.[1] It was unlikely that the German battle fleet would sail for at least a day. During the afternoon of 1 July, therefore, a lengthy teleprinter conference took place between Admiral Schmundt and General-Admiral Carls, as a result of which the latter returned to Schmundt control of submarine operations against PQ.17, until the fleet was ready to attack. Schmundt now had ten submarines lying off Jan Mayen Island waiting for the convoy to appear.* [2]

During the early afternoon, a signal was received by both the cruiser force and the convoy's escorts: it focused a disquieting light on the situation at Murmansk. As a result of heavy German air attacks, the Senior British Naval Officer reported, one-third of the town had been burnt down, and the British headquarters had been evacuated to the outskirts of the town; he could not recommend that any of the convoy's ships come to Murmansk as the defences were not adequate. The Admiralty immediately replied that all ships of adequate draught were to proceed to

---

* The tenth U-boat was *U-657* (Göllnitz). For the other nine, see footnote on page 30.

Archangel instead. Later, there was a further signal from White-hall to Tovey.

> Reconnaissance Trondheim failed, forenoon July 1st—unfit for photographic reconnaissance. As Force X was apparently not sighted owing to fog, it cannot have a diversionary effect. If you wish operation repeated, request you will make one word, 'Repeat'.³

Soon afterwards, they picked up Tovey's reply: 'Repeat'—so the dummy convoy manœuvre was to be attempted again. The mood in the American warships was now one of great excitement: 'The marines, as usual, came up to scratch. They were itching for a fight. Their two young Captains wore broad grins all day although some of the older sergeants, veterans of former campaigns, were a bit more serious.' Down in the wardrooms and in the communication office the specially wired radios were bringing dance music: Noel Coward was singing his new hit, 'London Pride', while the coding machines clattered out routine reports.

Lieutenant Fairbanks, observing and recording impressions all the time for his Admiral, wrote during the afternoon:

> The British Navy is under constant scrutiny by our professional 'sea dogs'. Its legendary superiority has, they say, gone. Its present state is a source of wonderment and discussion. How a great Navy, run by great sailors, could have allowed itself to fall behind in so many technical ways is more than our 'regulars' can understand. The hardships of three years' war, the shortage of materials and of manpower are only partial answers. Their accuracy in gunnery, quality, and types of ordnance, fire control, damage control and navigational aids are considered by our experts to be far behind the times. Their appreciation and use of naval aviation has caused them several unnecessary misfortunes. . . . They still remain great seamen, but one wishes that such worthy people, whose history is the history of the sea, had worthier tools.⁴

Soon after half-past two that afternoon, the enemy made his entrée. A distant aircraft was heard in the fog far behind the convoy. The anti-aircraft ship *Palomares*, keeping her radar beams well averted from hostile shores, picked up the aircraft as it approached from astern, and then the lookouts clearly saw it, a huge four-engined Focke-Wulf 200. No shot could be fired at the plane before it escaped. About an hour passed before the plane wirelessed its report to Norway. It came as a great relief to the escort commander, Commander Broome. The tension of waiting was broken. In particular, wireless silence could be relaxed. Broome believed that no method of controlling a convoy and its escort could compare with the simple radiotelephone. With no need for wireless silence now, he was able to get all the ships tuned in to his destroyer's radiotelephone frequency; and at 3.30 p.m. the convoy wirelessed Whitehall:

> One aircraft shadowing PQ.17 in position 71°11' North, 05°59' East.[5]

Broome also felt justified in breaking wireless silence again for a rather longer signal to the Admiralty, Hamilton, Tovey and the Admiral Commanding Iceland, reporting that two of the convoy's ships had been damaged north of Iceland and had had to turn back, and that the escort's oiler had also been holed and that he therefore proposed to exchange her for the 'Force Q' oiler, *Aldersdale*.

These lengthy wireless signals were all that the Germans needed to establish that it really was convoy PQ.17 that had been found. For while the Focke-Wulf's sighting report did not reach Admiral Schmundt in Narvik *for ten hours*, he had by 5.40 p.m. been informed by the German naval monitoring station at Kirkenes that the convoy which his U-boats were just beginning to report had been heard at 3.30 p.m. announcing that a shadowing aircraft had been sighted. Moreover a vessel with the convoy had thereupon transmitted a lengthy 'operational signal to the Admiralty and three further addresses', and this had enabled the monitoring station to obtain an extremely accurate fix on the convoy; it turned out to be very close to the position given by the first U-boat to sight Allied ships that afternoon.*

The first submarine to sight the convoy had actually been Lieutenant-Commander Max-Martin Teichert's *U-456*; at about 3.30 p.m. he had sighted over twenty-five merchant ships and at least four destroyer escorts, some of which caused him considerable discomfort shortly afterwards, for they had harried him with depth-charges for so long that he deemed it more prudent to

---

* The sighting report, timed 3.30 p.m., 1 July, was not passed to Schmundt by Lofoten Air Command until 1.25 a.m., 2 July.[6]

delay transmitting his sighting report until long after midnight. It was this caution which had made Teichert one of Schmundt's most reliable U-boat commanders; it was Teichert, in fact, who had torpedoed the cruiser *Edinburgh* two months before. But while *U-456* maintained its discreet silence for the time being, another U-boat in the patrol line, Lieutenant-Commander Reinhard Reche's *U-255*, had also sighted ships on the horizon, and half an hour after Teichert had made his first sighting, Reche wirelessed Narvik:

Light enemy forces are in position pinpoint AB.7166.

This was sixty miles east of Jan Mayen Island. It was the first report Schmundt had had of any naval units in the area, and he was considerably taken aback to find the enemy already so far to the east. The report from the naval wireless monitoring station at Kirkenes confirmed Reche's signal. Soon after Reche made his report, the British destroyer *Leamington* sighted him and warned *Keppel*, 'One submarine bearing 233° ten miles.' So the British now knew that they were being shadowed both by aircraft and submarines.

＊ 2 ＊

To Admiral Hubert Schmundt, studying the position at his floating headquarters in Narvik, it now seemed of supreme importance that his U-boats should not fall behind the convoy, already so surprisingly far to the east.[7] He wirelessed to all the 'Ice Devil' submarines:

All submarines not in contact with the enemy or on their trail proceed 50° at speed ten knots.

The weather in the U-boats' operational zone was still most unfavourable for any attack: there was a leaden sea and hardly any wind, there was a low layer of cloud and overcast and patches of fog alternated with sudden stretches of clear air where the visibility went up to fifteen miles and more. The submarine commanders found it impossible to attack—they were harried by the British escort vessels, forced down and bracketed with depth charges.

[56]

In mid-afternoon, Lieutenant-Commander von Hymmen's *U-408* reported that as the weather briefly cleared he had sighted the convoy but had been forced to dive by two destroyers. Von Hymmen's report meant that there were now at least two submarines in close contact with the enemy. Schmundt detailed these and two others to shadow the convoy, while the others worked ahead at speed to patrol a line across its path approximately midway between Jan Mayen Island and Bear Island; this was a technique of proven reliability. The eleventh of the U-boats assigned to the operation had flashed a brief 'reporting in' signal to Schmundt as it passed the latitude of 67° heading for the Barents Sea, and at a quarter to eight that evening Schmundt wirelessed this U-boat—Lieutenant-Commander Bielfeld's *U-703*—to make at full speed for the patrol line too.

The German Admiral now had all the parameters he needed to order the first rough deployment of his submarines, and at nine o'clock he wirelessed all of them:

> According to our wireless monitoring service and a signal from Reche, PQ.17 was at pinpoint AB.7166 at 4 p.m. Assume course north-east, nine knots.
>   Reche, von Hymmen, Teichert: shadow.
>   Timm, La Baume, Göllnitz, Bohmann, Brandenburg, Marks: occupy by 2 p.m. 2 July a patrol line extending between pinpoints AB.5155 and AB.5515.

The shadowing aircraft had by now lost sight of the westbound convoy. Two hours after he had sent this signal, Schmundt calculated that QP.13 would be crossing the submarines' operational zone at any time: he warned his U-boat commanders to let it pass, unless irresistible opportunities were offered to them. 'The victim is PQ.17.'

Like the Germans, the British Intelligence authorities maintained a series of highly efficient wireless monitoring establishments. The Admiralty had a cryptographic section capable of reading some of the German naval communications (up to a certain level of secrecy). Some signals were readily recognizable by their outward form; such were for example those sent by U-boats on making a sighting. At 6.30 p.m., Rear-Admiral

Hamilton's cruiser force was informed by wireless from Whitehall that an enemy submarine had sighted and reported PQ.17, and that more U-boats were concentrating to the east of the convoy.[8]

At this time, Admiral Sir John Tovey's battle fleet was cruising north-east of Iceland, steering north-westerly and southerly courses.[9] At six o'clock that evening, while some of his destroyers were away fuelling at Seidisfiord, a German long-range reconnaissance aircraft was sighted by the fleet; soon after, with the destroyers returned to his fleet, the Commander-in-Chief altered to the north-east to take up his covering position south of the convoy's tracks.

This was the enemy's first sighting of the Anglo-American battle fleet covering PQ.17: the Focke-Wulf 200 immediately wirelessed a report to the German North-West Air Command at Trondheim and they forwarded it with due delay to the German Navy.[10] The Allied fleet's composition was given as three battleships, one aircraft-carrier, six cruisers, six destroyers and three escort vessels, in a force some 120 miles north-east of Iceland— which was over three hundred miles from the latest position of the convoy—cruising at ten or fifteen knots in a south-westerly direction. As the weather had thickened, the shadower had lost the fleet at about 9 p.m. that night, at which time it was some forty-five miles north-east of Iceland. The aircraft had made minor errors in its reports, but it had estimated the positions and general scale of the force with great accuracy. That the Allied battle fleet was so far from the eastbound convoy suggested that it was not only to provide distant cover for the convoy, but also to insure against a suspected break-out by *Scheer* and *Lützow* into the Atlantic. General-Admiral Carls concluded significantly that 'it followed that the British were adhering to their previous procedure'.[11]

At present there was nothing to prevent the first phase of *The Knight's Move*—the fleet's move to advanced bases in northern Norway—from being launched: the Trondheim battle group was ordered to stand by at three hours' sailing notice as of noon next day, 2 July. By nine o'clock that morning, two of Admiral Schmundt's four shadowing submarines were still in close contact with the convoy, and six others were hastening to take up station in a patrol line across its path by 2 p.m. that afternoon. It was of

the utmost importance for the German Navy's planned fleet action
that the convoy be kept continuously in sight.

The sighting of PQ.17 on the previous day was the main item
discussed at Grand-Admiral Raeder's war conference in Berlin
during the morning. The German Naval Staff agreed that the
enemy had, as feared, delayed sailing both the westbound and the
eastbound convoys until the return of the notorious fogs of July.
That month was now upon them; how did it affect their chances
of success?

> Operationally we are considerably less well off than we might have
> expected to be in June [the German Naval Staff summarized].
> Even so it is extremely likely that our battle fleet will get its chance
> to strike, and it seems proper to adhere to the plans to transfer
> northwards the two battle groups, particularly as it is as yet im-
> possible to draw any conclusions on the probable intentions of the
> enemy's covering force, from such material as has come to hand.[12]

Raeder authorized Naval Group North in Kiel to issue the
appropriate orders, and the codeword was transmitted shortly
before 1 p.m. The Trondheim group, *Tirpitz* and *Hipper*, was to
sail at eight o'clock that evening; and the Narvik group, including
Scheer and *Lützow*, would leave their anchorages at Vestfiord's
Bogen Bay just four hours later. Arrangements were made for
Admiral Krancke, Raeder's permanent representative at the
Führer's East Prussian headquarters, to be kept fully appraised by
the chief of naval operations in Berlin on the enemy movements
and on all the orders issued by Kiel to the German battle fleet.

Very belated reports had by now reached Admiral Hubert
Schmundt in Narvik, giving him the results of the Air Force's
brief sighting of the convoy on the previous afternoon, and of
Lieutenant-Commander Teichert's more recent glimpse of the
merchant ships and their escort from his submarine some hours
later. During the early hours of Thursday, 2 July, Teichert had
again reported the convoy, now ploughing north-east at seven
knots; he had added that he was experiencing some difficulty with
the fog banks, and soon after he announced that enemy destroyers
were after him, and he was being forced to dive. With visibility
down now to only five hundred yards, Commander Reche was
also hard on the convoy's track, relying solely on the approximate

bearings given by his hydrophone equipment. Schmundt began to fear that his submarines might lose the convoy altogether before the Navy could attack with the battle fleet, and at his request the German Air Force intensified its reconnaissance patrols during the morning. They eventually sighted the convoy again at one minute past two that afternoon—thirty-eight merchant ships screened apparently by ten destroyers, steering a northerly course—and nine minutes later, Commander Broome was reporting the shadowing aircraft to London.*

Despite the accuracy with which air and submarine forces had now located both QP.13 and PQ.17, none of the Allies' heavy warships had been sighted by the Germans since the previous day.[13] On the other hand, as a result of the close submarine and shadowing aircraft contact with the eastbound convoy, fresh sighting reports were reaching Kiel on an average of one each hour.[14] Commander Teichert's *U-456* was still closely following the convoy, reporting PQ.17's course, speed and position with the greatest precision; by half-past two that afternoon, Commander Brandenburg's *U-457* was also in sight of the merchantmen. Shortly after 3 p.m. *U-255* launched a spread of two torpedoes at the convoy from outside the escort screen, forcing the American SS *Bellingham* to make an emergency turn forty-five degrees to starboard, but no damage was done.† [15] The anti-submarine vessels began dropping depth-charges, and the crashes of these weapons, the terror of the U-boat crews, continued to sound around the convoy's perimeter throughout the rest of the day. From the patrol line to the east of the convoy, *U-88* reported that he was following QP.13, the westbound convoy, but he was forced to dive by one of the German shadowing aircraft; when he had surfaced again, the convoy had gone. Schmundt ordered him to let it pass, and again signalled all the submarines to leave

---

* The German reconnaissance units operating against PQ.17 were: I./KG.40; I.(F)/22; I.(F)/124; II./406; III./906 and I./105.

† The torpedo log (*Schussmeldung*) of *U-255* stated, 'Firing data were estimated. Destroyer [target] must have heard torpedoes running or being fired. She turned hard to starboard after the torpedoes were fired. Subsequently attacked with depth-charges by destroyers and corvettes. Forty depth-charges.' I hold a complete set of these *Schussmeldungen* for PQ.17.

QP.13 unmolested. The victim was still PQ.17; it still had to be 'totally annihilated'; but so far not one ship had been sunk.

During most of 2 July, the thick weather blanketing North Cape had prevented most of the German's wheeled aircraft from taking off; of all the air bases, only Kirkenes with its *I./406* squadron of cumbersome Heinkel 115 torpedo-bomber float-planes was operational, and plans were laid between the Fifth Air Force headquarters in Oslo and the advanced headquarters at Kemi for an attack to be delivered by these planes late that evening.[16] At 2.38 p.m. Admiral Schmundt wirelessed the U-boats about the results of the air reconnaissance and about the Air Force's 'planned attack with seven Heinkel 115s', and half an hour later Commander Teichert was selected to keep shadowing the convoy and transmit homing signals for the aircraft.

Rear-Admiral Hamilton's wireless room could plainly hear the German shadowing aircraft carrying out homing procedure—broadcasting a series of '*A*'s, interspersed with a coded call-sign at regular intervals—and he was not surprised when information was received from the Admiralty that an 'air attack by torpedo-bombers' was expected to develop on the convoy at about nine o'clock that night. He despatched USS *Rowan* to the convoy to warn Commander Broome of the imminent air attack, refuel from the oiler *Aldersdale* and reinforce the escort screen. Later that afternoon, he was informed that the poor weather had again pre-vented any reconnaissance of the German warships' bases, al-though flights were now being flown continuously over them.[17] In fact the ships were still at anchor. Both the convoy and the cruiser covering force were blanketed in fog, with the cloud ceiling less than two hundred feet above sea level—ideal weather for torpedo-bomber attack.

✳ 3 ✳

The German Navy had always viewed with disfavour the Air Force's increasing interest in the torpedo as an airborne weapon for attacking enemy shipping. When it was decided early in the war to establish German torpedo-carrying bomber squadrons, no special torpedoes had been designed for them, and the early trials were conspicuous failures. The Naval Staff strenuously denied the Air Force access to information on naval torpedo developments, and when the Air Force attempted to collaborate with private industry on the design of suitable torpedoes, the Navy had deliberately impeded their efforts. Only in January 1942 had Göring obtained for the Air Force the right to open its own experimental and training establishments, and by the end of April there were, besides the Heinkel 115 torpedo aircraft of the German Coastal Command, twelve Heinkel 111 crews of the first squadron of *KG.26* waiting and ready at the newly constructed airfields of Banak and Bardufoss in northern Norway; by the time that convoy PQ.17 sailed, Coastal Command had assembled fifteen Heinkel 115 torpedo-floatplanes, and *KG.26*'s first squadron a further forty-two Heinkel 111 torpedo-bombers for the attack.[18]

At 12.20 p.m. on 2 July a Blohm & Voss 138 spotter plane had reappeared by the convoy, and within one or two hours two more planes had joined the convoy; through powerful glasses, these latter could be seen to be torpedo-carrying aircraft, not shadowers. The three aircraft continued to circle the convoy at a respectful distance for over an hour. Shortly, Commander Teichert's *U-456* was wirelessing back to Narvik that the convoy's merchant ships were hoisting barrage balloons.[6] The gunners stayed at their action stations for two hours, their eyes straining for the first signs of attack. Commander Broome signalled from *Keppel* that his radio room was picking up signals from the three circling aircraft, clearly homing in further aircraft on to the convoy. The attack came soon after half-past six, as two of the torpedo-bombers suddenly turned in towards the ships and raced in to attack only a few feet above the waves. Alarm bells shrilled.

6.36 p.m. Open fire. One torpedo seen to drop.

6.40 p.m. Steer 105°.

6.47 p.m. From *Keppel*: From unknown station—torpedo approaching convoy.

6.50 p.m. Red 160°. Two aircraft. Steer 100°.

6.51 p.m. Red 90°. Aircraft coming towards. Green 140°.

6.52 p.m. *Keppel* is firing at aircraft ahead.[19]

Amidst a chaos of orders, instructions, comments and warnings, the attack was over before it had begun: the two aircraft 'disappeared into mist ahead'.²⁰ There was one danger which could not be overlooked: that these long, tense runs into the convoy by the German planes were designed to distract the escorts' attention from the submarine pack snapping at the convoy's screen. At 6.56 p.m., however, *Leamington* was already broadcasting a warning of a new attack: 'Enemy aircraft are coming in to attack on a bearing 160°.'⁵

This time, the watching officers could see no fewer than seven torpedo-planes coming in towards the convoy from the starboard quarter. Four of the planes detached themselves from the rest, and came in at low level, their cannon firing at the ships which were putting up a curtain of anti-aircraft fire. One seemed to be heading straight for the Russian tanker *Azerbaijan*; the three rescue ships in the rear of the convoy, *Rathlin*, *Zaafaran* and *Zamalek*, aimed an intense hail of fire. *Zaafaran* managed to put one of the 4-inch HE shells from her low-angle gun right under the nose of the threatening plane,²¹ but *Zamalek* was badly hit by cannon-fire from the stricken bomber, the ricocheting shells smashing much of the glass in the wheelhouse of the little rescue vessel and injuring three ratings—a Bofors gunner and two gunners on the midship gunpit. The Bofors gunner had had one eye torn out by a fragment of one of the shells; Surgeon-Lieutenant McCallum—the ship's doctor—and a sick-bay attendant removed him and the two other gunners to the hospital fitted up in what had originally been one of the rescue ship's holds, and prepared to operate on them as soon as peace was restored to the convoy.²²

The Heinkel 115s were sturdy aircraft and those that had come within gun-range withstood more punishment than seemed possible. One of the American freighter officers afterwards reported, 'it seemed as though the ·50 calibre fire was doing little damage—the shot hitting the planes and bounding off'.²³ Only one of the bombers was mortally wounded, and that probably by the heavy shell fired by *Zamalek*'s sister ship, *Zaafaran*. The plane, piloted by the German squadron commander, had run the gauntlet of the maritime gun crews of the merchant ships as it flew straight on down between two columns of ships, but it limped right on through the advance screen of escorts, gradually losing height, until it suddenly nosed over and dived into the sea, right ahead of the convoy.

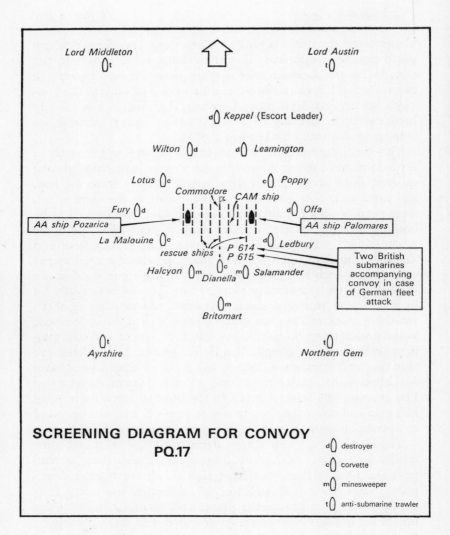

Lord Middleton
t

Lord Austin
t

d Keppel (Escort Leader)

Wilton d   d Leamington

Lotus c   c Poppy

Commodore   CAM ship

Fury d

AA ship Pozarica

AA ship Palomares   d Offa

La Malouine c

rescue ships   P 614   d Ledbury
                    P 615

Halcyon m   m Salamander
        Dianella c

Britomart m

Two British submarines accompanying convoy in case of German fleet attack

Ayrshire t

t Northern Gem

SCREENING DIAGRAM FOR CONVOY PQ.17

d destroyer

c corvette

m minesweeper

t anti-submarine trawler

Thirsting for blood, the warships of Broome's close escort at once headed for the floating bomber. Commander Broome signalled the Hunt-class destroyer *Wilton*: 'Aircraft shot down and in water', and added: 'Investigate!'⁵ Through binoculars, the destroyer officers could see the wretched German airmen clambering out on to the wing of their sinking bomber and struggling with a yellow rubber dinghy. It was possible to regard them as other than fellow human beings: these were the enemy. The airmen's plight could hardly have been more desperate. Two more destroyers were closing in on them from another quarter, possibly just over a mile away.

But then something happened of which PQ.17's survivors still talk in tones of awe and disbelief: a second Heinkel 115 suddenly appeared below the low overcast, and began losing height. Obviously it was going to land beside the wreck and dinghy in the sea, right in the path of the destroyers. *Wilton*'s captain, Lieutenant Adrian Northey, turned to his gunnery officer and asked if he wanted to take a pot shot: 'We aren't supposed to do this kind of thing in war, shooting at a man when he's down, but by Hell if we let him get away he may be back another day and sink the lot of us. Open fire!' The destroyer opened fire with her main armament on the downed aircraft, while she raced to close the range still further. Columns of water were thrown up all round the Germans as the shells exploded closer and closer. The other destroyers also opened fire.

The second Heinkel raced across the wavetops at zero feet towards the dinghy and the German airmen, and throttled back to a perfect halt amidst the giant spouts of salt water thrown up by the shells crashing down around them. Within moments the three airmen had climbed into the rescue plane; its pilot opened the throttles wide, and careered across the sea between the shell-bursts until it had gathered enough speed to lift off and vanish into the clouds.

The episode had happened so quickly it was over in a matter of minutes. *Wilton*'s guns ceased firing, and with that peculiar sense of disappointment that only the cheated hunter can understand returned to its station in the van of the convoy. They passed the empty wreckage and yellow rubber dinghy some minutes later. The Germans had lost their first encounter with PQ.17:

[65]

they had lost one aircraft, without claiming any hits on the ships. Nor had the submarines been able to penetrate the convoy's screen. The rumble of aircraft engines faded; the gunners collected the precious cartridge cases; the merchant ships edged back into their exact convoy formation once again. But the shadowing aircraft was still in company.

✳ 4 ✳

Late that evening, the two German battle groups left Trondheim and Narvik as planned for their advanced bases in Vestfiord and Altenfiord. At eight o'clock, just half an hour after the dramatic rescue of the ditched German airmen under the very guns of British destroyers, the *Tirpitz* group sailed, exploiting the Leads—the protected channels between the Norwegian coast and its tight fringe of offshore islands—for as far as they went.[24] Through the thickening swathes of mist, the battleship *Tirpitz*, the cruiser *Hipper* and their attendant destroyers negotiated the tight and tortuous Näröy Sound; even the *Tirpitz* made no use of the tug standing by, a further evidence of Captain Topp's outstanding seamanship. When the battleship had sailed for its nearly disastrous March sortie, the Norwegian pilots had warned Topp to give the treacherous Vegas fiord a wide berth; this time he eased the battleship right through it without difficulty. Topp had to abandon the shelter of the Leads only for the short stretch between Kaura and Grinna: he took it at a 25-knot run, crossing the gap in less than three-quarters of an hour.

By half-past midnight—the time the Narvik group weighed anchor in Bogen Bay—the mists had thickened, and dense fog was blanketing Tjeld Sound.[25] At a quarter-to-three, as Vice-Admiral Kummetz's flagship *Lützow* was nosing through the fog into the tightest part of the entrance to the Sound, the pocket-battleship touched bottom, extensively damaging her hull and flooding several watertight compartments.

Those versed in naval superstitions could enjoy their *Schadenfreude* now; it confirmed that all warships whose name are changed are under a curse in some degree. The battleship had been launched as *Deutschland*, but upon the outbreak of war Hitler had deemed it psychologically more prudent to have her renamed

Lützow: it would never do for a 'Deutschland' to be sunk or scuttled.* Now the *Lützow* had run aground, and had to be written off for the rest of *The Knight's Move*. Kummetz transferred his flag to *Scheer*, and sent the other unhappy warship back to Bogen Bay.

The Trondheim group fared little better: as the warships entered Vestfiord's Gimsöy narrows, three of the destroyers accompanying *Tirpitz* ran one after another into a submerged rock lying just off the deep-water channel incurring such damage to their propeller-shafts and screws that they were forced to drop out too. *Tirpitz* and *Hipper*—both closely following the main channel—avoided this uncharted obstruction. Norwegian mail-boats had used the same channels for decades, and even the shallow-draught Norwegian coastal warships had escaped injury; but the German destroyers, with their deep-thrashing screws, drew some three feet more than the Norwegian boats.

These casualties showed the Germans once again the hazards of using the Leads: they were inadequately charted and notorious for the swiftness with which unexpected fogs blotted out the narrower passages. The Germans took the casualties in their stride and reassured themselves that they need have no influence on the operation. Grand-Admiral Raeder learned of the setback at a small, highly confidential briefing session during the morning in Berlin: the Naval Staff stressed that regrettable though the dropping of *Lützow* from the operation was, it would have 'no bearing' on the execution of *The Knight's Move*; indeed, the ship's engines and armament were still fully serviceable, and her captain was requesting to be allowed to resume his rôle in the operation.[27] Naval Group North left a final decision on this to Admiral Schmundt in Narvik, but the latter heard the experts' reports on the damage, and ruled the possibility out altogether. *Lützow* had to return to Germany for four months of repairs.

By the time that the first battle group had left Trondheim on

---

* Cf. the note on Hitler's lunch-time comments on 4 July, when discussing this episode: he said he had rejected the idea of a battleship named *Adolf Hitler*, as it would be a disaster if he had to spend six months in dry-dock; and for the same reason *Deutschland* had been renamed *Lützow*, as 'the loss of a "Deutschland" would resound more strongly upon the German people than any other event'.[26]

the previous evening, three more U-boats had sighted the convoy, bringing the total up to five. During that night, however, the weather had thickened, and the campaign to keep the submarines down had begun in earnest: all night long, the depth-charges of the escort vessels churned the water, jarring the merchantmen and making sleep impossible for the three thousand officers and men manning the escorts and their charges. Lieutenant-Commander Heino Bohmann, who had been forcing his *U-88* ahead of the convoy all afternoon through the fog, had planned to deliver a textbook attack on it: he would submerge ahead of it, and rise to periscope depth once the anti-submarine screen had passed over him; twice he surfaced, but both times too soon, to find destroyers bearing down on him only a few hundred yards away on the beam. On the second occasion, the fog had closed in to two hundred yards by the time he surfaced once again, and this time the convoy had vanished. Commander Günther La Baume's *U-355* had a similar experience:

At pinpoint AB.4895 forced back by destroyer [he reported]. Contact again at pinpoint AB.5159 but sighted by corvette at pinpoint 5271 during convoy-overhauling manœuvre and forced to dive. Six depth-charges, no damage. . . .[28]

At 9.30 p.m., only *U-456* (Teichert) and *U-255* (Reche) had still held the convoy in sight; Teichert had reported that visibility was steadily deteriorating. Ten minutes later, after Reche had fired a spread of two torpedoes at a destroyer and missed, he surfaced to find that the convoy had vanished, leaving only *U-456* in contact. Visibility had remained poor, and at 10.30 p.m. Teichert was following the convoy only by its oil track and the soundings on his hydrophone gear. Then he had lost it altogether too.

The Air Force had held on until about midnight. Then the convoy had been swallowed up by the fog. The Allied heavy covering forces had still not been found by the Germans.

It was not until the following morning that submarines sighted the convoy again: this did not prevent the Admiralty from transmitting a 'Home Fleet Operational' signal at a quarter-past seven that morning, reporting that their direction-finding bearings had indicated that PQ.17 had been reported by the Germans at 4.47 and 6.37 a.m.; in fact, if anybody had reported the convoy it was not the Germans. The only U-boat signals transmitted during these early hours were by *U-456*, reporting at 3.30 a.m. to Narvik that he was still running in the convoy's oil track; by *U-355*, reporting his position (apparently well to the south of the convoy) and an improvement in visibility at 7 a.m., and by two submarines—*U-376* and *U-251* at 4.07 and 8.40 a.m. respectively—that they were down to their last 35 tons of diesel fuel, which would enable them to follow the convoy until about 30° East, at which meridian they would have to return to Kirkenes to refuel.

There again seemed to be some danger of the submarines falling behind the convoy. Schmundt radioed them at 7.48 a.m. giving them all the convoy's position, heading and speed as last ascertained at midnight, and informed them that he now intended to establish a new patrol line off Bear Island. Soon after, *U-255* and *U-456* both sighted large patches of floating oil, with tracks of oil leading from them; *U-255*, ploughing through fogbanks, with visibility down to two hundred yards, picked up convoy sounds far away on the port quarter: 'It's well known how far sound carries under water,' Commander Reche later explained.[29] He hastened to transmit an immediate signal to Narvik, and turned his craft in the approximate direction of the convoy sounds.

The other submarines listened steadily for further reconnaissance reports from Narvik. *U-88*'s hydrophone gear was faulty, but by dead-reckoning and on the basis of Reche's sighting report Bohmann worked his way forward until at 2.30 p.m. he was able to log: 'Convoy in sight again.'

One of the reasons why the submarines had found it difficult to relocate the convoy was that at about seven o'clock that morning, it had altered due east. During the convoy's approach to this turning point, Hamilton had purposely kept his force of four cruisers and three destroyers out of sight of the Germans, cruising in low visibility well to the north to avoid his force's being detected by any shadowing aircraft which might overshoot the convoy.[30] Hamilton had credited the Germans with sufficient insight to suspect that there would be cruisers covering the convoy, but by remaining hidden he intended to keep them guessing at his whereabouts. His original appreciation had been that to decoy Tovey's battle fleet, *Tirpitz* might be sailed in the direction of the QP convoy, now far to the south, while the two pocket-battleships, which Hamilton's force could fight, would deliver a separate attack on PQ.17, probably somewhere near Bear Island. The longer therefore that he remained unseen, the better were his chances of trapping the two pocket-battleships and bringing them to action. By midday on 3 July, however, it seemed that this appreciation had not been correct: *Tirpitz* had not been sighted heading for the QP convoy yet; and Hamilton was possessed of the 'uncomfortable feeling', as he put it, that he was now on the wrong side of PQ.17 for protecting it against surface forces:

> There was a possibility that the pocket-battleships might get in their attack and escape unscathed.[30]

He decided that the time had come to put into effect the second part of the Admiralty's 'general plan': the enemy should now be allowed to sight his cruiser force as soon as the weather cleared.

At 8.45 a.m. Hamilton accordingly turned his force to eastward, on a parallel course to the convoy's, while still twenty-five miles to the north of it. Within a short time the cruisers were ploughing through seas littered with several waterlogged ships' lifeboats and empty rafts—a sharp reminder of the punishment taken by PQ.16 at this spot at the hands of the German Air Force five weeks before. Some time later, the last doubts that the German battle fleet was to attack this convoy were dispelled, as the cruiser force received an urgent signal indicating that the German main units were at sea. At 2.20 p.m. a British Spitfire reconnaissance plane had broken through the clouds over Aasfiord, fifteen miles east of Trondheim, and found *Tirpitz*'s berth empty. The Admiralty signalled the cruiser force that photographic reconnaissance of Trondheim had shown the *Tirpitz*, *Hipper*, and four destroyers to be at sea. The patrols south of Iceland and in the Denmark Strait were strengthened to insure against a breakout into the Atlantic, and all available aircraft patrols were flown to find the missing German warships.[31] Narvik had still not been covered.

It was, in Hamilton's view, high time that the Germans learned of the presence of his force: visibility had by now increased to maximum, under a sky still totally overcast; the first signs of the convoy that he saw were the German shadowing aircraft, and then the convoy itself came up on the horizon, the tips of its masts looking like an uneven picket fence. He quickly turned his force away, hoping that the German aircraft had sighted and reported him to Norway. But by 5 p.m. there was still no Admiralty confirmation that such a report had been transmitted. The Germans seemed to have eyes only for the convoy.

As the German High Command now realized from the stream of sighting reports coming in, the PQ convoy intended to hug the ice-pack for most of its route, keeping as far to the north as was possible; PQ.17 was apparently now some ninety miles west of Bear Island, and it seemed to be heading for the passage between the island and Spitzbergen—the first PQ-convoy to sail north of Bear Island. The convoy, reported as comprising thirty-eight freighters in four columns, was hidden behind a screen of destroyers, and was towing barrage balloons. The sea's glassy surface still made it quite impossible for the submarines to come to close quarters with the merchant ships; they would have to content themselves with homing in the German aircraft. At 4.44 p.m., Schmundt wirelessed the only two submarines still in contact with the convoy: 'Main task—shadowing.'

It was indeed the Admiralty's intention that PQ.17 should give North Cape as wide a berth as possible. Some three hours earlier, Whitehall had wirelessed Admiral Hamilton the unexpected results of the latest aerial reconnaissance of the ice-barrier to the north. *London*'s Walrus aircraft was just about to be catapulted on an ice-reconnaissance when this signal arrived at 5.45 p.m.[32] A sortie the previous afternoon had shown that the passage between Bear Island and the ice-pack was ninety miles wide now, as the ice broke up and melted away; there was one patch of probably navigable loose ice in the convoy's path, and occasional small bergs about thirty feet high. Until now, Hamilton had no reason to suppose that the passage was more than forty miles wide, as shown by reconnaissance a week before. Hamilton said afterwards that the future was now 'very much more hopeful'. He cancelled the Walrus's assignment, and sent it instead to *Keppel*, the convoy's escort leader, with a signal directing Commander Broome to pass seventy miles north of Bear Island, and then aim for the 400-mile radius from Banak air base in Norway.

Keppel was oiling from *Aldersdale* when the aircraft approached, at 7 p.m.; this was the second round of refuelling already for the thirsty destroyers. Commander Broome watched the aircraft's Aldis lamp blink the new instructions to him, and also the information that Hamilton intended to remain thirty miles to the northward; finally, the American destroyer *Rowan* was to be returned to the cruiser squadron. At 8 p.m. Commander Broome altered the convoy's course to a more north-easterly one (53°).[33]

The Admiralty had meantime had the same idea as Hamilton and at 7.08 p.m. they had sent a signal ordering *Keppel* to pass at least fifty miles north of Bear Island. But when the Senior Officer of the escort signalled his amended convoy route to the Admiralty at 9.30 p.m., he had chosen not to carry out Hamilton's instructions, and was taking the convoy on a very much more easterly course than either Hamilton or the Admiralty had thought advisable in view of the danger of enemy air attack. There were grounds for arguing that it made very little difference from the point of air attack whether a lumbering, 8-knot convoy was three hundred or five hundred miles from enemy aerodromes. Broome was more anxious to make progress to the eastward in the beneficial low visibility on his current route than to waste time skirting round the outer limits of the German bombers' range.[34] Had not the Admiralty's orders a week before expressly stated that the convoy was to be kept 'moving to the eastward even though it is suffering damage'? Tovey subsequently supported his contention.

At about 9 p.m. a coded signal arrived from Whitehall advising Hamilton that *Tirpitz*, *Hipper* and four destroyers had definitely left Trondheim, but about five hours later the Admiralty added that although these warships were moving northwards, there was no immediate danger. Since the foggy weather in the Barents Sea was favourable to the convoy's passage, the Admiralty was taking no further action for the moment, but would await developments. In merchant ship and warship alike, an element of nervousness displaced the buoyant optimism of the previous nights, now that they were entering the probable battle zone. Many sailors avoided sleeping in their assigned quarters for fear of a midnight torpedo; the cooks and others who normally spent most of their time below decks found themselves places to sleep as high above the waterline as possible.[35] At 4.30 a.m. Hamilton signalled his force that they would maintain their present course until about six o'clock, when they would turn south until they reached the convoy, and then take up station on the convoy's southern flank—closest to Norway.

All the German warships were now at Vestfiord and Altenfiord, with the exception of the damaged *Lützow* and the three destroyers which had dropped out. The warships awaited only the codeword from Kiel to sally forth to attack the convoy; but Kiel could not act without the authority of the Naval Staff in Berlin, and Berlin was bound by the Führer's injunction that the Allied 'aircraft-carriers' were to be located before the attack, and rendered harmless.

By the late afternoon on 3 July, the German Naval Staff stood before the main decision, for such an Allied warship had been located, only to be lost again: at 1.50 a.m. a reconnaissance aircraft had sighted and shadowed for three hours a heavy enemy naval force, including an aircraft-carrier, some three hundred miles south-west of the convoy. The aircraft had in fact sighted Admiral Tovey's battle fleet as it was moving up to its covering position south of the convoy's tracks.* But an element of mystery had entered the German side of the story, as one hour after the initial sighting a second German aircraft claimed to have sighted a similar enemy force one hundred miles to the south-east of the first; apparently this second force also included an aircraft-carrier, and two battleships as well. This second force did not exist in fact; neither Tovey nor Hamilton (who was keeping his presence hidden hundreds of miles away to the north) reported sighting any aircraft at that time. The obvious effect of this wrong sighting on the German planning was to place a second 'aircraft-carrier' somewhere in Arctic waters—a carrier that had to be 'located' and neutralized before the German fleet could sail. A crippling element of uncertainty was introduced into the German decision-making.

The Germans realized at once the possibility of error: with considerable acumen, their air force operations staff set up the

---

* 'At 2.00 a.m. on 3rd July, the Fleet was . . . sighted by air reconnaissance, and shadowed until 4.30 a.m.' The two aircraft were both from *KG.40* reconnaissance wing, based at Trondheim.[36]

hypothesis that there was in fact only one force, which one or other of the two aircraft had inaccurately fixed; the total force might then credibly comprise *one* aircraft-carrier, two battleships, three cruisers and five destroyers. Notwithstanding Lofoten Air Command's loyal defence of its two pilots' faculties of observation and navigation, Admiral Schmundt also held that the concentration of two such heavy forces would be 'unlikely', and Naval Group North in Kiel also associated itself with this view, while warning that the presence of two such forces could not altogether be ruled out. It did not, for example, explain what had happened to the other heavy ships—one 'battleship' and three cruisers*—that had definitely been identified in the large force off Iceland two days before. Uncertainty and hesitation prevailed in Germany, even though at every level in the Navy—from Schniewind the fleet commander, through Carls right up to Raeder—it was not thought that such remote enemy force could seriously endanger the operation; in any case, the fleet's attack could be broken off at a moment's notice if necessary. The German Naval Staff was convinced that the movement of their two battle groups had not yet been detected by the enemy. Yet the Führer's restriction still stood, for the enemy aircraft-carriers, although found, had not been neutralized; and fog was preventing all attempts at re-locating the enemy's battle fleet.

During the early afternoon, therefore, General-Admiral Carls ordered Schmundt:

> Operate submarines low in fuel (especially Timm and Marks) against heavy enemy battle fleet, using the rest of their fuel for attack and return to nearest fuelling base.

Schmundt was greatly put out by this unrealistic order: while he, as Carls's subordinate, had to carry it out, he protested to Carls that nothing had been heard of the enemy fleet for ten hours; that the two submarines named were four hundred miles away; that he had planned to exhaust their remaining fuel in the operations against PQ.17 now approaching 'a decisive phase' and then return them to Kirkenes to refuel; and that operations against enemy fleets could more appositely be executed by submarines in greater

---

* Presumably Hamilton's force.

force and adequately fuelled for lengthy operations.[37] Carls did not reply to this for several hours.

At four o'clock that afternoon, Carls telephoned the Chief of Naval Operations in Berlin to ask for a decision one way or the other, on whether *The Knight's Move* was to go ahead or not. He suggested that in the meantime the *Tirpitz* group should move up from Vestfiord to join the other group at Altenfiord; both battle groups could then sail together, as circumstances permitted. The Naval Staff put this suggestion up to Raeder, but he was unwilling to approve even this without Hitler's permission.* He ordered first that a report be made to the Führer on this: while the report was to make it clear that he, Raeder, was aware that all the conditions had not been met, and that air reconnaissance had failed to establish clearly the enemy battle fleet's recent movements, the Naval Staff and Naval Group North both agreed that the *Tirpitz* group should be transferred to Altenfiord with the other battle group, to avoid wasting time if—and when—the order for the attack should be issued. Vice-Admiral Krancke was particularly instructed to make it plain that the Führer's permission was desired only for the provisional transfer, not for any attack itself as yet.

General-Admiral Carls expressly asked that the final order for the attack should be issued by 10 p.m. that night if possible. But although Krancke (Raeder's naval representative at the Führer's headquarters) made an attempt to see Hitler to place Raeder's request before him, he learned that the Führer was 'not available'.† Krancke reassured Raeder that, from the general tenor of Hitler's discussions with him, he was satisfied that there would be no objections raised from that quarter. Naval Group North was ordered to see to the transfer of the *Tirpitz* group from Vestfiord to Altenfiord at once.

---

* The real value, in terms of hours gained, by such a move is open to doubt: the battle fleet's advance would have been governed by the best speed of the pocket-battleship, which was at Altenfiord already; perhaps the psychological reason underlying Carls's suggestion was that he wanted his superiors to commit themselves, to resign themselves to an eventual sortie.

† Hitler had flown out of his Rastenburg HQ at 4 a.m. for an all-day visit to the HQ of Army Group South at Poltava.[38]

Convoy PQ.17 was already approaching the northern barrier of pack ice: shortly before seven o'clock, the Asdic trawler *Lord Austin* signalled an anxious warning to *Keppel* that she had sighted a 'suspicious vessel' ahead; but a few minutes later she corrected this to, 'iceberg in sight'. Half an hour later a second iceberg hove into view, and then a third. Soon the German submarines trailing the convoy were wirelessing back to Narvik that the convoy was surging at a steady 8 knots through fields of ice floes often jutting twenty-five feet and more out of the leaden sea.

At the same time, the Admiralty wirelessed the convoy escort:

Single D/F bearings at 4.21 and 5.10 p.m. suggest presence of enemy unit or units, probably U-boats, in the vicinity of PQ.17—probably shadowing.

That the Admiralty's submarine-tracking room was able to secure only 'single' direction-finding bearings on wireless transmissions in these hazardous northern waters must be borne in mind in a later context. Normally two bearings on an enemy transmitter would suffice to locate it; but in the waters north of North Cape, the position was less favourable as—for reasons not hard to divine —the Russians had refused permission for the British to establish a wireless monitoring station on their northern territory. At the time of PQ.17 only long-range and very narrow-angle bearings could be obtained on U-boat signals north of North Cape, and these were not adequate.[39]

By this time, the Anglo-American battle fleet was moving up to a new position, in readiness to strike at the German battle fleet. Admiral Tovey, who had been in 'considerable doubt' as to where the German U-boats were, had now gathered from the Admiralty that the submarines were congregating to the north-eastward near the convoy; at 5.23 p.m. the British Commander-in-Chief accordingly altered his battle fleet to northward, so that it would cross well astern of the convoy's tracks and avoid being sighted by any U-boats that might be straggling behind the main pack.[40] It was important that his fleet should not be detected moving up into its new covering position in the north.

Tovey calculated that the German surface attack on the convoy was unlikely to materialize before 6 a.m. next morning, 4 July, and by that time his fleet would be so positioned on the far side of the convoy that his aircraft-carrier would be well within air striking range. When the Germans appeared, his carrier-aircraft could suddenly pounce on the German heavy vessels and perhaps disable them long enough for his fleet proper to arrive and deliver the *coup de grâce*. The hook was baited; the trap was set; but would the Germans blunder in?

✳ 5 ✳

To the German Commander-in-Chief afloat, Admiral Schnie-wind, aboard his flagship *Tirpitz*, the continued delay in the arrival of the final codeword for launching the battle fleet's attack was by now both oppressive and inexplicable. Unaware of the telephone calls that were passing between Kiel and Berlin, and between Berlin and the Führer's headquarters, he could see no reason why the two battle groups—his own at Vestfiord, and the pocket-battleship *Scheer* at Altenfiord—should not leave at once. Both battle groups had anchored without further complication in their two advanced bases, the *Tirpitz* and *Hipper* at 2 p.m. in Vestfiord's Gimsöy narrows and the *Scheer* and her attendant destroyers almost four hours later at Altenfiord.[41] The destroyers had by now finished their refuelling programme.

At five o'clock, an aircraft catapulted by *Tirpitz* arrived at Narvik bringing three signals that Schniewind wanted Schmundt's nearby headquarters to transmit for him. To his consternation, Schmundt saw that the first of the three signals was the executive order for the launching of *The Knight's Move* at 10 a.m. next morning. Schmundt commented:

> Obviously the fleet has made a mistake, as Naval Group North has not yet issued the codeword ordering the attack.

Schmundt suppressed the signal. An immediate command-level teleprinter 'conversation' took place between Narvik and Kiel: Schmundt told General-Admiral Carls of the fleet commander's action, and of the other two signals he had received from Schniewind, one of which asked for closer information on the enemy's movements, while the other reported for the first time the damage suffered by the three destroyers—*Riedel, Galster* and *Lody*—in the *Tirpitz* group. Carls approved Schmundt's action in suppressing the premature sailing order, and promised for his part to secure an early decision on when the codeword should finally be issued.

Admiral Schniewind was signalled, 'Await the return of your ship's aircraft.'

None the less, fifteen minutes later, at 6.00 p.m., the German fleet commander had weighed anchor in Vestfiord, and *Tirpitz* and her consorts were putting out to sea.

The successful British reconnaissance of *Tirpitz*'s earlier berth at Trondheim sent a ripple of agitation through the teleprinter networks of the German Navy. The Germans realized that the Allied discovery that the *Tirpitz* was on the move would probably have a profound effect on their plans for covering the convoy's passage.

At about the time that *Tirpitz* was nosing out of Vestfiord, General-Admiral Carls sent a detailed signal to Schmundt, Kummetz, the Naval Staff, the Fifth Air Force and Admiral Schniewind:

Appreciation of situation as of 6 p.m.
1. Distant covering force last sighted 4.30 p.m. Probably only one carrier-force, but two not ruled out. Carrier-force possibly following eastwards.
2. Battle groups will accordingly first link up in Altenfiord; further decision follows.
3. PQ.17 sighted by submarines at pinpoint AB.3740 [West of Bear Island] at 3.25 p.m. Spitfire sortie over Aasfiord [Trondheim] at 2.20 p.m. may bear upon enemy's movements.
4. *Lützow, Riedel, Galster, Lody* have dropped out.—
                          Naval Group North. Most Secret.

Two hours later, Carls signalled the fleet commander, 'Transfer to Altenfiord. Decision whether internal or external route will be left to you. Decision on issue of codeword follows later. Report intentions.'*

Tirpitz, however, was not at anchor patiently awaiting orders from Kiel. At the time Carls's first signal arrived, the battleship was already advancing on the convoy. The second signal was already being transmitted when *Tirpitz*'s aircraft returned to

---

* The two signals originated at 6 p.m. and 7.57 p.m. respectively.[37]

Narvik; from its pilot Schmundt was shocked to learn that
Tirpitz's battle group had on Schniewind's own initiative sailed
at six o'clock. Upon receipt of General-Admiral Carls's order, the
group now changed course and headed for North Cape.* By
ten o'clock next morning, Saturday 4 July, the whole German
battle fleet was obediently lying at Altenfiord waiting for the
order to attack to reach them from Kiel.

Late on the evening of 3 July, Hamilton again felt it important
for the success of the Admiralty's general plan that the Germans
should be afforded another careless glimpse of his cruiser force,
and at nine o'clock he had accordingly altered to the south-east
to close to within twenty miles of the convoy.[32] At 10.15 p.m.
he sighted the convoy's barrage balloons over the horizon, and
almost immediately was himself sighted by two Blohm & Voss
shadowers. The convoy was passing only about thirty miles
north of Bear Island. Hamilton's dismay at Broome's disobedience
of his directive to steer the convoy seventy miles north of the
island was mollified by the news which reached him some minutes
later from Whitehall that the Germans had at last reported him,
'which pleased me considerably,' he reported to his Commander-
in-Chief.

Having achieved his purpose, he turned his cruiser force
parallel with the convoy once more, thirty miles to the north;
and he broke wireless silence for the first time to inform the
Admiralty and his Commander-in-Chief that he had been
shadowed, adding that he intended both the convoy and the
cruiser force to pass seventy miles north of Bear Island.

During the evening, the net of submarines began to close in on
the convoy: the U-boats made repeated attempts to come to close
quarters, but the patchy fog and glassy sea effectively thwarted
them. 'The conditions are the most unfavourable imaginable for

---

* *Tirpitz*'s plane brought the following signal for transmission to
Naval Group North in Kiel: 'I infer from your 5.49 p.m. orders to
proceed to Altenfiord. Proceeding externally as far as Naja, then
internally. Pinpoint Richard One at 1 a.m., minesweeper there. (2) As
at present informed on enemy, I support continuation of "*The Knight's
Move*" early tomorrow morning. (3) Urgently require clear picture of
enemy heavy forces' movements by then. *Fleet Commander*.'

submarines', complained Admiral Schmundt that night.[37] His U-boat commanders could clearly see the heavy merchant ships, and counted four of their barrage balloons waiting to be sent aloft. One by one Reche, Teichert, Bielfeld, Bohmann and Siemon picked up the convoy again; but none could attack. 'Numerous subs are closing in,' wrote the Second Officer of the American freighter *Bellingham* in his diary that night. 'Depth-charges have been jarring the vessels all day long.'[42] Half an hour before midnight, Hamilton's flagship catapulted its Walrus aircraft on an anti-submarine patrol astern of the convoy, at Commander Broome's request. Hamilton furnished the Walrus crew with a renewed instruction to Commander Broome to route the convoy four hundred miles from Banak airfield.

The Walrus, cumbersome, ugly and slow, was crewed by three Fleet Air Arm officers, and its top speed was just below that of the German Blohm & Voss 138 floatplanes of which there were now between two and four constantly circling the convoy, keeping at a respectful distance from its anti-aircraft defences. It was therefore no problem for *London*'s Walrus to fly into the convoy and to harass the U-boats impudently trailing it on the surface some miles astern; but when its fuel endurance was running low, the Walrus found itself unable to extricate itself and return to its cruiser, because one or other of the German shadowers pounced on it and opened fire on it each time. After several attempts, the Walrus pilot gave up and resolved to land inside the convoy, to be taken in tow by one of the escorts.

The plane still had its anti-submarine depth-charges with which it could not land, so as it came in over the convoy for the last time, its observer released the two depth-charges in a clear space of water. Unfortunately he had forgotten to drop them safe, and as the bombs hit the sea they exploded, convincing the bemused ships' gunners that this must in fact be a German plane. The corvette *Lotus* and trawler *Lord Middleton* both opened fire on the plane with their pom-poms.[43] The Walrus landed safely, nevertheless, and was taken in tow by the trawler, to wait for the weather to deteriorate sufficiently for it to rejoin the cruiser force.

The submarines continued to close in. Soon after midnight, Whitehall signalled PQ.17 that German aircraft were using beacon procedure to home in submarines on to the convoy, and they added that they had obtained several direction-finding bearings indicating that several submarines were shadowing and reporting the convoy.[5] But that was all; while the visibility even at midnight remained so good, the U-boats could not attack. The German Naval Staff noted without comment that none of the submarines had yet scored any victories against the convoy. When Admiral Schmundt renewed his protest at the order to two of his submarines to engage the enemy battle fleet although they were almost out of fuel, and the enemy was well to the west of the Lofotens, General-Admiral Carls replied tartly that as far as the remaining eight U-boats were concerned 'the lack of any kills so far makes it seem probable that with shadowing their repertoire is virtually exhausted—in which case eight submarines are enough.'[44] Schmundt retired to bed to lick his wounds.

During the night, the wireless officer of the *Bellingham* tuned in to Lord Haw-Haw, broadcasting from Germany. A notice was pinned to the ship's bulletin-board announcing that William Joyce had promised the American seamen that they would get a 'real display of fireworks' on their Fourth of July.[45] In the SS *Carlton* another seaman was reminded of the good old days back home: 'I realized,' he later wrote to his wife from a German prison camp, 'that this was the eve of Independence Day, and my daydreams rested on the memories of the fireworks and thrills that Baltimore enjoyed on every Fourth of July; and I wished then that I was there to see them. Oh God, how ignorant we are of the future!'

It was shortly after midnight that the German Naval Group North first learned that at 10.30 p.m. one of their aircraft had sighted what seemed to be a heavy enemy force cruising some thirty-five miles north-west of Bear Island, in the immediate vicinity of convoy PQ.17. Alas for the best laid plans, for the aircraft had reported Rear-Admiral Hamilton's force as comprising one 'battleship', one heavy and two light cruisers, and three destroyers. The German Naval Staff immediately realized that it was

possible that this is the convoy's close covering force of cruisers and destroyers, and that the identification of one of them as a battleship is a mistake.[46]

The 'battleship' was indeed really a cruiser, probably Hamilton's flagship; *London* had been modified to have two funnels, rather like *Duke of York*, and the confusion was understandable.⁴⁷ But as soon as the Germans even began to suspect the presence of a 'battle-ship' with the convoy, the Admiralty's carefully laid plan began to come unstuck. As General-Admiral Carls put it, if there were only cruisers covering the convoy then all was still well; but if there *was* a battleship in close company, then a raid by *Tirpitz* would have to be ruled out altogether, unless both the 'battleship' and any aircraft-carrier that might consequently be about could be neutralized.

It had to be assumed that the Allies either already had detected, or shortly would detect, the transfer north of both German battle groups. This left four possible courses of action open to the Allies. As the German Naval Staff saw them, these were:

1. turn their precious convoy back; or
2. move their battle fleet up so close to the convoy, and accompany it so far, that it will no longer be practicable for us to engage it with our own surface forces; or
3. if two battle groups *are* out there, keep one group with the convoy while stationing the other north-west of the Lofotens, in order to deprive our battle fleet of its tactical freedom, and attack it with carrier-borne aircraft; or
4. keep their heavy forces well out of the range of our bomber- and torpedo-aircraft, being thus compelled to leave the convoy's protection to a few light cruisers and destroyers. ⁴⁸

In the first case, the Germans would no longer be able to surprise the Allies, but on the other hand the convoy would either not reach its destination at all, or at least be delayed a long time. The second alternative would equally result in the Allies exposing their forces to German submarine and bomber attacks, while the third was hemmed in by such formidable imponderables that it would be unrealistic to risk the German fleet.

Only in the fourth and last situation envisaged did the Naval Staff see 'all the prerequisites basic to the operational plan for "*The Knight's Move*" satisfied.' This is the situation which would have arisen, had the British Admiralty's plan been adhered to.

As the hours of midnight passed—hours of darkness in Berlin, but of eerie brightness in the latitudes of Bear Island—the German Naval Staff waited tensely for the next reconnaissance report to confirm or deny the existence of vessels larger than cruisers in close company with PQ.17: 'If this force should not continue eastward, or if it should transpire that it does not consist of heavy units, the way would be open for our own battle groups to sail into the attack on 4 or 5 July.' But when the German shadowing aircraft looked again, there was no sign of the elusive cruisers: Admiral Hamilton's force had headed to the north again, satisfied that they had been sighted; and in Germany the doubts accordingly remained unresolved. At 2.20 a.m. Naval Group North telephoned Schmundt's office at Narvik and ordered a change in the emphasis of the submarine offensive for the time being: the U-boats were to concentrate on seeking opportunities of attacking 'aircraft-carriers and battleships'; shadowing the convoy and attacking its freighters were of secondary importance. The three submarines by now low in fuel were to return to refuel at once.

<h2 style="text-align:center">✳ 6 ✳</h2>

At about the same time, the lookouts in the convoy's merchant ships became aware that numbers of aircraft were circling the convoy. At 2.19 a.m. *Keppel* had signalled all the escorts, 'enemy aircraft are coming in to attack on the starboard side'.[5] The attack did not materialize at once, which may have been because the aircraft were having difficulty in sighting the convoy, now shrouded in a thick sea fog, with the cloud ceiling right down to only about two hundred feet. There was no breath of wind, and the sea was smooth save for the wash of the three score merchant ships and escort vessels steaming steadily to the north-east. The merchant ships could see nothing but the fog buoys trailed by the next ship ahead of them; but they were keeping almost perfect station none the less. Once an aircraft did break cloud and head across the convoy, barely thirty feet up; its pilot was perhaps as surprised as were the freighters' gunners, for the few ships which did have time to open fire scored no hits, and the plane dropped no torpedo. 'General quarters' was sounded on all ships.

For two hours, the aircraft engines could be heard muttering vaguely through the fog. Then, at 4.50 a.m., one of the aircraft, a Heinkel 115 torpedo-bomber of the Coastal Command *Staffel 1./906*, turned abruptly in from perhaps half a mile away, cut its

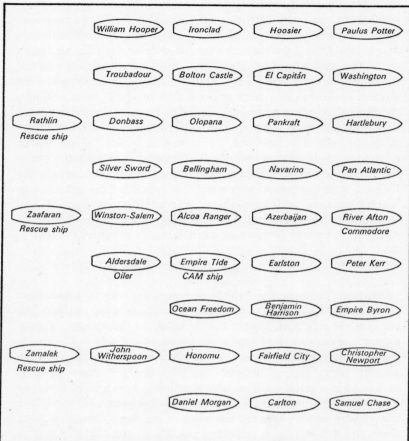

William Hooper | Ironclad | Hoosier | Paulus Potter

Troubadour | Bolton Castle | El Capitán | Washington

Rathlin
Rescue ship | Donbass | Olopana | Pankraft | Hartlebury

Silver Sword | Bellingham | Navarino | Pan Atlantic

Zaafaran
Rescue ship | Winston-Salem | Alcoa Ranger | Azerbaijan | River Afton
Commodore

Aldersdale
Oiler | Empire Tide
CAM ship | Earlston | Peter Kerr

Ocean Freedom | Benjamin
Harrison | Empire Byron

Zamalek
Rescue ship | John
Witherspoon | Honomu | Fairfield City | Christopher
Newport

Daniel Morgan | Carlton | Samuel Chase

LAYOUT OF MERCHANT SHIPS IN CONVOY PQ.17

BEFORE LOSS OF CHRISTOPHER NEWPORT EARLY ON 4 JULY 1942

engines, and glided silently towards the convoy, falling to a height
of less than thirty feet above the waves: its pilot saw the dim shapes
of three or four large merchant ships looming up grey across its
path, and swung round until his plane would head diagonally
into the starboard flank of the convoy. 'The plane was not heard
until it was seen', reported the Armed Guard officer of the
American Liberty ship *Samuel Chase* afterwards.[49] His ship was
right in the path of the attacking aircraft.

Aboard the SS *Carlton*, the next in line astern of the *Samuel
Chase*, in the extreme starboard column of the convoy, panic
broke out as the Heinkel was suddenly spotted gliding noiselessly
towards her through the luminous fog; when the aircraft was
only a very short distance from the column, it released two
torpedoes, then switched on its engines again to roar out of
range of the ships' guns. The torpedoes scudded rapidly towards
the leading ships of the starboard column. *Carlton*'s chief officer
shrieked for the helm to be put over hard to port, and the engines
went Full Astern; with the ship shuddering from stem to stern,
she lost way, the salt water boiling in a mass under the reversed
tread of the screws. The torpedoes missed the American's bows
by about ten feet, watched by a dazed ordinary seaman standing
lookout on the fo'c'sle head. The torpedoes sped diagonally on
through the gap between the *Carlton* and *Samuel Chase* to the
next column to port—column eight. The copper-yellow warhead
of one torpedo was clearly visible just below the surface of the sea.

Carlton sounded her siren to warn the leading ships in column
eight, but too late: the weapon was heading straight for the midship section of the 7,197-ton Liberty ship *Christopher Newport* at
the head of that column.[50] The ship's Armed Guard officer kept
his head and ordered the machine-guns to be turned on the torpedo racing towards them. The *Newport*'s merchant seamen
loading the guns lost their nerve and scrambled to the ship's port
side. One gunner remained at his post, directing a hail of bullets
at the torpedo; but the water deflected them and the torpedo
sped on. It slammed into the ship's engine-room, tearing a gaping
hole and knocking the steering gear out of action. A tongue of
flame and smoke licked momentarily out of the wound, and it was
all over. The gallant gunner who had risked so much was lying
unconscious on the deck, three men in the engine-room were dead

or dying, and the helpless ship was yawing out of control across the sixth and seventh columns of the convoy, narrowly missing collision with the other ships, before she wallowed right round in the opposite direction to that of the convoy, and slowed to a standstill.⁵¹ The surviving ships rolled past her, and the convoy was swallowed up by the fog.

Christopher Newport—code-number in the convoy, 'Penway 81' —wirelessed *Keppel*: 'Hit by aerial torpedo.' Commander Broome ordered *Leamington, Ledbury* and *Poppy*: 'Take all possible action to keep U-boats down.' Some of the escorts would have to stay behind to tend to, and if necessary finish off, the torpedoed ship and they could themselves fall an easy prey to any submarines; in fact none of the U-boats was in contact with the convoy now.

Her buzzers sounding 'rescue stations', Captain Morris's little *Zamalek* (1,567 tons) was already making for the American ship; her crew had needed no orders to abandon ship. Even before the torpedo hit, the vessel's lifeboats had been swung out ready: two of the four had been destroyed in the blast, but the other two were already pulling away from the merchant ship, which while she remained in sight showed no signs of settling at any time, according to the eye-witnesses.⁴⁹

Twenty-five minutes later, the rescue ship had picked up all the American's forty-seven survivors, including the Master, Captain C. E. Nash. It was a strangely varied crew: one of them, the bosun, was over eighty; while the youngest of the gunners was only seventeen. The seamen were headed, as they climbed aboard, by an elderly Scots engineer; behind him came a throng of laughing, shouting, happy seamen. Captain Morris had never seen shipwrecked seamen as exuberant as this; most of them were Negroes, and all of them seemed to be carrying little brown and grey suitcases as though they were going to the City; some of them were in their 'Sunday best', complete with collar and tie. All were dryshod, so smoothly had the abandonment and the rescue operation run.⁵² When Morris saw his seamen labouring to help the American crew aboard, loading up their suitcases and luggage, he finally lost his temper and shouted to his men not to mind about the baggage.

They were by now seven or eight miles behind the convoy, and only a corvette and one or two minesweepers had remained behind. The oiler *Aldersdale* was signalling that she was willing to take the crippled American in tow. Commander Broome ordered the corvette *Dianella* to stand by, and signalled the minesweeper *Britomart* 'Vet 81', meaning that they were to investigate the ship's state and report back. At 5.20 a.m., after Morris had picked up the last survivors, *Britomart* signalled *Keppel*:

Master of *Chris Newport* reports engine-room and stokehold flooded. Might float if bulkheads hold. Steering gear out of action.

Broome knew that there was no time for getting the Liberty ship under way again. He ordered *Britomart* to resume her station one mile astern of the convoy, and signalled *Dianella* to take a submarine over to the abandoned freighter and sink her. *P-614* fired one or two torpedoes into the ship, but the American showed no signs of sinking; *Dianella* even tried a couple of depth-charges, but they had equally little effect.[53] By now even *Zamalek* was disappearing over the horizon towards the convoy, so the corvette and submarine finally gave up their attempts at sinking the *Christopher Newport* and headed after them. The brand-new Liberty ship was left on the surface.

Aboard the rescue ship, Captain Morris ordered his Chief Officer to bring the American Master up to his bridge. He also ordered his Chief Steward to make a big pan of steak-and-kidney pudding, so that if his rescue ship were now hit, then at least everybody would have adequate sustenance for survival. Some moments later, Captain Nash was brought to see Morris with his Armed Guard officer; the little Welsh Captain suspiciously eyed Nash's heavy American service revolver strapped to his waist. Morris interrupted Nash's long-winded description of the loss of his ship to inform him that he could not allow the Americans to wear revolvers on his ship; would they please hand them to *Zamalek*'s Chief Officer, Mr Macdonald?

For a moment Nash could only gape; Morris was a good eighteen inches shorter than he was. He protested, 'Well good God, kid! What are we going to do? These are all nigger boys!' Morris quietly ordered Mr. Macdonald to collect their revolvers. Nash was shouting: 'They're all Negroes—if they start a panic, you have got to shoot them, you see.' Morris told him that there was not going to be any shooting in his ship; he further intimated that if the Americans disliked accepting orders from him, they could go back where he had found them—in their lifeboats. For a moment it was in the balance: then the two Americans unstrapped their guns and handed them over. Throughout the rest of the voyage to Archangel, during which at one stage *Zamalek* was under air attack for four hours continuously, not one of the Negroes showed the least signs of panic.

At 5.45 a.m., *Britomart*, by now closing the convoy, informed *Keppel*: 'One officer, two men killed in *Chris Newport*. *Zamalek* has 47 survivors.' As for the ship herself her former Armed Guard officer reported to the American authorities that she had 'sunk stern first, as result of gunfire of British escort vessel.'

The loss of the freighter had a second consequence: the noise of the torpedoes, the depth-charges and the increased movements of the escorts carried far through the medium of the water, and at 5.03 a.m., Commander Reche picked up the convoy on the sound-location equipment in *U-255*; it was the first indication of it since midnight. This, together with a report from the naval radio monitoring service that at 4.50 a.m. an aircraft had reported hitting a ship with an aerial torpedo, convinced Admiral Schmundt that the convoy would shortly be found again. At seven o'clock, *U-457* (Lieutenant-Commander Brandenburg) sighted a single merchant ship and a shadowing aircraft, having picked up convoy sounds an hour before. He switched on a signal transmitter for the other U-boats to home in on him, and closed the vessel himself. But the ship was lifeless and abandoned—it was the hapless *Christopher Newport*, which had successfully defied the efforts of both the German Air Force and the British Navy to sink her. At 8.23 a.m., having satisfied his curiosity about the freighter's identity, port of origin, and cargo, he put a torpedo in her and watched her sink.

The only Intelligence the convoy now received from Whitehall was a wireless message at 8.54 a.m. to the effect that the convoy had last been reported at 5.15 a.m., while direction-finding bearings had indicated that the convoy had been shadowed and reported 'throughout the night'. Once again this was not strictly accurate; but it was not the kind of error that caused damage. In fact by 11.30 a.m. both the German Air Force and the U-boats

were forced to admit that neither was in contact with Convoy
PQ.*17*

Independence Day had dawned: in London it was bright and
sunny; in the Arctic it was foggy, windless and cold. The temperature was now three degrees below zero, and still the convoy
had farther north to go. In the American merchant ships, the
tattered Stars and Stripes were hauled down and clean new
Ensigns were run up in their place. From the bridge of the British
cruiser *Norfolk*, the daylight signalling lantern was flashing a
Fourth of July greeting across to the American cruiser *Wichita*:

> Many happy returns of the day. The United States is the only
> country with a known birthday.

Captain H. W. Hill, USN, made the reply, 'Thank you. I think
England should celebrate Mother's Day.'

From his flagship *London*, Rear-Admiral Hamilton sent a more
formal greeting to the other cruisers and the three destroyers of
his screen:

> On the occasion of your great anniversary, it seems most uncivil
> to make you stationkeep at all, but even today Freedom of the Seas
> can be read two ways. It is a privilege for us all to have you with
> us and I wish you all the best of hunting.

It was a typically RN salutation; but underlying it was the grim
conviction that today was to be the day when they might well be
meeting the German battle fleet. A loyal Captain Hill replied,
'It is a great privilege to be here with you today in furtherance of
the ideals which 4th July has always represented to us and we are
particularly happy to be a portion of your command.' Celebration
of Independence Day, he reminded Hamilton, always required
large fireworks displays: 'I trust you will not disappoint us. . . .'

4

DECISIONS AND DISASTER
Saturday 4 July — Sunday 5 July

Hearty congratulations. The petals of your flower are of rare beauty.—
Admiral Pound to destroyer commander, having examined latter's
capture of a German U-boat's secret codebooks and papers,
intact, in May 1941

IT WAS NOW of overriding importance for the Germans to
establish exactly what the enemy's intentions were, so that the
German battle fleet could be sailed into the attack. On the
previous evening, General-Admiral Carls had rephrased the Navy's
requirements of the German Air Force in a signal to Fifth Air
Force headquarters: should their search for signs of the enemy's
heavy forces remain fruitless during the night, he asked the Air
Force to give him, at 5 a.m. and at 9 a.m. the next day—4 July—
'authoritative statements' on those sea-areas which had been
thoroughly swept by air reconnaissance and found to be devoid of
enemy units.[1] By mid-morning of 4 July, however, the Air
Force had lost convoy PQ.17 as well, while there was still no
news either of the suspected battle fleet, or of the heavy force
apparently accompanying the convoy—Rear-Admiral Hamilton's
cruiser force, in fact. The German battle fleet had perforce to
stay at anchor at Altenfiord.

It was not until shortly before 7.30 a.m. that the Air Force
found the convoy again—steering due east in 'five columns of
seven ships each'; the aircraft reported that there was a strong
escort screen, and strangely enough a 'double-decker' seaplane in
the convoy too—the Walrus which had had to be taken in tow at
about midnight by one of the trawlers. If the battle fleet was not
going to attack, it seemed to Admiral Schmundt (who was
unaware of this aerial sighting) important that his submarines
should exploit the situation as best they could. At 11.20 a.m., he
wirelessed all the 'Ice Devil' pack's submarines, from Narvik:

None of our naval forces [is] in operational area. Whereabouts of
enemy's heavy group at present unknown: this is to be main tar-

get of submarines as soon as it arrives. U-boats in touch with convoy are to stay on its trail.[2]

'Turtle' Hamilton's cruiser force was certainly entering its danger zone. His movements were still governed by the Admiralty's instructions given him a week before, to remain in a covering position until reaching the meridian of 25° East and then to turn back; he would very soon be crossing that meridian. Twenty minutes after Schmundt had signalled the U-boats to make the 'heavy force' their main target, Hamilton decided that the time had come for his cruiser force to be completely revealed to the enemy: he again altered course to close the convoy, and within an hour he was again being shadowed by a German aircraft.

Referring to the amended route which Commander Broome, the convoy's escort commander, had signalled to the Admiralty on the previous evening, Hamilton fully expected to pick up the convoy about thirty minutes after turning south; in fact, it took him an hour and a half to find it, for Broome had routed Convoy PQ.17 thirty miles further south of his promised route—thirty miles closer to the German air bases in Norway. By the time Hamilton sighted it, the convoy was already at 24° East, one degree short of the meridian at which he must turn back. He took his four cruisers and three destroyers ahead of the convoy, and remained there, zigzagging across its van some ten to twenty miles ahead of it.[3] 'Cruiser force in sight', wrote a corvette officer in his diary. 'A great morale booster.'[4]

Admiral Tovey's battle fleet was in the meantime heading almost due east, well to the north of the convoy, keeping out of range of the Norwegian air bases, but waiting all the time for the German heavy units to put in an appearance.

At the Admiralty in London, the Intelligence on the enemy's movements was still incomplete: as each side was now waiting for the other to make the first visible move, this was predictable. The Admiralty had originally assumed that the German heavy forces would attack the convoy to the east of Bear Island. The convoy had passed that island at midnight, and all that was known of the German heavy warships was that on the previous afternoon aerial reconnaissance of Trondheim had shown that *Tirpitz* and

Hipper were gone. In other words, they could be attacking PQ.17 by this coming midnight, or two hours later if accompanied by the rather slower *Scheer* and *Lützow* from Narvik; but all attempts to reconnoitre the latter port had so far been thwarted by fog.

At 11.16 a.m., the American naval authorities in London cabled to Washington a report on the latest developments with PQ.17: 'Visual reconnaissance confirmed by photographs of Trondheim reports *no* heavy units present. Admiralty believes that enemy heavy units' [move] to the northward is in progress.' Moreover the Admiralty had an Intelligence report graded by them as '*A2*' —a very reliable source—that 'warships are expected to attack PQ.17 between 15° and 30° East'. So there seemed little doubt that during the night of 4-5 July, the destruction of Convoy PQ.17 would commence.

It was in the light of this uncertain knowledge that the British First Sea Lord, Sir Dudley Pound, convened a staff conference that was to last, with interruptions, throughout the day until its desperate conclusion that evening. In the middle of the morning, Pound telephoned Admiral King's office in the Admiralty's Trade Division, and asked for Captain G. R. G. Allen to come to his room at once, dropping whatever he was doing. Allen was directly concerned with the organization of PQ convoys. When Allen entered Pound's room, he found a number of other high-ranking Admiralty officers present, including Rear-Admiral Rawlings, Rear-Admiral Brind and Vice-Admiral Moore.[5] Pound's question of Captain Allen was a significant one: 'Captain Allen, are the merchant ships of PQ.17 equipped with one-ship pads?' These were the simple encoding and decoding systems which could be used for communication with individual merchant ships.

Allen acknowledged that most of them were so equipped, so far as he knew. Pound continued, 'So if the ships were for some reason to be scattered, it would still be possible to communicate with them independently?' Allen affirmed that this was so. This brief conversation was the clearest possible indication that Pound, who had objected to the sailing of the convoy in the first instance, was still possessed of the idea of scattering it should the German battle fleet appear. Even so, until further Intelligence and primarily the aerial reconnaissance reports on the present whereabouts of the German warships came in, there was no firm action to which the First Sea Lord was prepared to commit himself.

At 12.30 p.m., the Admiralty wirelessed Hamilton informing him that unless he was ordered otherwise by his Commander-in-Chief, who was therefore also sent a copy of the signal, he was now to be permitted to proceed eastward of the meridian of 25° East after all, should the situation demand it. This was *not*, however, to be taken as urging Hamilton to proceed eastwards against his discretion.[6] As this signal reached Hamilton at the very time when he should have been preparing to turn back, he was greatly relieved to receive it.

As he privately confessed, he had from the outset despised the prospect of having to desert the convoy in the very waters where it would most need the presence of a heavier escort. Having attended both the Convoy Conference at Hvalfiord and the Escort Conference at Seidisfiord, he felt more than usually bound up with the convoy itself, and 'could not divorce' himself from its conduct and well-being. To Hamilton, it appeared that the present situation did demand that his cruisers should proceed beyond 25° East and he resolved in fact to remain with PQ.17 until 2 p.m. of the following day, which would be pushing the prudent limit of the two American cruisers' fuel-endurance: 'It was evident from the vague information concerning enemy main forces then available that it was my duty to remain with the convoy as long as possible,' he explained two days later.[7]

He sent the destroyer *Somali* to fuel from the oiler in the convoy, and with her he sent an icy signal to Commander Broome to the effect that he considered the convoy to be thirty miles to the southward of where it should have been; he again ordered the Senior Officer of the Escort to steer for the 400-mile radius from Banak, and to inform him of his intentions via *Somali*. The visibility on the surface was now maximum, with very brief patches of fog. Commander Broome obeyed Hamilton's instructions, and soon after (at 4.45 p.m.) the convoy's course was altered to north-eastward, causing complete confusion for about an hour, before its tight cruising formation was restored.

At 3.20 p.m., after reporting the only casualty so far—the SS

Christopher Newport, torpedoed by an aircraft that morning and 'sunk by own forces'—Hamilton informed his Commander-in-Chief and the Admiralty of the use he intended making of the Admiralty's offer:

First Cruiser Squadron remaining in vicinity [of convoy] until enemy surface situation clarifies, but certainly *not* later than 2.00 p.m. 5th July.

As though to stress the usefulness of his cruisers to the convoy, Hamilton simultaneously ordered two of *Wichita*'s aircraft to be catapulted, to maintain continuous patrols round the convoy to keep the U-boats down.

The Admiralty's offer to Hamilton had also been transmitted to Admiral Tovey, however, and he—indignant that this was a 'reversal of [the] policy agreed between the Admiralty and myself' on 27 June—determined that the four cruisers should not be exposed to unnecessary dangers. No information in his possession justified the change, and he signalled Hamilton at 3.12 p.m., categorically objecting to the Admiralty's intervention from afar:

Once the convoy is to the east of 25 degrees East, or earlier at your discretion, you are to leave the Barents Sea unless assured by the Admiralty that *Tirpitz* can *not* be met.

By this time, the convoy was in fact already east of 25° East; and at 4 p.m. Tovey's battle fleet altered to the south-westward to conform to the cruiser's withdrawal he had just ordered.[8]

Admiral Tovey's signal was hardly in the most glorious traditions of the Royal Navy: Hamilton knew this, and with his flag captain was keen to see some kind of a scrap with the German warships. Shortly after 6 p.m., he eventually answered his Commander-in-Chief's objections, but only evasively: he affirmed that he now intended to withdraw to westward at about 10 p.m., as soon as his destroyers had completed oiling in the convoy. ('I endeavoured', he wrote, 'to comply with the spirit of both signals' —i.e. both his Commander-in-Chief's and the Admiralty's.[9]) Admiral Tovey plainly resigned himself to Hamilton's obstinacy, for although he must have realized almost at once that by ten o'clock that night the cruiser force would be far—about 250 miles —beyond the 25° East meridian, he raised no further objection.

The Admiralty had arranged for continuous patrols up the Norwegian coast by a number of RAF Catalinas being ferried from Sullom Voe to Archangel; these sorties, which had begun three days before, had been reinforced by regular reconnaissance sorties by British shore-based units. Because of an aircraft accident, there had been no aerial reconnaissance of the fiords since 11 o'clock on that morning, 4 July, but Intelligence from other sources suggested that it was 'tolerably certain' that *Scheer* and *Lützow* were now at Altenfiord.* Of *Tirpitz* and *Hipper,* which had certainly left Trondheim by the time it had been photographed at 2.20 p.m. the previous afternoon, the 3rd, there was still no trace. Thus for all the Admiralty could know, all four heavy warships might by the afternoon of 4 July be at sea already and heading towards the convoy. Early in the evening, the Admiralty wirelessed a signal to Hamilton, referring to the earlier signals from Tovey and himself about how far the cruiser force should proceed to the east:

> Further information may be available shortly. Remain with convoy pending further instructions.

At 6.15 p.m., the destroyer *Somali* had returned to the cruiser force, now zigzagging just ahead of the convoy, and Hamilton sent the American destroyer *Wainwright* in to fuel. *Somali* had brought with her the amended route Broome was now following with the convoy—course 45°: Hamilton was satisfied that the escort commander was now obeying the orders issued to him.

✳ 2 ✳

At ten-thirty that morning, about the same time as *Tirpitz* was anchoring in Altenfiord and Captain Allen was being interviewed

---

* Roskill, *The War at Sea*, vol. ii, p. 139, mentions that 'there had been no verification of the photographic reconnaissance' which had revealed the departure of the German warships from Vestfiord (i.e. Narvik). But there had been no such reconnaissance, nor does he mention such a reconnaissance earlier.

The fact that the Intelligence from 'other sources' suggested that it was 'tolerably certain' that both *Scheer* AND *Lützow* were 'at Altenfiord' suggests that there had been a leak in German security before the latter vessel ran aground.

by Admiral Pound in London, the German Naval Staff had informed Vice-Admiral Krancke—Grand-Admiral Raeder's permanent representative at the Führer's headquarters—and the High Command's operations staff that the presence of a heavy force with the convoy stood in the way of launching *The Knight's Move*, and would continue to do so unless German aircraft or submarines could cripple these warships.[10] Convoy PQ.17 was being shadowed both by aircraft and by submarines now.

During the morning, still smarting under General-Admiral Carls's strictures about his U-boats during the night, Admiral Schmundt had proudly reported to the Naval Staff in Berlin that *U-457* had sunk the first freighter, *Christopher Newport*; he did not mention that this ship had first been crippled by the Air Force and was abandoned at the time of the attack.

In response to Carls's earlier request, the German Air Force had carried out an extensive reconnaissance of the waters to the west of Norway, covering the entire area up to the latitude of North Cape and Altenfiord (71°), but no trace of the enemy had been found. To the north of this, the reconnaissance was still incomplete. The War Diary of Naval Group North observed:

> Thus the sea surrounding the reported position of yesterday's aircraft-carrier force has been completely swept, and no trace of this force has been found. In all probability it has also proceeded northwards, and can be presumed to be at sea somewhere north of 71°N. This further underlines the impossibility of launching 'The Knight's Move' at the present time.[11]

Informing the German Naval Staff of this at 11.20 that morning, the Group had added that both German battle groups had none the less been put at three hours' sailing notice.

At noon, a German aircraft had sighted the Anglo-American cruiser force—as Hamilton had anticipated—and had correctly identified it as comprising four cruisers and three destroyers, although there was some confusion over their nationalities; no 'battleships' had been seen at all. The German Naval Staff correctly deduced that this was the convoy's close covering force: but if they briefly entertained hopes of sailing the German battle fleet after all, these hopes were shortly dashed, and the comedy of errors had begun again. At 1.27 p.m. *U-457* had sighted Hamilton's cruiser force heading eastwards, and half an hour later

Lieutenant-Commander Brandenburg further identified it as comprising 'one battleship, two cruisers and three destroyers'. Schmundt at once informed Group North of the sighting, and the various aircraft and submarines that sighted Hamilton's cruiser force up to about a quarter-to-ten that night reported nothing to dispel the impression that it included a battleship.[2]

Nor was that all. Although no aircraft-carrier had actually been located by the Germans, their shadowing aircraft had reported two 'torpedo planes' complete with 'torpedoes' heading east near the convoy at 6.30 p.m. The German Naval Staff was obliged at least temporarily to suspect the presence of an aircraft-carrier within striking range of the convoy. In fact these were *Wichita*'s two floatplanes, which had been catapulted on Hamilton's orders to keep the U-boats down.

✻ 3 ✻

While the German Navy had hesitated, the Air Force had arrogated to itself the duty of despatching convoy PQ.17.

By midday on 4 July, they would hold back their planned mass attack no longer, even though the possibility of a joint operation by torpedo and conventional bombers was ruled out by the weather. The Fifth Air Force decided that as the Navy was still vacillating on whether or not to operate its battle fleet in view of the Allied 'battleship' reported in the convoy's close covering force, they must launch the main air attack now if the convoy were not to pass out of bomber range altogether.[12]

During the morning, crews of three squadrons of Heinkel 111 torpedo-bombers were briefed at Bardufoss air base for the attack; these aircraft were long familiar to Londoners, as they had been the main workhorse of the German Air Force during the 1940 Blitz. Now converted to act as torpedo-bombers, they attacked from only a few feet above the waves, where they could release their torpedoes and then escape the wall of enemy gunfire as best they could.

The Heinkels' crews were told that convoy PQ.17 consisted of thirty-eight ships sailing in columns, in line abreast, with destroyers and other light escort vessels ahead and on either flank; two British and two American cruisers were not far to the west.

The plan was for one formation of the Heinkels to deliver a beam attack on the convoy's starboard flank while the remaining aircraft attacked obliquely from the rear; a small force of Junkers 88s supplied by Major Erich Bloedorn's *KG.30* Wing would launch a high-level bombing attack shortly before the torpedo attack proper began, to divert the ships' gunners from the extremely vulnerable Heinkels coming in at almost zero feet over the horizon. *KG.30* would also supply a Junkers 88 aircraft to rendez-vous with the Heinkel force and pilot it in the last few miles to the convoy.* Early that afternoon, the Heinkels took off at Bardufoss and headed northwards across the Arctic ocean.

As they vanished from sight, the German radio monitoring service picked up an Allied signal warning of an imminent air attack on PQ.17. The planes that were now coming in to attack with torpedoes were not the *KG.26* Heinkels, but Heinkel 115 floatplanes of the German Coastal Command squadron *906*. As soon as the aircraft were sighted by one of the convoy's anti-submarine trawlers, just before a quarter-to-five that afternoon, Commander Broome signalled all his escorts to 'close the convoy at best speed to give air support'. Three minutes later the air attack warning was sounded aboard the escort screen's vessels, and the Convoy Commodore ordered the merchant ships to man their guns and prepare for instant action; Flag '*Q*'—'air attack imminent'—went up in all the naval vessels. The ships of the escort closed in from their 3,000-yard stations to 1,000 yards from the nearest merchant ships.

During the two hours that followed, the German floatplanes circled clumsily round the convoy, trying to force a way into attacking range, or catch the gunners off their guard; but Broome's escort vessels were at their best and eventually the planes with-drew, some of them having jettisoned their torpedoes well out of the convoy's range. Several times during the next hour or two, the Allied sailors heard the sounds of aircraft circling overhead. Shortly before half-past seven three bombs hurtled down through the grey overcast and missed the U.S. destroyer *Wainwright* by a

---

* All three *Staffeln* of *KG.26*'s first squadron took part, involving 23 Heinkel 111-Ts in all, according to Brief Air Staff Report. The crews' briefing is described from the reports on the interrogations of the four German airmen shot down in the attack.[13]

Admiral Sir Dudley Pound,
First Sea Lord

Rear-Admiral L. H. K. Hamilton,
commanding the First Cruiser Squadron

Admiral Sir John Tovey,
Commander-in-Chief,
Home Fleet

Captain Jack Broome, who,
as Commander Broome,
led the First Escort Group in HMS *Keppel*

The American cruiser *Tuscaloosa* (foreground) and Admiral Hamilton's
flagship *London* at Scapa Flow, April 1942

Convoy Commodore J. C. K. Dowding
reports to Admiral Tovey

The battleship USS *Washington* and the cruiser
HMS *Norfolk* at Scapa Flow, May 1942

PQ. 17 assembling—Hvalfiord

A Convoy Conference. Commander Broome's telling cartoon
'Subscriptions in Advance', can be glimpsed at the rear right

On 27 June 1942, the convoy sailed. 'Like so many dirty ducks,
they waddled out past the nets and to sea'

Colonel-General Stumpff,
commanding the German
Fifth Air Force in Norway

dolf Hitler with Grand-Admiral Raeder,
Commander-in-Chief of the German Navy

Vice-Admiral Otto Schniewind,
German Commander-in-Chief afloat
in the battleship *Tirpitz*

General-Admiral Carls,
Admiral Commanding Naval Group North, with his Führer

Tirpitz

Lutzow

Admiral Hipper

Admiral Scheer

Tirpitz in Foetten Fiord, near Trondheim, on 15 February 1942.
A photograph taken by a low-flying RAF reconnaissance aircraft

The German air-raid on Murmansk on 1 July 1942
made it impossible to unload ships there.
PQ. 17 was therefore diverted to Archangel

Commander Reinhard Reche, commander of *U-255*

Lieutenant-Commander Heinz Bielfeld aboard his U-boat, *U-703*

bare 150 yards on the port bow, as she approached the convoy to refuel from the oiler *Aldersdale*. Captain Moon took the destroyer through the convoy's lines, and he could see the gun crews on the merchantmen tensely waiting at action stations for the next attack. He and *Keppel* patrolled the van of the convoy in a search for submarines, constantly alert for any renewed airborne attack. Flag '*Q*' still flew at the warships' mastheads. The escort vessels could hear the U-boats and shadowing aircraft broadcasting almost continuous homing signals now, so they knew that the biggest air attack was yet to come. Visibility on the surface had now increased to maximum, below a low cloud layer; the lookouts could see that not far ahead of them this low bank of cloud ended abruptly, with nothing but blue sky beyond.[14]

Since three o'clock that afternoon, Commander Brandenburg's *U-457* had transmitted a constant radio-beacon signal, while keeping the convoy under close observation. He reported that the cruiser force was standing off to the north-east of the convoy, with a 'destroyer shuttle-service' between them. In rapid succession during the afternoon, Bielfeld, Bohmann and Siemon also reported sighting the convoy as they closed in on *U-457*'s beacon. From Narvik, Admiral Schmundt wirelessed the 'Ice-Devil' pack that Bohmann and Bielfeld were to shadow the convoy, while Brandenburg was to beacon in other submarines on to what he still called the 'battleship force' (i.e. Hamilton's cruisers). At 4.12 p.m., Brandenburg reported that this heavy force was fifty miles north of the convoy, zigzagging like the convoy itself.[15]

In the meantime, Bohmann had taken *U-88* ahead of the convoy and delivered a further determined underwater attack. He had submerged in front of the convoy, allowed the anti-submarine screen to roll unsuspecting over him, then had surfaced to periscope depth. The sea was oily and smooth, so he had kept out of the convoy formation proper, firing a spread of four torpedoes as three overlapping freighters moved across his field of fire; he aimed at the foremast of the last ship. Nothing happened. He brought *U-88* rapidly round and fired her stern tube about twenty minutes later, taking the centre of three overlapping steamships as his target. Again the torpedo missed. Bohmann quickly submerged and let the rest of the convoy roll overhead.[16]

Commander Brandenburg continued to shadow the cruiser

force until late evening, while Bielfeld several times wirelessed to Narvik reports of the convoy's progress. Bielfeld was unable to attack because of the glassy seas and bright sunshine Schmundt commented that Bohmann's *U-88* had 'apparently found more favourable attacking conditions'. At about 10 p.m. *U-456* (Teichert) also reported in: his submarine was lying ahead of Hamilton's cruiser squadron as it headed east, and he was planning to attack.

By eight o'clock that evening, the twenty-three Heinkel 111 torpedo-bombers of the first squadron of *KG.26*, commanded by Captain Eicke,* were only a very few miles from convoy PQ.17, and closing in at 265 m.p.h.[13] Each aircraft carried two standard F4B aerial torpedoes, provisionally set with an 'angle of lead' to compensate for an assumed convoy speed of ten knots. The fine adjustment would be made as the convoy was encountered. As the aircraft reached a point some distance ahead of the convoy, which was hidden in a thin, low mist over the horizon, the promised Junkers 88 pilot-aircraft dived over the formation, and showed them the way to their target.

At about the same time, a number of Junkers 88s approached the convoy from astern at about a thousand feet; but before they could offer a serious diversion, they were driven off by the accurate gunfire of the escort vessels there.[17] The merchant ships and the naval escort vessels had remained at general quarters since the earlier attacks, and the escort screen had remained—rightly or wrongly—at its closed-in formation. In the hospital of the rescue ship *Zamalek*, the surgeon had just begun the delicate operation to save the sight of the gunner shot during the attack two days before, when the alarm bells shrilled again.

The cruiser force was by now just ten miles ahead of the convoy, with visibility extremely good. At 8.10 p.m. Hamilton signalled the convoy, 'How does she go?' and added a stern reminder about the convoy's proper course: 'Convoy is to steer 045° until further orders.' Commander Broome read more significance

---

* Eicke was actually only commander of the first squadron's 3rd *Staffel*, but the Gruppe's CO, Lieutenant-Colonel Hermann Busch, was acting as AOC North-West Air Command.

into this signal than Hamilton had intended and was left with the suspicion that the German battle fleet was moving up for its attack.[18] At 8.17 p.m. Hamilton wirelessed to the Admiralty in London the convoy's exact position, course and speed, and added that he was preparing to carry out an ice reconnaissance. *Norfolk*'s aircraft was readied for launching, and its two-man crew climbed aboard.

Minutes later, it was obvious that Captain Eicke's main Heinkel force had arrived, and the most dramatic of the air attacks on the convoy suddenly began. As the destroyer *Wainwright* was starting down the convoy's starboard flank, her radio direction-finder began to pick up a stream of 'A's on the convoy's starboard quarter, and almost at once a line of torpedo-bombers was seen on the horizon, very low down.[19]

'Stand by!' crackled the loudspeakers of one of the AA ships. At 8.18 p.m., the trawler *Northern Gem* signalled, 'Eight torpedo-bombers bearing 210 degrees, five miles.' Moments later, she corrected her count to ten torpedo-bombers. One of the AA ships began to broadcast the readings by powerful loud-hailer so that most of the convoy's ships could hear. At 8.20 p.m. *Ledbury* began signalling, 'Eight air torpedo-bombers 210 degrees, five miles', and then two minutes later, 'for eight read ten'. Suddenly all the escorts seemed to be blinking signals at once. The loudspeakers were booming, 'Bombers approaching . . . there's six of them . . . there's twelve . . . there's eighteen . . . good God, there's twenty-five!' The anti-aircraft ship lurched forward and altered course to head off the attack. Commodore Dowding signalled *Keppel* to ask if the convoy should make an 'emergency turn'; but it was too late for that kind of manœuvre now—half the ships would probably miss the signal altogether and Broome flashed back, 'I do not think it worth it.'[20]

From the bridge of *Wainwright*, Captain Moon could see the attacking torpedo-bombers splitting up into two groups—one coming in on the starboard quarter in line abreast, and the other circling round to attack the convoy on the starboard bow, seemingly at right angles to the other force. As the aircraft on the bow would have farther to go before launching their attack, while on the other hand it would be the more dangerous because of the additional run afforded the torpedoes by the convoy's advance,

Wainwright dashed out through the close-escort screen still bunched round the merchantmen, to try to head them off. The close-escort vessels similarly altered course, to bring their batteries to bear on the attackers, and all opened fire at once. Undeterred by the hail of low-angle shell fire and magnesium tracer bullets sweeping across the sea towards them—'when a gunner begins firing on a plane that is all he appears to see,' complained Moon afterwards—*Wainwright* continued towards the approaching bombers at over 32 knots. When she was standing out some four thousand yards from the nearest merchantman, Captain Moon swung hard round to port so as to bring the full weight of his starboard batteries to bear on the attacking aircraft. One by one these planes dropped their torpedoes, all short even of the *Wainwright*, and fled, causing the destroyer's captain some anxious moments as the sea around his destroyer became alive with the scudding torpedoes.

The consternation of the Heinkel pilots can be imagined. They had approached only sixty feet above the waves, coming in from the south-east in a comforting veil of mist; but this had whipped away as they had covered the last five miles in to the convoy, leaving the crews momentarily blinded by the sun. Those who now saw this destroyer barring their way turned tail and ran. One of them, Heinkel *1H + MH*, hurtled on towards the convoy, oblivious of anything but the ships; its crew saw only at the last moment that they were heading straight for a destroyer with all its anti-aircraft guns blazing at them. The observer panicked and released the port torpedo without making any further adjustment to it; before they could drop their second torpedo, they were caught in a hail of shell fire. One shell caught the aircraft's nose, and a second its port wing. The pilot, Lieutenant Kaumeyr, and his observer were wounded. The port engine choked to a standstill and fire broke out in the cockpit. The crew tried to bring the aircraft round to head back to Norway, but another shell hit its cockpit and the fire intensified. The observer jettisoned the second torpedo—the only one to hit the sea beyond the *Wainwright*—and the plane smacked into the sea about four thousand yards from the destroyer, on the convoy's starboard bow. They were not far from another destroyer, *Ledbury*. Captain Moon saw four German airmen climbing out into a rubber dinghy, and the bomber sank soon after. Commander Broome later made a nonchalant signal to the Americans in *Wainwright*: 'Thank you for your great support and congratulations on your anti-aircraft fire which impressed us all, and definitely left packing room for one in a German hangar.'

The sight of the ditched Heinkel seemed to have weakened the resolution of the remaining crews attacking PQ.17 from the starboard flank. The whole of this group's action was over within two minutes, and all the aircraft had jettisoned their torpedoes while still up to a mile from *Wainwright*. Before the bow attack was over, the second attack had begun from the convoy's starboard quarter, led by Lieutenant Hennemann, a *Staffel* commander who only a few weeks before had received a personal letter of commendation from Göring for having sunk 50,000 tons of Allied shipping.

On the starboard quarter there was no US destroyer standing boldly out to meet the attack, and it was here that the British tactics of closing up in face of air attack showed their unsuitability for torpedo attacks. Nine of the torpedo-bombers were able to press their attack to well within torpedo range. At 6,000 yards five turned off to port and the remaining four came straight in.

The noise now was terrific. The merchant ships were firing every defensive weapon they had, including 'pig-trough' rocket-launchers, parachute-and-cable rockets, Holman projectors, 4-inch guns, Bofors, machine-guns, Brownings, Oerlikons and Lewis guns. Two of the Heinkels headed straight for the American merchant ship *Bellingham*, and at 1,500 yards her guns opened fire. The after plane veered to port and dropped two torpedoes; the *William Hooper*'s forward ·50-calibre machine-guns opened up, scoring several hits on the plane, which was probably Eicke's. Its port engine began to smoke. A third Heinkel raced in, making a straight and level run, and dropped its torpedoes some five hundred yards away; the green-bodied weapons jumped once, then slid below the surface. The bomber continued for the ship, making straight for its wheelhouse; the ship fired off all her rockets at the German, but by then it was too late. As her Armed Guard officer looked back to where the bomber, its starboard engine now on fire, had come from, he could see the wake of its torpedoes streaking straight towards the deckhouse. One torpedo struck the ship and penetrated the starboard settling-tank before

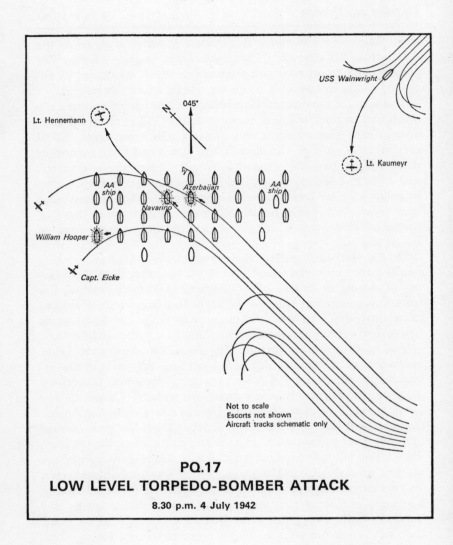

Lt. Hennemann

045°

N

USS Wainwright

Lt. Kaumeyr

AA ship

Azerbaijan

Navarino

AA ship

William Hooper

Capt. Eicke

Not to scale
Escorts not shown
Aircraft tracks schematic only

PQ.17
LOW LEVEL TORPEDO-BOMBER ATTACK
8.30 p.m. 4 July 1942

exploding; the starboard boiler was blown up through the engine-room skylight. The *William Hooper* began to settle in a cloud of flying asbestos and soot, and with a cacophony of noise coming from below.[21]

Few people saw the explosion, for all eyes were upon the apparent German squadron-leader's aircraft: this man, Lieutenant Hennemann, seemed to have singled out a ship in the heart of the convoy—'a very brave action', as Captain Moon later said—and to have shut his eyes to all else around him—the inferno of Bofors and machine-gun fire and tracer shell accelerating towards his plane as it roared in over columns six and five and four lower than the ships' bridges, even, and seemingly heading straight for *Bellingham*'s bridge; four of the ship's ·50-calibre machine guns were pouring a murderous hail of armour-piercing shells into the aircraft at point-blank range. The *El Capitán* alone pumped 95 rounds of ·30-calibre and 200 rounds of ·50-calibre armour-piercing shell from her Brownings into the plane; her first officer saw a little fist-sized ball of fire suddenly appear in the fuselage, and at once the whole plane was ablaze.[22] Hennemann's plane was far ahead of his comrades and he drew almost all the fire. The plane was so low that the merchant ships were caught in the cross-fire of their own Allies, and several casualties were sustained. One of *Empire Tide*'s gunners was struck in the thigh by a machine-gun bullet from another ship, and much of the ship's rigging, derrick spans and gun telephones was shot away. Another ship put a 4-inch shell into the bows of the indignant American *Ironclad*. As the Heinkel came up to *Bellingham*, the ship's Second Officer seized a Lewis gun and fired a dozen rounds at it until the gun jammed. Even as he watched, two torpedoes detached themselves from the burning aircraft, and starting 'skipping' through the water on a course converging with the ship's, easily visible with their green bodies and bright yellow warheads. One torpedo headed across *Bellingham*'s bow, missing it by ten feet, and the other headed straight for the midships of the British *Navarino* right in front of *Bellingham*. It struck the freighter under her bridge, and the crew started jumping overboard. Every window in the wheelhouse and bridge was smashed, and the ship suddenly took on a list to starboard as water cascaded into her No. 3 hold. The engine-room telegraph had jammed, and the ship fell off sharply to port.²³ Two of her lifeboats were hastily lowered and capsized. *Bellingham* had to haul out to starboard to avoid ramming the crippled *Navarino*, or running down the seamen floundering in the water. As *Bellingham* passed through the swimming seamen, one of them waved a fist and shouted 'On to Moscow . . . see you in Russia!'—which must have taken some courage in those icy waters.²⁴

Lieutenant Hennemann's blazing bomber crashed into the sea on the port bow of the *Washington*, the leading freighter in the second column. As the plane hit the sea, a roar of applause went up from the American cruisers in Hamilton's force, only a few miles away: 'We cheered as if we were in New York watching "dem bums" from Brooklyn', one of them reported.²⁵ And Rear-Admiral Hamilton, who had taken the cruisers towards the convoy when the Germans' attack had started, and had thus had a 'front seat in the stalls' throughout, commented more formally: 'In my opinion they are no longer amateurs'.²⁶ As the convoy surged past the burning wreck of the bomber, *El Capitán*'s crew clearly saw the airmen struggling inside their blazing cockpit. They were close enough to shout at the plane as it floated past on the starboard side; the seamen jeered and hurled insults at the dying enemy. There were no feelings of sympathy, and awe at this crew's courage was to emerge only in the cold afterlight of the battle.²⁷

As the gunfire reverted to the other attackers, their pilots threw them into violent snaking manœuvres, weaving from side to side to present more difficult targets; but none of them could emulate the gallantry displayed by Hennemann. One Heinkel released its torpedoes at the Russian tanker *Donbass*, trailing the convoy's third column; *Donbass*'s gunners fired at the torpedoes and deflected them. As the plane came in over *Olopana*, directly in front of *Donbass*, it met such a wall of gunfire that it broke off to port and raced out of the rear of the convoy over the crippled *William Hooper*, losing height and trailing a plume of smoke.²⁸ It looked unlikely to reach base, as it disappeared over the horizon. All the other aircraft dropped their torpedoes even while outside the close-escort screen, some of them so hastily that their torpedoes went in at bad angles and tumbled end-over-end towards the ships before sinking. Several more of the aircraft were hit: in one, the air-gunner was killed outright by the ships' gunfire. The sight of their leader's fate disheartened all of them. Lieutenant Hennemann's unquestionable bravery was posthumously rewarded by the Germans with a Knight's Cross; among the Allied records, there is not one ship's report which does not mention his brave attack in the face of certain death.

At 8.25 p.m. the attack was over. An observer aboard the destroyer *Wilton* wrote with trembling hand, 'One down—three merchant vessels hit.'[29] Apart from *William Hooper* and *Navarino*, only the Soviet tanker *Azerbaijan* in the middle of the convoy, astern of *River Afton*, had been torpedoed. From *Wainwright*'s bridge Captain Moon was watching as the tanker was actually struck by the torpedo: a sheet of flame enveloped its whole length to a height of about two hundred feet, then the flame quickly subsided to be replaced by clouds of smoke and steam. The torpedo's actual explosion had been inaudible, so great was the general tumult of gunfire.[30]

At 8.31, relative silence returned, broken only by the distant boom of *London*'s 8-inch guns, still firing at the departing bombers at extreme range. Lieutenant Kaumeyr and his three crewmen were being picked out of their rubber dinghy by the destroyer *Ledbury*; the charred wreckage of Lieutenant Hennemann's brave Heinkel and its perished crew were settling in the icy waters; *William Hooper, Navarino* and *Azerbaijan* were falling out of station, and three rescue ships and two minesweepers were dropping back to begin the hazardous rescue of their crews. Convoy PQ.17 had survived its biggest testing yet—not unscathed, but proud and undaunted by the ordeal.

On *Keppel*'s bridge, a signalman was again at Commander Broome's elbow, handing him a new pink naval message form. It was a signal Hamilton had made to him a few minutes before, at 8.40: 'Due to proximity surface forces, report when convoy is on 045°.'[31] How close were the German ships? Probably Hamilton did not even know himself. Broome signalled back that the convoy was already on the course ordered by the Admiral.

On the American warships' decks, liverwurst sandwiches, pie

and coffee were handed round by messboys. In the British escort vessels tea was served.[32] Flag 'Q' still flew, and the guns remained closed up at action stations. In the cruisers five miles away they could hear the crackling radiotelephone exchanges between convoy and escort. Broome was asking the Commodore how he was faring. Dowding replied, 'Still doing fine, thank-you—fine'.[33] Broome was proud of the convoy. It had 'gone from peace to bedlam and back to peace'. From the bridge of *Keppel* he scanned the merchantmen to see how they had borne the heavy German attack: 'steaming back through the convoy was a tonic,' he later wrote. 'Everyone was still in station, and the ships looked prouder than ever.'[34] The decks of every ship were littered with brass cartridge-cases and empty ammunition boxes; most of the ships had kept firing until their guns jammed or their ammunition was exhausted. Broome went down into his destroyer's chart-house, opened his diary, and indulged in a little boasting: 'provided the ammunition lasted, PQ.17 could get anywhere.' For eighty hours of intermittent air and U-boat attack, Broome's force of nineteen escort vessels had provided a very competent protection. The many U-boats—*Ledbury* alone had sighted seven —had scored no kills at all. On the horizon, the Blohm & Voss aircraft were still maintaining their relentless shadowing patrol. At 8.55 p.m., *Wainwright* finally headed for the oiler *Aldersdale* to refuel.* Throughout the attack, and much to Hamilton's surprise, the bombers had paid not the slightest attention to his cruiser force steaming ten miles ahead of the convoy—'yet another example of the singleness of purpose and short-sighted policy' of the Germans, he said.[35]

Morale in PQ.17 was now at its zenith, as several incidents could show: at the height of the attack, one of the two British submarines at the rear of the convoy—*P-614* (Lieutenant Beckley) —had made an anxious signal to Commander: 'Please may I go

---

* Throughout this dramatic air attack, an official photographer in the USS *Wainwright*, Frank Scherschel, was on deck taking a most remarkable series of photographs in which the attack by Hennemann and the torpedoing of *Azerbaijan* (wrongly referred to by *Life* magazine, who published the photographs on 3 August 1942, as an American merchantman) are graphically shown. They are published here between pages 194–195.

home to Mum . . . ?' At about the same time, the anti-submarine trawler *Ayrshire* (Lieutenant Gradwell) had nonchalantly enquired of her nearest neighbour, 'Are you happy in the Service?'* Again, the American freighter *Hoosier* had dealt summarily with one torpedo heading straight for their engine room by opening fire upon it, blowing up its warhead while still some way away; one of her officers rushed down into the Chief Engineer's room to tell him that he had all but been blown to bits, but that the gun crew had saved him in the nick of time by blowing the torpedo up. Without even looking up the engineer had dourly bellowed back, 'Well, keep a good look out and just keep blowing 'em up!'[37] The unfortunate *William Hooper*'s neighbour, the Panamanian *Troubadour*, adopted the same ploy: when an erratically weaving torpedo began heading for them, the *Troubadour* fired not only her ·30 Lewis guns at it but the 37-millimetre guns of the tanks on deck as well; after about seventy-five rounds had been expended on it the torpedo stopped, turned up on end, and sank from sight tail first.[38]

Even though the enemy had long departed, one ship's gun was still banging spasmodically away—in the bows of the tanker *Azerbaijan*, torpedoed but still afloat and falling astern of the convoy together with *Navarino* and *William Hooper*. The sea around them was dotted with lifeboats, rafts and swimming seamen: the gun crews of both *William Hooper* and the tanker had been knocked, or had jumped, into the sea, and only one of *Navarino*'s lifeboats had survived the blast. With their buzzers sounding 'rescue stations', the rescue ships *Zamalek*, *Zaafaran* and *Rathlin* were all closing in on them, and lowering their rescue launches.

From the rescue ship *Zaafaran*, officers had seen the Russian tanker engulfed in a mushroom of smoke, and had feared the worst; the second officer's launch headed towards the tanker through a sea covered with a thick layer of oil which they feared might ignite at any moment. But the Russian's bows slowly emerged from the smoke, and she showed little sign of sinking. She had been carrying linseed oil, not petrol. The heavy gun in the ship's bows, manned entirely by women, was still firing in the

* The corvette had replied that she wished time to consider her reply.[36]

direction of the long-departed bombers.* Behind the tanker, seven of the Russian's gunners were threshing about in the sea. *Zaafaran*'s motor launch was just picking them up, when an eighth man jumped into the sea from the tanker and swam in their direction. He was taken on board too. Apparently he was an OGPU officer, for he indicated to the British Second Officer that the launch was to be turned about and the seamen were to be returned to the Russian tanker. The British officer, James Bruce, ignored him, especially as one of the Russians left aboard the tanker was brandishing a healthy looking gun. Once all the seamen, some of them badly injured, had been picked up, the launch returned to the *Zaafaran*.

At the same time a launch lowered by the other rescue vessel, *Zamalek,* was nearing the wallowing Russian tanker from the other side. Making himself heard with difficulty above the noise of the tanker's 12-pounder, the British Second Officer, C. T. R. Lennard, asked the Soviet captain whether he and his men wished to abandon ship. The Russian officer became very agitated, and began waving his arms about: 'We don't want you! Go away!' *Zamalek*'s launch pulled away from the tanker; once, when Lennard looked back, he saw to his amazement that the Russian captain was firing a machine-pistol in the direction of the eight Russian seamen, who were making off in what he took to be a ship's launch.† Lennard steered his launch to where the burning *Navarino* lay, her engines stopped. He ignored the seamen in the lifeboat and on the rafts, for they were safe already; but he saw a sailor drifting idly in the sea, kept afloat only by a pocket of air

---

* The presence of women aboard Russian merchant ships was a constant source of wonderment. According to *Troubadour*'s Action Report, *Azerbaijan*'s captain was married to the chief engineer, and her chief officer to the boatswain; the stewards' department was manned entirely by women. It caused a minor sensation in nearby ships when word was passed round that *Azerbaijan*'s boatswain had had a baby.

† *Zamalek*'s Report, 4th July: 'Master of Russian ship *Azerbaijan*, though ship torpedoed, reported that he would rejoin convoy: ship not sinking. Some of her crew deserted her and were picked up by *Zaafaran*.' *Zaafaran*'s Report says that eight Russian seamen 'panicked and jumped overboard when their ship was hit', but this was not so.

in his oilskin. He hauled the body up: it felt cold and lifeless, and the eyes were fixed and staring. He pushed the man back into the sea, but one of the launch's crew, *Zamalek*'s carpenter, said that he had heard a groan. The man was hauled back in, and he was indeed found to be just alive.

The launch was raced back to its parent ship, while the seamen tore the sodden clothes from the body and wrapped it in dry blankets. The man was carried to *Zamalek*'s operating theatre, where Surgeon-Lieutenant McCallum stripped off the blankets: the man was stone cold, 'three inches through' he reckoned, but still just alive. While the sick-bay attendant gave artificial respiration, McCallum switched on two electrically heated blankets in the sick-bay's cot. Slowly, fitfully, the man began to breathe again. He was lifted on to the operating table, and McCallum checked the body functions as they gradually returned to normal. Within an hour, the man had almost completely recovered. Only one thing never returned to him—his memory. Who he was, how he came to be aboard this vessel, the circumstances of his rescue—all were a complete void in his memory.

For some hours he rested, wrapped in electric blankets in the cot of the sick bay; after that, he found his way to the *Zamalek*'s boiler room, where he made a little blanketed nest for himself on a ledge right on top of the boilers: 'He would not move from it,' McCallum later described, 'not even during the heaviest air attacks that followed. He never wanted to be cold again.'[39]

So that was the score: or was it? Three ships had been torpedoed in this first determined German attack on the convoy; but now, to everyone's amazement, the Russian tanker *Azerbaijan* signalled, 'No. 52 reporting in,' and limped after them.[28] Her engine-room crew had succeeded in repairing her damage, and within half an hour the plucky ship had regained her station in the convoy. The American *William Hooper* and the British *Navarino*, though still afloat even now, an hour after the attack, had been abandoned by their crews and were beyond repair. Commander Broome detailed the minesweepers *Britomart* and *Halcyon* to dispose of the two lame merchantmen by gunfire. The former had expended twenty rounds of semi-armour-piercing 4-inch shell on them, and left them 'sinking and on fire', when he received a signal from

Halcyon to rejoin the convoy. Commodore Dowding accurately reported that when last seen both ships were still afloat.⁴⁰

The convoy was by now ten miles or more away. The few small vessels that had stayed to pick up the survivors from the lifeboats and rafts dotting the sea were now exposed to acute danger from the patrolling German submarines.

One of the ten survivors from *Navarino* who had taken to a raft described how the ships of the convoy steamed past them, but nobody stopped to pick them up: 'The horizon emptied, and we were on a raft in the middle of the Arctic Ocean, and we began to fear that the others had reported that we had gone down with the ship. We saw one ship approaching, but it turned out to be a minesweeper hastening to catch up with the convoy. We knew they wouldn't stop for us, but we jokingly stood up and tried to "thumb a lift"; the men in the minesweeper, which passed less than two hundred yards away from us, crowded the rails and cheered us, but their ship did not pause. It had been an act of bravado on our part, but we would have liked it better had they stopped. . . .'⁴¹

Commander Broome had been busy tidying up the convoy when Hamilton's signal warning of the 'proximity of surface forces' reached him. He warned the two submarines to remain in the vicinity of the convoy and to endeavour to attack the German warships as they arrived, and he reformed his destroyers into two divisions in readiness for immediate attack or shadowing. There was still no further news, but he felt sure Hamilton knew more than he did. What next? In all probability the shadowing aircraft was at that very moment homing in the German surface forces. At 9.15 p.m. Broome radioed *Empire Tide*, with its Hurricane waiting to be launched from its catapult, 'Can you kill shadower?' By way of answer, the merchantman immediately hoisted the aeroplane flag, and the roar of the Hurricane's engine warming up reached Broome's ears.

Captain Morris's rescue ship *Zamalek* stayed long enough to make sure that in the chaos nobody had been overlooked, then he too set the engine-room telegraph to 'Full Ahead Both'. Every minute of delay increased the danger of submarine attack. At almost the last moment, he caught sight of *Navarino*'s raft drifting low in the waves a mile away with ten men on board, and at

9.20 p.m. they were brought on board. Almost simultaneously, the decision was reached in London which was to bring disaster to convoy PQ.17.

✳ 4 ✳

As the battered Heinkel 111s were returning to their base in northern Norway; and as the three British rescue ships were struggling to catch up the proud convoy, now marching once again in perfect formation across the Barents Sea, a report arrived at the Berlin headquarters of the German Naval Staff from the naval radio-monitoring station at Kirkenes: it had intercepted a number of British 'operational signals' which had been transmitted between 7 p.m. and 10 p.m. that evening from Scapa Flow and Cleethorpes, addressed to the Commander-in-Chief, Home Fleet, and the naval forces from Scapa Flow.[10]

The first, transmitted soon after 7 p.m., was the signal we have already met, warning Rear-Admiral Hamilton and Admiral Tovey that 'further information' might be available shortly, and ordering the cruiser force to remain with the convoy pending further instructions. Soon after, Hamilton had confidently ordered *Norfolk*'s Walrus seaplane to be catapulted on a 2½-hour ice-reconnaissance patrol. The aircraft was just about to be catapulted when *Norfolk*'s radio room telephoned up to the bridge that a further signal, MOST IMMEDIATE, was coming through from Whitehall. This was the second signal the Germans had intercepted. Captain Bellars asked Hamilton for permission to delay flying off his Walrus until the contents of the signal had been decoded; Hamilton refused, and the plane was catapulted off the cruiser.[42] Literally seconds later, the decoded signal was arriving on the bridges of the four cruisers and of Tovey's flagship, hundreds of miles to the west.

Timed 9.11 p.m., it read:

Secret. Most Immediate. Cruiser force withdraw to westward at high speed. . . .*

Norfolk's seaplane had not yet paid out her trailing aerial, and neither wireless nor searchlight signals succeeded in recalling her;

---

* There was a closing sentence.

the sailors lined the rails watching the little aircraft disappear over the northern horizon, its crew unaware that when they returned the cruisers would have gone.

Minutes later, a new Admiralty signal arrived, bursting like a bombshell on Hamilton's bridge. Timed 9.23 p.m., this one was addressed to the convoy's escort commander and Tovey too:

Secret. Immediate. Owing to threat from surface ships convoy is to disperse and proceed to Russian ports.

Seconds later, an even more urgent injunction:

Secret. Most Immediate. My 21.23B of the 4th. Convoy is to scatter.

To the two Admirals, this startling sequence of signals could mean only one thing: the German battle fleet was in the convoy's immediate vicinity and about to begin its attack.

Far from it: the enemy warships were still at anchor at Alten-fiord, and the Germans saw little prospect of their being used. While extreme anxiety still governed the Admiralty in London, resignation ruled the German Naval Staff in Berlin: at 5 p.m., General-Admiral Carls, growing increasingly impatient for a decision from Berlin, had indicated that within twenty-four hours the time for executing *The Knight's Move* would be up; if the fleet had not sailed by then, he planned to recall all the warships with the exception of *Scheer* and two destroyers to Narvik and Trond-heim. At eight-thirty that evening, as the big air attack on the convoy was ending, Grand-Admiral Raeder telephoned from Berlin agreeing to this course of action. And at the end of the day, the Naval Staff were still in two moods: while they correctly sus-pected that the two 'carrier-aircraft' sighted near the convoy were probably scout planes catapulted by Hamilton's cruisers, they were still forced to admit that there was no logical explanation for the behaviour of this cruiser force—to which all German sub-marines not shadowing the convoy had meantime been ordered to direct hostile attention. 'We can only hope that the hours of darkness and the early morning will bring some clarity in this respect,' the Naval Staff concluded.[43] Until then there was no prospect of their battle fleet weighing anchor.

The hour which had preceded the British Admiralty's transmission of the signals withdrawing the cruisers and scattering the convoy was the most dramatic in the experience of the British Naval Staff in London. During the early evening, the Admiralty had learned that *Tirpitz* had joined *Scheer* at Altenfiord, and this would put the Germans in the position to attack at 2 a.m. next morning, taking into account the latter warship's slower speed. It would be idle to speculate on how the Intelligence had reached the Admiralty; the Germans would have been convinced, had they known, that 'Norwegian agents' had wirelessed the information to London, and there was indeed a very efficient Allied Intelligence unit in the Altenfiord area.*

At about 8.30 p.m., the First Sea Lord, together with a number of other officers, descended to the 'Citadel', the concrete shelter constructed behind the Admiralty building in Whitehall to house the subterranean Operational Intelligence Centre; Pound's first visit was to Captain J. W. Clayton, the Centre's Deputy Director. A minute or two later, all of them, including now Clayton, walked along the corridor and packed into the office of Paymaster-Commander N. E. Denning, the principal Intelligence officer for operations of the German surface units. Into this room flowed virtually all Intelligence data on the movements of all German warships.

Admiral Pound asked him whether *Tirpitz* had yet sailed from Altenfiord. Denning replied that if she had, he was certain he would have heard of it. Pound persisted, 'Can you say for certain that the *Tirpitz* is still at Altenfiord, then?' The Intelligence officer replied that his sources were such that he would learn not that the battleship was at anchor, but only whether she had put to sea; in reply to a further question, he added that there was no evidence of the battleship's preparing to sail for the next few hours. Subsequently Denning was to blame himself for not having been able to put over to Pound with sufficient conviction his confidence that the ships were still at anchor. When the First Sea Lord finally left Denning's room he certainly gave the impression

---

* Thus Schmundt's 8 July order for the transfer of the damaged *Lützow* to Trondheim warned: 'From past experience it must be assumed that our naval units' movements are reported continuously by agents using W/T.'

that he accepted the commander's contention.[44] Later it became apparent that he had not.

Pound crossed the corridor into the Centre's Submarine Tracking Room. This was the equivalent of Denning's office, as far as the enemy U-boats were concerned: all the Intelligence and radio-monitoring reports on the whereabouts and activities of enemy U-boats promptly reached this room—a large chamber, dominated by a square table in the centre, and with charts of special areas on every wall. The room's commanding officer, Commander Rodger Winn, RNVR, was with Denning one of the most astute Intelligence officers produced by any of the three Services: he could detect every nuance of German submarine strategy even as it was being developed by the authorities in Berlin. German U-boat commanders soon learned that the ones who lived longest were the ones who transmitted least.

We have already noticed the extreme difficulties under which Winn's staff were labouring when trying to locate U-boats in the Arctic by direction-finding means; but now the picture forming in Winn's room was a most alarming representation of the dangerous situation developing for the cruisers in the Barents Sea. Commander Winn recalls having informed Pound that the U-boat situation was 'very serious indeed'.[45]

The first result of Admiral Pound's visit to the 'Citadel' was that by the time he and his entourage had returned to his first-floor room, he had resolved that the cruiser force must be withdrawn to the westward at once, as it could certainly not put up any lasting fight against *Tirpitz*, and—despite what Denning had assured him —the Germans must surely have sailed the *Tirpitz* squadron, or be on the point of doing so: there was no logical reason why they should not. At 9.11 p.m., the first of the three fatal signals was sent out, ordering Hamilton's cruiser force to withdraw to westward at 'high speed'. For a reason no longer exactly ascertainable, the signal was prefixed MOST IMMEDIATE, although there was no immediacy in the need for the force's withdrawal: they had fuel for another day's steaming eastwards. The stress on 'high speed' was the result of Pound's visit to the Submarine Tracking Room, where the German's change of emphasis for U-boat attack from the convoy to the cruisers had been reported to him; submarines were known to be lying across the cruisers' withdrawal route.

With Hamilton and the cruisers gone, Commander J. E. Broome, the Senior Officer of the Escort, would be the senior officer on the spot; Admiral Pound expressed great reluctance to unshoulder the burden for a major decision on to such a junior officer.[46] In any case, the Admiralty alone was in possession of all the relevant Intelligence, so it was the Admiralty that should make the appropriate decisions. The First Sea Lord inquired of each of the officers in turn, seated round the conference table in his room, what line of action he would support for the convoy to avoid being slaughtered by the German battle fleet during the night. He himself favoured its dispersal. But each officer in turn said that the convoy should not be dispersed yet, with the exception of Admiral Moore, the Vice-Chief of Naval Staff.[47] He alone expressed himself in favour of dispersing the convoy; indeed, it should be done immediately. Using chart and dividers, he argued that in five hours' time, the German warships could be attacking the convoy: this was not an occasion when the convoy could wait until the enemy ships actually appeared on the horizon, as in the famous *Jervis Bay* incident in 1940. Convoy PQ.17 was understood to be close to the ice pack to the north, so dispersal could be in a southerly direction alone, and this would bring the convoy's merchant ships right on to the guns of the attacking German warships. If the convoy was to be dispersed, it must be dispersed at once.[48]

According to the Director of Operations,[49] one of the younger officers present at this historic moment, the way in which Admiral Pound reached his final decision was almost melodramatic: the First Sea Lord leaned back in his leather-backed chair and closed his eyes—an invariable attitude of deep meditation when making difficult decisions; his hands gripped the arms of his chair, and his features, which had seemed almost ill and strained, became peaceful and composed. After a few moments the youthful Director of Plans whispered irreverently, 'Look, Father's fallen asleep.' After thirty long seconds, Admiral Pound reached for a Naval Message pad and announced, 'The convoy is to be dispersed.' As he said this, he made a curious but eloquent gesture to the others, indicating that this was his decision, and he was taking it alone; one can but admire his courage in reaching the decision in face of such opposition. That the decision was to prove wrong only lent the

[117]

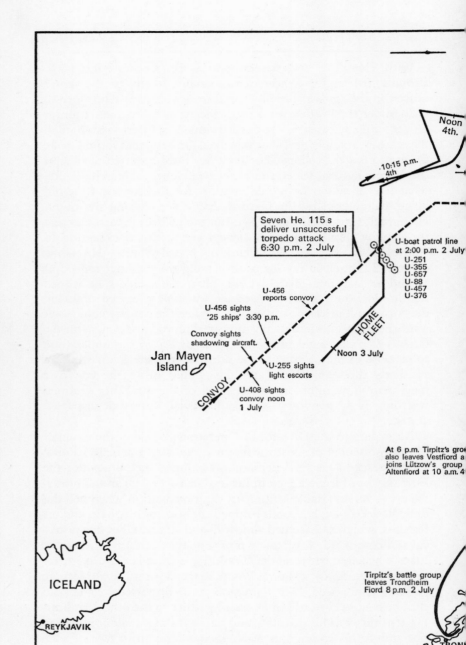

Noon
4th.

10:15 p.m.
4th

Seven He. 115 s
deliver unsuccessful
torpedo attack
6:30 p.m. 2 July

U-boat patrol line
at 2:00 p.m. 2 July
U-251
U-355
U-657
U-88
U-457
U-376

U-456
reports convoy

U-456 sights
'25 ships' 3:30 p.m.

Convoy sights
shadowing aircraft.

HOME FLEET

Jan Mayen
Island

Noon 3 July

U-255 sights
light escorts

CONVOY

U-408 sights
convoy noon
1 July

At 6 p.m. Tirpitz's grou
also leaves Vestfiord a
joins Lützow's group
Altenfiord at 10 a.m. 4

ICELAND

REYKJAVIK

Tirpitz's battle group
leaves Trondheim
Fiord 8 p.m. 2 July

TRON

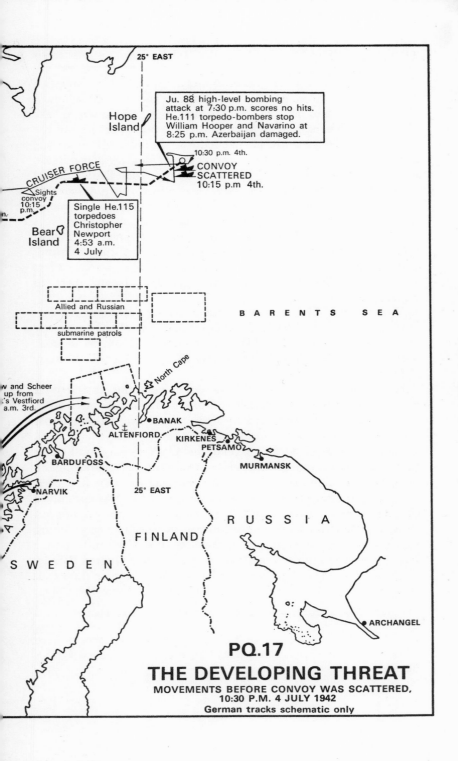

25° EAST

Ju. 88 high-level bombing attack at 7:30 p.m. scores no hits. He.111 torpedo-bombers stop William Hooper and Navarino at 8:25 p.m. Azerbaijan damaged.

Hope Island

10:30 p.m. 4th.

CRUISER FORCE

CONVOY SCATTERED 10:15 p.m 4th.

Sights convoy 10:15 p.m.

Single He.115 torpedoes Christopher Newport 4:53 a.m. 4 July

Bear Island

Allied and Russian

B A R E N T S   S E A

submarine patrols

North Cape

w and Scheer up from 's Vestfiord a.m. 3rd.

BANAK

ALTENFIORD

KIRKENES

PETSAMO

BARDUFOSS

MURMANSK

NARVIK

25° EAST

R U S S I A

FINLAND

S W E D E N

ARCHANGEL

PQ.17
THE DEVELOPING THREAT
MOVEMENTS BEFORE CONVOY WAS SCATTERED, 10:30 P.M. 4 JULY 1942
German tracks schematic only

more poignancy to it. The dumbfounded Captain Clayton slipped out of Pound's office and hurried down to the 'Citadel' again.

Admiral Pound himself wrote out the signal, ordering the convoy to 'disperse and proceed to Russian ports', because of the threat from surface ships. He handed it to Admiral Moore to see, and then it went down to the Registry for immediate transmission to Commander Broome, Admiral Tovey and Rear-Admiral Hamilton. No sooner had the signal gone down, than it occurred to Moore that there was an error in its formulation: 'disperse' meant that the ships would merely break formation and head in a bunch for Archangel, which would still leave them a worthwhile target for the enemy. Moore at once pointed this out to Pound, and informed him that the word laid down in the convoy orders was 'scatter'. The First Sea Lord agreed, 'I meant them to scatter.'

Vice-Admiral Moore swiftly drafted a brief second signal as a correction to the former, and to ensure that it reached the convoy coterminously with the 'dispersal' signal he prefixed it MOST IMMEDIATE. The new signal read, 'My 21.23B of the 4th. Convoy is to scatter.'*

Now the die was cast. The message went out at thirty-six minutes past nine. The signals, unforgettable as they arrived in rapid succession on the ships' bridges, were being flashed across the ether to the cruisers and PQ. 17.

When Captain Clayton reached the Operational Intelligence Centre nearly a hundred feet below ground in the 'Citadel' again, he related to Commander Denning the decision that had been taken. Denning urged his superior that the O.I.C. was convinced that the German warships had, for some unknown reason, not put to sea; nor was there any indication that they were even planning to do so in the near future. He prevailed upon Clayton to return once more to Pound's room, overlooking Horse Guards Parade, to persuade him to cancel the order for the convoy's dispersal. Clayton hastened aloft, and told Admiral Pound that the O.I.C.

---

* Had a closer scrutiny of the last signal been made by Hamilton and Broome in their agitation, it would have become obvious that it was essentially a correction of the former signal and this would have divested it of its apparent urgency. This can hardly be held against them, of course.

was satisfied that the enemy warships were still at anchor. Pound answered, 'We have decided to scatter the convoy, and that is how it must now stay.' There is some reason to believe that after dispatching the last signal, scattering the convoy, Pound had telephoned Mr Churchill to tell him what he had done (the extent to which the First Sea Lord was in awe of the Prime Minister cannot be over-emphasized); and that this was why he resisted Captain Clayton's suggestion.*

Clayton returned to the Citadel and related Pound's reply to Denning.[44]

* 5 *

At 8.43 p.m., it will be remembered, Commander Broome had received from Rear-Admiral Hamilton the first explicit warning about the 'proximity' of surface forces, and he had begun to prepare for the action that was to follow; at 9.47, twenty-three minutes before the Admiralty's two abrupt signals 'dispersing' and then 'scattering' the convoy reached him, Commander Broome had received an ominous report from the anti-aircraft ship *Pozarica*, with her superior radar arrays watching the rear of the convoy: 'Suspected formation, 230 degrees, 29 miles.'[50] That could be something coming from Norway.

Ordered now to scatter the convoy in such drastic terms, Broome needed no second bidding. At 10.15 p.m. he signalled the corvette *Dianella*, 'Tell submarines *P-614* and *P-615* to act independently and strike.'[50] When the corvette passed the signal on, *P-615* (Lieutenant Newstead) asked, 'Where the devil is the enemy?' Broome signalled back, 'God knows'.[51] The other submarine, commanded by Lieutenant Beckley, signalled Broome that he intended 'to remain on the surface'. A terse Broome replied, 'So do I.'[52] Their dispositions thus assigned to them, the two British submarine commanders decided to patrol north and south

---

* Commander Peter Kemp, who was Acting Deputy Commander of the O.I.C. that day and accompanied Pound through the Submarine Tracking Room and the main Operations Room, and into the Duty Captain's room, stressed to me (May 1963) that definite information that the *Tirpitz* squadron was still at anchor did not come through until some hours later.

of the line of the convoy's track and wait for the enemy warships to appear.*

The Convoy Commodore in *River Afton* refused to believe that this magnificent convoy was to be scattered without further ado, even though there was no enemy in sight: when Broome signalled the message across to him, Dowding thought there must have been some mistake, and he hesitated to pass it on to the freighters now keeping perfect station after the evening air attack. Broome was obliged to bring *Keppel* to within megaphone distance of the Commodore ship. He confirmed that the convoy was to be scattered. Only now, at 10.15 p.m., did the still incredulous Commodore hoist a red pennant with a white cross—Pennant Eight—on his signal halyards: on the bridge of every merchant ship, the officers reached for the codebooks. The pennant's listed meaning was: 'Scatter fanwise and proceed independently to destination at utmost speed.' Each ship was to set off on a different bearing according to a prearranged scheme; but each ship now seemed to be waiting for the others to move first. What lay ahead of them? Most had only magnetic compasses—inadequate for navigation in these latitudes—and some had only four obsolete light machine-guns as their armament. The fear of death lay like a pall over every ship. Finally, after the Commodore ship made the signal executive, the ill-armed merchant vessels slowly and hesitantly edged apart, 'like dogs with their tails between their legs', according to one of the Masters in his report. [28] Only *River Afton* was already surging ahead out of the milling merchantmen, as Commodore Dowding needed no further persuading that the German battle fleet was after them. To the ship's Chief Engineer he promised two cigars if he could coax an extra two knots out of his engines. [53] Poor *River Afton*: an elderly, creaking tramp—she was destined less than twenty-four hours later to meet the most horrible end of any of these merchantmen.

It was now that Commander Broome had to make one of the most unpleasant decisions of his career on the bridge of his

---

* They remained submerged until next day; reporting their positions to the Flag Officer Submarines (at Swiss Cottage) then, they were ordered by him to break off their patrol and proceed direct to the Russian naval base at Polyarnoe.

destroyer *Keppel*.⁵⁴ Whitehall had ordered the convoy to scatter, but what were the escort vessels of his command to do? The Admiralty had mentioned none of these, and no provision had been made in Hamilton's operational orders for an eventuality such as this.⁵⁵ Broome's first reaction was to make a signal to all the other escort destroyers: 'Join me!' At 10.18 p.m. he signalled to Hamilton the proposal that the convoy's close escort should join the cruiser force. Hamilton 'approved this as regards destroyers'.*
He had no hesitation in this, as the proper place for the destroyers was obviously with the forces which might meet the enemy attack, rather than with a scattering convoy; besides, this would still leave twelve anti-submarine vessels with the merchant ships.⁹ He was unaware of the step which Commander Broome—with no instructions to this effect—now took: at 10.20 p.m., on his own initiative, the commander signalled the remainder of his escort force:

All escorts from *Keppel*:
All convoy scatter and proceed to Russian ports.
Escorts, *negative* destroyers, proceed independently to Archangel.
Destroyers join *Keppel*.⁵⁰

The scattering merchant ships had thus been stripped of their last protection. At ten-thirty, Broome headed off towards the withdrawing cruisers in the east, taking his escort destroyers with him. The decks of every merchantman were crowded with bewildered seamen.⁴
At the time the cruiser force received the last of the Admiralty's fateful signals, the cruiser *Tuscaloosa* had still had one aircraft in the air and *Wainwright* was fuelling from the convoy's oiler. *Norfolk*'s Walrus had vanished over the horizon, and could not be recalled; the cruiser's captain proposed formally to Hamilton that he should

---

* Hamilton's Preliminary Report: 'It later became apparent that the Admiralty expected that the destroyers had remained.' Hamilton had served in destroyers for most of his Service life, and had recently given up the appointment of Rear-Admiral Destroyers, Home Fleet. At that time there was a great shortage of destroyers; he remarked to *London*'s captain that there was little Broome's destroyers could do to help a dispersed convoy.⁵⁵

Write across					
	12				55
	4/7/42.				60
	ALL DESTROYERS FROM KEPPEL.				65
	JOIN ME !!				70
	2032/4 ALL ESCORTS FROM KEPPEL				75
	ALL CONVOY SCATTER AND PROCEED TO				80
	RUSSIAN PORTS.				85
	ESCORTS NEGATIVE DESTROYERS.				90
	PROCEED INDEPENDENTLY TO				95
	ARCHANGEL.				100
	DESTROYERS JOIN KEPPEL = 2020Z/4				105
					110
	5th JULY 1942.				115
	P.Q. 17 ℗ ADMIRALTY FROM S.B.N.O.				120
	NORTH RUSSIA				125
	S.S EARLSTON IN ACTION WITH U-BOAT				130
	075° 43'N 038° 02'E at 1600C/5				135
	(1) SUBMARINE DISTRESS —				140
	VESSEL 075° 02'N				145
	038° 00'E TORPEDOED = 1556C/5				150

Keppel's signal, recorded on the pad kept by Lieutenant Frank Petter, of the corvette *La Malouine* be allowed to proceed eastwards to the agreed rendezvous with the Walrus fifty miles farther east, but furnished with what seemed such categorical orders from Whitehall, Hamilton was bound to 'regret' that this was impossible. The cruiser force carried on briefly to the eastwards as *Tuscaloosa*'s aircraft was recovered and then at ten-thirty Hamilton turned his force to the south-west, so as to steer between the scattering merchant ships of the convoy and the probable direction of the 'German surface attack'.[56] From *Wichita*'s bridge, Lieutenant Fairbanks surveyed the sorry spectacle of the scattering convoy:

> The ships are dotted around for miles. Some still burning and smoldering from bomb hits, while others are just getting up steam. Their smoke makes it look like huge black ostrich feathers are growing out of tubs.

As the cruisers approached the convoy, they saw Commander Broome's destroyers coming to meet them, accompanied by USS *Wainwright*: 'She comes boiling over the water at us looking very smug and self-conscious,' wrote Fairbanks. 'Wonder what happened to our young Ensign on the *William Hooper* who only had 90 rounds for his 4-inch guns?'[33] Broome led his six destroyers round at twenty knots, and headed off in line ahead to join Hamilton's cruisers and destroyers racing off to the south-west into a wall of fog. By 11 p.m. his destroyers were drawing very close to the cruisers. The destroyer *Wilton* signalled *Ledbury*, 'How fast are you going?' *Ledbury* replied, 'Full ahead.'[57] From the bridge of his flagship, Hamilton told Broome's destroyers not to rupture themselves—they were to cut the corners. At 11.18 p.m. Broome's destroyers took station astern of Hamilton's flagship, now heading almost due west. As the destroyers and cruisers passed the confused merchant ships at 11.30 p.m., Commodore Dowding wished Broome well: 'Many thanks. Good-bye and good hunting!' Broome signalled back to all his charges he was leaving behind, 'Sorry to leave you like this. Good luck. Looks like a bloody business.'[58]

The Admiralty had ordered 'high speed'. Rear-Admiral Hamilton increased to twenty-five knots. Soon the warships were speeding through the oil, débris and wreckage of the evening's big air attack. In preparation for what Hamilton also took to be the imminent action with the enemy, ships' buglers sounded 'general quarters' and the flashproof shutters began closing on the crews locked into the cordite and shell-rooms of the magazines beneath the cruisers' main batteries.

At Hamilton's request, Captain Don Moon, Senior Officer Destroyers, in *Wainwright*, reorganized all the destroyers into two flotillas, ordering them to form up in line abreast, ready to deliver a torpedo attack on the German warships 'at closest possible range'—less than 2,000 yards: 'in case of surprise contact at close range, attack without orders and exploit surprise to maximum'.[59] (Moon's plan overlooked the fact that Broome's two Hunt-class destroyers were purely escort destroyers, designed for little other than anti-aircraft and anti-submarine roles; they had no torpedo tubes.) The word that they were going into action spread rapidly through *Keppel*'s company; the sailors sat down to hasty meals, and began preparing their weapons for action.[60] Hamilton imposed strict wireless silence on the force. Shortly after midnight, the cruisers and destroyers ran into dense fog, and this was to persist for the next six hours.

The other convoy escort vessels had been flabbergasted by this turn of events, and their late Senior Officer's instructions had been anything but comprehensive. The fleet oiler *Aldersdale,* laden with 8,000 tons of fuel oil for the convoy's warships, tried to contact Broome by signal lamp as the destroyers raced past; Captain Hobson wanted to know whether to turn his oiler back, or to scatter with the merchantmen.[61] Commander Broome vouchsafed no reply.

Lieutenant Gradwell, captain of the armed trawler *Ayrshire*, recalled Hamilton's words at the escort conference a week before, to the effect that the convoy might well be the cause of another fleet action, 'perhaps another Jutland'. From the sight of the cruisers running off to the west, Gradwell drew what seemed the only possible conclusion. He gathered it would not be long before *Tirpitz* appeared over the horizon, and he ordered his crew to lash every available depth-charge to oil drums: his plan was to drop them across the battleship's path, if he could get close enough, then place *Ayrshire* squarely across her bows and blow the trawler up as they collided.[62] The captain of the anti-aircraft ship *Palomares* cleared lower deck and explained to all hands if they sighted *Tirpitz* they and two corvettes they had collected were to behave as though they were a cruiser and two destroyers, and head straight for the Germans to delay them while the merchantmen escaped. The Captain held a short service, and all hands not on watch were released to snatch what sleep they could.[63]

✳ 6 ✳

Was the decision for the cruisers to withdraw partly motivated by the First Sea Lord's realization that half the endangered cruiser force was American? Mr Winston Churchill offered this explanation in his post-war memoirs, first serialized in 1950 in the *Daily Telegraph*. There is nothing in the naval records to suggest that this was so. Although the passage of the memoirs describing the PQ.17 disaster was 'ghosted' by Captain G. R. G. Allen, one of the many authors who helped the former Prime Minister on this monumental task, Captain Allen has informed me that the unlikely explanation for Pound's actions was inserted by Mr Churchill himself, as 'he was trying to make excuses for his old friend.'[64] We are told that on occasion Mr Churchill was wont to invent such extenuating circumstances to mitigate the errors of his protégés.

Contrary to what the Official Historian suggests, Mr Churchill did not, however, know at the time that it was in fact Sir Dudley Pound who had taken the fatal decision to scatter the convoy. Allen said, 'When I told him [Churchill] one morning in 1949 that my researches among the official papers and my interviews with naval staff officers had yielded the information that Pound was responsible for these decisions concerning PQ.17, I could see real pain and grief written across his face; he had *not* known about it.' In the 'Churchill' memoirs, Allen accordingly wrote, 'So strictly was the secret of these orders being sent on the First Sea Lord's authority guarded by the Admiralty, that it was not until after the war that I learned the facts.'[65]

Whatever subsequent historians were to make of them, the effect of the Admiralty's signals on events in the Barents Sea was quite irreversible. As Rear-Admiral Hamilton privately explained soon after:

Although I had no intention of seeking action with the *Tirpitz*, it
seemed probable that I might not be able to avoid it. It is evident
that *Keppel* appreciated the situation in the same way, and his signalled intentions and my approval for the destroyers of the escort to
join me were based entirely on this inference. The scattering of the
convoy in waters infested by U-boats and enemy aircraft could only
mean the probability of immediate surface attack, and in these
conditions the proper place for the destroyers seemed obviously to
be concentrated with the forces which might meet that attack,
rather than being scattered with the convoy.[9]

He pointed out that he had provided for twelve anti-submarine
vessels to remain with the convoy, despite Broome's proposal that
they too should withdraw: 'I had no hesitation in approving that
the destroyers should join my force.'

Admiral Tovey made it clear in his report to the Admiralty
that he considered the actions of both Hamilton and the destroyers
ill-advised: 'The form of the signals ordering the Cruiser Covering
Force to withdraw and the convoy to scatter was such that it was
reasonable for C.S. One [Hamilton] to deduce that an attack by
the *Tirpitz* was imminent,' he admitted. He added that in these
circumstances he considered Hamilton to have been correct in
'ordering' the screening destroyers to join him:

Once he was clear of the convoy, however, and in default of further information to confirm his impression that the *Tirpitz* was in
the close vicinity, I consider that he should have released these
destroyers and instructed them to rejoin the convoy. Their value
for anti-U-boat purposes, even though the convoy was scattering,
would have been considerable, and if the enemy main units had
appeared the destroyers might have been a considerable distraction
and anxiety to them, especially in low visibility.[66]

Mr Churchill echoed this criticism in his memoirs: 'unfortunately,' he wrote, 'the destroyers of the convoy escort also withdrew'. Commander Broome, agonized by the implication that he
was somehow at fault in this, wrote in reply:

This statement may reasonably create the impression that the
destroyer force was free to remain with the convoy or to withdraw.
It was from no misfortune that the destroyers under my command
withdrew; it resulted from a direct order from the Admiralty to

[128]

scatter the convoy. This order could only have been justified by
the proximity of the enemy, and it demanded therefore that I
should concentrate my destroyer force with the nearby cruisers.* [67]

When Broome realized the terrible mistake that had been made,
a change came over him; he was a broken man for the rest of the
fast passage back to Londonderry.

At the time, Hamilton and all his officers still believed that
Tirpitz was at sea and advancing on the convoy's ships behind
them. The warships were still at action stations, and they were
still rushing headlong through the fog, heedless of the many small
'growlers' and icebergs infesting the sea; but still nothing happened. The events of the last few hours had had a shattering
effect on Hamilton's officers and men: assuming—as they all did—
that the Germans were about to pounce upon the scattering
merchant ships, they were running away from the enemy, and at
'high speed'.[3] Up to the time he had received the signals, Hamilton's belief had been that *Tirpitz* could not arrive at the convoy
before midnight at the earliest, or before 2 a.m. next morning if
Admiral Scheer was in company. The precipitate arrival of three
Admiralty signals, one prefixed IMMEDIATE and two MOST
IMMEDIATE, had left him convinced that the Admiralty had come
into possession of the 'further information' they had hinted at
two hours before, and that *Tirpitz* was at sea and in the near
vicinity of the convoy:[9] 'I acted accordingly.'[3] Had he known
otherwise, he would have remained with his force in a covering
position until the convoy was widely dispersed, and would then
have departed from the convoy's sight in a less painfully exposed
manner. 'I fear,' he told Tovey two days later, 'that the effect on
morale was deplorable.'[35]

It was indeed: an officer of the ill-armed American freighter
John Witherspoon wrote in his diary that night, 'Received orders
to disband convoy. It is unbelievable that we are being put on
our own without protection—some ships with no guns at all.

---

* Broome also wrote in *Make a Signal*, p. 149: 'The correct way to
scatter a convoy is explained in the signal book, but it is not explained
there or anywhere else how to round up a convoy once it has been
scattered.' Referring to the Admiralty's signals, he added with feeling,
'It seems that wireless telegraphy came forty years too soon for PQ.17.'

Everyone going every way on horizon. Some ships sticking two or three together. We are going off alone. . . . '[68]

What became of the twelve Royal Navy escort vessels left behind by their Escort Leader? It was in these that Rear-Admiral Hamilton had reposed his confidence for the salvation of at least some of the convoy's transports.

The corvette *Dianella* (Lieutenant Rankin) interpreted Broome's last orders literally, and was heading in a straight line for Archangel.[69] At 11 p.m. the anti-aircraft ship *Palomares* (Captain J. H. Jauncey) as senior escort vessel after *Keppel*'s departure, merely signalled all the escorts, 'Scatter and proceed independently';[70] but some time later she realized that in scattering the escorts she had left herself as denuded of anti-submarine protection as the merchant ships: she signalled the minesweeper *Britomart*, seven miles to the north of her, the one word 'Close' and then, ten minutes later, the instructions, 'Take station on my port beam, one mile. Course 077°, $11\frac{1}{2}$ knots.' Soon after, *Palomares* ordered the minesweeper *Halcyon* to take station on her other beam. *Britomart*'s Lieutenant-Commander Stammwitz afterwards observed, 'It seemed wrong that my anti-submarine minesweeper was being used only to escort a heavily armed anti-aircraft ship. But *Palomares* seemed more concerned with the safe passage of his ship than the merchant ships.'[71] The anti-submarine vessels were of course afforded excellent AA protection in this way.

The corvette *La Malouine* had initially shaped an easterly course with her sister-ship *Lotus*, the latter having newly oiled. 'Fog failed us when most needed,' wrote Lieutenant Caradus, *La Malouine*'s Asdic officer that night. The corvette *Poppy* was not far away, and *Ayrshire*, the little anti-submarine trawler of whom everybody had grown so fond, was in the distance. For two hours, those with naval codebooks worked on the continuing stream of cypher signals from Whitehall: 'Submarines were ordered to certain positions,' recorded Caradus, 'and we knew that the German fleet was at sea.'[4] By midnight the dispersal was complete, and so far apparently successful.*

---

* Even the corvettes were ill-equipped for navigating these latitudes. Caradus recorded that *La Malouine* signalled *Poppy* at this stage 'What is your DR [dead reckoning] position?' and received the reply, 'Hopeless!'

Hoping to salvage something from the convoy, the other anti-aircraft ship, *Pozarica*, had asked permission to take the seven northernmost merchant ships with her and five other escorts. The Senior Officer had signalled back a blunt refusal—the convoy was to scatter and keep as separate as possible. Faced with this, at 1 a.m. *Pozarica* requested the corvettes *La Malouine* and *Lotus* to provide anti-submarine protection to port and starboard of her. Together they set a north-easterly course, heading for the ice barrier at their best combined speed, which was of necessity restricted by the lower speed of the corvettes and their need to conserve sufficient fuel to reach the nearest land. *Pozarica*'s action caused some dismay in the corvettes. Ignorant, perhaps, of Captain Lawford's categorical orders that the convoy was to scatter, *La Malouine*'s First Lieutenant raged, 'We should burn the Ensign and put a yellow flag up.' He did not think the anti-aircraft ship should be escorted, and he expressed his disgust at the RN escorts' general 'lack of guts' by throwing a chair across the wardroom. From the vibration, all knew that the corvette was making maximum speed.

Lieutenant Caradus retired to his bunk until 4 a.m., fully clad in his kapok oilskin, and with an inflated life-vest as his pillow: 'Very tired but head full of thoughts and heart very heavy. Sleep wouldn't come.' Like all the seamen he had been on the alert for twenty-four hours and more; he wanted to keep abreast of the fast-moving events, but although the spirit was willing the flesh was weak. He remembered hoping that they would be hit before he woke up again.

Caradus was wakened by the words of the Morning Prayer. It was Sunday, 5 July. He was aware that the corvette's engines were now throbbing less. The rescue ship *Rathlin*, laden with survivors of the torpedoed *William Hooper* and *Navarino*, joined company and was given a station five miles on *Pozarica*'s port beam. At 8 a.m. the first ice-caps were sighted, looking unpleasantly like U-boats from a distance. There was a cold, biting wind and patches of fog. The cluster of vessels nosed in to within 800 yards of the ice and altered course to the south-west. They followed the ice edge all morning.

After receiving the order that all escorts were to make for Archangel, *Ayrshire*'s Lieutenant Gradwell had withdrawn to his charthouse, and examined the trawler's few charts of the area.

[131]

He decided there was little future in obeying Broome's order, as the Germans would be studying the same charts as he was and would immediately bar the route to Archangel either with submarines or with bombers, or with both.[72] The track to Archangel seemed to Gradwell to spell certain disaster. He resolved instead to steam to the north-west—in exactly the opposite direction—heading generally for Hope Island. It seemed improbable that the Germans would detect him there, and he hoped to be able to conceal his trawler alongside the island. 'I also thought', Gradwell reported deferentially a few days later, 'that I might escort one or two ships in that direction without defeating the object of scattering.'[73] He accordingly indicated to *Ironclad*, one of the merchant ships shaping in the most northerly direction after the scatter, to follow him. A corvette inquired of him, 'Where are you going?' Gradwell non-committally replied, 'To Hell. And the first one to come back, we hope.'[74]

Captain George Salvesen of the Panamanian freighter *Troubadour* had also set course for Hope Island, and a while later Gradwell caught sight of him heading to the north-west; although the Panamanian was making a lot of smoke, Gradwell saw in this an advantage rather than a disadvantage, for the smoke showed the freighter to be a coal burner, and this would help him out of a rather awkward situation. As the vessels drew abreast, the lieutenant hailed the freighter: 'Are you a coal burner?' The reply was that she was. Gradwell asked, 'What supplies have you got?' 'Six months.' Gradwell ordered: 'Come with me!' *Troubadour*, glad of the escort, joined company.

The three vessels proceeded together towards the north-west as the night passed. Gradwell was glad of his crew—fishermen for the most part, and tougher than any naval complement. He felt ready for any assault the Germans might be planning. At about 7 a.m. as they approached the northern ice-barrier, they came across yet another American merchant ship from the convoy, *Silver Sword*, running close to the great fields of ice-floes extending to the north. Gradwell realized, as he took this third freighter into his charge, that there was no hope of breaking through to the islands where he had planned to 'lie doggo'; and at eight o'clock that evening he signalled to the three ships that he was going to lead them into the ice to avoid detection by enemy aircraft.

This was an extraordinarily courageous action for a trawler captain to make: one false calculation and his ship would be crushed by the vast expanse of shifting ice. Gradwell had the Asdic dome removed from the underside of *Ayrshire*'s hull, and steamed at slow speed into the ice-floes, which became denser and denser as the ships pressed further to the north. All through that night and the following day the four ships ploughed on into the ice, the three freighter Masters trusting implicitly in Gradwell's good judgment. Finally the ice was almost too thick to break. The vessels were now some twenty-five miles from the open sea; on Gradwell's instructions they stopped engines, damped down their fires and blotted out every trace of smoke. He sent his First Officer, Lieutenant R. Elsden, RNVR, on foot across the ice to the other ships. With his authority, the gunners loaded and manned the guns on the M-3 tanks in their deck cargo, as well as their own ships' armament. In the event of a surface attack, the German raiders would certainly have encountered a most remarkable broadside.

This was not the only surprise that Lieutenant Gradwell had in store: on the way into the ice, *Troubadour*'s Master had investigated his paint-locker and found that he had an exceptionally large stock of white paint. As the ship's Armed Guard officer afterwards described:

> The *Ayrshire*'s skipper ordered all the ships to use as much paint as they could on their starboard sides, which were exposed to the direction of Norway. In a matter of about four hours all of the ships had carried out this order. The *Troubadour* was painted from stem to stern, from the water line to her foretop, in less than four hours. All of the deck cargo, deck-gear, hatches, superstructure, had been covered with this coat of white paint.[75]

So effective was this camouflage that they saw aircraft passing twenty miles away but failing to detect the little convoy.* Two of the vessels were only painted on the one side—'rather', as Gradwell later remarked, 'like playing Hamlet and Othello with a very small cast'. So long as they stayed in the ice they were concealed; and so long as they were concealed, they felt secure.

---

* On the evening of 5 July, the German Fifth Air Force reported to the Naval Staff in Berlin the position of the ice edge, and added: 'It will be impossible for ships to be in there. The pack ice extends 20–25 miles northwards, then there is solid ice.'

* 7 *

As Hamilton's cruiser force drew farther and farther from the scattering convoy, his British and American sailors' morale slumped. During the night of 4-5 July, the mystery deepened: the suspicion that the cruisers had apparently abandoned the convoy to engage enemy warships had not been dispelled; but now that the German warships had failed to appear why did the cruisers not turn back? They were still ploughing westwards at 25 knots. At one stage, as the warships raced out of a fogbank, the cruiser *Norfolk* saw a German U-boat sitting on the surface right in her path; Captain Bellars tried to ram it, but with klaxon hooting the submarine crash-dived and escaped below *Norfolk*'s hull.[42] These submarines—although Hamilton did not yet know it—were the only reason why his withdrawal had been ordered at 'high speed'.

The rumour began to circulate that the Royal Navy had been ordered to run away from the Germans; it spread like wildfire through the cruisers' lower decks. *London*'s Captain said later:

> I vividly recall one detail. I always lived on my bridge during these operations, and that night as I was having my evening meal on the bridge, my old chief steward came up to me, and as he cleared away my plate and cutlery he whispered to me, 'It's a pity, Sir, that we had to abandon that convoy . . .'. I knew then that the story was round the whole ship, and that something would have to be done to bolster the crew's morale.[76]

He told Hamilton that the ship's company would have to be informed in full of all that had happened, in order to kill the rumours. This Hamilton promised to do.

At 1.15 a.m. Hamilton signalled the other warships of his force a general explanation of the situation as he saw it, in an attempt to quell the growing dismay:

> I know you will all be feeling as distressed as I am at having to leave that fine collection of ships to find their own way to harbour. The enemy under cover of his shore-based aircraft has succeeded in concentrating a far superior force in this area. We were therefore ordered to withdraw. We are all sorry that the good work of the close escort could not be completed. I hope we shall all have a chance of settling this score with the Hun soon.[77]

The American Captain Hill replied from the senior US cruiser, *Wichita*, 'Thank you. I feel the same way.' From Hamilton's wording of the signal it is obvious that he still believed the German battleships were at sea. This impression was rudely dispelled two hours later: at 3.22 a.m. the cruiser force received from the Admiralty a message to the effect that reconnaissance had shown that enemy heavy units had moved from Trondheim and Narvik, and were 'believed' to be in the Altenfiord area.*[78] It was a cruel shock for Rear-Admiral Hamilton. Were the German warships not at sea, then, and already striking out amongst the scattered ships of PQ.17?

Whatever motives the Admiralty might have had for scattering the convoy, Hamilton realized that Commander Broome had attached his six destroyers to the cruiser force for no useful purpose whatever.

It was out of the question to send the destroyers back. The convoy's ships were by now too well-scattered—over 7,500 square miles of sea—for him to hope to achieve anything by returning Commander Broome's destroyers to them; the most they could do would be screen individual merchant ships, should they be able to find them. But by now they were already getting low in fuel. Hamilton considered that with the possibility of an offensive by the battle fleet against the German heavy warships, perhaps using the aircraft-carrier *Victorious*, the most useful service Broome's unhappy destroyers could perform would be to the Allied fleet. With this in view, Hamilton at 11.30 a.m. began a lengthy fuelling programme to ensure that all the newcomers were topped up with fuel from the cruisers, and within the next few hours four of the six had been completed.[3]

Commander Broome was equally aware of the complications he had caused by withdrawing his destroyers from the scattering convoy, and during the early hours of 5 July he communicated his uncomfortable feelings to the British admiral:

---

* Admiral Tovey's battle fleet received the news at about the same time. The War Diary of Commander, Task Force 99, Admiral Giffen, recorded this on 5 July: 'At 3 a.m. a message was received from the Admiralty stating that it was thought that enemy heavy units were north of Tromsö, but uncertain as to whether or not they were at sea.'

My final brief instructions to PQ.17 and remaining escorts were as follows: convoy scatter and proceed to Russian ports; remaining escorts proceed independently to Archangel; submarines remain to attack if enemy approaches before convoy dispersed, then act under orders of Senior Officer. *Palomares* has doubtless taken charge, but I feel I let my excellent escort down by leaving them thus, and therefore submit these hurried and inadequate instructions requesting they may be re-adjusted or amplified as necessary at the first opportunity.[79]

In the Barents Sea, nobody had 'taken charge'. With the few exceptions we have noted, each ship, escort vessel and merchant ship alike, was withdrawing at maximum speed, intent only on its own salvation. Filled with mounting foreboding, Hamilton that afternoon signalled Commander Broome again:

Had you any original instructions concerning the conduct of the escort when the convoy scattered? What led you to assume the destroyers should concentrate and act under orders of Senior Officer? Personally, I thoroughly approve of your suggestion.[80]

Encouraged perhaps by Hamilton's closing sentence, Broome replied:

No instructions. The suggestion to join your force was my own. My appreciation from slender information at the time was that action was probable in holding off enemy while convoy scattered, and that destroyers would be most useful under your orders.

His signal concluded with the sentence:

The decision to leave the remaining escorts was most unpleasant and I am always ready to go back and collect them.*[81]

---

* Since the war, a different interpretation has been placed on this signal by the Official Historian (Roskill, op cit., p. 141), who wrote: 'Broome, on the other hand, felt certain that [his destroyers] would be ordered to turn back to help defend the scattered merchantmen once the anticipated threat had subsided', and on the afternoon of 5 July he had 'signalled to Admiral Hamilton "I am always ready to go back", which message he "intended as a hint as to where I knew my duty lay".' (The quotations are from Broome's report, written three days later, when he was sadder but wiser.) It is true that Broome, in accordance with naval practice, came under Hamilton's orders as soon as he joined him, and could thus only 'hint'. But the full signal shows that Broome

In the two American cruisers, the 'retreat' left the sailors bewildered and bitter: 'What kind of High Command have we that with such great force in operation we cannot fight it out?' asked Lieutenant Fairbanks. 'Have the British become gun-shy? How can wars be won this way?' These were the angry questions heard throughout the US cruisers: 'it was the mood of the morning.'[33] Captain Hill sat in his chair on the bridge of *Wichita* staring blankly out at the bright and now so peaceful sea. He sensed the feeling of dismay spreading through the ship. The cruiser's printing press produced a special edition of the ship's newspaper relating the sequence of signals from the British Admiralty, and the events of the previous day. The editorial was blunt:

> No one can accuse us of ever having a faint heart, nor can anyone say the British lack 'guts': after all, they have been fighting this war for nearly three years; for one whole year they fought it alone, without Allies, without a trained army, and without equipment— their fleet spread thin around the seven seas of the world. Anyone who has seen the people of London, of Liverpool, Bristol, Portsmouth, Coventry or Southampton can testify to their worth. Anyone who has seen the Commandos in action, was at Dunkirk or at Malta, would be a good witness. No, we are kinfolk and Allies in more ways than one. We've only been at this game for seven months. We're fresh, and all we need is the chance—and we may be surprised at how soon that chance comes. In the words of a signalman 2nd class, 'We'll get those sons of bastards yet, by God!' And so we will![25]

It was an inglorious end to the first great joint Anglo-American naval operation.

At about the time that Hamilton and Broome were exchanging their worried signals, and *Wichita*'s printing press was producing the first copies of its special newspaper, Rear-Admiral Miles, head of the British Naval Mission in Moscow, was having a first 'hurried meeting' with Admiral Alafusov at the Russian Admiralty building in Moscow.[82] For both officers it was an unpleasant

---

was hinting that he wanted to go back and *collect his escorts*—no mention of the merchant ships. For the whole question of the scattering of the destroyers, see Appendix, page 305.

experience: Miles had been awakened in the middle of the night by his secretary, who had precipitately entered his quarters brandishing a copy of the Admiralty signal scattering PQ.17— the only one of all the thousands of Admiralty operational signals that Miles ever received; no sooner had Miles returned to a troubled sleep than he was reawakened, this time with the news that Alafusov, the Deputy Chief of Naval Staff, was demanding to see him at midday.

Alafusov was suffering from a severe bout of influenza and he had been roused from his sick-bed to deal with Miles. His face looked tired and drawn when the British admiral was ushered in, and he was 'sweating and shaking like a leaf'. Miles kept at a respectful distance. The Russian upbraided him for the British Admiralty's decision to scatter the convoy (they had apparently read the Admiralty's signals); the merchant ships, he told Miles, were being decimated, and the Russian monitoring service had picked up scores of distress signals from them. Admiral Miles's naval interpreter was hard-pressed to keep up with the Russian's flow of invective. Alafusov concluded by demanding that Miles secure from the Admiralty a complete and detailed explanation of what had happened; this was to be presented to Admiral Kusnetsov, the Russian Chief of Naval Staff, within the next few days. Kusnetsov had been ordered to report to Marshal Stalin.

As the PQ.17 affair had obviously been elevated to an exalted political level, Miles hurried back to his office and sent an urgent request direct to Admiral Sir Dudley Pound asking for the Admiralty's appreciation of the situation at the time of the decision to scatter the convoy.

THE BETTER PART OF VALOUR

Saturday 4 July — Monday 6 July

Has the British Navy no sense of glory?—Stalin, privately to Churchill, 16 August 1942

IT WAS SOME TIME before the Germans began to grasp what was happening to PQ.17. The wireless signals reaching the Narvik headquarters of the German Admiral Commanding, Arctic, from the U-boats showed puzzlement and indecision. Shortly before 1 a.m. on 5 July, Admiral Schmundt passed on to his U-boat commanders the results of the Air Force's latest reconnaissance:

> Air Force reports at 12.30 a.m.: convoy extended over twenty-five miles.[1]

An hour earlier, he had received a signal from Teichert's *U-456* announcing that the Allied cruiser squadron—four cruisers in two columns, with destroyers on either flank—had suddenly departed to the south-west; now Schmundt received a further puzzled signal from Teichert, reporting that by 11.15 p.m. parts of the convoy were making northwards past him, while the cruiser squadron was far to the south and strongly changing course again. Lieutenant-Commander Hilmar Siemon's *U-334*, closely following on the convoy's trail, had come across the scene of the big evening air attack and at about half-past midnight he found two ships torpedoed by the German Air Force, *Navarino* and *William Hooper*: at 12.45 a.m., *U-334* launched a torpedo at the former from a little over a thousand yards, but the ship turned over and sank before the torpedo reached her;[2] at 1 a.m. he fired two torpedoes at the other vessel, which still seemed perfectly seaworthy, and within five minutes of the explosion the vessel had sunk completely.

For some time after that, the U-boats' reports indicated that the convoy had been lost again, in a 'wall of fog'. But at 2 a.m. Teichert wirelessed that he had found scattered units of the convoy gathering near him and, soon after, Commander Brandenburg (*U-457*) reported that he had lost the cruiser squadron—which he was supposed to be shadowing—and could he have permission to attack the convoy's merchant ships which he now had in sight? Schmundt's office commented that it now seemed certain that the cruiser squadron had, as Teichert had reported, run off to the west. At 3.15 a.m. news came from North-East Air Command that an aircraft shadowing the convoy had reported an hour before that it seemed to have broken up into a northern group comprising nineteen freighters, three 'destroyers' and two corvettes, and a southern group of twelve freighters and a 'light cruiser'—which may have been a wrong identification of one of the heavily armed anti-aircraft ships. The aircraft had expressly confirmed that there were no heavy warships whatsoever accompanying the merchant-men.

Unworried by the dangers of wireless telegraphy now, the U-boat commanders kept up a steady running commentary for Admiral Schmundt as they began to hunt down the stragglers—a submarine's paradise: at 3.35 a.m. *U-456* (Teichert) signalled that he had sighted the convoy scattering; there were 'many unescorted lone freighters', steering north-easterly and south-easterly courses. Five minutes later a signal was received from *U-334* (Siemon) reporting he had sunk a damaged straggler—*William Hooper*—and had observed three ships sinking, including what might have been a heavy cruiser.* Five minutes later still, Commander Brandenburg's *U-457* signalled that he was chasing a lone freighter, and gave his position. So the signals poured into Narvik, all night long.

At 7.45 a.m., Teichert wirelessed Narvik that the convoy was widely scattered and heading south-east; it was apparently slowly regrouping, in improving visibility. Admiral Schmundt ordered all the 'Ice Devil' submarines to concentrate on attacking the 'little convoys' and lone merchant ships; but they were to revert to attacking the cruiser squadron should this reappear.

Below the surface of the Barents Sea two German submarines were already preparing for torpedo attacks: *U-703* was steadily overhauling the brand-new British merchantman *Empire Byron*, and *U-88* was manœuvring into position to destroy the American

---

* No cruiser had been sunk; the German Air Force subsequently made great play of the claim, however.

steamer *Carlton*. Captain John Wharton, Rear-Commodore of
PQ.17 and Master of the 6,645-ton *Empire Byron*, had finally
stretched himself out in an armchair in his day-room on the bridge
and fallen asleep; he had been at action stations for thirty-six
hours and more, and despite the cold daylight which had bathed
his ship all night, he had been unable to stay awake any longer.[3]
He had given his cabin to the lieutenant in charge of the maritime
artillery unit, as he and his men had been on the alert even longer.
The ship was carrying one of the first cargoes of the new Churchill
tanks to Russia; it was her second north Russian convoy duty.

At a quarter-past seven, *U-703* launched her first two torpedoes
at the target at a range of two miles.[4] Lieutenant-Commander
Bielfeld put the ship's speed at 10 knots, but both torpedoes passed
harmlessly ahead of her. No bells shrilled the alarm, so the attack
had passed unnoticed. Bielfeld believed the torpedoes had missed
astern, so he gave the target a speed of 12 knots and fired tubes
II and IV: the torpedoes missed even farther ahead. While his
crew hastened to reload tube I, he swung the U-boat round so as
to bring her stern tube to bear upon the vessel. An hour passed.
He had measured her speed now exactly—8 knots; she would
cross his periscope sights at right angles and only a thousand yards
away. At 8.27 a.m. *U-703* placed her fifth torpedo in the ship's
main engine-room. Bielfeld saw through his periscope a small
white puff of smoke from the after hold. Everybody in the U-boat
distinctly heard the metallic knock of the exploding warhead. The
ship settled slightly lower in the sea.

By the time the torpedo struck, Captain Wharton was so soundly
asleep that he never even heard the explosion. He was awakened
by the gunnery lieutenant shouting that the ship had been torpedoed; he refused to believe this, as he could hear that the ship
still had plenty of forward speed. Nevertheless he looked outside:
there was pandemonium as the crew were already struggling to
leave the ship; three of the four lifeboats had been lowered, and
the fourth was on its way down. Wharton went to the bridge to
see that all papers and documents were destroyed. The second
radio officer, a Manchester man, asked whether he should fetch an
emergency wireless for use in the boats, but Wharton told him the
set had already been sent aboard them. A dozen of the gunners
had been trapped below by the explosion, and above the noise of

rushing water he could hear their shouts and screams. There was nothing anybody could do to reach them.

Wharton dived into the sea. He was picked up by a raft, and transferred to one of the lifeboats. He ordered all the men to concentrate in two of the lifeboats, one of which had an engine. There were several bodies in the sea, one of which he recognized to his horror as being that of the young Manchester radio officer to whom he had spoken only minutes before. Twenty minutes after the attack, the ship's boiler exploded, tearing a gaping hole in the hull; the roar of water cascading into the ship was now deafening, and within not many more minutes she finally went down. Bielfeld had in the meantime impatiently fired yet a sixth torpedo at her, nine minutes after the fifth, but this went wide and vanished into the distance. As the ship went down, the nearby American Liberty ship *Peter Kerr* broke wireless silence to broadcast an SOS for *Empire Byron*; but they forgot to give the ship's position.[5] There were forty-two survivors all told; eighteen gunners and seamen had lost their lives.

Lieutenant-Commander Bielfeld ordered *U-703* to surface and moved across to the two lifeboats. Throughout the operation, he did not utter a word, but a tall blond officer climbed down on to the U-boat's deck, accompanied by a seaman in polished leggings toting a machine-gun, and began shouting to them. Captain Wharton had already ordered his officers to take off their uniforms, and not to betray his identity; the REME captain provided to advise the Russians on the new Churchill tanks, John Rimington, was reluctant to doff his magnificent pure-white duffel-coat and kept it on, while the lifeboats moved around, picking the survivors out of the sea. The blond German shouted, 'Don't they teach Merchant Navy seamen to row in Britain?'—a sarcastic reference to the difficulty the seamen were having using the unfamiliar oars to approach the submarine. When they were closer, he asked, 'Why are you fighting this war? You aren't Communists are you? So why do you risk your lives to take tanks to the Bolsheviks? Who is your captain?' Nobody stirred or answered.

The German's eyes fell on the rather distinguished-looking Chief Steward, but he hastily said that he was not the captain; finally, the officer saw Captain Rimington, and told him to step on to the submarine's deck; the Army captain's protests went un-heeded, and he was taken down below.[6] The U-boat commander then returned to the lifeboats an engineer his men had fished out of the sea. At the same time, the lifeboats were handed tins of biscuits and apple-juice, and a piece of sausage. 'How far is the nearest land?' asked Captain Wharton. 'About 250 miles,' answered the blond officer. A klaxon sounded within the submarine, and she submerged taking the captured Briton with them.*

Some time later, Admiral Schmundt received *U-703*'s victory signal in Narvik: 'Ten thousand ton *Empire Byron* sunk, pinpoint AC.2629. Cargo: tanks. Destination: Archangel. Captain John Rimington taken aboard as prisoner.... Convoy in rout. Heading 120 degrees. I am following hard.'[7] The fact that the convoy had been destined for Archangel was of no small importance to Schmundt, of course.

At about the same time as Schmundt was reading Bielfeld's signal, Rear-Admiral Hamilton, four hundred miles to the west of the *Empire Byron*'s drifting lifeboats, advised the captain of *Wichita*:

I understand one ship has been torpedoed. But on the whole the convoy has been scattered successfully.[8]

We have met *Carlton* before: an eccentric American freighter, she had shot down the British CAM ship's Hurricane during a German attack on convoy PQ.16, and she had been bombed and forced to turn back; she had narrowly missed being sunk by the airborne torpedo that had claimed *Christopher Newport* on 4 July. Now, laden with 200 tons of TNT, tanks and tank ammunition, she was plunging alone through the gently undulating sea towards Archangel. We have met too Mr James Akins, the voluble seaman who has described for us all these events that befell *Carlton*.

Of her 44-man crew (including eleven naval gunners) there was none who suspected that the enemy was at this moment so close to them: for three hours, Lieutenant-Commander Heino Bohmann's

---

* *Empire Byron*'s carpenter, Mr Frank Cooper, related in *The Times* (29 September 1942) how the engineer 'was shown over the sub-marine's engine-room by the commander and given wine, bread wrapped in silver paper and a sausage'. The U-boat commander had said he was sorry to sink the ship, but it was his duty.

U-88 had been closing in on her, gradually overhauling the speeding freighter; now, soon after 9 a.m., with visibility down to only eight hundred yards, Bohmann began the final attack manœuvre. His submarine barely moving forward, he took her up to periscope depth and prepared tubes I and III for firing. The first tube he aligned on the ship's foremast, and the second on a point some fifty feet forward of the aftermast.⁹ At 10.15 a.m., *Carlton* ran slowly across the crosswires of Bohmann's eyepiece, just six hundred yards away, and Bohmann fired both torpedoes. Thirty-three seconds passed.

On this morning, the last in *Carlton*'s four-month voyage from Philadelphia, Akins had been awakened at 9.45 a.m. to go on watch, and had just managed to consume some toast and coffee in the fifteen minutes before he went on duty.¹⁰ As he took over the wheel, he had seen a fogbank lying ahead, 'which I was hoping we could run into before a plane found us'. It was warm in the wheelhouse, so he took off his coats and boots. A quarter of a mile away, and seven fathoms deep, the U-boat's crew was listening to the dwindling murmur of the two torpedoes' screws propelling their warheads at a depth of ten feet towards their target. One struck home, for there was a distinct clang, but then the screw noises could be heard again, so there had been a detonator pistol failure.

Suddenly there was a violent explosion, and Bohmann saw 'a black mushroom cloud spurt up, completely obscuring the target.' Everything seemed to be falling around Akins. The second torpedo had struck home. He could not at first take in what had happened, as he had only had aircraft on his mind—never thinking of U-boats. He seized his coat and boots and rounded up all the navigation instruments he could for the lifeboats. Two of the three surviving lifeboats had been smashed by the torpedo, including Akins's. The ship's entire company would have to abandon ship in one lifeboat and the four life-rafts secured to the stays of the fore- and after-masts. The Second Officer and three others took the forward starboard raft, while James Akins and five others climbed on to the port raft. Commander Bohmann brought *U-88* round stern on to the crippled *Carlton*, and at 10.22 a.m. fired his stern tube at her. But the ship shuddered and began to move to port even as the torpedo left the tube, and it missed.

The raft with Akins aboard held on to the ship for some time, waiting for the Norwegian master, Captain Hansen; but he did not want to leave *Carlton,* not so much out of affection for his old ship as because *U-88*'s last torpedo was on the surface, running in erratic circles round her, missing the rafts and lifeboats by increasingly small margins. One of the less seasoned American seamen prepared to bludgeon the torpedo with an oar as it next passed, but the others successfully restrained him. Finally it ran down and sank. Hansen boarded the raft with Akins, then transferred to the lifeboat. At 10.50 a.m., as Bohmann was preparing to fire again, the seemingly indestructible *Carlton* rolled quietly over and sank by the bows.

The U-boat commander brought *U-88* up on to the surface. 'We all stood by, waiting to be machine-gunned,' wrote Akins. 'We had all been pumped so full of propaganda that they all did this. But it seems he took the name of the ship and left—he had a busy day ahead.' While on the surface, Bohmann wirelessed to Schmundt that he had sunk a 10,000 tonner, but he did not trouble even to ascertain her name.[11]

The *Carlton*'s crew assembled all the rafts round the boat and lashed them together; they picked up everything they could salvage from the water. A roll-call of the crew was held; all were accounted for but Fireman W. Pelt, Oiler Frey, and Fireman Stillwell, who had been on watch down in the engine-room. Some of the survivors were badly burned; they were moved to one of the rafts, where they could lie down. For about an hour the men rowed desultorily in what they took to be the direction of Russia. 'Everyone was now happy', reminisced Akins, 'as we figured our troubles were over. The Captain wanted to take the lifeboat with the nineteen men and head for help as they could manage much better alone. All hands voted *that* down, and we decided to stay together.' Nobody minimized the precariousness of their position now: for the present, the sea was a mirror, with only a gentle swell; but they were four hundred miles from land, and if a storm sprang up the men clinging to the rafts could not expect to survive long. For the time being, the sea was empty on every quarter—the horizon uninterrupted save for the chilling glimpse of grey icebergs.

* 2 *

By now, Naval Group North (General-Admiral Carls) had also been informed that a German submarine had sighted the cruiser force running off 'westwards at high speed'; there was still no news of the whereabouts of any 'aircraft-carrier force', and there still seemed to be some warships, although probably only light cruisers, with PQ.17's ships, which were reported to be widely scattered.[12]

As soon as these reports reached Kiel, Carls, determined to exploit this favourable situation immediately. His battle fleet would attack after all. During the early hours, Naval Group North formally proposed that provided the 'battleship' (wrongly) reported as being in the convoy's vicinity could be disposed of by noon, and provided there was no aircraft-carrier there, the *Tirptiz* group should ignore any aircraft-carrier threat altogether. The reasoning was sound: it did not seem likely that a carrier would advance into the zone of German air superiority; and any carrier would thus have to stand off so far that if *Tirpitz* were to delay its attack on the convoy until it was south of latitude 72°, the carrier-planes would have to operate at the limit of their endurance. The group again warned that for tactical reasons, the deadline for launching *The Knight's Move* was one o'clock that afternoon.[13] They asked for authority to issue the codeword for the attack at once, should the 'battleship' be successfully disposed of.

Grand-Admiral Raeder, mindful of the Führer's insistence that the aircraft-carrier be located and neutralized first, refused to condone this; and shortly after 9 a.m. Naval Group North was informed of this. But now the position was changed even more radically by another chance sighting by German aerial reconnaissance: at 6.55 a.m., the British battle fleet was found while in a clear patch between two banks of fog, retreating to the south west.* Here was the aircraft-carrier the Germans had been seeking

---

* At 10 p.m. on 4 July, Tovey had reversed the course of the Anglo-American battle fleet to the north-east to cover the withdrawing cruiser force against any German surface attack; but by 4 a.m. next morning he had estimated that Hamilton was clear of the 'danger area' and in fact some 160 miles south of him, and he had resumed the battle fleet's south-westerly course.[14]

—some 220 miles west-north-west of Bear Island, over four hundred miles from the German battle fleet's lair at Altenfiord, and eight hundred miles from the probable location of the fleet attack the Germans now planned.

The German Naval Staff correctly concluded from this sighting that the Admiralty had no intention whatsoever of exposing the heavy Allied warships and aircraft-carrier to attack by German torpedo- and bomber-squadrons based in Norway, and was therefore keeping them at a respectful distance from North Cape. Besides the Germans knew that the Allied fleet had been at sea since 1 July at least—it had been seen cruising off Iceland on that date—so it seemed likely that it would be forced either to break off operations altogether for lack of fuel,* or to take up a waiting position in the Arctic for completing from fleet oilers. The Naval Staff concluded that 'one need scarcely expect any real danger from the enemy's carrier group.'[15] Soon after 10 a.m., at about the time that *Carlton* was being torpedoed, Lofoten Air Command confirmed that there was no sight of any enemy forces in the area between 14°E and 26°E right up to the ice-barrier; this added still further to the growing confidence in Berlin.

Naval Group North had already placed the battle fleet at one hour's sailing notice from 9 a.m. At 10.52 a.m. the fleet was ordered to prepare to sail at a moment's notice, and Altenfiord was filled with noise as the German fleet weighed anchor and prepared to get under way. The sight of both Hamilton's and Tovey's forces withdrawing westwards had removed the last obstacles to the execution of *The Knight's Move*. From Kiel, General-Admiral Carls telephoned first the Naval Staff Operations Division and then Raeder himself to repeat his proposal for the battle fleet to attack regardless of any aircraft-carrier threat. This time, Raeder could only agree with Carls. His representative at the Führer's headquarters was directed to inform Hitler of the changed situation, and to ask for his approval for the operation.

At about 11.30 a.m., Vice-Admiral Krancke telephoned back that he had 'successfully accomplished' this mission. The Operations Division in Berlin forwarded this good news to Group North in Kiel ten minutes later, with the additional warning that the

---

* See page 195. Tovey was certainly low in fuel.

conditions on the attack's execution would still stand if there were to be no further favourable reports on the movements of the enemy's aircraft-carrier, or if the German battle fleet's movements were to be compromised by their premature detection by enemy air reconnaissance. One minute later, just over an hour before the deadline, General-Admiral Carls had already issued the agreed codeword* for the attack to begin.[16]

The prospects for an overwhelming victory now looked extra-ordinarily favourable to the Germans. In fact, with considerable strength of character, the Commander-in-Chief afloat—Admiral Schniewind—had once again not waited for the codeword to arrive: to gain extra time he had already left Altenfiord shortly after 11 a.m. and was proceeding through the Leads when the codeword authorizing him to weigh anchor arrived. And, despite the Group's orders signalled to him, stipulating that the 'Fleet is to leave [Leads] at Nordkyn'—i.e. as far to the east as possible—Schniewind adhered to his own plan to leave by the exit passage west of Rölvsöy, as he thought the risk of submarines was lesser there.[17]

Carls took over command of the U-boat operations for the duration of the fleet operation, and signalled Schmundt:

> Attack of our own heavy units on convoy planned for tomorrow noon. Time of this will be notified under codeword *Concord*. Sightings of enemy battleships, aircraft-carriers, aircraft, to be reported at once.[1]

At a quarter-to-one that afternoon, Kiel wirelessed a final appreciation of the enemy's movements to Admiral Schniewind, aboard his battleship: the Allied cruiser force was running 'westwards at high speed'; the carrier force was cruising at more moderate pace in the same direction, at least four hundred miles north-west of Altenfiord; no other heavy warships had been sighted right up to the ice-barrier for hundreds of miles on either side; the convoy, protected only by light escort forces, had disintegrated into two loose groups, with clusters of crippled freighters falling far behind. The German fleet's presence at Altenfiord had apparently

---

* The 'codeword' was in fact a complete sentence: 'Secret. The practice ammunition provided as per Naval Group North secret signal No. 3756 is withdrawn.'

not been suspected by the enemy. There were no German submarines lying across the battle fleet's own track; it would be plain
sailing for the Germans until midday of Monday 6 July, when the
raid on the merchant ships was timed to begin.

Even so, these were Germany's most powerful and significant
warships that were being staked, and none realized this more than
Grand-Admiral Raeder: over the telephone that morning, he
reiterated his anxieties to Carls, even now that the decision had at
last been made. In the spirit of Raeder's misgivings, Carls signalled
Schniewind as *Tirpitz* was already moving out of the Leads, an
unusual appeal for hesitancy and circumspection which must have
made the gallant Fleet Commander despair:

> A brief operation with partial successes is more important than a
> total victory involving major expenditure of time. Report at once
> if over-flown by any enemy aircraft. Do not hesitate to break off
> operation if situation doubtful. On no account grant enemy success
> against fleet nucleus.[12]

But there was nobody in the German Navy who did not now
believe that the most favourable light was already shining on the
German battle fleet. At three o'clock that afternoon, *Tirpitz,*
Hipper, Scheer, seven destroyers and two torpedo-boats finally
glided out of the Leads and into the open sea.

In the meantime, the German Fifth Air Force exercised its
reconnaissance and attack functions to the full. Preparations had
been made for the third squadron of *KG.30* Junkers 88s at
Bardufoss to join *KG.26* at Banak air-base as soon as the weather
permitted, so that they could carry out combined bombing operations against the convoy; but it now appeared that the convoy was
too widely scattered, and its fast vessels were heading for bad
weather areas with utmost speed.[18] That afternoon, the mass air
attacks began for the first time, as the Norwegian airfields were
now clear of fog. At 2.30 p.m. Schmundt's office in Narvik was
informed that frequent air-torpedo and bombing attacks were
taking place. Both North-East Air Command and Lofoten Air
Command lent weight to the attack, and during the afternoon all
three squadrons of *KG.30* and several torpedo-bomber aircraft
swept the Barents Sea, searching for the convoy's straggling
merchantmen.

All the more regrettable were the consequences of the Admiralty order scattering the convoy. Lieutenant Gradwell, whose small Asdic trawler had voluntarily collected three merchant ships and shepherded them into the ice-fields was the only officer who interpreted his orders in this way. As the ether filled with hapless victims' distress signals, the other freighters sought protection where they could. The corvettes were with the anti-aircraft ships *Palomares* and *Pozarica* which were making their own courses to the east.

The trawlers, as always, were the object of opprobium of all the other escorts: they were noisy, conspicuous and slow. Gradwell's First Lieutenant, Dick Elsden, had even composed a bawdy seven-verse lyric on the 'Trawler Boys', two of whose most apposite verses ran:

> Why, we're nothing but a tyro,
>   Haven't even got a gyro,
> And as for making smoke, well, bugger me!
> We just belch it up to Heaven
>   As we do our hot eleven,
> Keeping station on a PQ or QP.

> We are given types of gun
>   Little use against the Hun,
> And rounds of ammunition—bloody few,
>   Then sent out with destroyers
> Whose job is to annoy us,
>   As we help escort a QP or PQ.

The anti-aircraft ships soon found that the Asdic trawlers *Lord Middleton* and *Lord Austin*—besides making a lot of black smoke—were too slow for their liking. They signalled to ask their best speed, and the trawlers replied, 'Eleven knots'. Nothing more was said, but soon the trawlers were left behind.

Pozarica—with Mr Godfrey Winn aboard as a war correspondent for Beaverbrook Newspapers—had collected the corvettes *La Malouine* and *Lotus* and was running eastwards along the ice

edge with the rescue ship *Rathlin* trying to keep up and the
corvette *Poppy* not far away.[19] Early on the morning of the 5th,
the American freighter *Bellingham*, which had been on a converging course, had sighted this little cluster of ships and for all her
twenty-five years gradually overhauled them. After three hours
the anti-aircraft ship *Pozarica* ordered her to alter course forty-five
degrees to starboard because, according to Captain Lawford, the
course she was then making would have taken her into the ice.
The order was taken amiss by the *Bellingham* who flashed a curt
'Go to Hell' back to the Royal Navy; whereupon the anti-aircraft
ship signalled back 'Cheerio and Good Luck'[20] and moved away
from her. This resulted in some bitter comments by *Bellingham*'s
second officer.*

Other merchant ships had similar encounters with their
erstwhile escorts: we have seen how the anti-aircraft ship *Palomares*
had collected the anti-submarine minesweepers *Britomart* and
Halcyon and sped eastwards in solitary splendour. During the early
hours, to Captain Jauncey's embarrassment, the freighters *Fairfield City* and *Daniel Morgan* had caught up with him, showing a
surprising turn of speed; shortly after 6 a.m. *Benjamin Harrison*
had arrived, and three hours later *John Witherspoon* was there as
well—four American merchant ships clinging to the Royal Navy
escort vessels in mute appeal for protection. This cluster of ships was
shadowed all night long by German Blohm & Voss patrol planes,
obviously homing in submarines on to them. What happened then
is related in the official reports filed by the American Armed
Guard officers aboard the merchantmen: at 1 p.m., according to
John Witherspoon's officer, 'the escort altered course and advised all
the accompanying ships by blinker not to follow but to remain
on their own course'.[21] The *Daniel Morgan*'s officer reported to
his authorities, 'the naval escort left, ordering us to maintain
our course.'[22] And the *Benjamin Harrison*'s officer described
bitterly, 'The AA ship changed course and ordered us to keep
on our present course'.[23] Having shaken off the merchant vessels,

* *Bellingham*'s Armed Guard officer reported on arrival in Archangel: 'We were within three miles of an AA ship and three
corvettes doing thirteen knots; they moved away without waiting
for us.'

Palomares and the others moved off eastwards at superior speed.*

The four American ships ran for the shelter of a fogbank not far to the south-east of them. By 2 p.m. they were again being shadowed by a German Blohm & Voss, so just before the four ships plunged into the fog, *Daniel Morgan* swung round and fired her 3-inch anti-aircraft gun at the shadower in a steady barrage to prevent it from determining exactly the courses of the other three ships as they entered the fog.

As the *Morgan* stood alone outside the fogbank, the German submarine which had been shadowing her all afternoon moved into position for the final kill. This was *U-88*, the submarine which had sunk *Carlton* that morning; her torpedo tubes reloaded, she had submerged some miles away, and was now approaching *Daniel Morgan* under the surface.²⁴ Just as Lieutenant-Commander Bohmann was about to launch his torpedoes the American ship got under way again: the others had been safely swallowed up by the fog, so the *Morgan* now stood off alone on a course heading for Admiralty Peninsula, a point on the Novaya Zemlya coast. Commander Bohmann was obliged to wait, and then surface and resume the chase again.

At about three o'clock in the afternoon, while steering due east, *Daniel Morgan* ran out of the other side of the fogbank, and sighted *Fairfield City* steaming a parallel course to starboard. The *Morgan* was still unaware of any trailing submarine, but Commander Bohmann had found the ship again. As he began to overhaul the ship, three of *KG.30*'s Junkers 88s appeared overhead, manoeuvring into position to attack *Fairfield City*.²⁵ Once again the *Morgan* gallantly opened fire to divert the attackers' attention, but was unsuccessful: the first stick of bombs detonated close to *Fairfield City*'s starboard side, and a second bomber passed over, out of range of the *City*'s guns, and released a second stick, scoring a direct hit on her afterdeck. The third bomber placed its bombs

---

* According to his obituary in *The Times* (14 October 1958) it was for his work as Senior Officer of the Escort that Jauncey was awarded his DSO after PQ.17: 'With dogged tenacity he managed to collect and shepherd the few forlorn survivors, and by hiding these in the Matochkin Strait in Novaya Zemlya ultimately brought them to safety in Archangel.' There is no mention of the incident described in the text in *Britomart*'s report.

right on the flying bridge, killing everybody except the helmsman who was badly injured, and two men in the galley. Three lifeboats got away from the freighter, one of them badly damaged, and the burning ship sank soon after, taking its cargo of tanks to the bottom. The lifeboats set out on the long row to Novaya Zemlya, as *Daniel Morgan* disappeared over the horizon.

Three more Junkers 88s arrived, and together with the original three made a series of bombing runs over the *Morgan*, lasting over an hour; her captain kept the ship swinging to present a difficult target, and no bombs hit her. Her guns were fired at maximum rate. The crew began to show unmistakable signs of strain, having now been at their action stations for over twenty-eight hours without respite. After a brief interval, which gave them time to reload the guns' ready-use boxes, another group of five Junkers 88s arrived, rose into the sun and then attacked the ship in rapid succession. The gunners hit one, and it howled away over the horizon with flames streaming from one engine nacelle; its bombs fell fifty yards short on the starboard side. The second and third aircraft were also unsuccessful in their attacks. But the fourth dropped its bombs so close on the starboard quarter that the ship's plates were ruptured between No. 4 and No. 5 holds. She took an immediate list to starboard and began to settle aft. There was no response to the helm. The bombers broke off the attack, and vanished over the horizon. Through his periscope, *U-88*'s Commander Bohmann could see the merchantman steering an ungainly course and guessed that her steering gear had been put out of action.

Laden with 8,200 tons of steel, food, explosives, tanks and cars, *Daniel Morgan* had put up a braver fight than most, but now she was virtually defenceless. One seaman had been killed by blast, and a shell had jammed in the overheated breech of the ship's one 3-inch gun: most of the ·50-calibre ammunition was gone as well. Lieutenant Morton Wolfson, the Armed Guard officer, told the Captain of the position; satisfied that the wireless operator had got an 'air attack' distress signal away, giving the *Morgan*'s exact position, Captain Sullivan ordered his crew to stand by their lifeboat stations. Morton and two gunners continued their efforts to dislodge the shell from the gun's breech, but the shell parted from the case, and besides, some of the seamen had had enough anyway.

Without any orders to that effect, they lowered the lifeboats and cast off, leaving half the seamen and most of the gunners still aboard; one of the boats overturned in the panic, throwing its occupants into the sea. The Captain manœuvred the ship round on her engines, and brought her alongside the drifting lifeboats. They were hauled aboard and properly baled out: two men, including the Chief Officer, were drowned in the accident. As soon as the three lifeboats had been baled out, the entire crew abandoned ship.

Somebody must have sighted the second enemy for a radio signal was transmitted giving the 'submarine distress' prefix and *Daniel Morgan*'s position.[26] Commander Bohmann could hear knocking sounds on his U-boat's hydrophone gear, so he believed that there was still a skeleton crew aboard repairing the damaged steering gear. He fired a torpedo from tube I into the ship's port side, and saw a spurt of grey smoke from her hull; some minutes later, he fired tube IV into her engine-room, and he clearly observed the white columns of steam as the boilers burst. The ship sank slowly, and then began to crumple up to the accompaniment of much crashing and crunching; then she suddenly rolled over, and sank, leaving only the three lifeboats behind.[27] Bohmann entered in his log, 'Sunk her during repairs with two torpedoes.'

The American seamen saw a large German submarine rise from the depths and move towards them. As German sailors took photographs of the men in the lifeboats, an officer speaking English with the merest trace of an accent asked the American captain, 'What was the name of your ship? What was her tonnage? What was your cargo?' Lying valiantly, Captain Sullivan answered that they had been carrying a general cargo of food and leather. The Germans retorted that they did not believe him, but that was all. The Americans asked in turn the course to the nearest land. They were told to steer a southerly course. The U-boat followed them for some time, then set off on the surface in a renewed search for merchantmen.[28]

At about the same time as *Daniel Morgan* was being attacked and stopped by Junkers 88 aircraft, not far away an unseen enemy was also overtaking the American freighter *Honomu*, laden with

7,500 tons of steel, tanks, ammunition and foodstuffs: Lieutenant-Commander Hilmar Siemon's *U-334* was closing in, with tubes I, II and IV ready to fire. The ship was an ideal U-boat target; maintaining complete radio silence, and with ten men on watch, she was travelling at a steady 10½ knots and making no attempt at zigzagging.[29] By three o'clock on the afternoon of 5 July, *U-334* was lying in wait ahead of the intended victim, waiting for her to cross the field of fire; at 3.28 p.m., as *Honomu* waddled unsuspectingly across Siemon's sights barely 1,300 yards away, the U-boat commander fired the three torpedoes in a spread. Siemon's wireless operator followed the torpedo noises on the hydrophone gear for just over six minutes, so all had missed. They brought *U-334* sharply round to starboard, still submerged, and fired their stern tube at *Honomu* at 3.36 p.m.[30] Even as they did so, they saw a brown plume of smoke from the ship's No. 3 hold, and the ship's bows settled perceptibly deeper in the water. As the noise subsided, the hydrophone gear picked up what was unmistakably the sound of their stern-tube's torpedo, still running away into the distance, so somebody else had torpedoed *Honomu*. A few minutes later there was a second explosion, enveloping the whole ship in a cloud of smoke, and the vessel began to sink faster.

The second torpedo had hit *Honomu*'s No. 4 hold, and the ship began to break up. Thirty-seven of her crew managed to escape in the lifeboats, including Captain Frederick A. Strand; but nineteen men went down with the ship.[31] No sooner had the luckless *Honomu*, her fire-room demolished and her engines stopped, begun her last hundred-fathom plunge to the bottom, than three slate-grey German submarines surfaced. Two of them—*U-334* and *U-456*—were very close to the drifting patch of oil and wreckage left by their victim; and a third submarine, probably *U-88*, surfaced a quarter of a mile away. It was Lieutenant-Commander Max-Martin Teichert's *U-456* which had fired the striking torpedoes.[32] Teichert took his submarine alongside the lifeboats, and ordered the Master, Captain Strand, to come aboard; he was taken prisoner. The seamen were asked whether they had sufficient water, and they were handed tinned meat and bread by the submarine officers. They were told they would be picked up by destroyers a few days later. After interrogating Strand briefly about *Honomu*, Teichert reported to Admiral Schmundt: '3.30

p.m. at pinpoint AC.2937. Freighter *Honomu*, 6,977 tons. Tank parts. Fast escort vessels lost in fog.'[33] The submarines then headed off to the east, and were still visible sitting on the surface an hour and a half after the attack. Commander Siemon broadcast over *U-334*'s public address system to his crew that they would not be submerging any more. They would attack the next from the surface.

Honomu's radio operator had managed to send out three 'submarine distress' signals before his ship went down, and he had added the ship's position to the last.[26] Far to the north, the signals were brought to the bridge of the anti-aircraft ship *Pozarica*, following the ice-edge to the east.[34] Captain Lawford was awakened. He studied the signals, and decided it was impossible for them to go south to pick up the survivors: were the three hundred men of his command to be jeopardized for thirty or forty shipwrecked seamen whom they might never find because of fog?

By now the distress signals were falling 'thick and quick'. The corvette *Lotus* proposed that their little group of vessels should form a fighting unit again, and sail south to combat the enemy submarines and aircraft massacring the remaining merchant ships. Captain Lawford rejected the idea: 'I have been giving full consideration to this matter for half an hour and have come to the conclusion that the order to scatter was to avoid vessels falling into traps, and unless you feel strongly to the contrary in the matter I think we ought to stick to our original arrangements.'

The position of the solitary merchant ships was anything but enviable, and many of their Masters were torn between their responsibility for their crews and their duty to their Nation. Before each ship had sailed from America, its Master had been handed a letter from the Secretary of the Navy formally directing him that there was to be no surrender:

1. It is the policy of the United States Government that no U.S. ship be permitted to fall into the hands of the enemy.
2. The ship shall be defended by her armament, by maneuver, and by every available means as long as possible. When, in the judgment of the Master, capture is inevitable, he shall scuttle the ship. Provision should be made to open sea valves, and to flood holds and compartments adjacent to machinery spaces, start

[156]

numerous fires and employ any additional measures to insure
certain scuttling of the vessel.

3. In case the Master is relieved of command of his ship, he shall
transfer this letter to his successor and obtain a receipt for it.[35]

The cat-and-mouse game now being played by the German
U-boats was more than many freighters' Masters could endure,
however, and the seamen often needed little encouragement to
take to their lifeboats even before their vessels were attacked. The
report of the Armed Guard officer aboard the American Liberty
ship *Samuel Chase* tells in its own deadpan way of the strain felt by
these seamen, abandoned to their fate in PQ.17:

> On 5 July at 7 a.m. a black dot was seen dead astern which by
> 8.45 a.m. was identified as a German submarine. She was steaming
> on the surface and crossed to our starboard quarter and began to
> overhaul us on the starboard side. Then she disappeared from sight
> at 10 a.m. A ship—which we presumed to be the *Daniel Morgan*—
> was hull down on the horizon behind the submarine. She was
> seen to turn and head North.
> At 10.30 a.m., dead reckoning position 75°44′ North, 37°00′
> East, the Captain ordered engines Full Astern, and told all hands
> to get into the life-boats. All boats were away from the ship by
> 10.45 a.m. and they gathered and laid 600 yards from her. . . .

Surprisingly, the German submarine made no attempt to attack
this tempting target of a brand-new 7,000-ton Liberty ship drifting
helpless and abandoned in the Arctic. After two hours' waiting
in the lifeboats, the *Samuel Chase*'s Master gathered that there
would be no takers, and that he would have to finish the voyage in
his freighter after all. He and his Chief Officer took an engineer
party aboard to raise steam, and at 2 p.m. the lifeboats were taken
aboard again. The *Samuel Chase* was one of the few ships to survive
the disaster.

On another part of the Barents Sea a German reconnaissance
plane was circling an American merchant ship, most probably
fixing its position with exactitude. The *Alcoa Ranger*'s Master,
Lieutenant-Commander Hjalmar Christophsen, USNR, was one
of the many hastily commissioned merchant mariners whose
nerves had not yet been tempered by the rigours of war: although
the Focke-Wulf showed no signs of attacking, Christophsen 'gave

the order to display international flags meaning Unconditional Surrender'. He ordered the Stars and Stripes to be hauled down, and gave his crew the order to take to the lifeboats.[36] He had lost interest in shifting his cargo—7,000 tons of steel armourplate, flour, and a deck cargo of nineteen tanks—any farther on its long voyage from Philadelphia. It must be said that with only four light machine-guns the *Alcoa Ranger* was the worst defended ship in PQ.17 and would have been in no kind of position to ward off an air attack. In any event, the German plane made off in great embarrassment. The ship's Second Officer took command and asked for volunteers to sail her on, while the Master was confined below. At this, the Master apparently changed his mind, for he ordered the American ensign to be hoisted again and the guns manned, and later he resumed command.

Towards three o'clock a British merchant ship confronted with a similar kind of situation reacted very differently: about three miles away from *Earlston*, her First Officer, Mr Hawtry Benson, sighted what he took to be a 'growler'—a small grey iceberg almost completely submerged.[37] What was remarkable was that the 'iceberg' seemed to be steadily and almost imperceptibly over-hauling them. The U-boat's conning tower had been painted white on top, and as it drew nearer *Earlston*'s Master, Captain Hilmar Stenwick, could confirm Benson's suspicions. Visibility was very good, without a trace of fog in which they might hide their naked merchantmen. He gave his helmsman a new course to steer, and a signal was transmitted, 'SS *Earlston* in action with U-boat', giving their position.

'In action' because the naval gun crew manning the low-angle 4-inch gun on *Earlston*'s poopdeck had already opened fire on the submarine. The submarine was by now some 8,000 yards away, but closing on them at superior speed now that its commander recognized that he had been sighted. On the surface, the U-boat had greater speed than the merchant ship. Captain Stenwick ordered more speed, nevertheless, and all the off-duty firemen were ordered down into the stokehold to double-bank the firemen already on watch.[38] The ship began to vibrate strongly under the straining engines as they gradually picked up speed. A new signal was transmitted: 'SOS, SOS, SOS. SS *Earlston* taking action against submarine, steering 207°, submarine following. 3.09 p.m.'[39]

Their gun had fired several rounds at the U-boat, and the rounds were bursting successively closer to the conning-tower; the submarine began to submerge, and then vanished completely, still out of torpedo range. As long as it remained submerged, it had no hope of overhauling the speeding vessel. Of all the merchantmen in the convoy, this British vessel was the only one to keep its nerve in the face of a submarine attack and use the gun for the purpose for which it had been provided.

A score or more lifeboats and rafts were now riding in the gentle swell in the wake of the 'Ice Devil' submarines. At 5 p.m. seven Heinkel torpedo-bombers from *I./906* Coastal Command Squadron based at Billefiord seaplane base just south of North Cape passed low over the lifeboats, and the seamen heard sounds of explosions over the horizon soon after. The German seaplanes returned, their torpedo-racks empty. Their close interest in them alarmed the *Carlton*'s survivors, still clinging to their lifeboat and life-rafts after the loss of their ship that morning. The planes passed over them at a height of fifty feet, whipping up a curtain of spray as they did so. In James Akins's graphic vernacular, all thought it was 'curtains'. While six of the planes vanished over the horizon, the seventh banked and returned. Akins and another seaman stripped down to their underwear, ready to dive under their raft if the plane opened fire. It flew even lower over them— apparently to see if they were armed—then banked again and touched down on the sea, until it was taxying slowly round the cluster of rafts and the lifeboat only a few yards away.

With his engines still running, the pilot held up three fingers: three of the Americans were to swim across to the plane. The seamen, Stankiewicz, 'Big' McDonough and Higgens jumped off one raft into the freezing water and struck out towards the floatplane. They missed the taxying plane the first time, but the second time Higgens and Stankiewicz, climbed aboard; McDonough—a fat giant of a man weighing twenty-two stone or more—seemed to be in trouble with his trousers, which had fallen down and were preventing him from swimming. The plane circled again, with a German airman perched on one of its floats this time, wielding a boathook. He made several grabs at McDonough, who was by this time more under water than above; the American's comrades rocked with merciless laughter at his plight.[40] After several attempts, the Germans gave up and let him go. Promising to return, the plane skidded into the air. By the time the other seamen had salvaged McDonough from the waves, he was almost dead with the cold. They stripped him down and wrapped him in a blanket.

Sure enough, a large Dornier 24 hospital plane landed near them two hours later, having searched in vain for a 'ditched' Heinkel reported by a German reconnaissance plane. The Germans asked for any US Navy survivors among them; nine of *Carlton*'s Armed Guard personnel and one seaman were transferred to the plane. Three hours later, another plane landed and took on ten more men. The unfortunate ones left behind rowed some more to keep warm, while being careful not to move too far from their earlier position, 'in order,' as one put it, 'not to miss the next plane to Norway'.[41] After some time another German plane landed, and took the Chief Engineer Mooney, and Chico the messboy. That left seventeen. The seamen asked the pilot whether any more planes were coming out, but he regretted that there were not: his was the last. The remaining seamen transferred to the lifeboat, hauled the rafts alongside and transferred everything into it. Then they rigged up a small sail and set off for the Soviet Union, leaving their rafts behind.

Unhappy *Carlton* crew: everywhere misfortune took them, misfortune befell them. The German planes took their prisoners to Kirkenes, the naval base just east of North Cape from which the 'Ice Devil' submarines had sallied forth.[42] The seamen were placed into a prison camp along with hundreds of Russian prisoners and told they would be shot if they attempted to communicate with the Russians. Chief Engineer Mooney was closely interrogated by the Germans, who denied any responsibility for sinking his ship; one of the naval officers challenged him to explain why the alleged German U-boat had not taken Captain Hansen and him as Chief Engineer prisoner, for those were the orders of the German Navy. By clever innuendo he managed to persuade Mooney and several of the others that it was in fact a British submarine that had done the dirty work, seeing that the *Carlton*'s scatter course was apparently taking it towards Norway. Mooney afterwards admitted, 'It was a well-known fact that our captain, Reginald

Hansen, a Norwegian by birth, was a pro-German; and possibly he *was* heading for the Norwegian coast. . . . '

The *Carlton*'s survivors gave lengthy interviews to the German press, and their smiling—evidently relieved—photographs appeared in a big feature on the convoy disaster published by the German soldiers' fortnightly magazine *Signal*.[43] Nor was that all, for the germ of a propaganda idea had already been sown in the enemy's mind—an idea that was to cause the *Carlton*'s crew immense difficulties later on. It is clear from German naval records that the *Carlton*'s seamen warned the German High Command in good time that the whole convoy had been re-routed to Archangel because of 'non-serviceability of unloading facilities at Murmansk'.* The German newspapers were also able to publish a detailed list of the ship's entire cargo: '800 tons of flour; 400 tons of pork; 500 tons of tin; 500 tons of steel plate; 200 tons of shells; 50 tons of bullets; thousands of machine-guns and pistols and no fewer than 37 tanks including six 28-ton tanks of the General Grant type, fourteen 13-ton Canadian tanks and seventeen 20-tonners.'[44] Three days after the sinking, the German radio announced that 'survivors from some of these ships have given the most valuable information about the nature of their cargoes. It is now possible to form a picture of exactly what the Soviet

---

* Fifth Air Force War Diary. Cf. German Naval Staff War Diary, 6 July: 'Statements by the Captain taken prisoner from the steamship *Carlton*, sunk by U-boat on 5 July, confirm PQ.17's strength as 36 to 38 ships. It left Reykjavik on 28 June. . . . After heavy air attacks on the evening of 4 July, the convoy was scattered. Convoy Commodore issued the order for ships to scatter and make independently for port of destination. Heavy cruisers had not been seen since 4 July. The Captain feared that the German units *Tirpitz*, *Gneisenau* and *Prinz Eugen* had put to sea, and the cruisers were operating against them. The Captain knew nothing of whether the heavy British units were at sea. Apart from the aircraft carried by the cruisers, the convoy had no air cover. Prisoners witnessed the sinking by air torpedo and bombing raids on two American, one British and one Russian ship on 4 and 5 July. *Carlton*'s cargo consisted of six 28-ton tanks, ten 13-ton tanks and fourteen 20-ton crates, as well as 200 tons of explosives for powder manufacture and 200 tons of ammunition, and was *inter alia* taken on in Philadelphia, from which she sailed on 13 March. Further details in Fifth Air Force's despatch in *The Knight's Move* files.'

Union needs and is short of.'⁴⁵ And a broadcast to Latin-America announced, 'Survivors of the *Carlton* have supplied valuable information regarding the organization and escort of the Anglo-American convoy'⁴⁶; this was repeated over Radio Luxemburg and numerous other German home service stations.

To cap all this, a German propaganda station, transmitting as 'Station Debunk' by short-wave to America—and camouflaged as an American anti-Roosevelt station—included the following item in its news bulletin:⁴⁷

> *Stockholm*—Our listening posts learn from Sweden that two of our ships loaded with the newest U.S. tanks and heavy trucks arrived at Trondheim several days ago. These 8,000-ton vessels were part of the big convoy recently sunk by German planes and U-boats on the way to Archangel. Since they were only slightly damaged, one wonders why the American crews abandoned them. They were brought in by small German submarine crews, with the Stars and Stripes waving beneath the swastika. Men and officers of a German tank battalion have arrived to take over the 62 American heavy tanks and 132 trucks now being unloaded from the two American ships. One German officer said the new U.S. tanks are an improvement on the old, but not as good as the Russian or German.*

In an extraordinarily brief time the word had spread throughout the sea-going world that an American merchant ship called *Carlton* had surrendered to the Germans and run into a Norwegian port.

After the survivors had in fact been interrogated, they were embarked under constant guard on the German troop transport *Hans Leonhardt*; a few days later this transport sailed into Oslo, after several days' passage in convoy with two other ships down the Leads. The amazed Americans could only goggle at the strength of the escort the Germans provided for these three vessels—'and of all things we had air support too'. At Oslo they were transferred to a second troop transport, *Wuri*, making its last-but-one voyage between that port and Aalborg in Denmark. There they entrained for the main naval prison camp at Wilhelmshaven.

---

* The reference to *two* ships is puzzling, as only *Carlton* is named in other bulletins. By the time this bulletin was broadcast, however, the results of the interrogation of *Honomu*'s Captain Frederick A. Strand would also be on hand; Strand was certainly referred to later by German radio (see footnote, p. 292).

At Marlag-Milag Nord, *Carlton*'s crew found themselves despised and ostracized by all the other seamen. The word had somehow reached the camp that they had brought *Carlton* into Norway intact and surrendered her to the Germans. The Americans fumed but kept silent. 'With 5,000 British prisoners in our camp', said Mooney, 'it would be murder to mention that a British submarine was the only vessel in sight when we were torpedoed.'*

✳ 3 ✳

Where was the German battle fleet at this time? At three o'clock on the afternoon of 5 July, the German fleet—*Tirpitz, Hipper, Scheer* and seven destroyers—had emerged from the Leads at Rölvsöy and put out into the open sea. In Berlin, its prospects were viewed exceedingly optimistically: the Allied cruiser covering force and battle fleet had both been sighted heading westwards, and the 'warships' accompanying the scattering convoy's freighters could scarcely be more than a few isolated cruisers and destroyers. The eleven units in the German fleet should still be able to account well for themselves, even though the convoy was now so scattered, if they made effective use of the sightings being obtained by the aircraft and submarines.

The fleet had been under way only five hours when the Russian submarine *K-21* (Commander Lunin) patrolling off North Cape sighted the heavy warships. An immediate warning was broadcast:

Emergency. All ships. Two battleships and eight destroyers in position 071°24′ North, 023°40′ East. (1700B/5).[48]

---

* The rumour that *Carlton* had surrendered continued to gain currency as shipwrecked crews came in from as far afield as Murmansk and New York. Morison, p. 186, confirms, 'The tank-laden *Carlton*, steaming alone, was sunk by U-boat on 5 July. Most of her crew were rescued by submarine [*sic*] and the skipper gave the Germans valuable information. Prisoners from this ship, released after VE-day [*sic*] and returned to the United States, were responsible for some wild stories about the convoy.' Morison cites an article in the *New York Times*, 23 February 1945, as an example, based on interviews after their return aboard the Swedish liner *Gripsholm*. Subsequently *Carlton*'s crew were closely questioned by the F.B.I.

Aware that they had been sighted, but unaware that they had been 'torpedoed', as the Russian submarine commander at once claimed, *Tirpitz* continued with her escorts on her march to the north-east. Just over an hour later, a British aircraft patrolling the North Cape area also sighted the German battle fleet. A further signal was broadcast:

> Emergency. All ships. Eleven unknown vessels in position 071°31′ North, 027°10′ East. Course 065°, ten knots (1816/B5).

Finally, just before half-past eight that evening, the whole formation was again sighted by the Allies—*still heading north-eastwards towards the scattering convoy*—this time by H.M. submarine *Unshaken* (Lieutenant Westmacott). At 9.49 p.m. the news of the first of these sightings was received by Admiral Tovey's fleet,[49] together with news that a Russian submarine claimed to have scored two torpedo hits on *Tirpitz*.* The German attempt to slink out undetected into the Barents Sea could hardly have met with less success had they broadcast their intentions *en claire* to the Allies in advance.

In Berlin there was consternation: their radio monitoring service had picked up both the first two enemy signals.[50] The first reaction was that this very early sighting might enable the enemy's battle fleet to move up from the west in time to cut off the German fleet's withdrawal after the raid on the convoy.

Naval Group North in Kiel still did not consider the risk sufficient to warrant breaking off the operation altogether, although Carls was annoyed that the fleet had left the Leads at Rölvsöy rather than Nordkyn—with precisely the consequences he had wanted to avoid.[51] Even though the German fleet's sortie and direction of approach had been prematurely divulged, Carls pointed out that the enemy's fleet was a long way away and would not be risked in Norwegian waters; he imparted this opinion to the Naval Staff by telephone and teleprinter. But at the same time the Group informed Berlin that the enemy had begun

---

* Cf. Caradus Diary (*La Malouine*). 'Signal received that the *Tirpitz* had been hit by two torpedoes from a Russian submarine. Loud cheers when the mess decks were informed by bosun's pipe. Further signal—three destroyers have detached themselves and making due East and later South-East.'

strongly jamming German wireless traffic at 7.45 p.m., soon after
the sightings had been made; as a result wireless contact with
northern Norway had been blotted out. This was very sinister: it
was the first time that the enemy had adopted this procedure, and
the jamming was so effective that even after the Germans had
switched to another circuit they could make themselves understood only with great difficulty. *Tirpitz*'s radioroom had picked
up the first signal, but claimed they had been unable to forward it
to Kiel because of the jamming on their frequency.[52] The German
Naval Staff considered that the sudden emergence of this jamming
was proof that the British Admiralty had been 'apprised' of the
sailing of the German battle fleet.

A telephone conference was at once held between Raeder's staff
in Berlin, and Naval Group North in Kiel. The latter was finally
persuaded that the enemy could bring up his heavy units and aircraft-carrier after all and cut off the Germans' line of retreat. This
conclusion sprang from the seemingly inevitable assumption that
the Allies would be prepared to risk anything to engage a target
as tempting as that presented by *Tirpitz*, *Hipper* and *Scheer*.

Naval Group North was presented with three alternative
courses of action: either to proceed with the operation and accept
the risks; or to proceed with an operation so brief as to prevent
the enemy from cutting off its retreat in time; or to call off the
operation altogether and leave the convoy's destruction to the
U-boats and aircraft.

As we now know, the first course of action would have been
devoid of danger for the Germans: the Home Fleet rejected an
Admiralty suggestion that it should engage *Tirpitz* at this time.
But General-Admiral Carls in Kiel recognized that if the Führer's
conditions were to be adhered to, the operation must be called off,
as a confrontation with carrier aircraft could not be avoided with
complete certainty. Even so, both Naval Group North in Kiel and
the Naval Staff's operations division thought that if the Führer's
condition were to be lifted, and Carls were to be given absolute
freedom of action, the risks involved in continuing the operation
were entirely commensurate with the rewards that offered themselves. A final decision was left to Grand-Admiral Raeder.

'Fully conscious' of his responsibility to the Führer when it was
a matter of 'risking our few valuable ships', Raeder ordered *The*

Knight's Move to be broken off. The risks were too great to be justified by what few successes the fleet might still enjoy against a convoy already decimated by German aircraft and U-boat attacks. At 9.15 p.m., Naval Group North, using the top-secret enciphering prefix *KR-KR*, wirelessed to Schniewind the one word *'Break'* (*Abbrechen*). Carls reported to Raeder soon after that Schniewind had been ordered to turn back, and operational command of the Arctic U-boats reverted to Admiral Schmundt. The German battle fleet turned back in silence at 9.50 p.m., and with Schmundt making frantic preparations to receive the premature returners, re-entered the Leads at 3.30 a.m. on the following day.

The German Naval Staff commented: 'A second attempt to bring our heavy ships into action against the traffic to Murmansk and Archangel has proven unsuccessful. Every sortie attempted by our heavy surface units is burdened by the Führer's desire to avoid at all costs the risk of losses or defeats.' It was obvious that such operations could only be launched when there was no real risk, especially from aircraft-carriers. These conditions had been satisfied during *The Knight's Move* to an extent scarcely likely to be repeated in future PQ convoy operations. Regrettable though the effect of the recall had been on the morale of the German sailors, even General-Admiral Carls was forced to admit that the decision had been correct: 'If the operation had been partially carried out, from 8 p.m. 5 July to 1 a.m. on the 6th, it would probably have led to an air attack [on our fleet] if our force had failed to find quickly the three ships which are believed to have reached Murmansk.'[53]

The order to break off the operation was certainly a bitter disappointment to Admiral Schniewind. He believed that the main reason for the failure to sieze the opportunity to attack earlier was the far-flung character of the German naval organization: he urged that the tactical headquarters (Group North) should be transferred to a site closer to the actual zone of operation in the Arctic than Kiel.[54] Admiral Schmundt was at one with him on this, advocating that either the tactical command should be given to him in Narvik, or that Group North and its operations staff should transfer to the Arctic Circle itself.[55] Naval Group North rejected the suggestions, and drew attention instead to the importance of maintaining close liaison with the Naval Staff headquarters and the political authorities in Berlin and at the Führer's headquarters.[56]

Schniewind argued that only by having the two tactical headquarters—of Navy and Air Force—located close together in the northern theatre could momentary opportunities be seized and exploited. Above all, there was the possibility that 'adequate heed' would then be paid to his own requirements of the Air Force, for the co-operation between the two services had been demonstrably lax during *The Knight's Move*. While he recognized that as the convoy operation progressed the co-operation between the aircraft and the U-boats improved, and that during the German battle fleet's brief sortie it had had adequate air cover, Schniewind was disappointed that the Air Force had failed to maintain close contact with the enemy's heavy covering forces, although he had expressly asked for this.

> I see the reasons for this as being a certain degree of understandable hesitancy in the Air Force to divide their own limited forces available, and to detach reconnaissance planes to shadow enemy heavy forces, particularly when there is a carrier in the vicinity.
>
> Once again we see the great disadvantages we labour under, lacking as we do our own Fleet Air Arm.*[57]

Reichsmarschall Göring for his part expressed his inability to understand why the Navy had called off the battle fleet's attack. When the Naval Staff learned of this from an aside by General Bodenschatz, it was suggested that the Führer should be put in the picture as to why the battle fleet had turned back. Grand-Admiral Raeder rejected the suggestion as 'uncalled for'.[58] Admiral Schniewind, who was equally exercised by the difficulty of

---

* It is interesting to read in Admiral Tovey's Report (11 July) on the Home Fleet's operation precisely the same sentiments: 'The operation provided a striking illustration of the handicap imposed on the proper conduct of sea operations through inadequate air co-operation. On the one hand, the enemy disposed of a numerous and efficient force of long-range reconnaissance aircraft, timing and adjusting his offensive moves by their reports. On the other hand, we were operating without any effective air co-operation, enjoying only such information as originated from Intelligence sources.'

explaining his fleet's withdrawal to 'outsiders' proposed the following dishonest formula: 'The heavy enemy force, including an aircraft-carrier, accompanying the convoy was obliged to turn back by the movements of our own heavy battle group, and this facilitated the convoy's attack by submarines and aircraft. The objective of our own heavy ships' sortie was completely achieved.'[59] It was doubted whether such an explanation would be convincing to 'outsiders', least of all to the U-boat and bomber crews.

Grand-Admiral Raeder was quite clear in his own mind about the reasons why he had stopped the attack. The war was going so favourably for Germany on every front that he had wanted at all costs to avoid the kind of reverse that the loss or damaging of a big German warship would entail. Besides, the main convoy battle had already been fought and won by aircraft and submarines.[60] Subsequently, he tended to divert attention from the part his own staunch adherence to the 'fleet-in-being' concept had played in the decision to withdraw, and in post-war histories the Führer has received more than his just share of the blame.[61]

There could be no question of repeating *The Knight's Move* against one of the next PQ convoys—their stratagem had been displayed too clearly to the enemy for that. Nor, on the other hand, was it likely that the Allies would risk running PQ convoys on the same scale as PQ.17 during the summer months. Group North mooted the suspicion that while the British would not drop the convoys altogether, they would revert to smaller fast convoys of six or seven ships, hugging the ice as far as Novaya Zemlya perhaps, and then creeping down to Cape Kanin using fog as much as possible. Admiral Schmundt recommended that the focus of future attacks be switched to the westbound QP convoys, as they were only moderately escorted by naval forces, while the strategic objective of sinking enemy shipping tonnage would be attained just the same. Raeder agreed that this was worth consideration.[62]

It certainly seemed unlikely that a comparable disaster could be inflicted on any PQ convoy after PQ.17: 'These successes were made possible only by the Convoy Commodore's incomprehensible action in scattering the convoy, thereby giving my submarines the chance to come within range of unescorted merchant ships,' said Schmundt. And the Naval Staff in Berlin, wrestling with the same enigma, concluded that the conduct of PQ.17

operations by the Allies had been so disastrous that only the Americans could have been in command. They gravely warned, 'Without doubt the British will resume command and control the escort of the next PQ convoys after their bad experience with the Americans in command of PQ.17.'

Immediately after the returning battle fleet anchored at Altenfiord, the Flag-Admiral Cruisers—Vice-Admiral Kummetz—proposed that they repeat the sortie at once, if necessary with only some of the warships. Recognizing that the convoy's remnants were still well to the north, and that even though the German battle fleet had been sighted the Allied fleet had *still* stayed west of 15° East, Schniewind agreed and signalled Naval Group North's headquarters:

Consider situation particularly favourable for repetition of sortie.[63]

The request was turned down, on the grounds that the whereabouts of the enemy's heavy force had still not been established beyond doubt; that 27 of the 38 merchant ships had already been claimed sunk; and that as the remainder were widely scattered there was no worthwhile target for such a sortie. Besides, the German destroyers would encounter fuel difficulties attacking targets so far to the north.

Similar requests by Commodore Bey,* the destroyer flotilla commander, to be permitted to operate with seven destroyers against those convoy remnants still afloat, and by the *Hipper*'s Captain Meisel, to be allowed to take his ship and four fast destroyers out into the eastern Barents Sea, were not forwarded by Admiral Schniewind, their fleet commander, as Raeder's objections still held good for them. After refuelling, the German battle fleet sailed again at 6 p.m., and headed south to Narvik, unaware that on the charts in the British Admiralty's operations rooms they were still flagged as advancing on the helpless merchant ships.

---

* Who commanded the battleship *Scharnhorst* at the time of her heroic last fight in December 1943.

6

A DUTY TO AVOID DESTRUCTION

5 July – 6 July

The ice came so fast upon us that it made our haires staire upright upon our heades, it was so fearful to behold.—Gerrit de Veer, *Voyage of William Barents to the Arctic Regions, 1594*

FIVE O'CLOCK ON THE AFTERNOON of 5 July 1942: of the thirty-five merchantmen which had set out from Iceland, three had turned back and eight had already been sunk by German aircraft and submarines. Forty-seven Merchant Navy officers and seamen had already lost their lives, but the disaster still had not reached its climax. Before another half hour had passed six more merchant vessels and the fleet oiler *Aldersdale* would have been attacked by bombers and sunk or abandoned. Already the American *Peter Kerr,* laden with foodstuffs, tanks and bombers, was blazing from end to end and lifeboats were pulling away from her across the oily sea.

The ship had proven a tougher target than most of them. Two hours before, she had been attacked by no fewer than seven torpedo-bombers, dropping a total of thirteen torpedoes, and had still survived.* Her Master, Captain Butler, knew that salvation lay in zigzagging, and as his vessel had headed almost due south at over 11 knots, he was constantly changing the vessel's speed and zigzag pattern. After two hours, the torpedo attack had ended; but then four Junkers 88 dive-bombers came in from the south-east and attacked from over 4,000 feet, far above the range of the ship's guns. The bombers were from Captain Willi Flechner's unit, *V./KG.30.* Thirty-six bombs were dropped, three of which scored direct hits, setting fire to No. 3 hold, the deck cargo and the ship's wireless room. The remaining bombs were all near misses, knocking out *Peter Kerr*'s steering gear and flooding the forward part of the ship. As the fire got out of control, Butler

---

* One of the attacking torpedo-bombers had subsequently picked up the *Carlton*'s first survivors.

gave the order to abandon ship. The crew escaped in two lifeboats. The ship continued to blaze for some time, and then blew up and sank, leaving only the two lifeboats on the sea. The wooden-legged Chief Engineer said, 'Thank God I had my good leg on!'[1]

The airfields in northern Norway were now at last clear of fog, and the wheeled Junkers 88s had been able to take off *en masse*: all three squadrons of *KG.30*—sixty-nine Junkers 88s—were in the air, scouring a vast expanse of sea for the scattered merchant ships, and picking them off one by one.* First reports back to Norway spoke of the ships being scattered across 130 miles from north to south, while some of them were even hugging the ice-barrier; there could be no talk of any kind of organized anti-aircraft defence.[3]

After the convoy had been scattered, few of the merchant ships had obeyed their scatter order literally: Captain J. Holmgren of the American *Hoosier*, for example, had opened his sealed orders and headed for the next rendezvous position he found in them, in the bewildered hope that he would find the whole convoy re-formed there as if by magic.[4] But magnetic compasses are un-reliable instruments in those northern latitudes, and Captain Holmgren eventually abandoned the plan and ran instead at full speed towards the north-west coast of Novaya Zemlya. In the 5,203-ton *Bolton Castle*, Captain John Pascoe had steered a north-easterly course in order to draw out of the range of the German bomber squadrons operating from Norway; more from an instinc-tive reluctance to face the Arctic alone than from any deliberate disobedience to orders, two more ships had formed up on the British vessel—the Dutch *Paulus Potter* and the 5,564-ton Ameri-can freighter *Washington*, already leaking from previous attacks. The latter's Master had seen with dismay how 'the trawlers and anti-aircraft ships ran away at superior speed' as the slow merchant ships began to scatter, and decided that safety still lay in numbers.[5] Captain Sissingh, the Dutch ship's Master, had met Captain Pascoe while their ships were loading in adjacent berths in Glasgow, and a strong friendship had been forged between them; the Dutchman had closely surveyed the British freighter and had

---

* Captain Willi Flechner was awarded the Knight's Cross, as were squadron commanders Captain Erich Stoffregen (killed 14 January 1943) and Captain Konrad Kahl.[2]

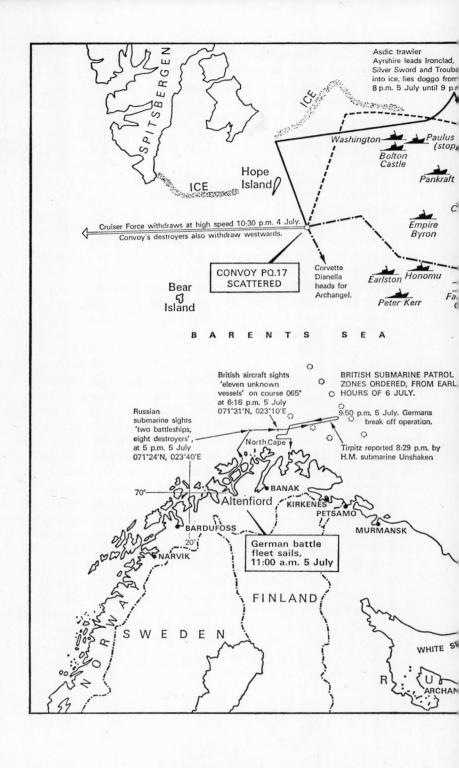

ICE

SPITSBERGEN

Asdic trawler
Ayrshire leads Ironclad,
Silver Sword and Trouba
into ice, lies doggo from
8 p.m. 5 July until 9 p.r

Washington ▲   Paulus
Bolton   (stop
Castle

Pankraft

Hope
Island

Empire
Byron

Cruiser Force withdraws at high speed 10:30 p.m. 4 July.
Convoy's destroyers also withdraw westwards.

Earlston   Honomu

Fa

CONVOY PQ.17
SCATTERED

Corvette
Dianella
heads for
Archangel.

Peter Kerr

Bear
Island

B A R E N T S   S E A

British aircraft sights
'eleven unknown
vessels' on course 065°
at 6:16 p.m. 5 July
071°31'N, 023°10'E

BRITISH SUBMARINE PATROL
ZONES ORDERED, FROM EARL
HOURS OF 6 JULY.

Russian
submarine sights
'two battleships,
eight destroyers',
at 5 p.m. 5 July
071°24'N, 023°40'E

9:50 p.m. 5 July. Germans
break off operation.

North Cape

Tirpitz reported 8:29 p.m. by
H.M. submarine Unshaken

70°

BANAK

Altenfiord

KIRKENES

PETSAMO

BARDUFOSS

MURMANSK

20°

NARVIK

German battle
fleet sails,
11:00 a.m. 5 July

FINLAND

S W E D E N

WHITE S

N O R W A Y

R   U

ARCHAN

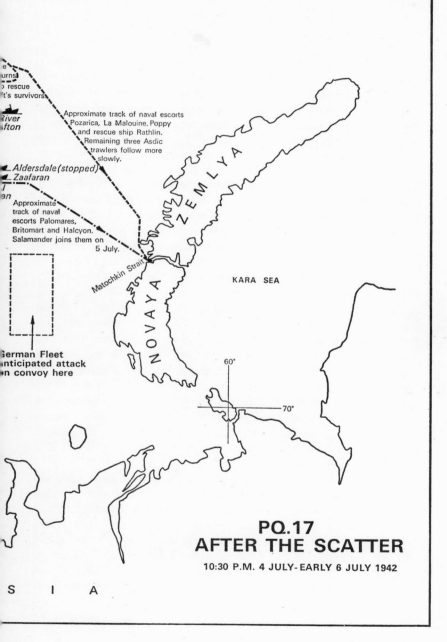

e
urns]
o rescue
't's survivors

River
fton

Approximate track of naval escorts
Pozarica, La Malouine, Poppy
and rescue ship Rathlin.
Remaining three Asdic
trawlers follow more
slowly.

Aldersdale (stopped)
Zaafaran
an

Approximate
track of naval
escorts Palomares,
Britomart and Halcyon.
Salamander joins them on
5 July.

German Fleet
anticipated attack
on convoy here

Matochkin Strait

Z E M L Y A

N O V A Y A

KARA SEA

60°

70°

S   I   A

PQ.17
AFTER THE SCATTER
10:30 P.M. 4 JULY–EARLY 6 JULY 1942

not failed to be impressed by the *Bolton Castle*'s heavy armament, which included a 4-inch anti-submarine gun, a Bofors, and four Oerlikon and four light machine-guns.

Originally there had been a fourth vessel tailing them, the American freighter *Olopana*. This old-timer could barely make 9 knots, and as nobody had wanted to fall back to her speed, she gradually dropped back over the horizon. As the three other ships headed north, they found their way barred in the small hours of the morning by the ice-barrier, stretching as far as the eye could see, and glittering in the rays of the midnight sun. Captain Pascoe decided to turn east along the edge of the ice, but after a few hours of steaming the three heavy-laden ships found their passage barred by a new wall of ice. They were forced to head south-eastwards, every hour bringing them closer to the German air-fields. 'We kept getting radio reports of ships attacked. Many submarines and torpedo planes were reported at positions ahead of us,' recorded *Washington*'s Armed Guard officer.⁵ The ship had 350 tons of trinitrotoluene in the port side of hatches 1 and 2, so he advised the Captain to keep very close to the ice floes to protect that side from submarine attack.

At five o'clock, the lookouts sighted a lone Junkers 88 flying high above them at some 13,000 feet. *Bolton Castle*'s gunners prepared to man their Bofors guns, but held their fire when it seemed that the aircraft had not noticed the three ships. But the Junkers went into a dive, and swooped down on the *Washington*, its machine-guns rattling. A row of holes was drilled in the ship's superstructure; dents appeared in the pill-box only a few inches from the Armed Guard officer's head. The bombs landed about fifteen yards off the ship's starboard quarter; the ship was shaken but undamaged. *Washington* transmitted an 'air attack' signal and gave her position.

Pascoe knew that it would not be long before more German aircraft arrived, called up by the first one. He ordered *Bolton Castle*'s four lifeboats to be swung out, but not lowered; if the worst came to the worst, he would have perhaps only a few minutes to supervise getting seventy seamen and gunners safely into the lifeboats. He also summoned his boatswain and carpenter, and confided in them that he expected the ship to be sunk within the next few hours: they were to make an unobtrusive additional check that the lifeboats were properly provisioned with food and water.[6]

Half an hour later, it was obvious that his forethought had been justified: a starboard lookout reported that several more Junkers 88s were approaching. The aircraft were from Captain Hajo Herrmann's notorious third squadron of *KG. 30*, specially brought up from Bardufoss to Banak, the most northerly air base in Europe. One aircraft swooped on the *Washington*, its bombs lifting her hull partly out of the water; several other aircraft followed at once. The ship's crew counted twenty-one bombs hitting the sea near them. *Washington*'s steering gear was knocked out, the ship began to take water and Captain Richert gave orders to abandon ship. A wireless signal was transmitted to this effect, repeating their position.

Captain Pascoe resigned himself to his fate; he made no attempt to take evasive action when the bombers next came in. The aircraft were attacking not from one direction but from several, and from different altitudes. An aircraft dived out of the sun on them, and dropped a stick of bombs right on the ship. The second of the three bombs penetrated No. 2 hold, containing hundreds of tons of cordite. For a moment *Bolton Castle* forged on, ignoring the direct hits; the ship did not shake, and Pascoe did not even hear the detonation as the bomb exploded in the hold. But as he looked through the bridge windows, the world suddenly went green: a brilliant flash blinded him and he heard a roar lasting some seconds, like a mighty waterfall. The cargo of cordite had ignited —not as an explosive with shattering violence, but 'like a giant Roman candle'. From *Washington*'s lifeboats, they saw the mushroom cloud where *Bolton Castle* had stood, barely a quarter of a mile away; but the prayer died on the men's lips, for as the cloud drifted away the British ship was still there. The heat had melted the steel hull, and the hatch cover had just vanished. 'The bridge windows buckled, twisted and melted away in the heat.' Pascoe went forward and leant over the gaping hole where the cordite had been stacked. The hold was empty, but he could hear the sound of water rushing blackly in below.

At the same time, the bombers straddled the third of the ships, the 7,168-ton *Paulus Potter*, disabling her steering gear.[7] Her crew escaped safely in four boats, as did the crew of the *Bolton Castle*.

Within a very few minutes, three ships had been lost; but there had been no casualties.

The eight Junkers 88s descended to only a few feet above the waves, and roared in triumphant formation over their three victims, firing incendiary bullets into the abandoned hulks, while German war reporter Benno Wundshammer, crouching in one bomber's cockpit, took photographs of the scene. [8] As the aircraft disappeared, *Washington* began to burn, and *Bolton Castle* slowly stood up on end and sank; *Paulus Potter* looked unscathed.

The weary American freighter *Olopana*, some way behind them, was still afloat, seaworthy and manned, thanks to a ruse adopted by her excellent Master, Captain Mervyn Stone. When the first lone Junkers 88 attacked him half an hour before, Stone ordered nearly all his men to abandon ship in the lifeboats, leaving only a skeleton crew aboard: three men carried out the entire manning of the engine-room, the Second Officer manned the hand steering-station aft, and two other men prepared to lower the last rafts should the ship be hit. 'The British gunners unhesitatingly declared they would defend the vessel to the last,' and also stayed aboard. As the aircraft made its first pass, Stone ordered smoke-floats to be ignited on the ship's decks forward, midships and aft, and within a few moments the whole vessel was enveloped in thick, choking fumes, making the Second Officer's task at the exposed steering-station aft extremely unpleasant. In any event, the German aircraft made off, and left the ship alone after this, apparently believing that they had hit her. [9]

Now once again the story of this convoy is interrupted by one of those almost unbelievable episodes that serve to elevate it above other naval operations of the Second World War. After the yellow wing-tipped aircraft had returned towards Norway, the Masters of *Bolton Castle* and *Paulus Potter* conferred on their next best course of action. Pascoe, the Briton, announced that he intended to row his lifeboats towards the Russian coast, some 400 miles to the south-east; but his Dutch friend, Captain Sissingh, observed that since according to his chart the nearest land was Novaya Zemlya, it made more sense to take his lifeboats there. Pascoe tried to persuade him that the shorter journey was in fact the more dangerous, as it would take them through regions of extreme cold close to the ice-barrier. The Dutchman was adamant: he wanted to find dry land as soon as possible. Pascoe sadly shook hands with the Dutchman and bade the Dutch crew farewell.

Shortly afterwards, the *Olopana* came on the scene, anxious to rescue the survivors of the three stricken ships. Captain Stone afterwards reported to Naval Control in Archangel: 'The *Olopana* headed in the direction of the vessels burning on the horizon, to pick up survivors. The *Washington*'s boats were the first encountered; but the crew were so shaken up that another session of dive-bombing was the last thing they desired.' The American seamen in the lifeboats were convinced that it was only a matter of time before the unescorted *Olopana* was also sunk. They refused to set foot on another merchant ship:

> Only the captain boarded us, and after an examination of the chart agreed that Moller Bay, Novaya Zemlya, should be his objective. He requested a boat compass-check.
> Proceeded to [lifeboats of] *Paulus Potter*, Dutch. She had fought off the same group of planes, for an hour and had been badly smashed about by near misses; finally, engines stopped and taking water, she was abandoned. The crew of the *Paulus Potter* were in four lifeboats, one a motor-boat. We chased after them, and when alongside inquired if they had anyone injured, or did they wish to come on board? To both queries the answer was negative. They did request cigarettes, bread and lubricating oil. These wants were provided for, and the Dutchmen cast off to join the *Washington*'s lifeboats, also headed for Moller Bay.
> The *Bolton Castle*'s lifeboats were sailing away to the south and showed no desire to contact us, so we proceeded north.

Captain Stone concluded that the British crew were equally unenthusiastic about being rescued by his ship; Captain Pascoe has since confirmed that nothing was farther from his mind at that time than the desire to board another merchant ship in those seas.[6] Thus, to the already grim saga of Disaster Convoy PQ.17 was added the story of how one hundred and fifty ship-wrecked seamen elected to drift for weeks across the expanses of the Arctic ocean in open boats rather than once again set foot aboard an unescorted Allied merchantman.

A hundred miles or so to the south, German bomber aircraft

were preparing to attack a small group of naval vessels which had been heading eastwards for Novaya Zemlya. The two 1,500-ton rescue ships *Zamalek* and *Zaafaran*—former Cypriot and Syrian coastal cargo and passenger boats—had stayed together after the order to scatter had been passed to the convoy, as between them they disposed of a not inconsiderable fire-power against attacking aircraft: two 12-pounders, two 40-millimetre Bofors quick-fire guns, eight 20-millimetre Oerlikons and two machine-gun turrets. By five o'clock on the afternoon of 5 July, the two vessels were still within sight of each other. *Zamalek*'s Captain Morris wrote in his log that his ship was 'receiving SOS's constantly from ships all around—aircraft and submarine'. He was not unlike a Welsh terrier in character: he was short, and brisk in his movements, his hair was dark and his eyes were small and fierce. He spoke with a pronounced Welsh sing-song intonation, raising his voice to a high squeak when impatient, but gruff and slow when addressing his crew. He had been born and raised in the little towns of Pwllheli and Abercynon, and he had never strayed far from the sea all his life.

How different was Captain Charles McGowan, the dour Scots Master of the rival rescue ship *Zaafaran*, also employed by the General Steam Navigation Company. At thirty-nine, McGowan was no older than Morris; but technically he was the senior, having gained his own ship in the company sooner. There was no love lost between the two, and a feud surprising in its intensity had broken out between the two little rescue ships and their crews. Soon after five o'clock on the afternoon of 5 July, McGowan signalled Morris that he was planning to head for the White Sea alone, as his ship was being held up unnecessarily by the slower *Zamalek*, which was still heading eastwards for Novaya Zemlya.

It was true that McGowan's ship was about half a knot faster than Morris's, probably because Morris was carrying a small cargo of anti-submarine bombs. The Welshman grudgingly admitted that his rival had the better Chief Engineer too; but that, as he remarked to his officers, was scarcely McGowan's real reason for sheering off to the south-east now. It was rather more likely that *Zamalek*, with her older engines, was making too much smoke for safety; and that was why he was nervously edging away. Captain Morris still believed that safety lay in numbers, and barely an hour later he was relieved to run across a small group of ships, including the 8,402-ton fleet oiler *Aldersdale*, the British merchantman *Ocean Freedom* and the Royal Navy minesweeper *Salamander*. Morris signalled the latter, 'May we join you?' *Salamander* welcomed the addition of a rescue ship to his party.[10]

At five-thirty, four Junkers 88s came in to attack this small group of vessels. The first three attackers were so demoralized by the group's combined fire-power that their bombs fell wide, throwing up harmless fountains of sea water. The fourth aircraft alone ventured right in, dropping its bombs from about 6,000 feet. They exploded obliquely under the *Aldersdale*'s cruiser-stern and engine-room; the oiler began to take water amidships.[11]

The Chief Engineer reported to the oiler's Captain Hobson that the engines were out of commission, and could not be repaired at sea. Hobson considered his position: his ship had sustained no casualties and rescue was near at hand; but his tanker was completely immobilized. He decided to abandon ship forthwith, collected all the confidential papers from the ship's safe and put them together with a quantity of British and Icelandic money into the weighted bag supplied for destroying them, and hurled the package overboard. The minesweeper *Salamander* hove to and took the entire crew off the oiler; but seeing how the *Aldersdale* showed no sign of settling, Hobson sent his Chief Engineer back aboard to re-examine the engines. Perhaps the oiler and her 8,000 tons of fuel oil could be salvaged after all.

Zamalek's Second Officer, Mr Lennard, had been watching the disappearing *Zaafaran* as it headed south-east over the horizon. He could see a number of aircraft buzzing round it like wasps round a jampot, very low down; he could near nothing, but visibility was remarkably good. Suddenly Captain Morris was in the starboard wing of the bridge with him, shouting 'McGowan has had it!' His rival's rescue ship was right over the horizon by then, but they could see her masts slowly heeling over, and then suddenly and dramatically her bows in the air, sticking up like a log on end. Morris ordered his ship's helm put over to starboard, and to his signaller he said, 'Tell that anti-aircraft ship we want anti-submarine protection to go and pick up survivors. If they refuse, quote the regulations book at them.' *Palomares*, far away, detached *Britomart* for the purpose.

Ten miles to the south, Captain McGowan was supervising the rescue of his crew and passengers from the sinking *Zaafaran*. He and his First and Second Officers saw the lifeboats away, and told the crew to get as many rafts away as possible. Then they too left the ship, over the port side. 'I noticed one of our rafts with no one on it,' said the Second Officer later, 'and I jumped into the water and swam a few feet to the raft. As I arrived at the raft so did one of our firemen. He was singing *How deep is the Ocean, How high is the Sky*. It's hard to explain, but from that moment, come what may, I knew we would win through.'[12] As the rescue ship went down, he and the engineer propelled their raft round it with their steel helmets, picking up seamen from the water. Shortly afterwards one of the RN escort vessels arrived, and hailed them. It requested the 'name of ship, when attacked and where ship was now'.

By three minutes past seven, all the survivors had been picked up by Captain Morris's rescue ship, a total of ninety-seven men. There had been only one casualty. Two minutes later, the little convoy—which now included *Zamalek*, *Ocean Freedom*, and *Britomart*—headed eastwards after the disappearing anti-aircraft ship *Palomares*. A cold meeting followed between Morris and his rescued rival on *Zamalek*'s bridge, Captain McGowan's demand to take command of his junior's ship was refused outright by Morris. McGowan stumped down the companionway to the little ship's hospital, where without a word to the surgeon-lieutenant he poured himself a steaming hot bath, using up the hospital's entire supply of hot water for the afternoon.*

The need now was for speed. Somewhere under the sea's surface U-boats must have heard the turmoil of the bombing attack, and at this very moment they might be manœuvring into position. Lieutenant-Commander Mottram of *Salamander* told the damaged *Aldersdale*'s captain that there was only one choice open to him— either to take his crew back aboard the oiler and try to restart her

---

* McGowan and his Chief Engineer were both awarded the DSO for PQ.17; Morris also gained a DSO. The rivalry between the two rescue ship skippers ended only when McGowan lost his life after his next command, the SS *Sunniva* (also General Steam Navigation Company) was sunk with all hands on her first Atlantic convoy as a rescue ship in January 1943.

engines, or to give her up there and then. Hobson said that there must be no question of leaving the tanker afloat for the Germans to take as a prize to Norway. Mottram gave him five minutes to decide.[13] Captain Hobson's Chief Engineer advised that he could not restart his engines, as they had shipped too much water in the engine-room. Hobson decided the oiler would have to be sunk.

Salamander endeavoured to sink the tanker with a stick of depth-charges under the engine-room, as her single 4-inch gun had jammed. The charges were well laid, but although the tanker heaved slightly it showed no signs of breaking up. Mottram tried to set it on fire by shooting up the aviation-fuel tank with his machine-guns, but the bullets just ricocheted from the steel plating. *Aldersdale* was left afloat, and to all appearances un-scathed. The little *Zamalek* convoy, with the anti-aircraft ship *Palomares*, the minesweepers *Britomart* and *Halcyon* and the fast merchantman *Ocean Freedom*, was already ten miles ahead of *Salamander* as she sped with *Aldersdale*'s unhappy survivors towards Novaya Zemlya and safety.

Three German submarines were still trailing the British *Earlston*, some way to the west of *Zaafaran*'s grave. They were keeping a wary distance between themselves and the Briton, who had already discomfited one U-boat with her anti-submarine gun.

From the merchantman's bridge, the First Officer had seen the bombing of *Peter Kerr* to the south, and they had shaped a more northerly course since then. In her holds were several hundred tons of explosives, and crates of ammunition as well. She survived until late afternoon, when a flight of returning Junkers 88s spotted her, and attacked from astern. Three bombs hit the sea off the ship's bows, throwing up a wall of water into which the *Earlston* plunged. She shook herself free, and Chief Officer Benson struggled waist-deep through the water to inspect the damage; he shouted to the Captain that the plates would hold, and had begun making his way back to the bridge when a lone Junkers 88 roared in at bridge height from the starboard bow, dropping a single bomb into the sea just by the vessel's port side. The engines stopped, and the ship slowed to a standstill. The three submarines stopped too, and waited.[14] Captain Stenwick's wireless operator broadcast an 'air attack' distress signal, and he ordered his crew to abandon ship. As the crew pulled away in the two lifeboats, they could see steam pouring out of the engine-room ventilators and the ship settling lower in the water. Scarcely had they put a quarter of a mile between themselves and the ship, fearing that the explosives in No. 2 hold would blow up, than two submarines surfaced on *Earlston*'s starboard bow within a few moments of each other—*U-334* and, most probably, *U-456* who three hours before had torpedoed the American *Honomu*. A short while later, yet a third submarine surfaced, not far from the other two. Commander Siemon's *U-334* began to close in fast on the helpless vessel. When she was still 1,300 yards away, he fired tube II at her, aiming at the freighter's empty bridge. The torpedo struck abreast the after mast; the ship listed slightly, but stayed well afloat. Siemon fired tube III, but the torpedo missed; he fired tube IV, his submarine now barely seven hundred hards away.[15] The torpedo sped towards the British ship, and the seamen in their lifeboats saw with trepidation that it was heading straight for No. 2 hold. The white trail of bubbles extended to the *Earlston*'s flanks abreast the foremast, and stopped.

For an instant of time, nothing happened. Then Siemon, watching from *U-334*, saw a pillar of smoke about 200 feet high billow up, preceded by a blinding blue flash. The heavy naval steam launch which had been strapped in a cradle on top of No. 2 hatch was picked up bodily by the explosion and hurled a quarter of a mile across the sea. The ship broke in two, and the bows sank almost at once. The air was filled with the terrible sound of the heavy cargo—the Churchill tanks, anti-aircraft guns, and trucks—tearing loose in the holds, and the groaning of the ship's members under the unintended strain. Then the stern section slid under the sea with a roar, leaving only the barrage balloon, which had been stowed on the after deck, floating on the sea for a few seconds as the cable paid out from the ship foundering beneath it. Then that too was plucked beneath the waves, as though by an invisible hand. Ninety seconds had passed since Hilmar Siemon had fired his third torpedo.

The British ship's Master, Captain Hilmar Stenwick, was ordered on to *U-334*'s foredeck. He asked what would become of his ship's lifeboats, but received no satisfactory reply. He disappeared into the bowels of the submarine. The three U-boats moved off on the surface, their officers shouting congratulations to each other on their good hunting so far. The latest victory was signalled to Admiral Hubert Schmundt in Narvik.

Within moments, a German sailor in the conning-tower of *U-334* shouted that an aircraft was coming in to attack them. It passed low overhead and released two bombs which detonated not far from the starboard side of the U-boat; but the attack had not come so fast that the submarine officers were not able to identify the attacking aircraft—it was a Junkers 88, a German plane. The U-boat trembled in the blast, and everything loose flew out of its supports; the floor-plates were torn up, the diesel engines were unseated and one ballast tank fractured. A fine spray of water entered the boat, and the lights went out. A voice in the conning-tower yelled, 'Abandon ship, the boat is sinking!' The aircraft returned, and machine-gunned the submarine from very low altitude—'fortunately,' one of the submarine crew later said, 'she had no more bombs left'. Then the plane left them, leaving the submarine to right herself as best she could.

U-334's steering gear had been jammed, and she was unable to submerge.[16] Not far away, Commander Brandenburg's *U-457* also reported that all manner of aircraft were executing bombing-runs on his submarine.[17] Lieutenant-Commander Siemon wirelessed details to Schmundt, and recommended that *U-456*, who was with him and had currently lost contact with the enemy, should be detached from the operation to escort *U-334* back to Kirkenes naval base. Schmundt agreed, and ordered the two U-boats to observe wireless silence all the way. He arranged for escort vessels and tugs to stand by at Kirkenes, and sent a detailed report to the Naval Staff in Berlin. The Fifth Air Force conducted an investigation of the incident, and copies of its report also went to Berlin, but the matter was dropped without the culprits being found.[18] A third U-boat, *U-657* (Commander Göllnitz), also had to return to Narvik as there was a leak in one of her diesel fuel bunkers.

The damaged *U-334* ran into Kirkenes two days after the attack on her, escorted by two Messerschmitt 110s and two mine-sweepers. While *Earlston*'s Captain Stenwick was held under loose guard below decks the U-boat's crew paraded to receive the congratulations of the local senior officer. Commander Siemon was questioned more closely on the 'possible' American heavy cruiser he had reported seeing sink after the heavy air attack on the convoy on 5 July. He described how he had seen a magazine explosion in a big ship, which at once began to list; from its superstructure and mast he took it to be an American warship. It had been twelve miles away. Schmundt forwarded the report to the Naval Staff; Naval Group North commented that the onus of proof was on the Air Force.[19]

A few days later, Captain Stenwick reached Marlag-Milag Nord, the naval prison camp in Germany; there he met *Carlton*'s survivors. Two of the American seamen described to him how the aircraft in which they were flying had broken off to attack an 'enemy submarine' with its machine-guns, *en route*. Stenwick told them that he had a shrewd idea which submarine it was.*[20]

✳ 2 ✳

During the afternoon, the 'Ice Devil' U-boats' operation had been controlled by Naval Group North, and Schmundt had been directed to sail the three refuelled submarines commanded by Timm, Marks and von Hymmen—*U-251, U-376* and *U-408*—as soon as possible, to attack any crippled ships lying north of North Cape and in the latitude of Bear Island, well away from the German battle fleet's projected zone of operations. During the late afternoon, several submarines, including Lieutenant-Commander Bielfeld's *U-703*, wirelessed Narvik that they were chasing lone merchant ships.[22] Soon after the *Tirpitz* operation was broken off, U-boat control returned to Schmundt.

Many miles to the north, the Royal Navy's escort vessels were still making way at maximum speed. The anti-aircraft ship *Pozarica* was steaming eastwards along the ice-pack accompanied by three corvettes and a rescue ship, so close to the ice that they could

---

* It is interesting to note the comments of Mr Walter Stankiewicz, one of *Carlton*'s seamen flown back to Norway. Interviewed by German reporters at Kirkenes, he said: 'During the flight, the Germans gave us pullovers and track suits to put on. Then they fed us with cakes, as we were half frozen. It was my first flight, and frightfully interesting. I sat right up in the bomber's nose, surrounded by glass. I kept wanting to let fly with the machine-gun in every direction, I was so delighted.'[21]

hear the 'resounding crack' each time the ice floes broke away. Several miles behind and now completely out of sight, the American freighter *Bellingham* followed. The escort vessels' radios were unable to pick up either the Admiralty or the BBC direct, but German propaganda wireless broadcasts were coming through loud and clear.

All had received the first signals reporting that two German battleships and eight destroyers had been sighted putting out to sea, and soon afterwards they had picked up a further signal locating the German battle fleet just 350 miles away to the south-west of them, and coming their way.[23] By now the ether was full of distress signals even without the German fleet. 'The radio-man beat a path to the bridge with a continuous stream of distress calls, all to the south of us', wrote *Bellingham*'s Second Officer in his diary.[24] 'The Commodore-ship [*River Afton*] was calling that she had been struck by three torpedoes causing great loss of life, and the remainder were taking to the lifeboats. They were thirty miles away from us.' Every few minutes calls were being received of submarine or air attacks: the trap was sprung, and it seemed that there was to be no escape for any ship.

In the corvette *La Malouine*, the radio operator picked up wireless distress signals from *Earlston, Daniel Morgan* and *Silver Sword*, and from three other ships that failed to identify themselves, all well to the south. The little group of escorts maintained their speed.[25] At 14 knots, the corvette's fuel would last for only three more days. 'Enemy torpedo planes were having a piece of cake on the scattered ships which were being attacked about 100 miles away,' wrote a *La Malouine* officer that night. 'Complete destruction of the convoy is the German intention—and we in *La Mal[ouine]* might have been able to help the odd merchant vessel, but were too occupied protecting a well-armed anti-aircraft ship. A sore point with us all.'[23]

Night closed in again on the Arctic, but again it was a night without darkness—a night without stars. The sun shone clearly on Captain Mervyn Stone's American freighter *Olapana*, as she plodded slowly along the ice-barrier, far behind even *Bellingham*, on an easterly course. 'In the early hours of 6 July,' reported Stone, 'we came upon an unforgettable sight: the *Pankraft*, the vessel which had been ahead of us in the convoy, was ablaze in the ice. Smoke was billowing from her midships house, and flames licking by her No. 4 hatch. Behind was the sun shining over a vast expanse of ice.'9 Both the ship's lifeboats were half a mile away, stuck fast in the icefield; both were empty. Where was the *Pankraft*'s crew?

Laden with TNT, 5,000 tons of crated aircraft parts and a deck-load of bombers, the ship had been following the same ice-barrier on the afternoon of 5 July six miles astern and within sight of the American ship *Bellingham*, when at five o'clock she was bombed from over 4,000 feet by three Junkers 88s—a part of a flight of six guided to their victim by two Focke-Wulfe 200 reconnaissance aircraft.26 The 5,644-ton freighter had been visible for miles because of her smoky engines, and as she hastened without any attempt at zigzagging through the drifting ice she had had no room for evasive action. The sun was dead astern and visibility unlimited. After the third bombing-run, the *Pankraft*'s Master, Captain Jacob Jacobson, decided to abandon ship. According to the survivors, he gave no orders to that effect, but with the Chief Officer was among the first to take to the lifeboats. The Second Officer stayed aboard, directing operations to the last, seeing the lifeboats and rafts away. The wireless operator stayed long enough to broadcast an 'air attack' signal, and added: 'Hit by bombers.'27 Then he left the ship in haste, making no attempt to destroy the confidential British papers in his office. One Junkers 88 roared in low as the last lifeboat was about to pull away, and sprayed the decks of the deserted ship with incendiary bullets; the gallant Second Officer was killed before he could reach the lifeboat.28 The boats pulled away from the *Pankraft*, leaving her to her fate.

The German aircraft had then headed towards *Bellingham*, and towards *Winston-Salem*, one and a half miles on her port quarter, just as they entered a low fogbank. The seamen heard the howl of descending bombs, and three exploded harmlessly on an ice-floe half a mile away from *Bellingham*. When she emerged from the fogbank about an hour later, she was again attacked by a single plane. She fired her 4-inch low angle surface gun into the sea, and the geyser of water seems to have scared the aircraft away. *Bellingham*'s safety valves were screwed down, and vibrating in every joint her speed was gradually coaxed up to over 15 knots: convoy sailing orders show her rated maximum to have been only

12. The rescue ship *Rathlin* fell into sight, and the merchantman thankfully joined company.[24]

Far to the east, the anti-aircraft ship *Pozarica*'s radio officer had picked up *Pankraft*'s distress signal and took it to Captain Lawford. Lawford was reluctant to go to the ship's aid: uppermost in his mind were the urgent signals reporting the positions of the German battle fleet as it headed north-east towards them. The officers of the accompanying corvettes were anxious to turn back, but the captain of *La Malouine* felt his place was with the AA ship. 'After hearing six SOS messages from merchant vessels, the No. 1 and all but one of us—other than the captain, who did not have to express an opinion—agreed we should go with *Lotus* or go alone,' wrote one of the corvette's officers that night. 'Again No. 1 flew into one of his Irish tempers at having to suffer hearing the SOS's and doing nothing but escort a ship capable of looking after herself.' *La Malouine* stayed with *Pozarica,* but her sister-ship the corvette *Lotus* signalled the AA ship that she was going back alone to search for survivors, whatever Lawford might decree. As her signalled intentions were broadcast to *La Malouine*'s seething crew, a great cheer went up for their sister-ship's gallantry.*[23] Lieutenant Henry Hall, captain of *Lotus*, brought his corvette round and headed back towards the position given in the last distress signals.

The last sighting report had put the German battle fleet 350 miles to the south-west, but closing the distance rapidly. 'This caused heavier hearts and a full discussion with all officers present on bridge, and with Novaya Zemlya plans in front of us.' At eight o'clock, the three naval vessels altered course, heading now direct for Admiralty Peninsula on Novaya Zemlya, 220 miles away. The latest report now was that the enemy was 260 miles away, and steering a more easterly course which would cut them off, perhaps even before they could reach the island. At midnight, *Pozarica* altered course to southward, heading now for Matochkin Strait instead of Admiralty Peninsula. Shortly afterwards, she and her consorts ran across the American freighter *Samuel Chase,* whose relief at sighting the heavily armed anti-aircraft ship and her

---

* *La Malouine*'s captain, Lieutenant Bidwell, was awarded the DSC for PQ.17.

anti-submarine escort can be imagined. The relief was short-lived. Before the Americans could draw breath, *Pozarica*'s signal lamp was warning them not to use their wireless—evidently she had picked up a transmission from somebody. The Americans signalled the Royal Navy, 'We were intercepted to southward three times today but lost him, in the fog, steering northward. May we accompany you?' A glance at the convoy sailing order showed that the American freighter's maximum speed was 10 knots. Captain Lawford signalled her, 'I am proceeding Matochkin Strait, Novaya Zemlya. Suggest you do the same at utmost speed. *Von Tirpitz, Hipper* and six destroyers steering 060 degrees from North Cape at 22 knots.' Again the importunate American asked, 'Can we accompany you?' The anti-aircraft ship answered: 'My course and speed 102 degrees, 14 knots.' *Samuel Chase* said, 'Thank you.'[29]

Of this brief exchange, the Armed Guard officer aboard the merchantman reported: 'He informed us that he was heading for Novaya Zemlya at his utmost speed. A few minutes later he told us he was heading for Matochkin Strait and advised us to do the same. Owing to his greater speed we finally lost sight of him.'[30] A dense blanket of fog descended, a blessed relief to the British sailors in their ordeal. But still *Pozarica* did not slacken speed. A signal was sent to Lieutenant Hall in *Lotus*, directing him to head for Matochkin Strait as soon as his search for survivors was completed.[23]

Hall reached the site of the attack on *Pankraft* after two hours' hard steaming to the west, at about 7.45 p.m.[31] The first sight his crew had of the abandoned ship was enough to show that the American had evidently run into an ice-field and stuck fast before being bombed. The vessel was partially obscured by steam rising from her superstructure, and the lifeboats, crowded with a largely Philippino crew, were some distance from the ship in the open sea.

Without wasting a moment, Hall collected all twenty-nine men from the two lifeboats, urging his sailors to get them aboard as quickly as possible as *Lotus* was completely alone in this vast expanse of ice and ocean.[32] Then he ordered the gun crews to open fire on *Pankraft* and sink her. As the corvette's pom-pom and 4-inch gun were brought to bear on the ship and opened fire, the

doomed freighter's Master gave a shout of fear and leapt for the
scrambling nets from his lifeboat. The pom-pom was thumping
shells into the merchant ship from only a few hundred yards
away, and *Lotus* was drawing closer; *Pankraft*'s superstructure
was now well on fire. Jacobson besought Hall to order the guns
to cease fire: he had over a thousand tons of high explosive in his
ship's cargo. Lieutenant Hall's corvette withdrew as smartly as
her engines would allow.

The *Pankraft* continued to burn for over twenty-four hours,
finally blowing up at six oclock on the morning of 7 July with an
explosion so loud that it was heard even by Lieutenant Gradwell's
private convoy far away to the west.[33] By the time *Olopana* stum-
bled across the blazing *Pankraft*, her empty lifeboats had been
blown into the loose ice-floes by the same south wind that
eventually forced Gradwell's four ships to break their way out.

Three torpedoes had struck *River Afton*, and her fate was the
worst of all.

After scattering his convoy at 10.30 p.m. the previous evening,
Commodore Dowding's ship had kept religiously to her north-
easterly scatter course until she met the ice-barrier; then, in thick
fog, she had groped her way eastwards, making for the coast of
Novaya Zemlya. She never made it: during the day, the weather
cleared, and at two minutes past ten on the evening of 5 July,
Commander Bielfeld's first torpedo struck the ship's engine room.
Through his periscope, *U-703*'s commander saw a small white
puff of smoke rise from the vessel's stern, and the ship gradually
slow to a standstill: 'no signs of settling'. He and his crew clearly
heard the explosion, forty-four seconds after the torpedo was
launched.[34] So did Captain John Rimington, the British army
officer taken prisoner twelve hours before from an earlier victim's
boats. On the freighter's deck, Bielfeld could see large crates,
tanks and aircraft.

In *River Afton*, an indescribable confusion was breaking out.
Her Master, Captain Harold Charlton, had given the order to
abandon ship, and some gunners were already struggling to lower
the starboard lifeboat; the port lifeboat had been destroyed by the
blast. To Charlton's consternation, Commodore Dowding expressed the belief that the ship was still seaworthy. Charlton

COD   V   ADM.

S E C R E T   PASS TO R.G.S.S.
ADDRESSED ADMIRALTY FOR · MWT.
MASDROSBEG ADRIRARDYFF M W T

noted
↙tłł 16/7/42 .

FROM S T O ARCHANGEL

CORRECTION

PLEASE INFORM OWNERS RIVER AFTON FOLLOWING 11 MEMBERS OF CREW

LOST, LONGSTAFF, WOOD, ROLFE, PRITCHARD, BREEN, HAINSWORTH,

MASON,, WATSON, COULL, BRIDGER, WALLER.

‒‒‒‒‒‒‒‒

8 D.E.MOMS. RATINGS, WILLIAMS, BANHAM, JESSOP, BROOK HOLDING,

CARVER KIRK HEAF. COMMODORES STAFF. WALLACE WALTON ALSO PASSENGER

LT. WATERSTONE R.N.V.R. =

0945/14 ++

C WA OWNERS RIVER

NEJ   B3

ADM   CAN I H=3 - EQ AQRT79

CAN I HAVE ADDRESS AFTER PASS TO R G S S OVERTYPED ERE

ADDRESSED ADMIRALTY FOR M W T

TKS

ADM   COD

R 2340/15

EJD VA

The Sea Transport Officer's signal to the Admiralty giving the losses in
River Afton

reminded him that he was the ship's Master. Dowding persisted that if a ship was sturdy enough to withstand a torpedo without showing any signs of settling, she was fit to go anywhere; he was a veteran with considerable convoy experience—he had taken the very first PQ convoy through to north Russia. Dowding said he would radio for a corvette to come and take them in tow: *River Afton* and her cargo were worth millions of pounds, and it would be wrong to abandon her.³⁵ Captain Charlton reiterated that he was still the ship's Master, while Dowding's prerogatives as Convoy Commodore had lost their substance when the convoy as such ceased to exist. As a veteran of two north Russian convoys, he knew a doomed ship when he saw one. If the Commodore wished to stay aboard, then that was his own responsibility.

The gunners and other seamen had almost got the starboard lifeboat down now. Other seamen had slipped two rafts, but they had promptly floated away with nobody on them. Captain Charlton took his leave of Dowding and cast off from the *River Afton* in a jollyboat, taking some of his men with him. Dowding and his staff of Royal Navy signallers stayed stubbornly aboard, resolved no doubt to organize the ship's salvage themselves. The ship's radio officer, George Garstin, also stayed aboard, continuing to transmit distress signals, but he could get no acknowledgement of them, so he feared they had not been picked up.

A number of Charlton's officers had also ignored his orders to abandon ship, and were trying to rescue the engineers trapped below. The first torpedo had detonated in the engine-room below the water line. The Fourth Engineer had just gone below to take over the watch from the Second Engineer, and had reached the generator platform when the torpedo struck: the heavy generator had rolled over on top of him and crushed him. The vessel's South African Second Engineer lay with both legs broken in the engine-room, which was flooding fast. The Chief Engineer, Edward Miller, at once organized a rescue party to bring out the Second Engineer, taking with him the Liverpool Chief Steward Percy Grey and his nineteen-year-old assistant cook Thomas Waller.³⁶

At this moment, *U-703*'s second torpedo struck *River Afton*'s engine-room, killing all the rest of the crew below. The starboard lifeboat was capsized by the blast, and all the gunners were thrown into the sea. Chief Engineer Miller was trapped by a smashed mooring winch, which rolled over and pinioned his leg; but with the help of the others, he freed himself and pressed on with the Second Engineer's rescue. Dowding returned to the ship's bridge, and destroyed his official papers; he saw that Captain Charlton had left his secret papers there, so he placed them in a weighted box and threw them overboard as well. Then he went to the engine-room skylight, where Miller and his rescue party were trying to get the engineer out. They had found him lying on the fan platform just above the foaming water flooding into the engine-room. The young assistant cook, Waller, climbed through the engine-room grating on a rope and put the unconscious engineer into a sling for hoisting aloft. With extreme care, the engineer was hauled out through the grating by the radio officer, Dowding, and a number of others. The Chief Engineer placed his injured colleague on a stretcher on one of the ship's rafts on the main deck. Dowding gave orders to all the men still aboard the ship to stand by the rafts, but not to slip them until the ship went down.

The seas around the ship were swarming with struggling men, some with life-jackets, but all swimming for their lives. Captain Charlton and Lieutenant Cook, a middle-aged sea-transport officer who had been on his way to a posting in Russia, were moving round the ship in their jollyboat, and hauling seamen out of the sea, until the little boat could take no more.

Commander Bielfeld had turned *U-703* away to the west, but saw to his annoyance that his victim had still not begun to sink twenty minutes after the first torpedo had struck home. At 10.22 p.m. he fired his third torpedo at *River Afton*, as Commodore Dowding and his men stood by their rafts; the torpedo struck the ship cleanly on the starboard side of No. 5 hatch. The brave young assistant cook Thomas Waller, who had been left in the engine-room after rescuing the Second Engineer, was killed outright. Hatch-boards and crates of cargo were thrown violently into the air, and everybody could hear the thunderous noise of the sea cascading into her holds. Dowding shouted that the rafts were to be slipped, and he himself climbed on to the small raft bearing the wounded engineer, the Chief Steward and another man. They could feel the ship rolling over to starboard, but then she suddenly began to sink stern first. Dowding's raft was carried across the deck, which was awash by now, and fouled the derricks and the hatch covers, which were being blown off by the air pressure building up beneath them. The doomed *River Afton*'s bows reared up above them; she began to slide backwards into the sea. Water was pouring over them from the superstructure and the horrified Commodore saw the foremast bearing down on him, as the raft to which he and the others were clinging was forced off the sinking ship. As the ship plunged, the mast caught their little raft and capsized it, throwing Dowding, the injured engineer and the others into the icy sea.

The sea was empty now save for the jollyboat and the flotsam of wreckage and human life clinging to the scattered baulks of timber and rafts. Dowding swam back to the raft, and picked up the wounded engineer, by now more dead than alive, and two young cooks. Close to him he could see a large raft with about nine men, and a smaller one with three wireless officers and another man. 'Some distance off' was the jollyboat with Captain Charlton, and there was the upturned lifeboat with about half a dozen men clinging to it: Charlton towed a small raft over to them, and they climbed aboard. All attempts to right the lifeboat failed. There was no compass or food of any sort on the rafts, and only four paddles between all five rafts. In his crowded jollyboat, Captain Charlton saw a fireman dying before his eyes. He eased the body into the sea and mumbled, 'dust to dust, and ashes to ashes'—all that he could remember of the Service for Burial at Sea.

U-703 surfaced only briefly. One of her officers asked some men on a raft the name of their ship and her cargo; in good English he said he was sorry he had had to do this, and regretted that he could not take anybody into his submarine. He handed over a large sausage and water, and told them to steer eastwards for 200 miles, when they would make Novaya Zemlya. 'Without paddles, this would have been a difficult job', commented Dowding. Then *U-703*, keeping on the surface, disappeared in search of further prey. Several hundred yards from Charlton's boat, Commodore Dowding found some small smoke floats on his raft, and these he cut free with his jack-knife and opened. Dense reddish-brown

[193]

smoke billowed out, but it drifted low and heavy across the glassy sea. It looked like the end for all of them.*[37]

Ten minutes after Bielfeld's third torpedo struck *River Afton*, William Joyce was broadcasting from Germany the first details of the Arctic convoy battle. He concluded by mocking that there were a number of questions that the Russians should ask themselves about British and American promises of military aid:

1. what proportion of the war material despatched to Soviet ports will ever arrive?
2. in view of the admission made by Mr Lyttleton and Mr Churchill in the Commons concerning the British policy of preferring quantity to quality in armaments, how much of the war material that *has* arrived can be worth unloading? and
3. when is the Second Front going to materialize . . .?[38]

✳ 3 ✳

At half-past six that evening, an hour and a half after the German battle fleet had first been sighted putting to sea, the British Admiralty wirelessed Admiral Sir John Tovey that if the Germans were to sight the Home Fleet steering eastwards, it might make them reluctant to risk their own warships so far to the east as the convoy would soon be. Tovey, receiving the Admiralty's signal at about seven o'clock, was reluctant to adopt the measure as he thought it essential to continue on his present south-westerly course for his destroyers to refuel. Nevertheless, he did make arrangements for the course of his fleet to be temporarily reversed to the east should an enemy reconnaissance aircraft be detected approaching.[39] In the meantime Hamilton's cruiser force

---

* *River Afton*'s late owners, Hunting & Son Ltd., informed the author that they understood that Captain Charlton had 'a number of disagreements' with Dowding, and this was why Charlton received no recognition at the time. Dowding was awarded his CBE for the next homeward convoy, QP.14, when he again ended up on a raft (*London Gazette*, 13 October 1942). Charlton was awarded a DSC in December 1944 (*Lloyd's List*, 20 December 1944). Miller, Grey and Garstin (the radio officer) were awarded Lloyd's War Medal for Bravery at Sea (*Lloyd's List*, 7 October 1942 and 31 August 1943).

KG.30's Ju.88s could not press home their attack on PQ. 17
on 4 July because of the fire-power
of the merchantmen and their escorts

Late on 4 July the Heinkels of *KG.26* attacked PQ.17.
Lieutenant Kaumeyr's aircraft was shot into the sea
by the USS *Wainwright (see page 102)*

Lieutenant Hennemann led a second attack from astern.
Before his aircraft was brought down one of his torpedoes
struck the British freighter *Navarino*

Another torpedo hit the Russian tanker *Azerbaijan*. When the rescue ship *Zamalek* moved in *(below)*, eight Russian seamen deserted the tanker in a lifeboat

HMS *Keppel*

Lieutenant Gradwell

Paymaster-Commander
N. E. Denning, Admiralty
Intelligence Officer

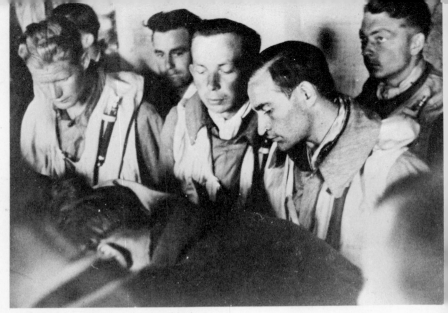

Ju.88 bomber crews being briefed before
a sortie against PQ. 17 on 5 July 1942

Ayrshire under the gun of an American tank
broached open on the deck of *Troubadour*.
A photograph by Ensign H. E. Carraway

Two lone merchant ships of PQ. 17, spotted by Ju.88s
after the convoy had been scattered.
The one below, scudding along close to the ice pack,
is possibly the American freighter *Fairfield City*

(above and left) The sinking of *Bolton Castle*, and two
boat-loads of her survivors *(see page 175)*

Carlton's happy survivors, as seen by readers of *Signal*.
Captain Roy Hansen: 'Tell your commanders, I hope German sailors are treated as well
in the States as we are here.'
'Big' McDonough: 'The trousers I am wearing were given me by a German airman'

Captain O. C. Morris and (*above*) the crew
of his rescue-ship *Zamalek*

Paulus Potter, abandoned

Two photographs taken from Commander Siemon's *U-334* show *Earlston's* barrage balloon marking the spot where the freighter sank, and survivors approaching the U-boat (*see page 182*)

had just been sighted by a German Focke-Wulf, and he learned shortly after from the Admiralty that his force's position had been reported back to Germany with great precision; he was conse- quently able to break wireless silence at 6.30 p.m. to report to Tovey the composition of his force.[40] It was only now that the Commander-in-Chief learned that Hamilton had all Broome's escort destroyers with him, and that some of them had over 75 per cent of their fuel remaining.

At about eight o'clock, the Admiralty wirelessed its latest grim appreciation to the naval escort vessels:

> Most likely time of enemy surface attack now tonight of 5–6 July or early tomorrow morning, 6 July. Enemy may strike 065° in direction of North Cape.[41]

Soon afterwards, they learned that a Russian submarine, *K-21*, was claiming to have 'torpedoed' *Tirpitz*. Requests were signalled to two RAF squadrons to search for her, at 8.45 p.m., and at 9.06 p.m. the Admiralty wirelessed the Commander-in-Chief an urgent request to reconsider whether, if *Tirpitz* really was damaged, she might not present an attractive target for the tor- pedo-planes of his aircraft-carrier *Victorious* once he had com- pleted refuelling his destroyers.

Tovey was unimpressed by this suggestion. He could see no practicable opportunity for striking at the 'crippled' German battleship; *Tirpitz* could make the return passage almost entirely under short-range fighter cover, while there were more than enough Junkers 88s in the north to deal with any Albacores that might be despatched to attack her along those parts of her route outside short-range fighter cover. It was in any case difficult to believe that the Germans would make the passage, especially if the battleship was damaged, unless they had first arranged fighter cover in advance, and unless German air reconnaissance had ensured that the Home Fleet was not in the offing.

One may criticize these arguments in retrospect as exaggerating the capacities of the German Air Force for escorting naval units and for executing reliable reconnaissance operations; but one must respect Tovey's final argument—that his own flagship, *Duke of York*, was too short of fuel then to engage in such an operation, and he was not willing to divide the Fleet before an operation so close to the enemy shores. In any case, as we now know, the whole German battle fleet had turned back towards Norway some time before ten o'clock that night, and all of them —including the undamaged *Tirpitz*—were safe at anchor again by the early hours of 6 July.

The first two RAF reconnaissance squadrons had by 1.45 a.m. found of course no trace of any damaged *Tirpitz,* but a third squadron was requested to carry out an immediate reconnaissance of the same area. The German Naval Staff, whose radio monitoring service intercepted and decoded the signals to the squadrons concerned, was at a loss to understand why they were being directed to search for an unnamed damaged 'battleship', as the German fleet had been recalled before it could bring any enemy battleships to action. Finally they assumed that the British must still be searching for the heavy cruiser the Germans had 'sunk' during the evening air attack on 4 July, and there the matter rested.* 42

Rear-Admiral Hamilton's cruiser force received the news that *Tirpitz* might have been damaged, and that *Victorious* might be operated against her, shortly before ten o'clock that night: Hamilton decided that *London* and *Norfolk* could be of most use

---

* Adolf Hitler was obviously informed of this. Discussing PQ.17 with Ribbentrop and a foreign diplomat (Ambassador Gerede) on 13 July, he reverted to the subject of the Russian claim to have sunk *Tirpitz.* 'A Russian lieutenant had apparently declared he had seen the ship sink with his own eyes. But as the *Tirpitz* was lying safe and sound in a Norwegian fiord, and he (the Führer) was even considering whether or not foreign journalists should be invited to visit her, either the lieutenant concerned must have lied, or the sinking concerned was of an English battleship; the latter possibility did exist, inasmuch as wireless messages had been intercepted in which the whereabouts of an English battleship were urgently inquired after.'—Protocol Nr. Füh. 24/42 written by Ambassador Schmidt, in German Foreign Office archives.

German Home Stations broadcasts at 7 p.m., 11 July, made similar comments. 'While the London authorities are busy counting the number of ships which reached port out of the thirty-eight that set out, it might be worth their while to check the number of Anglo-American escorts—heavy cruisers and battleships', as the only explanation of the Russian canard was that they had torpedoed a battleship of their allies.

to Tovey by topping up the remaining destroyers with fuel, and
he began by topping up *Somali* and *Fury* while the USS *Wainwright*
fuelled from *Norfolk*.[43] But no further use was made of them.*

Whether or not *Tirpitz* was at this time drifting crippled off
the Arctic coast of Norway, of one thing the Admiralty was
certain: three highly circumstantial and independent sightings
had been made of an enemy battle fleet, including at least two
battleships, steering north-eastwards on a bearing of 65° into the
Barents Sea, where they would probably begin picking off the
the merchant ships one by one in the early hours. What possible
cause could there be for breaking the operation off? With their
superior air reconnaissance the Germans would by now have
learned that Tovey's fleet and the cruiser squadron were running
westwards, hundreds of miles away, and that nothing heavier
than corvettes still remained with the scattering merchantmen.

At 2.30 a.m. signals were wirelessed to Admiral Bevan, the
Senior British Naval Officer in north Russia, to Admiral Miles in
Moscow and to Captain G. O. Maund, the SBNO at Archangel,
warning them that it was possible that a German surface attack
would develop on the defenceless merchant ships, and asking
them to arrange for a search for survivors by all available means,
including any Catalina aircraft in north Russia not required for
searching for and shadowing the enemy units.[44]

At the same time, the British Admiralty despatched what was,
one assumes, the most desperate signal of the war to the vessels
of PQ.17's one-time escort force, still obviously believed by the
Admiralty to be screening some of the scattering merchantmen:

MOST IMMEDIATE. Attack by enemy surface forces is probable in
next few hours. Your primary duty is to avoid destruction to enable
you to return to scene of attack to pick up survivors after enemy
have retired.[45]

Fifteen minutes later, they made one last attempt to stave off
the apparently imminent disaster: at 2.45 a.m., they signalled

* Captain Bellars (*Norfolk*) wrote to Hamilton, 8 July: 'I must say
that I was surprised that *Wainwright* had to be fuelled twice. We are
thinking of cutting off the '*k*' from our name and calling ourselves
Norfol'—a typical fleet auxiliary oiler's name.

Admiral Tovey urging him to reconsider the proposal that he should steer eastwards, in order to *threaten* the Germans with being cut off if nothing more, if the weather conditions were such that his fleet was likely to be sighted by enemy aircraft. Admiral Tovey was reluctant to comply: the weather was still overcast and visibility was low. Even so, at 6.45 a.m. he did alter the Home Fleet's course to north-eastward, and he ordered Hamilton's force to join. At 7.45 a.m., a lone enemy aircraft droned high overhead, obscured from view by the layers of cloud. Tovey tried to attract the enemy's attention by gunfire and by scrambling fighters, so that the German's curiosity would be aroused and he would report the Home Fleet's eastward course to his superiors. The aircraft passed on unawares.

By 10 a.m. Hamilton's force was in sight of the battle fleet fifteen miles off Jan Mayen Island, and at 10.40 Hamilton took station on Tovey's flag, with a wet wind blowing. After four hours of this unrewarding cruising to the north-east, with the weather still unfavourable for the enemy's air reconnaissance, Admiral Tovey reversed the Home Fleet's course again. The Allied battle fleet, like the German one, headed for home.[46]

Not all the Royal Navy's escort vessels had the codebooks necessary to decipher the Admiralty's signal recommending them to 'avoid destruction'.[47] They pursued their separate ways in blessed ignorance.

Not so the anti-aircraft ships: to the officers and men of the *Pozarica* and the two corvettes escorting her, it seemed certain that the end could not be far for them. They were still over two hundred miles from the safety of Matochkin Strait, but they could go no faster. After the Admiralty's earlier signal, announcing that the most likely time of German surface attack on them was during the coming night or early morning, had burst like a bombshell on *Pozarica*'s bridge, Captain Lawford called a grim conference in his charthouse. All agreed that it was now out of the question to try to reach Archangel direct. Their only hope of survival was to make for the nearest point of land and perhaps even go ashore with the remaining stores, with the intention of making their way south on foot, 'real Shackleton stuff'. Lawford returned to his bridge, and called the two corvettes alongside in turn and repeated the signal to them aloud through the loud-hailer. He told them the course he was proposing to steer, and that the speed would be fourteen knots, the flotilla's maximum. Finally, Lawford cleared Lower Deck and explained that all three ships would form up in line ahead, in order to give the impression of a larger force if sighted in silhouette through the mists by the enemy.

Pozarica signalled the corvette *La Malouine*:

> The enemy is expected to attack early tomorrow, 6 July. When we come within range of their heavy ships we shall turn towards them and fire as long as we can. Suggest that those off watch get sleep and make their Peace. But with God's help we shall survive.[48]

In every man's mind, the paramount thought now was, when would the enemy be sighted? *La Malouine*'s officers knew that their one 4-inch gun would do little more than make noise and keep them occupied until the enemy fleet's salvoes sank them; they were not afraid, they were angry that they had been forsaken like this.

After the Admiralty's signal had been received, Lieutenant Caradus wrote one of the most moving passages of his private diary, in *La Malouine*: 'No. 1 and self think this signal the last straw. We will be slaughtered if we don't get through Matochkin [Strait]—sunk off Novaya Zemlya or sunk in the Barents Sea. *Pozarica* talks to Captain over loud-hailer and leaves us with little doubt that the end has come. Everyone is becoming silent. Petter is in the R/T room checking that every signal is picked up—anything that might give us a clue. Am weary and cold even with electric heater in cabin. Writing this up with four hours' sleep ahead.' Before he turned in, he saw the supply assistant sitting in the galley flat reading the New Testament; his action station was ammunition supply, the most thankless in the ship. 'Spoke to him for a few minutes. Told me he was ready to die if it was God's will. Lay on my bunk and prayed. Fell asleep, again hoping that whatever happened it happened while I was asleep.' The information at the Admiralty, he suspected, must be very 'vague'.[49]

The sun rose at 4 a.m.—not that there had been any night. The boatswain's mate called him to the watch again, tired and very frightened. '[Ship] still doing 150 revs. Made my way to bridge wondering what the latest signal reported—or if there was any news at all. On my way saw group of about 12 huddled round funnel with tin hats and life-jackets on—pathetic sight in our predicament.' The latest position of the German destroyers was only 160 miles away, and they still had over 180 miles to run to Matochkin Strait, twelve hours at their present speed.

Far behind them Lieutenant Hall's corvette *Lotus* was returning eastwards at speed from her rescue of the *Pankraft* survivors. A lookout reported 'tall pillars of smoke' coming from over the horizon, as though a ship was on fire. It was not far off the course they were steering, so Hall decided to investigate. As they approached, the smoke columns grew shorter until finally they vanished almost altogether—short, stubby puffs of thick brown smoke being emitted from the smoke pots which Commodore Dowding had set not far from his raft some hours before. If a weird Arctic mirage had not so magnified this tiny smoke signal, *River Afton*'s survivors would surely have perished within the next few hours. They were already in a pitiful condition. Commodore Dowding, a steward and a cabin boy had shared a Carley float for three hours since the loss of their ship, and the few survivors were distributed among rafts and the one small boat. As the corvette covered the last hundred yards, she seemed to be ploughing through a sea strewn with débris and bodies.[50]

As Captain Charlton's small jollyboat drew alongside, the seamen were almost too tired to reach for the scrambling-nets. Two in the bows made hardly any movement at all: one was the badly injured Second Engineer, his cap over one eye and unable to speak; the other was an officer looking after him. As the boat came alongside the corvette, witnesses in the corvette saw the officer try to speak to the engineer, and then begin taking things out of his pockets; he slipped a ring off the man's finger, and climbed aboard. The engineer was left alone in the boat. Lieutenant Hall shouted to know what the delay was about. The sombre British seaman asked if they could bring the body aboard to give him a decent burial at sea. Hall told them to leave the man in the boat, and cast off; he thought that if a submarine had sunk the *Afton*, it might well still be lurking nearby to torpedo any vessel rescuing the survivors. Of the fifty-nine officers and men who had sailed with *River Afton*, twenty-three—including all the gun-crew —were dead. Both Commodore Dowding's RN staff officers had perished, as the ship made her final plunge.* [35]

For PQ.17, 5 July had been a massacre. Around midnight, *U-703* wirelessed to Admiral Schmundt in Narvik: 'Pinpoint AC.3568. 5,479-ton *River Afton* sunk. Cargo, aircraft and tanks. Three torpedoes.' He had added that he still had 75 cubic metres of diesel fuel, so he was good for some time yet. At about the same time, *U-408* ran out of Narvik to join the attack, her tanks full and her crew eager for action. Commander Bielfeld's sinking of *River Afton* brought up to six the number of ships despatched by the U-boats of the 'Ice Devil' pack during the day. Schmundt particularly praised the improved co-operation between Air Force and submarines, apart of course from the regrettable Junkers 88 attack on *U-334*. [51]

By the morning of 6 July, reports reaching his office showed that surviving ships were widely scattered and well to the east of the 40° meridian. Soon after midnight, air reconnaissance had reported sighting two merchant ships and two apparent 'destroyers' heading almost due east for Novaya Zemlya, and probably for Matochkin Strait; they may well have been the anti-aircraft ship *Palomares* and such of the convoy's ships as had been able to keep up with her, in fact. Such a wide detour to the east seemed to confirm, in Schmundt's view, what *Carlton*'s Master had revealed to the Germans: the convoy's destination had been Archangel, 'in which case,' Schmundt commented, 'the submarines still have excellent prospects of successful operations.'

During the small hours, Naval Group North informed Schmundt that it had been their intention to direct the U-boats to follow the convoy's track within to about eighty miles of the Russian coast, and then to turn round and sweep back along the convoy's path as far as fuel would permit, killing such cripples and stragglers as they came across. Admiral Schmundt's office agreed that this was a good plan. Shortly before 6 a.m., the Air Force's midnight sighting report was passed on to the

---

* Three more of *River Afton*'s crew perished when the minesweeper *Leda* went down on the return convoy, QP.14.

submarines, and Schmundt ordered those with no contacts to sweep southwards between the 42° and 48° meridians, turning back upon reaching the latitude of 70° North. He ordered La Baume's *U-355* to transmit a meteorological-report flash, and added for the information of all of them: ' *"Concord"* has been dropped.'

✳ 4 ✳

Rear-Admiral Hamilton's cruiser force had taken station on his Commander-in-Chief's flag during the course of the morning.

At first he was ordered by Tovey to proceed with his force to Iceland, but some hours later he was directed to take *London* to Scapa Flow with the Home Fleet, leaving the rest of his force to proceed to Iceland without him.[43]

Before they finally parted company, Admiral Hamilton signalled to the three other cruisers his own explanation of what seemed to have gone wrong, as there was still no explanation from Whitehall. At one stage he had even toyed with the idea of addressing each of the ships' companies in person, so urgent did the morale position seem; but now he invited each Captain to make it quite clear that their force had been 'acting under orders of a higher authority' throughout—an authority with, it seemed, full knowledge of the facts and issues involved.

> Our retirement [he signalled] was made at high speed in order to avoid contact with a superior force once we had left the convoy. Contrary to expectations, the enemy has produced all his heavy ships supported by shore-based aircraft at a time and in an area where defence by our own heavy ships is out of the question owing to the lack of shore-based aircraft on our side.[52]

Captain Bellars replied from *Norfolk*, 'I hope we will have better luck next time.'[53] The American Captain Hill (*Wichita*) signalled, 'It was a pleasure and a privilege to have been under your command.'[54] To Bellars Hamilton replied, 'I am sorry we are not going to meet and talk things over. Now I have got things in perspective I am thoroughly happy about the prospects of PQ.18.'[55] And to the American warships he signalled, 'I am sorry we were not allowed to have a battle. Perhaps PQ.18 will give us a better run for our money. So far the convoy appears to have incurred few losses.'[56]

THE NEW LAND
6 July – 14 July

My ship and cargo are now in a harbour of the Soviet Union—Captain
W. Lovgren, Master of the US freighter *Winston-Salem*, after
running her aground and abandoning her in a bay on an Arctic
island

N OVAYA ZEMLYA—'the new land'—is a pair of Arctic
islands six hundred miles long, divided by a narrow,
fissured channel called Proliv Matochkin Shar about four
hundred miles from its northern end. The islands form the eastern
boundary of the Barents Sea.

For the greater part of its length, 'Matochkin Strait' runs between
high and rugged mountains, and in places the ships' fairway is
narrowed to only seven hundred yards by banks of alluvial sand
on either side. Along all its fifty mile length there were in 1942
only three sparsely inhabited settlements; Lagerni settlement in
the west and the Polar Geophysical Laboratory and Matshar radio
station at the north-eastern end.[1] It was for this inhospitable
passage through from the hostile Barents Sea into the Kara Sea
that most of the escort vessels and merchant ships had independently set course after the scattering of Convoy PQ.17. It seemed
unlikely that the German battle fleet, or even its destroyers, would
be able to follow them through the strait into the Kara Sea.

The first ships to sight the massive and forbidding islands on
6 July were the Royal Navy's escort vessels screening the anti-
aircraft ship *Palomares*, including the minesweepers *Britomart*,
Halcyon and *Salamander* and the rescue ship *Zamalek*, with 153
survivors now crowding her decks. One merchant ship, *Ocean
Freedom*, had managed to keep up with them. At 11 a.m. they
sighted land—a sight which many of the seamen had thought they
would never see again. On Captain Jauncey's orders *Britomart*,
who knew these waters well, sailed far ahead carrying out an anti-
submarine sweep as the little convoy passed the difficult entrance
into Matochkin Strait. Her captain later reported:

Britomart was not challenged on passing Stolbovoi point, so I proceeded at seven knots. When off Lagerni settlement, I stopped to allow a small motor-boat with a Russian naval officer to come alongside. The boat, with a crew of one seaman, was armed with a machine-gun which the officer directed against the ship. He did not speak English, but I made him understand that we were not an invasion fleet, and that we required anchorage. The officer then left for the shore, and I proceeded to report situation to *Palomares*.[2]

By half-past two the remaining ships of *Palomares*'s group had followed the minesweeper in, and were at anchor off Lagerni settlement in five fathoms of water. Two hours later, Jauncey called a conference aboard his anti-aircraft ship, and discussed whether they should attempt to break out into the Kara Sea, or wait a while where they were and take the shorter west coast route into the White Sea and Archangel. *Britomart*'s Lieutenant Stammwitz interjected that from his own experience the strait would be blocked by ice at the other end, where conditions were always very different from those at the western entrance where they now were. On Jauncey's instructions, the Walrus seaplane which they had picked up two days before was readied for a short reconnaissance flight up the strait, and took off; it returned soon after with news that there was indeed no passage, as the strait was blocked by ice.[3]

The other anti-aircraft ship, *Pozarica,* had continued to make for Matochkin Strait all night long. She and her flotilla had been making their best speed for thirty-six hours. When they were still some way from the entrance to the Strait, at 1 p.m., she stopped and detailed the two corvettes *La Malouine* and *Poppy* to circle round her giving anti-submarine protection. 'Tension built up quickly with the ship's company over the delay,' recorded Lieutenant Caradus of *La Malouine*, who understood that the halt was due to trouble with *Pozarica*'s engines. Nobody knew where the German battlefleet's destroyers were now. The corvettes' radios had ceased to function at this distance, and *Pozarica*'s was receiving only a few isolated signals.

At 2 p.m. land was finally sighted. The British seamen could clearly see the glaciers, the snowcaps and the many bays. 'Very barren and uninviting, but almost with "Welcome" written along it.' Three hours later, they sighted Cape Stolbovoi with its little red buildings and made out the well-concealed entrance to the strait. At 6 p.m. they were entering the strait itself with engine-room telegraphs at Slow Ahead, thankful for the leading-marks and other navigational aids provided by the Russians. They pre-pared to anchor in Pomorskaya Bay on the right-hand side of the entrance to the strait, but no sooner had the order to let go the anchor been given than they saw *Palomares* and her escorts anchored in the opposite bay near Lagerni settlement.[4]

A fatuous exchange of signals followed between the two sister-ships:

Palomares: 'Welcome to *our* base.'
Pozarica: 'May we anchor in your back garden?'
Palomares: 'Certainly. Anchor on my port bow where our guns can command the entrance.'[5]

As the newcomers re-anchored opposite the settlement, they could see bare wooden buildings ashore, a number of men, women and children, and several large dogs. Ships' telescopes were handed round, but there was little else to see. The one desire was for sleep, after so many alarums and excursions. But at 7 p.m. the corvette *La Malouine* was ordered by one of the anti-aircraft ships to weigh anchor and proceed out into the Barents Sea to pick up any of the convoy's merchant ships that could be found and lead them into the strait. It was obviously now felt that the escort force which was gathering in the strait should try to assemble the merchant-men and reform convoy for the rest of the passage to Archangel.

Far out to sea, the convoy's fastest merchantman, *Hoosier*, was heading due south towards the White Sea entrance, when she sighted an American Liberty ship at 5.30 p.m.—*Samuel Chase*—heading east at full speed. Her lifeboats had been swung out and lowered almost to the sea. Thinking that the *Chase* was in distress, *Hoosier* signalled to inquire if she needed assistance. The other replied that she did not, but that a German task force of sub-marines, destroyers and possibly a heavy cruiser was in the vici-nity. As *Hoosier* drew closer, she learned that the other ship was heading east towards Matochkin Strait, and she decided to alter course for the strait as well.⁶ The Panamanian freighter *El Capitán* had also planned to lie low in Matochkin Strait until the hue and cry had died down; and *Benjamin Harrison*, who had originally been making for Moller Bay, had also changed course for the strait, and soon afterwards caught sight of the other three merchant ships heading for the concealed entrance.⁷

La Malouine rounded the four ships up and formed them with difficulty into a single line. There was a full gale blowing outside the strait, and the corvette's captain had great difficulty giving each ship instructions over the loud-hailer: 'The crews were greatly excited,' wrote Caradus. Each greeted the tiny corvette with a terrific cheer as she drew alongside.

By ten o'clock that night, the four ships were safely at anchor in the strait. One of *Samuel Chase*'s crew had gone insane during the previous two days. He was transferred to a rescue ship for medical supervision.⁸ In the hours that followed, the ancient 11-knot trawlers *Lord Austin*, *Lord Middleton* and *Northern Gem* also plodded into the strait, making much smoke as they did so.⁹ The worst ordeal of the Royal Navy was over. Here in Matochkin Strait they were relatively safe from surface attack. All the warships were anchored in positions from which their 4-inch armament could be brought to bear on the entrance to the strait.

In the escort vessels, the gun crews gained their first sleep for several days and nights, and the talk reverted to the events of 5 and 6 July and the Admiralty's signal about their 'duty' to avoid destruction: 'Seamen, stokers and petty officers all agreed that during the night of 6th July they had been "shot to pieces" several times over. There had been fear. The minutes passed like days— they weren't hungry or thirsty, but Cook said gallons of tea were drunk nevertheless.' Then there was that air attack two days before—150 aircraft attacking over a three-hour period: 'Our Pom-Pom gun aft had been continually jamming and only 150 rounds had been fired. The Oerlikon guns were effective, but the Pom-Pom could well have been replaced by more Oerlikons. During one lull the Supply Officer read aloud from the New Testament to three other ratings. The RDF [radar] worked perfectly; the Asdic was used little and was upset by the closeness of the destroyers from time to time.' And then, in the midst of the reminiscences, a nagging question-mark: 'We will want to know why the ships were scattered.' Lieutenant Caradus concluded his diary for 6 July by asking whether the corvettes could have done more: 'Perhaps we will hear the full story from SBNO Archangel —if we get there.'⁴

As the day drew to a close, the corvette *Lotus* came slowly in, looking like a Margate pleasure-steamer with three-score survivors crowding her rails; she got a terrific reception. *River Afton*'s survivors were transferred to one of the anti-aircraft ships, and *Pankraft*'s were put aboard one of the American merchantmen. Commodore Dowding elected to stay in *Lotus*. From midnight onwards, corvettes patrolled the entrance to the strait with Asdic, watching for the possible infiltration of a German submarine. There was no sign of the trawler *Ayrshire*, for whom *La Malouine* and other ships had formed 'quite a liking'. So there were altogether seventeen ships sheltering in Matochkin Strait now; unfortunately, only five of them were merchantmen.

Where were the other merchant ships? At least seven of them were in the northern waters of the Barents Sea, skirting the icefield and heading at their maximum speeds for the coast of Novaya Zemlya. At their head was the American Liberty ship *John Witherspoon,* laden with tanks and ammunition; behind her, in a disorderly procession strung out over 150 miles, were *Alcoa Ranger*, the catapult-aircraft merchantman *Empire Tide, Bellingham, Hartlebury, Olopana* and *Winston-Salem*.

At 10.45 a.m. *Olopana*'s crew spotted a Focke-Wulf aircraft approaching, a huge four-engined bomber. As they manned their gun, fire and boat-stations, all now expected that the end had come: Captain Stone ordered an 'air attack' signal to be broadcast with his ship's position, so sure was he that this was the end. He also jettisoned all the secret codebooks in a weighted bag and told the wireless operator to add this fact to the signal. The aircraft did not, however, attack. After circling the ship several times, it made off. 'We decided he had radioed in for attack planes', said Stone afterwards, 'and gave ourselves three or four hours respite.'¹⁰ All day long, his lookouts remained posted, and the gun crews stayed at action stations, but no attack materialized.

The *I./KG.40* Focke-Wulf reconnaissance bomber returned to its base at Trondheim, and by 11.30 a.m. its radioed sighting report was already lying on the desk of the German Admiral Commanding, Arctic, at Narvik—Admiral Schmundt. The Focke-Wulf had reported sighting seven ships altogether 'probably PQ.17's fast spearhead', all apparently hugging the ice and heading for Novaya Zemlya. Shortly afterwards, the German radio monitoring service confirmed the position of ships there, no doubt in consequence of *Olopana*'s distress signal.[11] Admiral Schmundt ordered all those submarines well up in fuel to be prepared to operate against these seven ships; they were each to transmit a flash signal (*Kurzsignal*) giving their positions to enable him to mount the attack.

During the early hours of 6 July, far to the west of Matochkin Strait, a very generous Fate had led the Soviet tanker *Donbass* to the very spot where the late *Daniel Morgan*'s three lifeboats were drifting. Captain Pavlov invited the American seamen aboard. Although physically exhausted from seventy-two hours' continuous action stations and a night in open lifeboats as well, the American gunners volunteered to man the tanker's forward 3-inch gun, and the seamen stood extra lookout watches. The tanker resumed her southerly course heading straight for the White Sea. Soon afterwards, Pavlov had cause to be grateful to the Americans: a single Junkers 88 delivered two dive-bombing attacks on the tanker; on the second dive, the American gun crew put a shell so close to the diving aircraft that it turned away and made off, one engine sputtering, and losing height.[12]

In the meantime, the 7,180-ton *John Witherspoon* had run out of the fogbank in which she had been sheltering for the previous ten hours, at about 5.30 a.m. Like the *Morgan*, she had been one of the freighters who had vainly tried to keep up with the anti-aircraft ship *Palomares* and her anti-submarine escort on the previous day until they had altered course and broken away from her. As the *Witherspoon* emerged from the fogbank, she caught sight of a German U-boat on a parallel course on the horizon. The submarine dived, leaving the Americans in no doubt of its intentions. A running fight ensued, in which the American freighter's 4-inch surface gun fired nineteen rounds at the periscope wake closing in on them. Gradually the U-boat was brought astern of the freighter, and she fell back. The gun ceased firing.

By 12.30 p.m. *John Witherspoon* believed herself to be twenty miles off Novaya Zemlya, and her Master, Captain Clark, decided to make a dash straight for the entrance to the White Sea. He brought the ship round on to an almost southerly course.[13] The weather was now bright and clear, with only a slight swell.

At 4.40 p.m., *U-255* (Lieutenant-Commander Reinhard Reche) fired a spread of four torpedoes at her, and his thirty-hour chase after this obstinate freighter was over. From eight hundred yards away, he saw a 200-foot pillar of smoke mushroom out of the ship. The ship lost way and veered to starboard. She began to blow off steam, but showed no signs of settling.[14] Reche prepared to fire a fifth torpedo from his stern tube.

Later the ship's Second Engineer wrote:

6th July: Captain decided to head for White Sea and try to run for it. At 4.40 p.m., while I was on watch, submarine fired torpedo into holds number 2 and 3, and a second torpedo into holds number 4 and 5. Orders to abandon ship. Secured engine and crew sent up on deck. When I arrived on deck, all boats that were usable [were] away except the chief officer's. Jumped into his boat and made off from vessel. Submarine came up and put another torpedo in ship which broke in half and sank.

Commander Reche had watched the ship's death-throes from some way off. One of his officers filmed the lifeboats with a ciné-camera while another kept a machine-gun trained on their occupants. Reche saw the fore- and after-mast incline slightly to each other and knew the ship's back was broken. *John Witherspoon* sank like a stone soon after. Reche took *U-255* alongside the lifeboats, looking for the Captain. His officers gave the American seamen cigarettes, water and cognac, and told them which way to steer to avoid a pack of ice lying in their path to the White Sea. 'We lost one man, a sailor—Otis Lydinge—who was drowned,' wrote the Second Engineer in his diary. 'We pulled him out of the water, looked at him, seen he was dead and let him go back in. Ships had been going down all around us, and the wireless operator told me that some guys would get off the air to let the others who were sinking faster send out SOS's.'[15]

Commander Reche did not broadcast a victory signal to Narvik: his very purpose in firing four torpedoes at the American ship had been to prevent her from getting off a distress signal, and in this he had been successful. He wanted nothing to betray where he was lurking now.

What was greeted at higher levels as 'close co-operation' between aircraft and submarines had its bitter moments for the submarine commanders. At 12 knots, the 5,411-ton American *Pan Atlantic* had been heading steadily southwards for the entrance to the White Sea.

Her Master, Captain J. O. Sieber, had had seven lookouts posted, each furnished with binoculars; she was keeping wireless silence, and no other vessel was in sight. Her chances of reaching Russia had seemed good, but below the surface of the sea at least two submarines were already manœuvring into attacking positions, each unaware of the other's presence. The ship was laden with tanks, steel, nickel, aluminium, foodstuffs, two oil stills and —for some reason which people knowing the Soviet Union's capacity for explosives' manufacture will find hard to understand— a considerable quantity of cordite. One of the submarines was Commander Bohmann's *U-88*, which had sunk two of the convoy's ships on the previous day. Early that morning he had sighted smoke clouds on the horizon a hundred miles off Matochkin Strait, and on investigating he had found a lone merchantman beneath them steadily ploughing southwards. He had persisted in his chase throughout the morning and afternoon, often plunging through banks of fog, covering a hundred miles in the southwards chase. Now, at 6 p.m., he was manœuvring into position for his attack.[16]

At 6.10 p.m., however, a single Junkers 88 dive-bombed *Pan Atlantic*; two bombs struck the hold containing the cordite, and the ship's bows were blown off, bringing the foremast down on her pilot house. No distress signals could be sent out, so sudden was the attack, and within three brief minutes the furious U-boat commander had seen his prize slip beneath the waves, taking twenty-six of her crew with her and casting the rest into the sea.[17] A second angry U-boat commander watched the same spectacle from not far away—Commander Bielfeld, fresh from sinking

River Afton. His *U-703* had also been hunting the freighter all morning and afternoon; during the morning he had fired two torpedoes at her, having estimated the target's speed with the greatest possible precision. Both had missed. At 6.45 p.m. he surfaced and wirelessed to Narvik that his victim had now been 'sunk by an aircraft'. He had only one torpedo left, and 68 cubic metres of diesel oil.[18] Bielfeld's report meant that of the original ten submarines available to him, Schmundt would soon have only six fully operational. But three more, their torpedo-racks full and their fuel tanks brimming, would shortly be joining the attack— *U-251, U-376* and *U-408*.

They would have little chance of finding the enemy except by patrolling a line south of the merchantmen's last reported positions. According to the latest air reconnaissance, there was an ice-barrier at the southern end of Novaya Zemlya, extending to the entrance to the White Sea; the ships would have to skirt round this to reach Archangel. Admiral Schmundt directed the three new submarines to take up adjacent patrols at the western end of this ice-barrier, ready to catch these last few ships just as they believed that they were safe. The existing submarines he allowed to continue their freelance activities a little longer.[19]

In the Fifth Air Force's view, there were now ten to twelve ships at most surviving from convoy PQ.17; some of these were heading north-eastwards, while others were heading south-east and due south. 'Armed reconnaissance' was continuing.[20] The first squadron of *KG.26*—the unit that had launched the intrepid low-level torpedo attack on the convoy on 4 July—attempted to mount a second large-scale operation against all the surviving freighters during the afternoon, and in particular against a small group of four vessels sighted off the north-west coast of Novaya Zemlya; but the weather deteriorated and no ships were found at all.

Late on the evening of 6 July, Naval Group North telephoned Admiral Schmundt's office with a report that an aircraft had sighted the British tanker damaged the previous day, drifting and abandoned in the northern reaches of the Barents Sea. Its cargo of oil would be of the highest value to the Reich. Group North suggested that she should be taken in tow by a submarine. Schmundt must have choked to hear his superiors suggesting such an

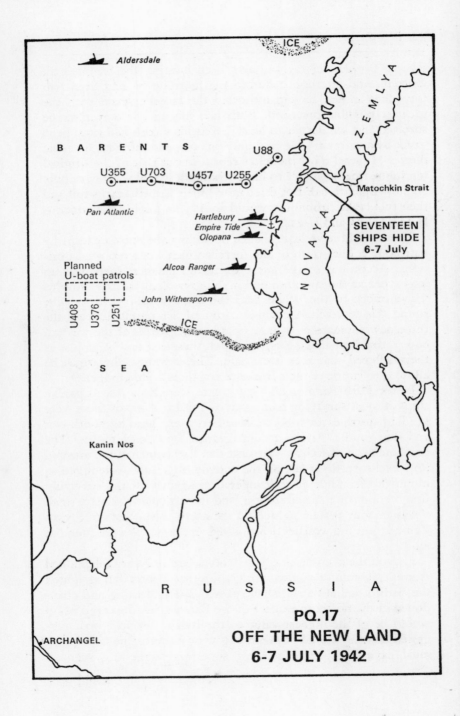

ICE

Aldersdale

B A R E N T S

Z E M L Y A

U88

U355   U703   U457   U255

Matochkin Strait

Pan Atlantic

Hartlebury
Empire Tide
Olopana

SEVENTEEN
SHIPS HIDE
6-7 July

N O V A Y A

Alcoa Ranger

Planned
U-boat patrols

U408 U376 U251

John Witherspoon

ICE

S E A

Kanin Nos

R U S S I A

ARCHANGEL

**PQ.17
OFF THE NEW LAND
6-7 JULY 1942**

operation. The tanker (*Aldersdale*) was very far from the closest submarine, and in any case the suggestion was 'technically not feasible'. Kiel insisted that the tanker must be dealt with one way or another.

At 11.40 p.m. Admiral Schmundt wirelessed his submarines:

1. Reche [*U-255*], Bohmann [*U-88*] and La Baume [*U-355*]— report position;
2. La Baume—search for tanker reported drifting at pinpoint [AC]3571 by Air Force at 8.30 a.m.[19] *

An hour later, Schmundt received word from Commander Reche that at 11 p.m. he had not been far off the southern island of Novaya Zemlya, but several hundred miles from the crippled *Aldersdale*. At the same time a belated signal reached Schmundt from the young submarine commander Günther La Baume of *U-355* reporting that he, Bohmann (*U-88*) and Bielfeld (*U-703*) were waiting not far west of Reche's *U-255*, with the intention of operating jointly against any groups of ships or stragglers that might now run across their sights. The weather was favourable, he added, although fogbanks were hampering them from time to time.

The German High Command now believed that there were no more than about seven ships remaining from the convoy. On the evening of 6 July, the German Naval Staff recorded,

This is the biggest success ever achieved against the enemy with one blow—a blow executed with exemplary collaboration between air force and submarine units. A heavy laden convoy of ships, some of which have been under way for several months from America, has been virtually wiped out despite the most powerful escort, just before reaching its destination.

A wicked blow has been struck at Russian war production, and a deep breach torn in the enemy's shipping capacity. The effect of this battle is not unlike a battle lost by the enemy in its military, material and morale aspects. In a three-day operation, fought under the most favourable conditions, the submarines and air force have achieved what had been the intention of the operation 'The Knight's Move', the attack of our surface units on the convoy's merchant ships.[21]

---

* Brandenburg had reported his position earlier that evening.

As 6 July drew to a close, Schmundt had heard nothing that might lead him to suspect that seventeen ships were now sheltering in Matochkin Strait; all attention was concentrated on those that were still at sea. If the German victory claims so far were accurate, how could there possibly be more ships elsewhere?

By the early hours of 7 July, the mood among the lone merchant ships, still struggling towards Novaya Zemlya, was distinctly ugly. As Captain Stone, Master of *Olopana*, recorded, some members of his crew had been without sleep for three or four days, and in the engine-room 'certain unlicensed personnel were particularly upset'. His ship, laden with explosives, phosphorus, lorries and high-octane petrol,* had been heading along the ice-barrier for three bays shown on his charts behind Cape Speedwell, where his men could get some rest; but now that they had been sighted by a Focke-Wulf reconnaissance aircraft they would have to abandon that idea. When they reached the bays, they found them blocked by ground ice, and the uninhabited, mountainous country bordering them was the most inhospitable and forbidding the seamen had even seen: no place for castaways, but still less a venue for a ship without any chart of these waters. The only sailing directions his ship possessed advised all ships to keep five to eight miles off the coast of Novaya Zemlya, as it had not been properly surveyed.

With the last prospect of sleep now gone, the trouble among the seamen in *Olopana* grew. Captain Stone summoned them to his mess room, and 'suggested' to them that their position was rather more healthy than that of the hundred or so seamen they had left drifting in the open sea in lifeboats thirty-six hours before, three hundred miles out to sea. 'I was assured they were feeling better about the situation,' Stone wrote.

During the morning, he discussed with his Chief Officer the pros and cons of heading for Moller Bay, on the south-western coast of Novaya Zemlya, and seeking refuge there for several days. According to the sailing directions, there was a small inhabited

---

* Again it is a matter of some surprise that explosives and petrol were being shipped over such a dangerous route to the Soviet Union, one of the world's largest producers of both commodities, when that country needed heavy armaments and aircraft to a far greater degree.

[214]

settlement there, with a ship calling once every September. Captain Stone unsealed his secret orders: they listed certain rendezvous positions in the Barents Sea, through which the convoy would normally have passed; ships were also warned against 'cutting corners'.* Stone could only read this as a warning that large tracts of the sea were mined; would not Moller Bay have been mined by the Russians too?

On the other hand, during July in these parts, on average nineteen days were fogbound. Stone was inclined to accept the risk of the open sea, and the refuge offered by fog, rather than chance the uncertainties of an uncharted bay. He would head due south down the coast, keeping the recommended ten miles out to sea; then he would make a dash for the White Sea. 'The unknown factors,' he commented, 'were that two vessels had been torpedoed south of us that day.' One had been heard to broadcast that she had been hit by three torpedoes—most probably *John Witherspoon*. The other had radioed only that she had transmitted a distress signal, but the signal itself had not been received. Their unknown attacker was the risk that Captain Stone was taking, as he quelled the incipient mutiny below his decks and told his men he was heading straight for the White Sea.[10]

The increase in the number of sightings of merchant ships heading towards Novaya Zemlya raised in Admiral Schmundt's mind the possibility that they might be planning to break through Matochkin Strait into the Kara Sea; he thought it more likely however that they would scuttle southwards along the western coast of the massive islands, as far as the White Sea. He proposed to stake his operational submarines on this belief. When Bohmann in *U-88* reported during the morning that he intended to search for a ship sighted by the Air Force just to the north-west of the entrance to Matochkin Strait, and then move somewhat closer inshore, Schmundt did not interfere. In this way Bohmann would be well placed to trap any vessels planning to break out through Matochkin Strait, as well as those just creeping down the coast.

---

* Cf. the secret instructions for a 'Straggler's Route' issued by Commander A. C. Roberts, RN, Naval Control Service Officer, Iceland: 'It is imperative that you should adhere strictly to the route and make no attempt to cut corners.'

By 12.30, indeed, it seemed to him that freelance operations promised little further success: he wirelessed to La Baume and Bielfeld that after the former had finished off the crippled *Aldersdale* and the latter had dealt with a freighter whose incautious wireless manners had enabled the German monitoring service to position her with great accuracy, they and three other submarine commanders—Brandenburg, Reche and Bohmann—were to establish an east-west patrol line, each U-boat patrolling a beat (*Schlag*) of forty miles, with the line extending right in to the *northern* side of the entrance to Matochkin Strait.[22] What he did not realize was that by the time he issued this order, the strait itself was already full of fast vessels which had reached it the previous day, and only a very few were still plodding down from the north.

As Commander Reche's *U-255* was heading northwards up the coast of Novaya Zemlya early that morning to take up station, he sighted two ships headed towards him, about forty miles from the place where he had torpedoed *John Witherspoon* the day before. He rapidly brought his U-boat into firing position, and emptied tubes II and IV at the second of the two ships, the American freighter *Bellingham*; the first had already passed out of his field of fire. One of the torpedoes hit the ship, punching a hole in her starboard side; but the torpedo's warhead failed to explode, and *Bellingham* escaped before Commander Reche's eyes.*

Almost at once, Reche then sighted another lone freighter, *Alcoa Ranger*, steadily approaching over the northern horizon at 13 knots and making no attempt at zigzagging. Ninety minutes later, a single torpedo from Reche had torn a large hole in the ship's No. 2 hold, and the ship 'settled forward slightly, then lost way blowing off steam'. The ship's crew abandoned ship during which operation 'the Master used very poor judgment and no leadership', according to the Armed Guard Report. Reche was now down to his last three torpedoes, and he could not afford to

---

* According to *Bellingham*'s officers, the torpedo's detonator exploded but not its booster charge. It punched a dent in the bulkhead 'the size of a tin hat' only four inches from one of the ship's ribs, about fourteen feet below the water line. The jolt was sufficient to throw several members of the crew off their feet and smash the ship's crockery. Had it not hit near the support, the torpedo would probably have gone right through.[23]

use one on the *coup de grâce*.[14] The U-boat surfaced and fired six
rounds from its gun into *Alcoa Ranger* from a short distance
away.

> Then the submarine came alongside the Master's lifeboat and [its
> officers] asked in broken English the name of the ship, destination
> and cargo [which he noted as 'aircraft'], gave land direction and
> took pictures; inquired as to whether the lifeboats had sufficient
> provisions, and disappeared on the surface in a southerly direction.[24]

The ship sank four hours later. Far away to the north, the
British merchant ship *Empire Tide* had emerged from the fog just
in time to see the American ship hit even as the British officers
surveyed her through binoculars. Not far from the torpedoed
ship, they saw no fewer than three German submarines sitting on
the surface, one of which detached itself from the rest and began
heading at speed towards them. *Empire Tide*'s Master, Captain
Harvey, needed no prompting. He immediately rang telegraphs
for 'all possible speed', hauled the vessel round tightly to the
north-west and retreated up the coast. Only when he was satisfied
that he had shaken off his pursuer did he turn away from his
headlong flight, nosing into Moller Bay (also known as Mali
Karmakulski). It was not mined, as *Olopana* had feared, and here
Captain Harvey hid his bulky merchant ship behind an island,
resolving to lie low there until the British naval authorities could
send sufficient escort forces to ensure his ship's safe passage to
Archangel.[25]

✳ 2 ✳

The first of the convoy's ships to reach north Russia was not
a merchant ship but one of the Royal Navy's escort vessels—the
corvette *Dianella*.[26] She had berthed at Archangel early on 7 July.
Her commanding officer, Lieutenant Rankin, was immediately
summoned by Naval launch to Norway House, to explain to
Captain G. O. Maund what had happened to PQ.17. Maund was
Senior British Naval Officer, Archangel.

All that Maund had so far received were the signals of many
merchant vessels in distress, and a series of garbled messages from
the Admiralty, among the latest of which was that from the First

Sea Lord requesting Maund and Admiral Bevan—the SBNO North Russia—to arrange for a search for any survivors by all possible means. Lieutenant Rankin saw a sheaf of Naval messages on Maund's desk. The latter explained to him that the situation appeared to be that there were up to ten ships out in the eastern Barents Sea, and probably twice that number below it. Somehow, he had to organize the rescue of survivors as best he could. He had appealed to Captain J. H. F. Crombie, RN, to despatch his First Minesweeping Flotilla to round up as many survivors as possible and escort the remaining ships to port; this task Crombie had sternly refused to undertake, explaining that his flotilla was at north Russia for minesweeping duties. Crombie's seniority was actually greater than Maund's, so there the matter had to rest.

Maund urged Lieutenant Rankin to turn his corvette round and conduct a lone, and extremely hazardous, search for lifeboats. Rankin agreed to take his ship out as soon as a minor radio fault had been repaired and she had been refuelled.

Over in Polyarnoe, the SBNO North Russia, had only one elderly fishing trawler allocated to his command. She was skippered by a Captain Drake, RNVR, of Plymouth. Bevan asked the Russians to send out vessels to pick up the Allied seamen, but they replied—probably truthfully—that they had no ships available for this task. Captain Drake volunteered to take his unarmed trawler out alone. Bevan was able to give him only a rough idea where to find survivors; then that plucky officer sailed with one young doctor and a week's supply of provisions, to look for the lifeboats from the convoy's casualties.[27] At midnight the corvette *Dianella* also backed out of her berth at Archangel, having taken on 235 tons of fuel oil, enough for an eleven-day rescue voyage: two small naval craft, independently commissioned with the task of searching several hundred thousand square miles of sea.

Early on the afternoon of 7 July, a special announcement was broadcast on all German home service stations, preceded by the ritual fanfare and drums. The BBC's confidential monitoring report stated that 'exceptional prominence' had been given to the announcement, the German High Command's first communiqué on the convoy battle, issued from the Führer's headquarters.[28]

Special Announcement.

The High Command of the Armed Forces announces: since 2nd July 1942 a large-scale operation has been carried out against enemy convoy traffic bound for the Soviet Union, by air and naval units in the waters between North Cape and Spitzbergen, 300 miles off the northern Norwegian coast.

Bomber formations and German submarines attacked a large Anglo-American convoy in the Arctic Ocean and destroyed the major part of it.

The convoy consisted of 38 merchant vessels and was carrying a cargo of aeroplanes, tanks, ammunition and foodstuffs. It was bound for Archangel and was very strongly protected by heavy enemy naval units, destroyers and corvettes. In close collaboration between the Navy and the German Air Force, one heavy American cruiser and 19 merchantmen totalling 122,000 BRT were sunk by bombers, nine ships totalling 70,400 BRT by U-boats, making a total of 28 ships of 192,400 BRT.

The remainder of the completely dispersed convoy continues to be attacked. A large number of American sailors was rescued by rescue planes and taken prisoner.[29]

The German claim that a 'cruiser' had been sunk led to a hilarious exchange of signals between the three cruisers of Hamilton's force heading for Iceland. Later that day HMS *Norfolk*'s Captain Bellars signalled the two American heavy cruisers keeping perfect station close to him: 'German radio claims one heavy American cruiser sunk with convoy. Which of the two of you is it?' With easy naval humour, *Wichita*'s Captain Hill flashed back: 'Rank has its privileges, so it must have been the *Tuscaloosa*.' When Bellars countered that he was certain that the *Norfolk* hadn't been sunk, as he did not feel a bit like a ghost, Hill sceptically replied that his cruiser had been 'attending *Norfolk*'s wake all afternoon.'[30]

In Matochkin Strait, Tuesday 7 July had dawned fine, with the sky cloudy and the horizon clear. At 1 p.m. Commodore Dowding called a conference of the Masters of the five merchant ships and the escort vessels aboard the anti-aircraft ship *Palomares*, while the corvette *Lotus* maintained an anti-submarine guard on the entrance to the strait. Some of the Masters, headed by Captain John Thevik of *El Capitán*, advocated that the ships should all lie up in

Berliner Ausgabe

189. Ausg. / 55. Jahrg. / Einzelpreis 15 Pf. / Auswärts 20 Pf.

„Freiheit und Brot"

Berliner Ausgabe

Berlin, Mittwoch, 8. Juli 1942

VÖLKISCHER BEOBACHTER

Kampfblatt der nationalsozialistischen Bewegung Großdeutschlands

Der Vernichtungsschlag gegen den großen Geleitzug im Eismeer

Trotz stärkster Sicherung 192400 BRT.!

Verfolgung der Sowjets wird über Woronesch hinaus fortgesetzt

Berlin, 7. Juli.

Wie an anderer Stelle näher ausgeführt, ist mit der Einnahme von Woronesch durch die deutschen Truppen ein Schwerpunkt der feindlichen Wehrwirtschaft in deutsche Hand gefallen. Durch Gegenangriffe von Norden versuchte der Feind die vordringenden deutschen Kampfverbände aufzuhalten. Die Bolschewisten wurden jedoch unter schwersten Verlusten geschlagen und zurückgeworfen. Die bei diesem Kampf als vernichtet gemeldeten 61 feindlichen Panzer, unter denen sich 42 Panzerkampfwagen modernster Bauart befanden, unterstreichen die Bedeutung, die dem Besitz der Stadt von den Bolschewisten selbst zugeschrieben wird.

Die Angriffsoperationen der deutschen Truppen sind weiterhin in erfolgreichem Fortschreiten. Eine Angriffsgruppe setzte die Verfolgung der geschlagenen Bolschewisten fort. Der Feind leistete in dem Kampfraum nur unzusammenhängenden Widerstand in Anlehnung an Waldstücke oder sonstige günstige Geländeabschnitte. Eine andere deutsche Angriffsgruppe konnte wiederum einen feindlichen Kampfverband einschließen, die Ausbruchsversuche der abgeschnittenen Bolschewisten zurückschlagen und einen weiteren Brückenkopf über den Don bilden. Im Verlauf der Kämpfe hatten die Bolschewisten sehr hohe Verluste an Menschen und Material.

Bei den siegreichen Kämpfen, die zur Einnahme von Woronesch führten, griff die Luftwaffe durch Einsatz von Kampf-, Sturzkampf- und Zerstörerflugzeugen in die Erdkämpfe ein. Trotz teilweise schlechter Wetterlage wurden Panzerbereitstellungen und zäh verteidigte Ortschaften westlich von Woronesch ebenso wie der feindliche Nachschubverkehr wirksam mit Bomben angegriffen. Durch die Zerstörung mehrerer Donbrücken mit Bomben schweren Kalibers, sowie durch wirksame Tiefangriffe wurde der Nachschubverkehr des Feindes unterbrochen

Während der rollenden Angriffe der Kampf- und Sturzkampfflugzeuge, die auch das Stadtgebiet, die Rüstungswerke und die Bahnhofsanlagen von Woronesch immer wieder bombardierten, beherrschten deutsche Jäger den Luftraum über dem Kampfgebiet und vernichteten in Luftkämpfen über 100 bolschewistische Flugzeuge. Zahlreiche weitere feindliche Flugzeuge wurden durch Flakartillerie zum Absturz gebracht, die sich auch bei diesen Kämpfen an der Niederringung stark bestückter Bunker und Widerstandsnester des Feindes erneut bewährte.

ER will Europa regieren

Woronesch — Sewastopol — Eismeer

VB. Berlin, 7. Juli.

Der Mittag des 7. Juli hat zwei äußerst bedeutsame Sondermeldungen gebracht: Im Zuge der neuen deutschen Offensive an der Ostfront ist Woronesch, die große bolschewistische Industriestadt östlich des Don, gefallen und der Strom selbst, wie aus dem OKW.-Bericht hervorgeht, überschritten worden. Die im Raume von Kursk-Charkow eingesetzten deutschen Armeen und Luftstreitkräfte haben damit bewiesen, daß ihre Stoßkraft — entgegen den zuversichtlichen Prophezeiungen des Feindes — durch den harten Winterfeldzug nicht im geringsten geschwächt worden ist. Die außerordentlich schweren Verluste an Panzern und Flugzeugen, die die Bolschewisten in dieser Schlacht bereits erlitten haben, lenken die Aufmerksamkeit der Welt in verdoppeltem Maße auf die Vorgänge, die sich in den letzten Tagen im Nördlichen Eismeer abgespielt haben: Wieder ist ein großer anglo-amerikanischer Geleitzug, vollbeladen mit hochwertigen Kampfmitteln und nach Archangelsk bestimmt, von der Luftwaffe und unseren Unterseebooten zusammengeschlagen worden. Das bedeutet zunächst eine wertvollste Entlastung für die deutsche Ostfront, der die versenkte Riesenmenge von amerikanischen Waffen nun niemals entgegentreten wird — es bedeutet aber auch ein weiteres tiefes Loch in dem knappen Bestand an feindlichem Schiffsraum.

Noch niemals ist aus einem einzigen Geleitzug eine so große Tonnagemenge herausgeschossen worden!

Wir geben in folgendem den ersten genauen Bericht über die Fünf-Tage-Schlacht im Nördlichen Eismeer, der jedoch lediglich die Erfolge der Luftwaffe schildert; über die Taten der deutschen Unterseeboote, die allein 70000 BRT. auf den Grund schickten, liegt noch keine Schilderung vor. (Vergl. Bilder auf Seite 3!)

Das Ende von Sewastopol

Von unserem nach Sewastopol entsandten Sonderberichterstatter Kiekheben-Schmidt

.... 7. Juli 1942.

Niemand, der es erlebte, wird jemals das Schlachtfeld von Sewastopol vergessen können. In hoffnungsloser Totenstarre, in scheinbar endloser Gleichförmigkeit wölben die kahlen Kalksteinfelsen ihre plumpen Leiber in weiter Runde. Die Augen schmerzen im Anblick der grauen, weißen und gelblich-braunen Gesteinsmassen, über denen erbarmungslos die heiße Sonne südeuropäischer Breiten brütet. Das spärliche Gras der steinigen und staubigen Erde ist versengt, und nur in den tieferen Tälern zwischen den Hügeln wuchert in dichten Massen mannshohes hartes Gestrüpp, das sich hangaufwärts in magerem Buschwerk zwischen dem Geröll verliert. Das einzig belebende Element in dieser flimmernden Hitze und steppenhaften Dürre sind die blauen Buchten des Schwarzen Meeres, das sich am fernen Horizont in den Himmel verliert, zu Füßen der baumlosen niedrigen Küstengebirge jedoch tief ins Land hineingreift.

Um diese leuchtenden Wasser entbrannte der Kampf, denn an den Rändern der Meeresarme liegt Sewastopol, der große, von der Natur ausgezeichnete Kriegshafen der Sowjetunion, der den Seewege zur Ukraine und zum Kaukasus umsäumt

Völkischer Beobachter's front page, 8 July 1942

the strait until the hue and cry had died down, and then sneak down to Archangel. The high cliffs on either side would afford some protection from dive-bombing. The warships' officers, and particularly the two anti-aircraft ships' captains, had other views: firstly, it was understood that a force of German destroyers was out hunting for them; once one German aircraft had spotted the seventeen ships in the strait, the enemy could mine the entrance or block it with submarines, and then indulge in an orgy of high-level bombing. While the sea outside the strait was invariably foggy, the strait itself seemed to enjoy unusually fine, clear weather. Captain Thevik suggested that the Germans would think twice before attacking such a hornet's nest, but he was voted down.

The other ships' captains argued that the last signals that had been received from London could only mean that German surface ships were out searching for them; and the escort vessels' captains agreed that the two AA ships should be able to create a sufficient diversion. Commodore Dowding had in the meantime radioed to Archangel a request that they be given fighter escort for the latter part of their journey.

After Lieutenant Bidwell had returned from the conference, his corvette *La Malouine* steamed out to take up anti-submarine duties off Cherni Island. The sky was deceptively blue, but the air had a frosty clarity. In front of the assembled ship's company, the corvette's Irish First Lieutenant dived over the side clad only in bathing trunks, for a swim. He barely floundered back to the Jacob's ladder. He was carried aboard, purple with cold and speechless with shock. With the heaters working full blast to little effect in their cabins, the seamen switched on the radio and heard the BBC news report that Alexandria was still being held. Then they picked up the German bulletins, giving the latest news of PQ.17: 'German radio claimed 29 ships sunk out of 38—the remainder were being hunted.'[31]

The ships' anchors came up clean and free of mud from the bottom of the strait. Shortly after 7 p.m. on a perfect evening, the minesweeper *Britomart* nosed out of the strait and carried out a final anti-submarine sweep. Soon after, the little convoy—newly disciplined and with a new formation—put out to sea with the intention of heading due south for Cape Kanin Nos and the entrance to the White Sea. *Lotus*, with Dowding aboard, led the convoy, with *Halcyon* as Senior Officer, Escorts. A trawler was appointed 'rescue ship' as *Zamalek* now had 154 survivors on board. Several seamen took photographs of the strait as they left, in the fond belief that they would never see it again.

They had covered 1,600 miles in their dangerous voyage from Iceland; the toughest 900 miles were still to come.[32] It was only a remnant of PQ.17, but all the same there were still five merchant ships which had somehow to break through to Archangel.

There was some despondency about the little convoy's prospects: the navigating officer of one of the minesweepers discovered that the course set by *Palomares* (who had taken over Commodore's duties) on advice radioed by the SBNO North Russia was given in all the reference books as being unnavigable at this time of year because of fog and ice.[33] Sure enough, as they steamed out of Matochkin Strait, dense fog closed in on them. One of the freighters, *Benjamin Harrison*, lost the convoy and ran back into the strait for shelter. There was some suspicion among the naval escorts that she had 'probably deliberately disappeared on her own'. On their radar screens, the escort vessels could see the ships becoming more and more dispersed in the terrifying fog. The nervous strain became unbearable, as the fog thickened and the temperature dropped:

> Continuing on a southerly course [wrote Lieutenant Caradus in his diary] and hugging the coast. Signal received that *Dianella* and three Russian destroyers *en route* to join us. Fuel remaining at 8 a.m. was 76 tons. Milk powder is now rationed. Porridge is off and bread is rationed. Potatoes are reduced and rice is being built into the meals. Fate of [anti-submarine trawler] *Ayrshire* is frequently discussed.

The corvettes operated their radar non-stop—a great boon in the dense fog; but its loud whine was a source of constant irritation to the crews. At one stage *La Malouine* sighted the dim shape of a ship looming up through the fog ahead, and approached to investigate, 'guns at the ready'. The shape took substance and became the trawler *Lord Middleton*, falling far behind her station in the convoy. Trawler and corvette were equally relieved to

identify each other. The whole convoy began to straggle and lose
formation. Within a few hours, they were picking up a new series
of distress signals from stricken ships. It was little comfort to
Captain Thevik to know that he had been right: the distress signals
were from ships attacked by submarines directly across the route
the convoy was taking towards Archangel, five miles off the coast
of Novaya Zemlya.

Soon after noon on 7 July, Commander Reche had radioed to
Admiral Schmundt the news of *U-255*'s latest kill: 'Pinpoint
AT.4876, two freighters disappeared southwards. Have sunk
Alcoa Ranger, ex New York, 5,116 tons—aircraft. Big merchant
vessel broke away to north-west just beforehand. Am following
hard.' The 'big merchant vessel', *Empire Tide*, had hidden in
Moller Bay and Commander Reche lost sight of her; but other
ships began to appear on the northern horizon, and he set course
after these.

It will be remembered that just before 2 p.m. Schmundt had
wirelessed to the U-boat commanders La Baume, Bielfeld, Brandenburg, Reche and Bohmann orders to establish a patrol line
across the northern approaches to Matochkin Strait; the young
Lieutenant-Commander La Baume had also been detailed to finish
off the crippled oiler *Aldersdale* first. An hour or two afterwards,
however, *Aldersdale* was sighted by Commander Brandenburg's
U-457, and he gave her the *coup de grâce* with one well-aimed
torpedo, before moving off to take up the patrol zone assigned to
him by Schmundt.

Schmundt's tactics had assumed that most of the surviving
ships of PQ.17 still had to come down the north-western coast of
Novaya Zemlya and either enter or pass Matochkin Strait, and it
failed to take into account that at that very moment seventeen
ships might be passing out of the strait, to the south of the patrol
line. A signal arriving from Bohmann's *U-88* at 5.30 p.m. voiced
the first fears that they might be laying their trap too late;
Bohmann, stationed just off the northern side of the entrance to
Matochkin Strait, suggested that the 'convoy fragments' had
already slipped through the net. In a sweep of Cape Sukhoi Nos
he had found nothing. He accordingly asked permission to operate together with La Baume against the crippled British oiler,

[223]

unaware that Brandenburg had settled that score. Schmundt commented, 'In view of the small number of vessels surviving from the convoy, it would seem most promising for the U-boats to operate against those targets already sighted, and to abandon the idea of occupying these patrol zones.' So far only La Baume—who had just signalled to this effect—and Reche had sighted the enemy, so Schmundt radioed:

> *Admiral Commanding, Arctic, to 'Ice Devil':*
> All operate against ships reported by La Baume and Reche. Transmit shadowing fixes and homing signals even for single merchantmen.[22]

La Baume's oiler affair, he added, had been dealt with.

It is not hard to imagine Günther La Baume's anxiety as this signal was laid before him. He had had a most unfortunate convoy so far: he had had six depth-charges thrown at him on the 2nd; he had lost the convoy completely on the 3rd; in thick fog on 4 July he had found Bear Island far from where it should have been by his reckoning. During 5 July, his U-boat had set upon a number of stragglers, but had been surprised by an escort vessel in the fog. He had been given the inglorious job of stalking and sinking an abandoned tanker, and even that small morsel had been snatched from him by another U-boat now. Finally, at 2.50 p.m. on 7 July he had sighted his first live enemy freighter, a fast merchantman scurrying due south past the entrance to Matochkin Strait and very close inshore.[34] He set off in chase after the vessel, and began closing in on her: surely he was not now to be cheated of his prize at the last moment yet again?

Through his periscope he could see that the ship was armed with two heavy guns and several anti-aircraft guns. There was a letter 'H' painted on her funnel. From eight hundred yards he emptied all four main torpedo tubes at the luckless vessel, and hauled *U-355* sharply round to starboard. For forty-seven long seconds, his wireless operator followed the torpedo noises as they ploughed towards their victim, running two fathoms below the surface of the sea.[35]

＊ 3 ＊

When we see an Allied ship despatched, as we have seen twenty
sunk in the course of this one convoy, it is difficult not to grow
callous—not to steel oneself unconsciously to the familiar tragic
sequence of torpedoing, sinking, and the sad calling of the roll
in the lifeboats. But when this twenty-first ship goes down, it is
time to recall sharply and vividly that it was not the ships and
cargoes that were being tortured, it was primarily the human
beings who manned them who were suffering. They were ordinary
seafaring men, whose jobs by their nature were more hazardous
than most; but they were also men with characters, with families
and with private hopes and ambitions. There were the brave and
the not so brave. But they were people whose passing, as in this
ship, would leave problems and sorrow for someone, somewhere.
This description of the end of the *Hartlebury* can symbolize the
story of each and every one of the ships that 'stayed at sea', as
the German submariners put it of their own fallen.

The brief encounter off the coast of Novaya Zemlya displayed
all the grim and pitiless traits of naval warfare at its most cruel.
Captain George Stephenson, Master of *Hartlebury*, had already
been awarded the OBE for ramming an enemy submarine with
another ship on the outward passage in mid-Atlantic some months
before. He had not stopped to pick up survivors, and when on the
return voyage his ship had been singled out by U-boats from the
very heart of the convoy's formation, he swore with grim pride
that they had sunk him as an act of vengeance for their drowned
comrades.

Commander La Baume saw his torpedoes hit, one after another,
and through the curtain of spray he watched the ship list to starboard and slow to a halt. The ship's Third Officer, who kept a
dramatic diary of the tragedy, described:

7th July. 7.40 p.m. Torpedoed. Had just relieved second mate for
tea, and walked out on bridge, and literally walked into torpedo
which exploded immediately below: terrific crash, everything went
black, and was drenched by solid wall of water coming from
'monkey island' bringing with it all kinds of debris.

Struck heavily on head by something and stunned, my one

[225]

thought being to get to other side of ship before the second torpedo struck her—great presence of mind, this. Crawled through wheelhouse which was deserted and washing with water, and got on other side just as second torpedo exploded. This time my feet left the deck clear and I landed flat on my back.[36]

The First Officer, Mr Gordon, was also thrown to the floor, one arm twisted awkwardly under him; but he was still alive. Inside the radio room, the radio officer had been knocked unconscious by a heavy amplifier falling upon him. The ship's radio was smashed beyond repair.

The first torpedo had blasted a big hole outside the crew's quarters, and as half a dozen stewards ran out they fell one after the other into the gaping crater in the passage. The second torpedo threw a wave of water which bowled over the Oerlikon gun-platform mounted on the monkey island above the bridge, sweeping the five gunners into the sea; the platform itself had collapsed on top of Captain Stephenson, who had rushed out into the wing of the bridge after the first torpedo struck.

Together with a Marine corporal, the First Officer managed to rescue the Master from beneath the twisted steel and concrete blocks pinning him to the deck. Stephenson—a small, solidly built Yorkshireman—seemed to be unhurt apart from a savage gash on his head. Swearing profusely, he tore off his soaking uniform and found a dry overcoat.

The ship was listing heavily, and both engines had stopped. The decks had been 'corrugated' by the force of the explosion, and the boilers were blowing off steam. The resulting painful whistle drowned every other sound. Before Captain Stephenson could order the crew to abandon ship, they had rushed the two lifeboats. Each could hold thirty-six men, and the ship had a total complement of fifty-nine including the gunners and the naval signals staff (*Hartlebury* was Vice-Commodore in PQ.17). The starboard lifeboat had, however, been crushed by the second torpedo explosion, and the seamen had rushed the port lifeboat, whether that was their station or not. Several began struggling with its release gear.

Captain Stephenson ran aft to see that the rafts there were released, while the First Officer let himself down the forward bridge ladder to release the life-rafts stowed on the foremast shrouds. With his one sound arm—the other having been injured by the first torpedo blast—Gordon awkwardly struck at the single hook-and-toggle retaining the port raft, while somebody else took care of the starboard one. The raft suddenly swung into the sea; Gordon dived after it and climbed aboard. The painter would not free itself, so he cut the raft adrift with a pocket knife.³⁷

The raft slipped free, and as *Hartlebury* was still under way the ship drifted past him. As his raft drew abreast of the midships, the First Officer saw a scene which made his blood run cold: the one sound lifeboat had collapsed into the sea while full of seamen, and was still being dragged along by the ship by its after fall. The lifeboat had capsized, and righted itself, and now it was completely awash with water, with only its bows and stern showing above the low waves. All around it, the sea was alive with the drifting, struggling seamen who had been spilled out. The Third Officer, Needham Forth, had reached the port lifeboat and given a cadet orders to lower away on the falls:

> Unfortunately Cadet C—— let go the forward fall, sending the nose of the lifeboat crashing into the sea, where she filled right up, throwing several of the fools who had jumped into her into the water.
> This terrible accident caused a panic.

Had the lifeboat been empty when lowered, the accident would probably not have happened. In the meantime, another disaster had occurred amidships: a number of the remaining cooks and firemen had succeeded in swinging out one of the ship's two jollyboats on the single gangway davit, and they had even managed to lower it into the sea with three or four men in it. The boat rapidly sank beneath them, as they had forgotten to put the plugs in. It fell astern, to be washed ashore on the coast of Novaya Zemlya, empty, several days later.* One of the men who perished with it was the twenty-year-old third radio officer, who had just come off duty when the torpedo struck. This officer, Mr George Storey, had lost his father in an air raid on Sheffield, and just before *Hartlebury* had finally sailed for PQ.17 his mother had begged the

---

* The *Hartlebury*'s empty jollyboat was put to good use by the ship-wrecked crews of *Olopana* and *Winston-Salem*.

first radio officer, Mr Richard Fearnside, to 'take good care of George' because she had 'nobody else' but him.[38]

Hartlebury was now settling fast, and falling off to starboard. Fearnside struggled out of his wrecked radio room and ran to the starboard side, where some men had successfully launched a raft from the stern. There were already thirteen people on the raft, designed to hold only eight or nine at most. The raft was below water, and most of the men were up to their chests in water as Fearnside climbed aboard. They refused to find room for him to sit, and for the rest of the night he and three others were forced to stand. This saved their lives.

First Officer Gordon's raft made fast momentarily to the flooded port lifeboat. Eight men climbed down a wire rope one after another to the swamped lifeboat, walked across its thwarts and climbed aboard the raft, barely wetting their feet in the process. With a full complement of nine men, Gordon cut his raft adrift.

The Second and Third Officers appeared at the rail overhead just as the raft began to drift away. There were still a score of men aboard the stricken ship, with no rafts or lifeboats to take them off. Their only hope now lay in the single large flooded lifeboat, still being towed slowly along by its after fall. The Third Officer and many others slid down ropes into this boat.

> My only hope was the port lifeboat [he described] now full of water, and hanging by the after fall, with several of the crew inside and apparently dozens shouting and crying in the water. Slid down a rope and got aboard. All of us up to our waists in icy water.

Ten minutes after firing the first four torpedoes, La Baume fired a fifth from *U-355*'s stern tube at a range of a thousand yards. He saw for himself the tall plume of spray and smoke billow four hundred feet into the air, and the funnel and bits of superstructure blown into the sea. The ship's back was broken. *Hartlebury* immediately took a violent list to port:

> Third torpedo struck home right abreast of us, lurching the side of the ship right over us, and we all thought she was coming right over on us. Able Seaman Dixon, a worthless type of individual at any time, was shouting and screaming about us all being doomed.

[228]

Third Officer Needham Forth was last but one to climb aboard the flooded lifeboat, sliding down a steel rope which had originally held the lifeboat in its cradle. The others began to shout that the ship was rolling over, and he jumped the last few feet. Harold Spence, the ship's young Second Officer, was already climbing down hand over hand into the boat when an eighteen-year-old assistant steward in the boat, Arthur Spuhler, grabbed an axe and hacked away the one rope still binding the lifeboat to the doomed merchantman. The strands suddenly parted, and the lifeboat dropped back astern. The hapless Second Officer was left suspended over the sea, with only the waves below him.

The score or so seamen in the swamped lifeboat tried desperately to bale out the water, but every little wave swamped back over the lifeboat's gunwales; only its buoyancy tanks could be holding it afloat at all. With a single oar, the Third Officer tried to pull the heavy boat round to head into the waves, but by himself it was impossible. He wrote: 'Everybody else was apparently resigned to their fates.' He knew that so long as the lifeboat remained as crowded as it was, there was no hope of making it seaworthy.

Soon after the third torpedo struck, the ship broke into three sections, and began her final plunge. As the stern section sank, the poop-deck was levered into the air, and the seamen saw a single figure running desperately up the sloping deck towards the stern, now high above the waves. The stern rose higher and higher, until the motionless screws were forty feet above the sea. Water was still cascading off the sinking ship, and the seamen could see right through the bottom of her No. 5 hatch, where the last torpedo had struck. All eyes in the lifeboat followed the figure as it climbed over the stern rails and tottered across the ship's stern, now almost horizontal, to jump into the sea far below: it was Captain Stephenson.

He landed close to the Third Officer's lifeboat, which picked him up. As Forth turned round to have one last look at the dying *Hartlebury*, he saw another man aboard her, climbing the ladder from the main deck to the bridge. At the top of the ladder, the man turned round, and they saw it was the Second Officer, Harold Spence, who had been left hanging in mid-air when the lifeboat had been cut adrift. They saw him stripping off his life-jacket, his coat and finally his cap. He had resigned himself to his fate. As the merchant ship finally plunged groaning beneath the waves, the last sight they had of him was of a figure waving to them from the bridge. Then the waves poured over him. [39] It was one small personal tragedy in the vast canvas of this disastrous convoy: Spence had been married just ten days before the *Hartlebury* had sailed from Sunderland on her last voyage.

A thick sea mist had sprung up: out of this swirling mist, its engines purring, appeared the German submarine *U-355*, the icy water running off its back and half a dozen sailors crowding its conning-tower. Lieutenant-Commander La Baume commented that night that it was not a sight for weak stomachs, as very many of the merchant seamen had lost their lives, and the position of most of those on the rafts and in the lifeboat was quite hopeless. *U-355*'s Second Officer approached one of the rafts, the Chief Officer's, and asked the ship's tonnage, name and cargo; all these questions were accurately answered. The submarine officers gave the men on the raft a course for the nearest land, while machine-guns were constantly trained on them. Then a roll of black bread wrapped in silver paper was handed over, together with a bottle of gin and a bottle of rum, and the raft was pushed away.

The situation now was that apart from one or two rafts with only one or two seamen on them, there were two life-rafts and one lifeboat carrying all the ship's survivors. The Chief Officer's had nine men aboard; the radio officer's had fourteen all told, and there was the one flooded lifeboat, with twenty seamen sitting almost totally immersed in it, including the Captain and the Third Officer. The latter officer's diary takes up the story:

In the midst of all our troubles, the submarine now approached, looming up out of the mist.

Keeping well clear of the lifeboat, the submarine's officers asked for the Captain. Stephenson had already warned his crew not to divulge his identity, and he certainly did not look an officer in his bedraggled overcoat. The seamen began to hope that the Germans would pick them up, at least long enough for them to empty out the lifeboat and make it seaworthy; but the

Germans were in an aggressive mood. A voice shouted the familiar taunt from the conning-tower: 'You're not Communists are you. Then why are you fighting for the Communists?' Then *U-355* sheered off, afraid perhaps that if they approached too closely they would sink the wretched craft altogether. A signal reporting their victory was wirelessed to Admiral Schmundt at Narvik.*

Submarine surfaced and came up to us [wrote Needham Forth in his diary] but only to ask ship's name, and then cleared off, leaving us in such a state it seemed at the time to be one of the cruellest things possible.

To the men on Chief Officer Gordon's raft, the Germans had given bread and liquor. More important than that, they had told them that they were barely three miles offshore. To the seamen in the Captain's lifeboat, however, they had given nothing and said nothing. Left alone in the silent mist, nearly all the seaman gave up the ghost and died in the next few hours. Forth's diary continues:

The crew began to die one by one now: first, fireman Hutchinson; then mess boy; AB Clark; poor old Sibbit—'Sparks' and a fine fellow; then 16-year-old cabin boy; then AB Dixon and Hansen. These were all dead inside two hours, and had to be unceremoniously pushed overboard to lighten the boat. A little later, chief engineer; galley boy, another fireman died; and by midnight chief and second stewards, cook, a gunner and OS Jessen had also gone. What a tragedy, and only three miles from land. All went the same way, became sleepy and mind wandering slightly and then eyes glazing over and finish—and apparently not a bad death.

Very bad shape myself, had stayed up to waist in water trying to handle oar for an hour and I was slowly aware of the fact that I was going the same way as the others—the water having a stupefying effect on me.

So I struggled out and scrambled up among the gang in the bows, where we huddled together, with boat rolling and severe waves washing along her whole length. Everyone cramped together, frozen, feet absolutely stiff and white.

---

* Conscience was perhaps pricking the young U-boat commander when he noted in his Brief Report five days later that *Hartlebury*'s cargo was 'tanks, aircraft, for Russia.'

Weather calmed down at midnight, but not before I had been
badly sea-sick on top of other discomforts. There were now only
five of us left: Captain Stephenson, myself, AB May, fireman Storey,
assistant steward Spuhler.

Later, the Third Officer expanded upon this grim outline of
events. Geoffrey Dixon, who had been among the first to go, had
not been in the boat more than an hour before he started going
off his head; he began to rave that they had no hope, and they were
all going to die. He had been sitting up to his armpits in water.
After a time, he began ducking his head under water, trying to
drown himself; the others had restrained him, but after a while he
had seemed to drift off to sleep. Gradually his eyes had opened,
and from his awkward position the Third Officer guessed that
he was dead. He and another seaman lifted the unfortunate Able
Seaman over the side of the boat into the sea, and pushed him
gently under.

Many of the firemen had come straight up from the stokehold,
and were clad only in vests and shirtsleeves. They were the first
to go.

Sibbit was the next to drift off in this way that I noticed: he had
been a church-fittings salesman before the war. He was cool, calm
and collected, but just gave up all hope. He wasn't even sitting
immersed in water, sitting as he was right up in the bows. He fell
asleep, and the next moment I noticed he wasn't normal any more.

Spuhler, the young steward, volunteered to swim with a line
around his waist to a nearby raft which looked more seaworthy
than the boat. He had swum only half-way when his heavy
clothing began to drag him under. They hauled him back barely
alive into the lifeboat on Stephenson's orders. Spuhler lost both
his feet as a result of this gallant attempt.

As the dead British seamen were slipped one by one over the
lifeboat's gunwales in melancholy procession, the boat began to
lift out of the sea, and when the others baled out the water it no
longer swamped back in. By early morning, there were only the
five of the original twenty seamen left in the lifeboat, too weak
and depressed to care much about survival. Even so, with a super-
human effort by the sole surviving fireman, John Storey, they
managed to get the lifeboat's mast partially stepped, and to run up

the orange canvas sail. But despite their feeble struggle, they could not get the mast completely vertical, and the sail did not fill with enough wind to drive the boat forwards. Without uttering a word, fireman Storey jumped over the side of the lifeboat and swam away into the mist. The seamen hardly gave him a glance as he floundered out of sight. They called out weakly to him twice, but made no effort to put about after him. Now there were only four.

Death had reaped a rich harvest among the fourteen men on Radio Officer Fearnside's raft as well. The men who had reached it first had forced the last four to stand; only these four survived the night. The first one to die had been a fireman, dressed only in a vest and trousers; the next was a galley hand, clad in thin kitchen clothing.

All the time that these men were dying, the Second Engineer, Joseph Tighe, was mumbling and moaning. He kept on singing the Twenty-Third Psalm over and over again, *The Lord is my Shepherd*, which he knew off by heart. Then he began to cry that he wished he was home in Glasgow. He was the last to die. He drifted off to sleep, and we tried to keep him awake, rubbing his feet, shaking him, talking to him, but it was no use.'38

Some hours later, a small raft with one of the naval gunners in a khaki duffel coat drifted close to them. He made no response to their shouts, and appeared completely dazed. When the two rafts drew together, the radio officer saw that another rating was lying dead on the bottom of the raft. The body was tipped out, and the food and tablet boxes were broken open; gradually the spirits of the five surviving men began to revive. For two more days their raft bobbed and swayed about among the waves, while all around them the mist obscured the horizon. Then the fog lifted, and they saw that they had been drifting in and out of a small bay on the coast of Novaya Zemlya all the time; the shore was barely a mile away, and they could see a large American ship beached two miles along the coast. The Americans put out a boat with four men aboard, and these took the raft in tow.

The nine seamen who had abandoned *Hartlebury* on the Chief Officer's raft had fared considerably better after the U-boat had left them. Not one of them had succumbed; Chief Officer Gordon had passed round the bottles of German liquor at regular intervals, and with land only three miles off they knew that they would not be at sea for more than a few hours. They erected a small canvas shelter for themselves, broke open a can of whale oil they had found in a locker, and within half an hour all of them were massaging their feet with the oil as a precaution against frostbite.

In the early hours of the morning, they came across the flooded lifeboat, the shadow of death still hanging heavily over it.

> We saw a lifeboat appearing out of the mist, with its sail half up and half down, and we moved over to it with our paddles. We found it was our lifeboat, which had been full of water and sinking when we left the ship. It had the Captain and Third Officer and two others and a body on board. We got rid of the body, and with my men in fairly good shape as we were we soon baled it out, rigged the sail properly and picked up the land.[37]

Gordon had his compass with him, and he knew where the land was because the U-boat commander had told him. As the lifeboat's four survivors were recovering with tots of brandy, biscuits, condensed milk and Horlicks tablets, the lifeboat nosed through a narrow bar into a little bay with a flat and rocky island in it. Here the shipwrecked seamen landed and set up camp. The island was barren, but there was plenty of driftwood, and soon the Chief Officer had organized a tent from the canvas sail cloth, and was boiling milk and corned beef over an open fire. The U-boat's gift of black bread was shared round, and Naval discipline was again enforced, with regular watches and the posting of lookouts. There were meals of goose-eggs and pemmican soup. At the same time, Chief Officer Gordon organized searches for other inhabitants.

The days passed, sunny, but breezy and cold. The fog gradually cleared, and three days after the sinking the Chief Officer reported that he had sighted an American ship aground ten miles away. Within a very few hours, these seamen—the last of *Hartlebury*'s survivors—were also safe aboard the big merchant ship. Of the fifty-six men who had sailed with the British merchant vessel, only twenty had survived. A year later, La Baume's torpedoes claimed their thirty-seventh victim as Captain Stephenson died of his head injuries—the only merchant ship's Master to die on convoy PQ.17. The German submarine service had exacted its revenge.[40]

On the evening of the *Hartlebury* tragedy, William Joyce was again broadcasting to Britain a long and gloating description of the desperate situation in the relations between the Soviet Union and her Western Allies now that the Germans had wiped out PQ.17, with all that it meant for the fighting on the Eastern Front.[41] And from Wilhelmstrasse in Berlin came the official comment that 'British and American armaments works which are supposed to be working for Russia are actually busily producing war materials for the Germans to send to the bottom of the sea'.[42]

✳ 4 ✳

The submarine 'kills' of 7 July brought their score to thirteen vessels claimed from PQ.17, totalling 94,000 tons. But during the evening, as we have seen, the weather worsened again and widespread fog set in. The three U-boats taking up station across the entrance to the White Sea—Timm, Marks and von Hymmen—were reporting dense fog, which left little prospect for finding further merchantmen, crippled or otherwise. Admiral Schmundt accordingly planned to call off the submarines' hunt for the convoy's remnants at midday on the 9th. In the meantime, he decided to establish a second patrol line with the remaining operational submarines, at present working freelance along the coast of Novaya Zemlya. Half an hour before midnight on 7 July, Schmundt drafted orders to Brandenburg, Bielfeld, Reche and La Baume to occupy a patrol line somewhat to the south of the other three U-boats in the White Sea, provided that they had not in the meantime made contact with the enemy. Commander Bohmann's *U-88*, which was now low in fuel, was ordered to return to base.[43]

The patrol zones to which Schmundt was assigning these four U-boats would in fact have been impossible, as they coincided with the field of pack-ice barring the eastern half of the entrance to the White Sea. In any case, one of the four was already closing on a new victim: after losing *Empire Tide* during the afternoon of the 7th, Commander Reche had continued northwards up the coast of Novaya Zemlya, only to sight late that evening yet another freighter hurrying south past him. He turned south to follow her, thereby missing by the narrowest of margins sighting the little convoy of seventeen ships which had emerged from Matochkin Strait a few hours earlier.

Throughout the evening, Reche continued the long process of overhauling his victim, while out of sight. An hour before midnight he radioed Narvik that he was chasing a straggler heading southwards close in to the south-western shore of Novaya Zemlya. For two hours he accompanied the unsuspecting vessel southwards, overhauling her in a wide circle. Then he submerged across her path and ahead of her. His victim was the Matson Navigation Company's 6,069-ton *Olopana*. The moment had come which those hundred or so men in the lifeboats from *Washington, Paulus Potter* and *Bolton Castle* had so clearly anticipated two days before. From less than seven hundred yards, still submerged, Reche carefully fired tube III at the freighter's midships, right below her funnel.[14] At five-past one the one well-aimed torpedo slammed into the ship's main engine-room from the starboard side, and *Olopana*'s twenty-two years of voyaging were over.

Her Master, Captain Mervyn Stone, had just finished a short conference with the Chief Engineer and the Second Officer when the torpedo struck. Again there was a brief 'delay' before its warhead exploded—one may suspect that this was another faulty torpedo—but when it did, all the bulkheads caved in and the ship began to settle at once. Reche was certain that the torpedo had hit, for the ship was blowing off steam and slowing to a halt; but she was still on an even keel. He could not afford a further torpedo, so he ordered *U-255* to surface, and her gun crew to stand by.

The vessel staggered [Stone reported to Archangel Naval Control] and felt as though she had received her death blow, as indeed she had. Lights went out and water was pouring on the main deck into quarters. I made my way on to starboard deck, and then up to boat deck. The starboard boat had been thrown in the air, all equipment was blown out including thwarts. On the port side, the boat had been lowered too hastily, and the emergency radio antenna had become fouled in the forward boat fall block. Result was, after end of boat was in water and swamped.

Some of the crew were attempting to bale out boat and cut forward fall. I gave orders to launch and take to rafts, and then turned my attention to making sure that the distress message was sent out. Charles Schultz, USNR (first trip to sea), deserves commendation for his devotion to duty regardless of his safety. I requested that the message be repeated and gave him the ship's position; these messages went out on the ship's main antenna.[10]

The submarine surfaced some two hundred yards away, as the rest of the crew of the sinking freighter escaped on rafts from the starboard side of the ship. Three men had been killed in her engine-room, one man had jumped overboard and been drowned, and a British gunner had been lost overboard when the wall of water thrown up by the torpedo swept over the ship's decks. A sixth man was also missing.

Commander Reche ordered his crew to open fire from the 88-millimetre gun on the U-boat's foredeck. Twenty rounds were fired into the port side of the ship, and twenty more into her starboard side to speed her sinking. Reche wanted no trace left of her to warn off future victims. *Olopana* sank by the bows soon after.[44] A signal went to Narvik reporting the sinking, but by this time Reche had learned from his radio room that a distress signal had been transmitted by the victim.

U-255 was last seen on the surface heading 'at fast speed' for her new patrol zone across the White Sea entrance, while behind her tossed the crew of the *Olopana* on their rafts and floats, to await their fate in these lonely waters.

For the Master of the 6,223-ton American merchant ship *Winston-Salem*, Captain Lovgren, the sudden loud distress signal transmitted by the *Olopana*, torpedoed only a few miles ahead of him, was the last straw.[10] He turned his elderly freighter into the nearest bay—Obsiedya Bay—and headed through the fog towards the shore; the ship surged at right angles to the beach, and ran hard aground on a sand bar. Lovgren ordered the breech-blocks of every gun in the ship to be cast into the sea, and all the ship's secret papers were burned. The captain and his crew lowered the ship's lifeboats into the shallow sea, loaded them up with cigarettes and provisions from her cargo, and set up camp in a disused lighthouse not far away. This was the mysterious 'American ship' to which the first survivors of the *Hartlebury* tragedy struggled some hours later (page 234).*

It seemed certain that there was to be no salvation for any ship. The nearer the surviving ships came to their goal, the White Sea, the more determined the enemy's attack became; in each man a new struggle developed—a struggle between the will to survive and the will to win through. A single Focke-Wulf 200 found the 5,345-ton freighter *Bellingham* (Captain S. Mortensen) at about half-past two that morning, accompanied only by the British rescue ship *Rathlin* about a mile ahead of her. Both ships were in the open sea and heading straight for Archangel, with about twelve more hours to go. *Bellingham*'s crew first sighted the giant four-engined reconnaissance bomber on their starboard quarter. Their eyes were so strained from lack of sleep, the glare of the ice-barrier and the constant search for the enemy that at first they thought the approaching speck was just a bird; but its course was too steady, its intent too obvious for that.

'General Quarters' was sounded on the under-armed freighter, as the huge bomber circled once round its prey, losing height, and then vanished in a cloud bank astern.

The next time it appeared it had increased speed and was heading in to the ship, straight as an arrow, on its port quarter. The ship's Second Officer tried to fire the Lewis gun on the bridge, but it jammed at once, so he dived for cover in the steel wheelhouse. *Bellingham* opened a crackling fire with her three puny ·50-calibre machine-guns and a Browning, but the bomber seemed to shake off the tiny bullets, and came roaring on only a few feet above the waves, its 115-foot wingspan darkening the sea as it raced towards the ship. The plane's own 20-millimetre cannon had begun firing now in an attempt to drive the ship's gunners away from their guns.

---

* *Winston-Salem*'s Armed Guard officer, Lieutenant Robert Chitrin, was called upon to account for this extraordinary episode, and his report has been available to this author. In it he claims that the grounding was accidental, that nine days passed before the guns and ammunition were thrown overboard, and that every attempt had been made first to refloat *Winston-Salem* (Armed Guard report, 1 August 1942). The reports of the *Olopana*, *Washington* and *Hartlebury* survivors are in strong conflict with this version.

Then the miracle happened. One of the ship's machine-gun bullets must have punctured a sensitive spot in the bomber's fuselage, for when it still had a hundred yards to come, its starboard outer and port inner engines began to smoke, and flames began to tear two gaping holes in the fuselage. One of the plane's cannon shells split a block of wood some fifteen inches above the head of one of the gunners, and another exploded the ship's ammonia tank. There were three explosions astern of the ship, where the bombs had fallen about twenty yards away, knocking one of the machine-gunners on to the deck below.

As the Second Officer looked over the edge of the wheelhouse, the German bomber thundered past only a few feet away and just above him; he saw its rear-gunner crouching in his perspex gun-turret at the rear, directing his cannon along the length of the ship, obviously unaware that the plane's fuselage was now a mass of flames. The crackle of the ship's machine-guns died away. Before the astounded American seamen's eyes, the Focke-Wulf suddenly lost height and ploughed into the sea two hundred yards off the *Bellingham*'s port bow, breaking up at once, while a pillar of black smoke shot up out of the floating wreckage.[45]

The American's gun crew were 'shouting like a carnival full of children' at this unexpected victory. White fumes were billowing out of *Bellingham*'s engine-room from the burst ammonia tank, driving the choking engine-room crew on deck; two of the men had been blinded by the gas. The rescue ship *Rathlin* turned back, but the Americans waved them away and sent a party below decks with respirators to man the engines. *Rathlin* moved over to the wreckage of the German bomber to pick up its crew, but all six men were floating outside in the water, perished.[46] Fifteen minutes later, the two ships were under way again. Now there were only 160 miles to go to Cape Svyatoi Nos and the entrance to the White Sea.

On 8 July, the full story of the PQ.17 disaster broke in the newspapers throughout the length and breadth of occupied Europe, coupled with another notable victory, the capture of Voronezh on the Eastern Front. It was the convoy disaster which continued to hold the Reich's front-page headlines for the next three days, and continued indeed as a main propaganda item until far into the following month.* It was a story on which the Germans could hardly miss. On 8 July, the *Völkischer Beobachter* published a circumstantial account of the battle, blow by blow; when the Allies issued a *démenti* soon after, the Germans countered with the name and photographs of the merchant ships that had been sunk and details of their cargoes. The British press stayed silent.

At lunchtime at the Führer's headquarters on 8 July, it was obvious that Hitler was elated by the operations in the Arctic, despite the German battle fleet's failure to intervene. Martin Bormann afterwards noted how 'especially pleased' his chief had expressed himself that by all accounts all but six of the convoy's thirty-eight ships heading for Archangel had now been sunk. Hitler told Bormann that on the day before, when the news had been that only 'barely two-thirds' of the convoy had been sunk, he had suggested that the victory should be marked by a special Roosevelt cartoon in *Kladderadatsch*, a comic periodical. As it was primarily American war material that had been sunk, they ought to depict an American worker handing up tanks, aircraft and the like to the President, who was promptly dropping the lot into the sea from a suitably elevated position. Underneath the cartoon, they could put a mocking couplet:

> *We do not work for pay or gold,*
> *We work to build a better world!*

He added that anybody who owned a shipyard now in America really was sitting on a gold mine.[47]

✳ 5 ✳

In the cruiser force, a shocking exchange of signals had been decoded, picked up from the Admiral Commanding Iceland and a section of QP.13, the westbound convoy from Russia that PQ.17 had passed a week before. It seemed that half of convoy QP.13 had proceeded to the United Kingdom, and the other half had just been rounding the 'home stretch' on the west coast of Iceland on 5 July, in a thick fog, when within three minutes the Senior Officer's ship and four merchantmen blew up, and two

---

* See, for example, the editions of *Völkischer Beobachter* published on 7, 8, 9, 10, 11, 17, 18, 23, 28 and 31 July and 2, 11 and 22 August.

more were seriously damaged in explosions: the convoy had been guided into an Allied minefield off Iceland by mistake. The news caused a groan of dismay in the American ships: 'It seemed to our officers inexcusably stupid—fog or no fog,' commented Lieutenant Fairbanks. 'It is beginning to look as if blunders were the rule rather than the exception.'[48]

A long way to the south, the British cruiser *London* trailed behind Admiral Tovey's flagship back to Scapa Flow, and Rear-Admiral 'Turtle' Hamilton retired to write what must for him have been one of the bitterest letters of his career to his Commander-in-Chief: 'I must confess,' he wrote, 'I hated leaving that convoy of fine ships on the night of the 4th when every indication was that they were going to be shot at by Tirpitz and party almost immediately.' Now, however, he fully realized the 'correctness' of the Admiralty's decision.[49]

Hamilton knew only too well the major line of criticism that would be invoked against him as a result of Commander Broome's orders to his escort destroyers to withdraw; he did not flinch from meeting the criticism. 'I felt that they were of much more use to me than being scattered with the convoy to be mopped up singly.' And with great prescience he added, 'As things have turned out, I may be severely criticized by the Admiralty, but judging the situation on the spot, with action against superior forces imminent, I feel my decision was correct.'

The Home Fleet arrived at Scapa Flow on the afternoon of 8 July. There was no doubt that Hamilton's cruiser captains fully supported him. On the same day, *Norfolk* arrived at Hvalfiord with the two American cruisers, and Captain Bellars wrote a long and friendly letter to Hamilton admitting that his ship's company had been 'hopping mad' about the events of 4 July, and he had gone so far as to address them publicly using Hamilton's revealing signal of the 6th* as a basis for his address.[50] Rear-Admiral Hamilton knew that some similar action was urgently expected from him: 'judging by the feeling on the lower deck of *London*,' he had informed Tovey, 'the sailors were very upset about leaving the merchant ships and "running away at high speed from the convoy".' No sooner had *London* berthed at Scapa, than Hamilton

---

* Page 202.

went ashore to see his Commander-in-Chief, fully aware that he would be facing something of a trial, but hopeful nevertheless of being able to carry his point of view across.

Admiral Tovey filled in for him the part of the story he did not know, and Hamilton was horrified to realize the real enormity of the blunder. He coldly wrote to his Commander-in-Chief afterwards:

> It would have been a great assistance to me had I known that the Admiralty possessed no further information on the movements of the enemy heavy units other than I had already received.[51]

That afternoon, he and his Flag Captain, R. M. Servaes, went ashore alone together to climb the hills bordering on the Flow. They exchanged little conversation until they had reached the top, and stood gazing out over the Home Fleet at anchor. Then Hamilton said, 'Well I suppose I ought to have been a Nelson. I ought to have disregarded the Admiralty's signals.' Captain Servaes shook his head and said that even Nelson could not have ignored a series of signals like those.[52]

On board *London*, the loudspeakers announced 'Clear Lower Decks. Everybody aft!' Division by division, the whole ship's company fell in and marched to the quarter deck, where they waited breathlessly to see what was about to happen. A blackboard had been set up with an outline map of North Cape and the Arctic. After a while the sailors were called to attention, and Rear-Admiral Hamilton appeared. He had them stood at ease, and addressed them through a microphone.

What followed was surely unprecedented.[53] Admirals are not given to explaining their actions to the lower deck. Hamilton began:

> I propose to be quite frank with you, but don't misconstrue any remarks I make as being a criticism of the government, of the Admiralty, or of the Flag Officers of the Fleet.

He put the whole history of the PQ convoys to north Russia into perspective. He reminded *London*'s company that in 1941 they had themselves transported Lord Beaverbrook on his mission to Moscow—the genesis of these convoys—and he stressed the

importance of their continuation, even at the expense of heavy
losses.*

He continued:

As the weather in northern Norway improved, the German air
attacks increased exactly as every Flag Officer had visualized.
Unfortunately, the ice is farther south in the early part of June. Fleet
opinion was against convoy PQ.16 going until the ice had receded,
but was overborne by the political considerations. Consequently
PQ.16 ran and came in for a hell of a time east of Bear Island,
being attacked by two hundred aircraft altogether.

Admiral Hamilton recalled to the company the *Bismarck*
episode, to show how greatly Britain's future would be jeopardized if ever *Tirpitz* should break out into the North Atlantic:

I want to bring it home to you that when a PQ convoy is running,
the C-in-C has other problems to worry about as well.
   Things began to boil up on the afternoon of the 4th, when it was
discovered by reconnaissance that *Tirpitz* and *Hipper* were at sea,
and we were ordered to scatter the convoy and withdraw at high
speed to the west. I have never hated carrying out an order more in
my life. . . .

As he said this, a great cheer went up from the ship's company,
and it was clear that Hamilton had won them over. He had difficulty in making himself heard for some time. Then he continued:

I felt—as I know all of you felt—that we were running away and
leaving that convoy to its fate. If the decision had been left to
me, I would have stayed and fought—and I should have been
wrong. You have got to put personal feelings on one side, and
consider the question in cold blood as a matter of strategy: if we
had been engaged in the Barents Sea, it might have incurred the
C-in-C's coming there and being forced to engage the *Tirpitz*
in face of attacks by German aircraft. We might well have suffered
a major disaster.

---

* As in the case of his speech at the convoy conference, an almost
verbatim note of Hamilton's speech, headed 'London, ship's company
8th July', in typescript, was among Hamilton's papers. He clearly
wanted an exact record of what he did in fact say; the reader is invited
to judge the effect of his opening gambit, quoted above, for himself.
The sailors were also warned,'Must not write home about what I'm
going to say.'

THE DESTRUCTION OF CONVOY PQ.17

Hamilton concluded sombrely that he would be surprised if more than half of the convoy's ships arrived; but when one looked at what had been achieved in seventeen convoys, he thought they would all have to admit that the risks and losses were worthwhile.

At 10.30 p.m. that night, William Joyce again broadcast from Germany to his millions of listeners in Britain, commenting now on the Admiralty's 'deathly silence' on convoy PQ.17's losses: 'As time goes on,' he added, 'it must be realized even in Britain that the German war communiqués state nothing but the facts. There is no reason to doubt the accuracy of the reports of the destruction of this convoy.'⁵⁴ And in a further attempt to draw the British authorities into making an announcement confirming PQ.17's losses, the 'New British Broadcasting Station', a thinly disguised German transmitter operating ostensibly from British soil, asked plaintively, 'What about the Arctic? The public is getting very dissatisfied at the failure of our government to give any reply to the Nazi claim to have wiped out an important convoy carrying supplies to Russia. . . . '⁵⁵

Whitehall very properly refused to give any comment on the German claim to have virtually annihilated the convoy, and certainly did not attempt to refute it. For that matter, Whitehall was still unaware how many of PQ.17's ships had been lost, in spite of widespread searches by a few Catalinas and other aircraft of Coastal Command based in north Russia, and by a few isolated vessels like the corvette *Dianella* and Captain Drake's trawler.⁵⁶ That evening, the Cabinet decided that a long-anticipated Debate on the shipping situation, scheduled for 16 July, would now be held in Secret Session; the decision surprised many MPs, and their uneasiness was not assuaged by Sir Stafford Cripps's assurance next day that they would realize when they secretly learned the facts that the decision had not been arrived at because of a Government desire to conceal unpleasant facts. Several Members, including Mr Arthur Greenwood and Mr Emanuel Shinwell, protested that the whole purpose of the Debate had been to set the public mind at rest; the decision to hold it in Secret Session would have the very opposite effect. But the Government would not be dissuaded.⁵⁷

Towards midnight on 8 July, Admiral Hubert Schmundt

decided to alter his U-boats' tactics for what he took to be the closing phase of their operation. During the latter hours, he had received reports that ice was blocking much of the entrance to the White Sea. Commander Bielfeld had signalled, 'Big field of dense pack-ice at pinpoint AC.9380. Fog. Visibility one to ten miles.' And La Baume (*U-355*) had reported, 'My progress to patrol-zone badly delayed by necessity to skirt round pack-ice fields at pinpoints 9390 and 9380.' He was down to his last 16 cubic metres of fuel.[58] Assessing the position on the basis of the signals reaching him, Schmundt guessed that there were no further prospects of success for his submarines patrolling near this ice. No ships had crossed the two patrol lines he had set up with his six remaining operational submarines; *U-88* and *U-355* were both returning, short of fuel. He decided on a change of tactics: the entire submarine force would march back in line abreast, raking over the latter part of the convoy's general route since it scattered, crossing certain check-lines at fixed times. In this way they would account for any crippled stragglers too.

A few minutes before midnight, he ordered the six remaining 'Ice Devil' U-boats—Marks, von Hymmen, Timm, Bielfeld, Brandenburg and Reche—to begin this final sweep at three o'clock next afternoon, crossing one 'check line' each twelve hours in a broad curve northwards up the coast of Novaya Zemlya, and then due west, almost as far as Bear Island.[59] This was a tactic which no enemy trick could counter, but little was expected from it. 'The operation can be said to be over', affirmed the Naval Staff that night.[60]

Passing southwards down the coast of Novaya Zemlya was the little convoy that had left Matochkin Strait on the evening of the 7th. After nosing out into the Barents Sea, it had formed up into two columns of merchant ships, four in all, screened by a dozen escort vessels. At a quarter to ten on the morning of the 8th, they passed through a large patch of oil and wreckage marking the resting place of one of *U-255*'s victims—probably *Alcoa Ranger*.[2] In dense fog, the four freighters—*El Capitán, Hoosier, Samuel Chase* and *Ocean Freedom*—continued to plunge due south, heading for the entrance to the White Sea. The fog persisted throughout the day as they hugged the south-western coast of Novaya

Zemlya. Even so, every hour was bringing them ten miles closer to their final destination, Archangel.

The First Officer of *El Capitán*, the oldest ship in the convoy, was on the bridge at 4.30 p.m. that afternoon, when suddenly the anti-aircraft ship directly ahead started blasting off her siren in a prearranged ice-warning.[61] In mounting crescendo, the other ships joined in—their sirens, bells and whistles shrieking in dull cacophony through the dismal fog. *El Capitán*'s engines were thrown from Full Ahead to Full Astern, and the ship lost way, creaking and groaning in every plate, but not soon enough to avoid the broad expanse of white fading into the grey fog ahead. She and several other ships ploughed for hundreds of yards into the brittle pack before finally shuddering to a halt. When the crashing and screeching subsided, a momentary silence descended on the ships; and in the midst of that vast waste *El Capitán*'s First Officer heard the shrill note of a boatswain's pipe. He pulled out his binoculars and peered ahead, sighting nothing at first, but then—as a scarcely perceptible breeze gently shifted the veil—he glimpsed a tiny red sail two miles away in the midst of the tightly packed ice. Captain Thevik came on the bridge, and confirmed that there seemed to be a lifeboat stuck fast in the ice. While the other ships set about backing out of the ice pack *El Capitán* nosed forwards, forcing a way through the splintering and bursting ice until the little lifeboat was close by. The boat had drifted into the ice fifty-three hours earlier, and had been unable to extricate itself. Nineteen survivors from the American *John Witherspoon* were lifted out from beneath the red sail which they had lowered and fashioned into a windbreak; some of them were badly injured.

Sound carries far in those cold, dry latitudes. But had the American officer not blown his whistle at precisely the moment when the freighters' engines were stopped, all the survivors would have suffered a terrible end. As he was carried aboard, the First Officer pressed the whistle into the hands of *El Capitán*'s First Officer, as a memento of this encounter. As the freighter now reversed out of the ice's clutch, relays of seamen began to massage the survivors' limbs with whale oil. By the time the escorts and merchant ships had extricated themselves from the ice, the convoy as such was at an end; the fog was as thick as ever, and there had been so many course-alterations and diversions in the last few hours that navigation by dead-reckoning had ceased. At times their speed was reduced to 8 knots and less, and zigzagging was impossible.

The anti-aircraft ship *Palomares* radioed all the ships to report their present locations by wireless, and all dutifully reported in except the minesweeper *Salamander*, who thought any wireless transmission at this stage most ill-advised. She maintained a discreet silence. At seven o'clock that evening the minesweeper *Britomart* sighted *Lotus*, with Commodore Dowding aboard, and together they tried to round up the lost merchantmen; but two hours later further ice was encountered, and visibility was down to only eighty yards in the fog. Such ships as had now grouped around them changed course to the north, but found that the ice was getting thicker instead of looser—a navigator's nightmare; they seemed to be in a cul-de-sac of ice. They turned east again, and eventually found open water in the early hours of 9 July. Now they were able to proceed cautiously northwards once again. It seemed that the Russians had given their Senior Officer a course leading straight into a massive barrier of ice coming from the Kara Sea, barring the eastern part of the entrance to the White Sea; this was, of course, the same ice the German U-boats had encountered a few hours before.

There was no alternative: the freighters and their escorts would have to make a long detour to the north-west, drawing all the time closer to the German air bases in Norway—and nearer to the three U-boats stationed by Schmundt at the western end of this ice-barrier. At 2 a.m. on the 9th, the fog suddenly lifted, and *Britomart* and *Lotus* were joined by *Halcyon* as they proceeded along the ice-edge; two hours later they found *Samuel Chase* stuck in the ice, and shepherded her to the open water. In the hours that followed, two trawlers, *Lord Middleton* and *Northern Gem*, and the merchant ship *Ocean Freedom*, were also sighted and ordered to close.[2] The corvette *Lotus* found the twenty-three survivors of *Pan Atlantic* in an open lifeboat, and took them aboard; but that was all. There was no sign of the other ships. The convoy had been effectively halved.

The two other merchant vessels and their escorts, including the rescue ship *Zamalek*, the two anti-aircraft ships and the corvette

[247]

La Malouine, continued along the ice-edge, making more ground to the westward than those whose progress we have just examined. For them, the fog persisted. *La Malouine*'s Asdic officer, Lieutenant Caradus, wrote in his diary: 'Awakened at 4 a.m. by engine-room telegraph. The R.D.F. was still operating—the continual whine loud and annoying to say the least. Revolutions were down to 50–60, i.e. 5½ knots.' At about a quarter-past five, the fog cleared rapidly and they could see the ice-edge about five miles to port; not far off, the ice came to an abrupt end and beyond that lay the open sea again. Now the extended line of ships could see each other again; but three minesweepers, a trawler and two merchant vessels had vanished in the fog. A new 'little convoy' was formed, consisting of the corvettes *Poppy, Lotus* and *La Malouine*, the two AA ships, the rescue ship *Zamalek* and the Asdic trawler *Lord Austin*, all escorting just two freighters, *Hoosier* and *El Capitán*. Between them, as the fog lifted, signal lamps began to flash, and almost at once the port side lookout in *La Malouine* reported to the bridge an unidentified object slightly abaft their beam two miles away. The corvette made for the object at full speed, and anti-submarine stations were manned. But two lifeboats with red sails came into sight, and within ten minutes willing hands were helping twenty-nine more survivors from *John Witherspoon* to climb up the scrambling-nets into the corvette.*

As the corvette turned to rejoin the convoy at cautious speed, to conserve her dwindling fuel reserves, hot meals and a change of clothing were issued to the exhausted American seamen, who had been three days in their lifeboats. 'Their rescue', wrote Caradus,

---

* Godfrey Winn, in *PQ.17*, gives the impression that it was *Pozarica* who had rescued the *Witherspoon*'s survivors. Not so. Cf. the private diary of *John Witherspoon*'s second assistant engineer: '*7th July*. In motor boat, ran out of gas and are rowing at times to keep warm. First assistant Swanson had his hand over the side with his glove on—seal came up and snatched glove from his hand. Cold feet mostly in boat. I recommend that everyone massage feet every 30 mins. which we are doing. *8th July*: Still in lifeboat, connected up with Captain's boat. He came over to ours and we hooked on to 2nd mate's boat which had a sail. *9th July*: Picked up by HMS *La Malouine*, which with HMS *Poppy* and a couple of minesweepers and trawlers were escorting two ships, the SS *El Capitán* and the SS *Hoosier*.'

'was nothing short of a miracle. Had the fog persisted for another five minutes and had a less experienced lookout been on watch, these twenty-nine survivors in two small open boats would not have been seen.'⁴ What ponderous mechanism had decreed that this ship's crew should thus be rescued by two such remarkable Acts of Providence we shall not know. Certainly, her crew were not specially marked by virtue or saintly character. They fell asleep as soon as they lay down, at various places in the corvette, and seemed little to appreciate their great fortune. Lieutenant Caradus found one of them asleep in the officers' small bath, and ten more had taken over the wardroom and forced the wine cupboard, and were lying about the floor in drunken stupor. The bath's tenant awoke when Caradus saw him there. The Lieutenant later described:

> He had an amazing collection of nude postcards and obscene flicker photos. He pushed these cards and photos into my coat pocket. It was when I got to my cabin, after stepping over men sleeping in groups in passage ways, that I saw what I had been given. Flicking the photos gave the motion-picture effect of sexual intercourse. I nearly vomited.

The RN Lieutenant returned the man's property to him at once, and was profusely thanked for returning the crew's 'girlfriends'. The seaman said that he wouldn't go anywhere without them.

There was little sleep for these frightened men. At 8.15 a.m., *Lotus* dropped a pattern of depth-charges at a suspected U-boat, but without success. It became very cold indeed, although the sun was shining. By 11 a.m. ice was forming on the signal halyards and on the guard rails. *La Malouine* had only one quarter of her fuel left now, and food was strictly rationed; the situation was the same in the other ships. At 1 p.m., the temperature dropped even lower as they ran back into dense fog, a fog which was to blanket their movements all afternoon and evening.

While Moscow radio announced that day that 'the convoy reached our port safely',⁶² the first congratulations were already arriving at Naval Group North's headquarters in Kiel for achieving its destruction. Colonel-General Dietl, Commanding General of the 20th Army in Norway, signalled his 'heartiest congratulations' for the decisive relief this victory would bring to the

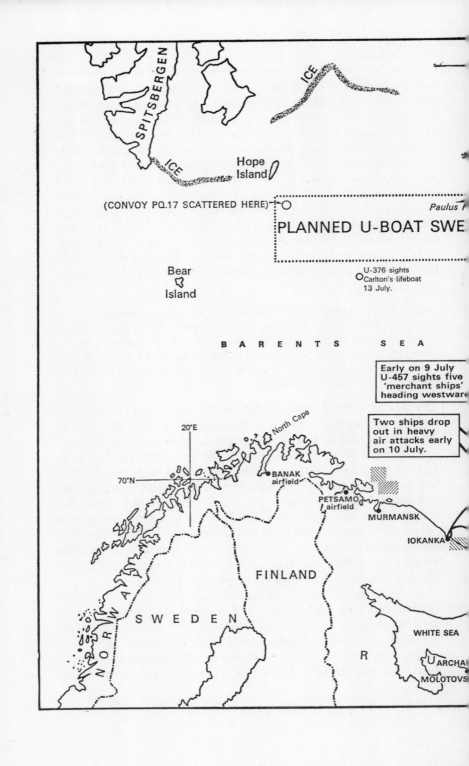

SPITSBERGEN

ICE

ICE

Hope Island

(CONVOY PQ.17 SCATTERED HERE)

Paulus

PLANNED U-BOAT SWE

U-376 sights
Carlton's lifeboat
13 July.

Bear Island

BARENTS SEA

Early on 9 July
U-457 sights five
'merchant ships'
heading westwar

Two ships drop
out in heavy
air attacks early
on 10 July.

20°E

North Cape

BANAK
airfield

70°N

PETSAMO
airfield

MURMANSK

IOKANKA

FINLAND

SWEDEN

NORWAY

R

WHITE SEA

ARCHA

MOLOTOVS

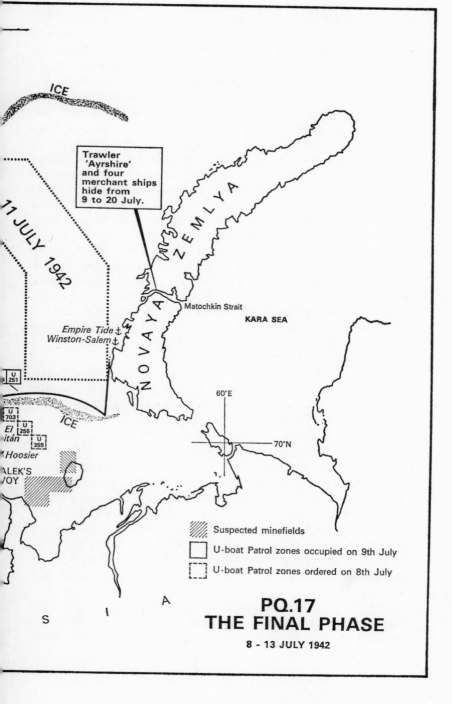

ICE

Trawler 'Ayrshire' and four merchant ships hide from 9 to 20 July.

11 JULY 1942

N O V A Y A   Z E M L Y A

Matochkin Strait

KARA SEA

Empire Tide ‡
Winston-Salem ‡

U
251

U
703

El
itán

U
255

U
358

Hoosier

ALEK'S
/OY

ICE

60°E

70°N

S   I   A

//// Suspected minefields

☐ U-boat Patrol zones occupied on 9th July

⌐⌐ U-boat Patrol zones ordered on 8th July

PQ.17
THE FINAL PHASE
8 - 13 JULY 1942

German armies fighting on the eastern front; his own Army sent greetings to its brothers-in-arms, the gallant U-boat crews.[60]

The German Naval Staff in Berlin already considered the operation to be at an end. But all Admiral Schmundt's orderly plans for the six remaining U-boats to rake back round the Barents Sea were shattered by the signals which reached him during the latter part of 9 July. At about 10.45 a.m. Commander Brandenburg (*U-457*) urgently wirelessed to him that he had 'sighted a convoy of up to five merchant ships' heading almost due west past the ice-barrier at the mouth of the White Sea. During the afternoon and evening, *U-703*, *U-376* and *U-408* all picked up this little convoy, or sections of it, heading westwards in dense patches of fog; they were transmitting homing signals for the other U-boats to follow. *U-376* was depth-charged unsuccessfully while trying to attack, and *U-408* fired two torpedoes at one ship, but missed.

All this was a great shock to Hubert Schmundt. He commented, 'This means that a major portion of the convoy has been located, contrary to expectations.' And he added, 'Apparently not all the freighters the Air Force claims to have sunk, *have* sunk.'[63] He began to consider what he should now do.

As the ships in the rescue vessel *Zamalek*'s little convoy finally swept out of the dense fog at a quarter to nine that evening, heading almost due south now that the ice-barrier had been passed, lookouts reported an enemy submarine trailing them on the surface, six miles astern of them. Captain Morris suggested to *Palomares* that it would be more prudent to hug the ice in the blessed fog belt, and thus avoid being observed by the enemy. He received a snotty reply, directing him to maintain station and carry out the Commodore's instructions. No attempt was made to detach a corvette to harass the shadowing U-boat, which Morris strongly suspected was beaconing in German aircraft at that very moment. Probably the submarine-chasers were too low in fuel to engage in a prolongèd U-boat hunt. In any event, two German aircraft were sighted soon after, and 'action stations' was sounded.[64]

They were only shadowing aircraft, but they must have observed that there were by now two splinter groups from the original little convoy—one comprising *Zamalek* and the other heavier escorts, shepherding the freighters *El Capitán* and *Hoosier*, while about fifty miles behind them there followed *Samuel Chase* and *Ocean Freedom*, escorted by four smaller escorts. 'Fog never was with us when it could have helped us,' recorded Lieutenant Caradus in his diary at this time. At 10 p.m., *Zamalek*'s convoy still had some 480 miles to run to Archangel.

Captain Morris's forebodings would have been confirmed, had he been in Admiral Schmundt's headquarters at eighteen minutes to ten, for the signal despatched by the U-boat at 8.45 p.m. was just reaching him. The U-boat was Commander Reche's *U-255*. Reche had reported: 'Convoy at pinpoint AC.9543, heading south. Three destroyers [*sic*] and two escorts in front, with three freighters behind them. Am transmitting homing signals. Visibility outside fog fifteen miles.' The way was thus prepared for the most violent and dramatic air attack of the whole convoy operation. The ice-barrier had forced the ships to come much closer to the Norwegian airfields, and in particular that at Banak, than had been foreseen. Within an hour, Reche was wirelessing that the convoy was now on a south-westerly course heading it towards Banak airfield at 10 knots.

On Banak airfield itself, nearly forty Junkers 88 dive-bombers were being hastily bombed and fuelled for the final sorties to put an end to this importunate remnant of PQ.17.[65] Reche advised Narvik that there was little wind, and the visibility was now up to about twenty miles; two Blohm & Voss aircraft were already circling the convoy. Ten minutes before midnight, he reported in again: the convoy was still heading methodically south-westwards, with five escorts in line abreast preceding three merchantmen. Then he flashed, 'Junkers 88s coming in to attack. Will continue to transmit homing signals. [Distress] Signals are being jammed.'

✳ 6 ✳

Shortly before midnight, the first 'action stations' for several days was sounded on the Allied merchant ships in *Zamalek*'s little convoy. Enemy aircraft were approaching, seventy miles away. The dreaded Flag '*Q*'—'air attack imminent'—was flown in the convoy again. This time every seaman knew just how tough the fight would be, for they were very close indeed to the German airfields, and they need expect no respite. They were only 140 miles from Murmansk when the first five Junkers 88s arrived from Banak airfield a few minutes before midnight. Cotton-wool was handed round by the sick-bay attendants for those without rubber ear-plugs, and those ships that were crowded with survivors formed them into supply and re-ammunitioning parties to keep them occupied. A beautiful sun illuminated the evening sky as the *II./KG.30* aircraft were first sighted, twenty miles away, climbing from a thousand feet; the seamen saw at once that they were not the expected torpedo-bombers. Soon the aircraft were wheeling overhead, picking out the most rewarding targets.[66]

Then the five aircraft plummeted down on the ships near the centre of the formation, swooping from their starboard side. The bombs all missed, but threw up huge fountains of water between the ships. All the ships' guns had opened fire, and the noise was terrific; yet the scream of falling bombs had still been heard, despite the sailors' ear-plugs. 'Our bloody Pom-Pom gun jammed again,' wrote Caradus. Already there were fresh waves of aircraft upon them, switching their tactics, coming in from several quarters at once, and attacking the escorts as well as the merchant ships. Then an aircraft peeled off and hurtled down on the 5,060-ton American freighter *Hoosier*, in the centre of the pattern. According to her Armed Guard officer,

They went into a dive, pulling out at approximately 3,000 feet and releasing their bombs. The gunners manning the ·50-calibre machine-guns opened fire although it was realized that at that range their fire would be ineffective; about 3,500 rounds of ammunition were expended.

The first stick of three bombs dropped into the water approximately fifty yards on the port bow of the ship; no damage was inflicted. The second stick of bombs hit the sea about five feet from the boat deck on the starboard side. Considerable damage was inflicted by this blow to the ship and equipment. Several men in the gun-crew were knocked on to the deck.

The third stick of bombs struck on the port side just abaft of the beam, approximately twenty yards away. It was believed that some of the ship's seams had been opened. The chief engineer went below to determine if the ship could continue to be operated; he concluded that it could not. Planes were still flying overhead, and there was a submarine on the surface, distant about 15,000 yards.

The ship, having lost way, was now alone. The convoy proceeded onward. The captain thereupon gave the order to abandon ship.[67]

The *Hoosier* was on an even keel and did not look as though she was finished. Another Junkers 88 bombed her and again missed, but she was an old ship and could not take much more of this punishment. The corvettes *Poppy* and *La Malouine* were detached to minister to the freighter's needs. The latter corvette stopped in the midst of *Hoosier*'s lifeboats and took all the American seamen on board; *La Malouine* now had no fewer than 129 survivors packed between her decks.

As an RNR officer, Lieutenant Bidwell was an ex-Merchant Navy officer, and he knew full well what 'salvage' meant. He took *La Malouine* close alongside the deserted *Hoosier*, and said, 'No. 1, I think we can take her in tow.' A boarding party was put on the American, consisting of the corvette's First Lieutenant, *Hoosier*'s engineers and those from the late *John Witherspoon*, with orders to try to restart the ship's main engines. The attempt met with no success. But the First Lieutenant reported to Bidwell that the ship was seaworthy, and would keep afloat. There was an air of excitement in the corvette as the news passed from mouth to mouth. Towing gear was prepared, and a line was put aboard the American freighter. Their sister-corvette *Poppy* was circling slowly round them, standing anti-submarine guard.

Then lookouts spotted the U-boat only four miles astern of them, and closing in. The tow was smartly dropped, and the boarding party taken off. Bidwell made as though to attack the U-boat, but his fuel was low, and on the surface a U-boat was faster than he was. There were no aircraft to force the submarine to submerge. The matter was decided for him in any case by an R/T signal from the escort commander, directing him to sink the *Hoosier* and rejoin the convoy. He withdrew a short distance, and opened fire on the deserted but seaworthy freighter with his corvette's 4-inch gun. He fired one round after another into her, until she was engulfed in flames; but still she refused to sink. Some of the *Hoosier*'s survivors stood weeping on the corvette's deck to see this bitter spectacle; others were depressed only by the knowledge that it would now be even longer before they saw the United States again. Convoying is seldom spectacular, and often dull; but to have to sink one of one's own ships in the face of a jeering enemy was 'sufficient unto the day'.⁴ From *U-255*, Commander Reinhard Reche was wirelessing Narvik that he could see a ship blazing while two escorts were standing by; the rest of the convoy was vanishing over the southern horizon, with three shadowing aircraft circling round it.

Hour after hour, in perfect bombing weather, the Germans pressed their relentless attack on the surviving ships of the little convoy in their final dash for Iokanka and the entrance to the White Sea. A total of thirty-eight Junkers 88s from the first and second squadrons of *KG.30* were taking part in the operation, from Banak airfield. The aircraft were now coming in to attack from out of the low glare of the midnight sun, making them almost impossible to spot in time.

These were the first determined dive-bombing attacks these ships had suffered, and the effect on the sailors was shattering. In one corvette, a rating who was otherwise a 'fine ordinary seaman' suffered mentally, and had to be locked into a cabin for the rest of the action. Again the Senior Officer signalled to Archangel a request for fighter cover to come out.⁴ * Just two or three fast fighter aircraft would have made all the difference. The merchant ship and her mighty escort were now not many miles from the Russian coast. At 1.50 a.m. a single Junkers 88 dropped three bombs only forty feet astern of the *El Capitán*. The afterpeak began to take water, and the gun crew's quarters were flooded, but the ship—the only merchant vessel left with them now—persevered.⁶⁹ An RAF Flight Lieutenant lay on his back on the monkey-island of the rescue ship *Zamalek* shouting directions to the Captain as each bomber came into attack them; Captain Morris was passing them on to the helmsman and the

---

* According to Lieutenant Caradus (*La Malouine*), the signal was delayed for twelve hours by the Russian authorities. Other officers had at that time a distinct impression that 'the Russians were not unhappy to see our ships sunk'. In particular Allied naval officers were puzzled to find cargoes from previous PQ convoys still standing on Russian quays when new convoys arrived.⁶⁸

little ship was weaving in and out of the great plumes of salt water thrown up by the bombs.

The two anti-aircraft ships had exhausted almost all their ammunition, and were unable to put up a barrage any longer. One had fired 1,200 rounds of 4-inch anti-aircraft shell in this time. No aircraft had been shot down, but some had evidently been damaged. Each aircraft was taking it in turn to attack, peeling off in leisurely fashion as though this were only a practice bombing-range. They were clearly concentrating on *El Capitán* and the rescue ship now. Over the horizon, the sailors glimpsed a Catalina aircraft, but it wisely turned back very quickly when it saw the battle. As each German aircraft retired, its bomb racks empty, a fresh one arrived from Banak to take its place. *Zamalek*'s guns and pig-trough rocket-launchers were fired non-stop; seamen stood by to reload the pans as each one was emptied. As the helm was continually thrown over at full speed, Captain Morris knew that the ship's engines would not stand the punishment much longer.

A bomb hit the sea barely twenty feet from her bows throwing up a wall of water in which *Zamalek* rammed head on. The shock was so violent that the ship's pregnant cat had a miscarriage, her two abortive kittens were irreverently baptized 'Blohm' and 'Voss' and thrown into the sea. For a moment it seemed as though the ship must surely sink under the sheer weight of hundreds of tons of water descended on her foc's'le. Three feet of sea crashed down her companionways, and her compasses were unshipped by the shock.

The nerves of the eight Russian seamen they had picked up on the 4th could take it no longer. They crowded on to the foredeck, while their Second Officer began tugging at the release gear of a raft strapped to the rigging. The raft slid into the sea with a splash on the end of a short painter, and the Russians began clambering over the rails into the sea. Captain Morris shouted furiously, 'Somebody shoot that sod. It's all right, the ship's not sinking!'

His own Second Officer leapt on to the foredeck, threw aside the panicking Russians and hacked the raft adrift. On the boat-deck, where the other 150 survivors had prudently forgathered, there was a rush for the lifeboats. Morris's chief officer, Mr Macdonald, seized an axe from one of the lifeboats and kept the mob at bay. Within a minute the crisis was over: the rescue ship was upright, but still swinging violently to avoid the bombs being aimed at her. One particularly wild swing brought her close to the AA ship *Pozarica*, and the latter nervously signalled Captain Morris not to come so close, as they were trying to draw the enemy's fire.

Shortly before three o'clock that morning, 10 July, *Zamalek* was finally stopped. A heavy bomb detonated just twenty feet from the starboard side, and Captain Morris felt the sign he had been dreading: the steel deck under his feet stopped vibrating to the throb of the two main engines. Gradually the vessel lost way and fell out of the convoy, a helpless, sitting target for the Germans. With both hands Morris seized the engine-room telegraph and rang four times Full Ahead, and four times Full Astern. It was his private signal to his Chief Engineer to bring the engine-room crew up as fast as he could.

But the sky was quiet and the air was still. The Germans had withdrawn. For four hours the battle had raged, but now it was over, or so it seemed. The Chief Engineer and his men were clattering up the steel companionway from below, when the naval signaller shouted to Morris that *Palomares* was making a signal to them: she was, he said, signalling that she was reluctant to come back to *Zamalek*'s assistance.

This roused Morris's Welsh temper to its limits. He determined to show the anti-aircraft ship whether they were finished or not. He turned to his dazed Second Officer and ordered him to give his Chief Engineer his compliments and tell him that the ship was all right. 'Can he get the engines started again?' The officer did not reply, but stood there looking vacant. Morris slapped his face and shouted at him to make haste. He must have known that only a miracle could save them, but he was determined to achieve the impossible. He marched excitedly up and down the bridge, and encouraged the lookouts to keep their eyes peeled for U-boats.

In the engine-room there was chaos: the four-hour hail of bombs had smashed just about everything that was smashable. The light-bulbs throughout the ship were broken, the dynamo had a broken bed-plate, the keeps of the propeller-shaft were splintered and the oil pipe taking fuel to the settling tank had fractured. Even the lavatories and baths had smashed. But now *Zamalek* had not one but three Chief Engineers—her own and those of *Christopher Newport* and her late rival *Zaafaran*. As soon as the ship's plight became known around the ship, the other ships' entire engine-room personnel mustered in the blacked-out engine-room, although they knew that if a submarine put a torpedo into her their chances of survival down there were very slim.

At 3.04 a.m., Commander Brandenburg wirelessed Narvik that he had sighted the convoy under heavy air-attack, and his *U-457* was now working its way ahead of them.[70] Time was running out for the rescue ship, but at twenty-past three the grimy and sweating *Zamalek* Chief Engineer reported to Captain Morris that he had repaired the dynamo and replaced the oil-pipe; the ship's hull was leaking badly, but the main engines were both restarted, and the battered rescue ship slowly got under way again, at a maximum speed of 10 knots, heading for the southern horizon, where the German Air Force had already resumed its attack.[71]

The last minutes of *El Capitán*, an elderly oil-burner flying the Panamanian flag, with a Norwegian Master, British First Officer and a fifteen-nation crew, had now arrived. At a quarter to six that morning, as tea was being served by the gallon in the escort ships, a lone, yellow-tipped Junkers 88 aircraft arrived and knocked out *El Capitán*. Three bombs sufficed, placed close to the starboard side of the engine-room and abreast the bridge. The engines stopped, and the ship slowed to a halt. 'If the Russians want war material they should bloody well send us fighter protection,' commented Lieutenant Caradus bitterly,[72] as the merchant ship fell back out of the convoy's formation: some 'convoy' now, with its last freighter gone!

The *Capitán*'s First Officer volunteered to go below and see for himself what had happened. The engine-room telegraphs were broken, and the voice-pipe produced no reply. In the stokehold he found a clear four feet of water. The sea valve had been blown in, and the fuel and water pipes to the main engines had been ruptured. The Third Engineer came out, drenched in black fuel-oil and water, shouting that the water was coming up to the fires. Captain Thevik quickly mustered everybody on deck, including the nineteen *John Witherspoon* survivors they had picked up. Fire was breaking out below decks, but nobody was trapped. Thevik ordered his crew to abandon ship.[61]

He and his First Officer had long before made the best possible provision for being sunk, by adapting the two ship's lifeboats to enable them to sail back to Iceland, or even to Scotland should need arise. The first officer had made a gaff and a boom for his boat, laced a bright orange sail and added a jib and keel to enable him to tack into the wind. Captain Thevik made a Bermuda rig for his lifeboat, and both stocked their craft well with fishing lines, charts, ·22 hunting rifles and tarpaulins to shelter their passengers from the elements. How ironic that now that they were indeed cast adrift in these two magnificently equipped lifeboats, they were picked up after barely five minutes by the trawler *Lord Austin*, which had raced back to the scene, attracted by the smoke from the burning ship. All Commodore Dowding's wirelessed appeals for fighter protection, in code at first and then in desperation in plain language, had gone unheeded.

Now once again there were only eight naval vessels left as the burning *El Capitán* fell back over the horizon. The ship had been laden with four Boston bombers and eight Valentine tanks as deck cargo, and 7,500 tons of machinery, leather, tallow and general *matériel de guerre*, none of which would now reach the Soviet Union.

Captain Thevik was almost in tears at the loss of his fine old ship. 'I think it was you,' he reminisced to his war-time Chief Officer years later, 'who got hold of *Lord Austin*'s chief officer and asked him for a drop of rum for the old Captain as he was about all in. So I sat up in the bunk and took it easy, and the midnight sun was looking in at the porthole. My very good chief mate was sleeping on the sofa and the poor little *Lord Austin* was ploughing steadily on towards the entrance to the White Sea—and the Jerries were likely gone home for a glass of beer. And my good old ship *El Capitán* on her way down to the bottom of the Barents Sea...'.[73]

The battle was over. In the escort ships, Flag '*Q*' was hauled down. 'Secure from action stations' was piped around them. More gallons of tea were being brewed, and the gunners' parties were already checking over their guns, refilling the magazines and counting and collecting the cartridge-cases. Now that the two last lame freighters had been disposed of, the escorts could increase speed, and did, to over 11 knots as they headed for Iokanka, the small Russian port outside the entrance to the White Sea.

As the rescue ship *Zamalek* gradually caught up with the speeding convoy, Captain Owen Morris saw that the anti-aircraft ship *Pozarica* was altering course and coming close alongside. For a moment he toyed with the idea of signalling *Pozarica* not to come too close, as he was trying to draw the enemy's fire. Then he saw that the anti-aircraft ship's crew were tumbling out of hatches and companionways, and off gun-platforms, into the wing of her bridge and were lining the rails of the ship, dwarfing the tiny *Zamalek*. The AA ship's company was 'manning ship': not only that, for as the two ships slowly closed on each other, rising and falling in the gentle seas, the Royal Navy doffed caps, held them high and roared themselves hoarse for the gallant rescue ship which had come out of the jaws of hell. It was so unexpected that Captain Morris found himself choking with emotion. The anti-aircraft ship's powerful Ardente amplifier was crackling, and then the voice of a woman, many times amplified, boomed out across the short stretch of water dividing the two ships, bellowing a line from a famous war-time song, *'Oh, What a Night it was, Really was, Such a Night . . . !'*

Captain Morris ordered the *Zamalek*'s Red Ensign to be dipped in acknowledgement; then his crew gave the anti-aircraft ship three cheers for its protection. 'See you in Archangel,' he bellowed through a megaphone to his opposite number on the bridge of the slate-grey warship, and the two vessels moved apart.

The latter stages of the air attack on the *Zamalek* convoy had been seen from afar, but not heard, by the crews of the two merchant ships following far behind them, *Ocean Freedom* and *Samuel Chase*, escorted by two RN minesweepers and two Asdic trawlers. At 2.56 a.m. they had seen disembodied AA shell-bursts in the sky and several aircraft wheeling over some object beyond the southern horizon; the attack on *El Capitán* was also seen and, many hours afterwards, they saw a sudden explosion and the *Capitán* sinking.[2] Half an hour later, at 9 a.m., the minesweeper *Britomart* saw a single German submarine sitting impudently on the surface, trailing them on a parallel course four miles on their starboard quarter. The submarine stayed there for about an hour, and then vanished.

The submarine was probably Commander Reche's *U-255* again. He had certainly been following these six ships for over two hours when he was first sighted, and he had already radioed details of this new group of ships to Narvik. An hour after Reche's first report, Commander Bielfeld (*U-703*) was also reporting sighting a group of two merchant ships and four escort vessels, heading south-west towards the White Sea, so Schmundt's office was in no doubt but that a second group of ships existed. Two further signals lay on Admiral Schmundt's desk when he entered it that morning, 10 July: *U-376* had finished off *Hoosier*, laden with tanks; and Commander Timm (*U-251*) had torpedoed a second freighter, which accounts for the sudden explosion in *El Capitán* seen by the following ships. Air Force reconnaissance sighted the burning *El Capitán* and the surviving ships soon after. Timm reported to Narvik that his U-boat was suffering from a faulty diesel compressor and could barely submerge, and Reche had lost the enemy by now. By this time, however, Commander Brandenburg's *U-457* had also found the convoy being trailed by Bielfeld, a group of two merchantmen and four escorts, and he radioed its position to Narvik.

The target had thus been definitely located, but it was right on the 69th parallel, south of which the U-boats had been instructed not to proceed. Admiral Schmundt decided that if the submarines were in contact, they should be allowed to exploit the situation to the full. At 11.26 a.m. he wirelessed the 'Ice Devil' pack:

According to aerial reconnaissance 7.41 a.m., blazing freighter sighted at pinpoint AC.9797. Permission granted to operate to within 30 miles of coast, or line between Cape Kanin Nos and Svyatoi Nos.

Naval Group North in Kiel also recommended that the U-boats should be allowed to follow their quarries into the jaws of the White Sea. But beyond Cape Kanin even they thought the risks too great. Schmundt, in the meantime, was obliged to assume that quite apart from this latest little bunch of ships, the possibility of still further stragglers coming down from the north could not be ruled out.[63]

At 11.07 a.m. sixteen Junkers 88s of the first squadron of *KG.30* and the experimental squadron from Petsamo thundered in to make the final attack on these six ships, concentrating their venom on the two large merchant vessels. The aircraft arrived when the ships were just north of Iokanka, and delivered a series of terrifyingly accurate attacks from well above the ships' gun-range.[74] Twenty miles to the south-west, watchers lining the decks of the ships in *Zamalek*'s convoy were witnessing an amazing spectacle, refracted by the layers of air of different temperature so common in these parts: they had heard by radiotelephone that the six ships were only some twenty-miles behind them, and when they scanned the north-eastern horizon they had seen the bombing attack just begin. Each bomb hitting the sea had thrown up a pillar of water, which was so refracted and inverted that it became a huge mushroom of spray to the distant watchers. Suddenly, high in the sky, there were ships, *upside down*, suspended on 'mushrooms' of salt water. 'It was all so silly,' wrote one watcher. 'There were spikes, cones, pyramids, pillars—all very beautifully suspended for many, many seconds. My Captain said to me, "Cook's Tours can't boast of that attraction." I knew it was refraction—so did we all. Perhaps we were at the perfect distance for a perfect view. Here before our eyes was a sight for poets—not for seamen. Here was something that could rouse from sleep the whole of the ship's company, and that is a fine compliment far above the words of any poet.'[75]

After ninety minutes of determined dive-bombing, with several near misses on both ships, the attack ended. *Samuel Chase*'s engine had stopped, all her steam lines had been severed and her auxiliaries cut off, and the compass had been blown out of its binnacle.[76] The Germans claimed that she 'sank within a few hours'. But now her escort were more than ever determined to cheat the Germans of this last prize, and a minesweeper and an Asdic trawler were detached to stand over the crippled American; the minesweeper took the heavy merchantman in tow, while *Ocean Freedom* raced on alone to Iokanka with *Britomart* and *Northern Gem* escorting her.[77] Three minutes before 1 p.m. a single Junkers 88 came roaring in, and straddled the British freighter so accurately that her compasses were unshipped and her Master, Captain William Walker, was badly injured in the hip by a bomb splinter. But as the sea water poured off the ship she righted herself and her engines were still running; and land was coming into sight at last. A compass could be dispensed with now.*

The Germans claimed that the Briton was so badly damaged by two 'direct hits' with 1,000-pounders that she could be 'considered destroyed'. The Fifth Air Force summarized, 'Thus the surviving ships of the convoy which were trying to reach Iokanka were annihilated.' But *Samuel Chase* and *Ocean Freedom* were not to be cheated of victory so easily. A Russian flying-boat flew low over-head, and turned back to the coast again, obviously fetching reinforcements. *Britomart*'s captain stationed the Asdic trawler ahead of the blind merchantman to pilot her, while he himself continued his anti-submarine sweep around them.

At half-past one that afternoon, the two merchant ships were sighted again by the amazed German aerial reconnaissance, 120 miles east of Murmansk and proceeding separately, each accom-panied by 'patrol boats'. Eighteen more Junkers 88s were scrambled from *II./KG.30*'s base at Banak, detailed to finish off these troublesome freighters. But at 3.45 p.m., as the bombers rose above the horizon of the enemy's radar system, German radio monitors heard a British unit ashore transmit a warning of immi-nent air attack on 'convoy "Competent"' ten miles north of Svyatoi Nos, and an hour later they heard Murmansk radioing the unwelcome news 'Fighter cover for "Competent" has been scrambled.'[78] As the eighteen Junkers 88s were about to swoop on the two merchant ships, many miles apart by now, a swarm of Russian Pe.3 and Hurricane fighters appeared and beat them back. The German aircraft returned to Banak, thwarted, savaging a destroyer and a stray coaster on their way back.

So it was only now, after the ships had covered 2,500 miles from Iceland, and in sight of the Russian coast, that the Soviet Union was forthcoming with its defences. Soon after, two mine-

---

* Captain Walker of *Ocean Freedom*, Captain F. W. Harvey of *Empire Tide* and Captains Banning of *Rathlin* and Morris of *Zamalek* were awarded the DSO for their heroism in this convoy. This military decoration had not hitherto been awarded to any Merchant Navy officer or seaman (*London Gazette*, 29 September 1942). They were also awarded the Lloyd's War Medal for Bravery at Sea (*Lloyd's List*, 31 August 1943). See also footnotes on pages 180 and 194.

sweepers from Captain Crombie's First Minesweeping Flotilla, *Hazard* and *Leda,* came into sight. The minesweeper *Britomart* gave them the position of the crippled *Samuel Chase* and proceeded towards Iokanka with the British *Ocean Freedom.*

At Iokanka, the eight escorts of *Zamalek*'s convoy were waiting for them. They had anchored there shortly before noon, but there was no oiler waiting for them. It was warm and sticky. The officers and men had not been out of the kapok suits for four days, ever since leaving Matochkin Strait. Before they left for the last sheltered leg of their voyage to the White Sea and Archangel, a signal reached the escorts that two Russian destroyers at Iokanka had offered to show them the way to the entrance to the White Sea. The Royal Navy's ships weighed anchor at 12.30 p.m., grateful for this added protection, with the Russian destroyers leading the way. The Russian destroyers were weird ships with their guns all in separate mountings and all facing aft. Outside the port entrance, the destroyers 'showed them the way' to the White Sea, and turned back to their berths. The corvette *La Malouine*'s Captain recovered his astonishment in time to signal them by 10-inch projector, 'Hope you get back safely.' But there was no acknowledgement of this from the Russian destroyers.

All the ships proceeded in single line ahead towards the Gorlo —'neck'—the entrance to the White Sea. By midnight, a Russian minesweeper force had joined company, and a Hurricane fighter and a Stormovik bomber were circling overhead. For the first time in many days there was a slight darkness. It began to rain heavily, and the ice disappeared. Moscow Radio announced that Soviet airmen had shot down thirty German aircraft that day, and repeated that the convoy had arrived 'safely'. To which a Portuguese propagandist replied, 'It would appear then that the ships which were sunk have finished their voyage under water.'[79]

This was the end of the story for the rescue ship *Zamalek.* If any single ship ever deserved to have a film made of her life, it was Captain Morris's sturdy vessel, whose life from her passenger-carrying days in the Levant to her ignominious end in 1956— scuttled in Port Ibrahim by the Egyptians after Suez, and cut up by United Nations salvage engineers after the settlement was reached—was more colourful than any fiction. On the next convoy after PQ.17, one of the Russian ships' officers rescued by *Zamalek* gave birth to a baby in the vessel's operating theatre; but that is another story.

Early on the afternoon of 11 July, *Zamalek*'s little convoy swept proudly down the Dvina river, past the saw-mills, the ferry-boats packed with silent women workers, and the thousands of logs floating in the river. Some of the villages gave them a rousing cheer as they passed; others remained silent. At four o'clock, *Zamalek* berthed in the minareted port of Archangel, 2,490 miles out from Seidisfiord; before he could be stopped, the American seaman who had been transferred to them insane four days earlier jumped overboard and swam the last few yards to the shore. Captain Maund, the British Senior Officer, personally boarded the rescue ship to greet her Welsh Master.

The rescue ship *Rathlin* and the American freighter *Bellingham* were already there, together with the Russian tanker *Donbass*. (The latter owed her survival in no small measure to the American seamen she had rescued. Though at the extreme limit of physical endurance, they had manned one gun, brought another into service and fought continuously at action stations for several days and nights until the tanker reached Molotovsk; a high-ranking Soviet government official personally thanked Captain George Sullivan for the unselfish effort of his crew.[80]) One day later, the American freighter *Samuel Chase* also limped into Molotovsk.

'Three ships brought into port out of thirty-seven,' Commodore Dowding reported to the naval authorities in Archangel on the 13th. '*Not* a successful convoy.'[81]

✳ 7 ✳

There were still a score or more lifeboats, and many rafts, scattered about the Barents Sea, some still several hundred miles from the nearest land. Five days after *Carlton* had been sunk, on 10 July, her survivors saw the first sign of human life: a lone aircraft came over the horizon, and turned out to be an RAF Catalina, probably taking part in a search operation. There was little wind, and the sea was glassy smooth, so the American seamen expressed some hope that the flying-boat would land and pick them up. The aircraft circled the lifeboat several times, then dropped a package into the sea nearby: it contained a rubber life suit, corned beef and biscuits, and a message reading 'Help is on the way'. Unfortunately, most of the seamen took this cheering news literally, and within the next few hours they consumed a goodly quantity of their food and water rations in a bacchanalian celebration feast. Then they settled back to wait for the rescue, which never came. [82]

As far as the German Air Force was concerned, the operation was over. Colonel-General Stumpff, of the Fifth Air Force, telegraphed to Reichsmarschall Herman Göring on 12 July:

Herr Reichsmarschall!

I beg to report the destruction of convoy PQ.17. During reconnaissance executed on 12 July over the White Sea, the western passage, the Kola coast and the waters to the north of the coast, not a single merchant ship was observed.

Photographic reconnaissance of Iokanka showed that no ship belonging to PQ. 17 has reached that port. I report the sinking by the Fifth Air Force of: one cruiser; one destroyer; two escorts totalling 4,000 tons; 22 merchant ships totalling 142,216 tons. [83]

Of these sinkings, the lion's share was claimed by the Junkers 88 units. The cost of this victory was remarkably low; the Junkers 88s had flown only 130 sorties, dropping just 212 tons of bombs; the Heinkel 111-T torpedo-bombers had flown forty-three sorties (of which twenty, on 5 July, were abortive) dropping a total of forty-six aerial torpedoes, and the Heinkel 115 torpedo-bombers had flown only twenty-nine sorties (of which six were abortive) resulting in the expenditure of fifteen aerial torpedoes.

Only five aircraft had failed to return during the whole operation, of which the crew of one (a Heinkel 115) had been recovered in the daring rescue under the guns of British destroyers, while the crew of another (a Heinkel 111) had been picked up by the destroyer *Ledbury*. Two other Heinkel 111s had returned to base with fatal casualties aboard from ships' gunfire. The remaining missing aircraft were the Focke-Wulf 200 brought down by the gunners of the *Bellingham*, one Blohm & Voss shadower and one other Heinkel 111 lost during the big evening attack on 4 July, and subsequently credited with having crashed his bomber on an American cruiser (*U-334*'s sighting of a 'sinking cruiser' could not otherwise be explained). [84]

At about the same time as *Zamalek* was docking at Archangel, Admiral Miles and his interpreter were being ushered into Admiral Kusnetsov's room by Admiral Alafusov. Kusnetsov was the Soviet Chief of Naval Staff, and his office was in the new Admiralty building in Moscow. 'We had a very interesting discussion about convoys afterwards,' Miles cautiously noted in his diary. That morning, he had received from Admiral Pound what in his opinion was a very unconvincing explanation of the PQ.17 decisions taken in Whitehall, and had paraphrased it as accurately as possible for the Russians. The interview was 'chilly'; but afterwards the Soviet Chief of Naval Staff led Miles and the interpreter out of his cavernous office, and into his adjoining ante-room, where over caviar and cognac he commiserated with the British admiral for having been landed in such a position by his superiors.[85] The Russian was probably mellowed by the news that both the Russian ships in the convoy had in fact escaped destruction.

In London, it seemed that only a handful of the ships would ever arrive. When Mr Maisky, the Soviet Ambassador, called on Mr Eden on 14 July to ask whether there was any news of the convoy, the British Foreign Secretary could only tell him that what news there was was very bad; only five ships out of the forty-odd which had sailed had got through, and it was possible that two more might yet do so. Out of 600 tanks, only about a hundred had arrived. Maisky, with more verve than tact, asked Eden what plans the British had for the next convoy. The Foreign Secretary rejoined that the British Government had learned a lesson from the last one; Admiral Pound held the belief that if he were on the German side, he could guarantee that not one of the next convoy's ships would reach port. It was, said Eden, no help to the Russians for the Allies to send convoys out and have nearly all the ships sunk.[86] The Admiralty felt it would be necessary to cancel all further PQ convoys until the autumn. This kind of answer did not satisfy the Russians: Admiral N. M. Harlamov, head of the Soviet military mission in London, made no attempt to hide his indignation about the fate of PQ.17, and Mr Churchill was finally obliged to ask Eden to call a meeting between the Admiralty and Soviet government representatives. Two weeks passed without the meeting being called.[87]

8

FIRST BACK FROM HELL
6 July — 21 July

The more law that comes to sea, the better, and let litigation look after itself.
—Senior British Naval Officer, north Russia, to an ex-barrister
Lieutenant who had saved three merchant ships, 15 July 1942

IN ARCHANGEL, many anxious voices were raised about the
fate of the Asdic trawler *Ayrshire*, commanded by Lieutenant
Leo Gradwell. The trawlers that had been requisitioned for
convoy escort duties were not the most popular of the Naval
vessels, but this one had inexplicably inspired a high degree of
fondness, ever since leaving Iceland. We last saw her many days
ago, on 5 July, steaming slowly northwards into the ice, while
three merchant ships—*Troubadour, Ironclad* and *Silver Sword*—
trustingly followed her in. In obedience to Gradwell's commands,
they had painted their vessels white, and listened in anguish to
the wirelessed appeals for help being broadcast by the less fortunate vessels to the south of them. Many of the distress
signals had given no indication of the nature of their attackers
and, unable to decipher the signals from the Admiralty, Gradwell
could only assume that the German battle fleet was marauding
in the Barents Sea. This strengthened his resolve to lie low until
the wave of distress signals had died down.[1]

During 6 July, however, the wind changed to southerly, and
the heavy ice began to show signs of packing against the ships.
Lieutenant Gradwell decided the time had come to edge through
the ice-field and out to sea again, following the technique he had
found laid down in the navigation manual: steaming very slowly
towards the ice, until the bows just touched it, and then giving
the engines a sudden burst of power so that the ship rode up on
top and the ice broke under its weight.[2] Sometimes the ice was
alarmingly thick, and refused to break. Gradwell ordered the
sixty men in his crew to run together backwards and forwards
along the deck, rocking the trawler until the ice cracked. If
the the worst had come to the worst, he was prepared to

depth-charge the ice-field. At nine o'clock that night, after two days in the ice-pack, the four ships of Lieutenant Gradwell's private convoy broke out into the Barents Sea again, and set cautious sail for Novaya Zemlya.[3]

For two days and more they skirted in almost continuous fog along the ice-edge. On the 7th they heard *Pankraft* blow up, and later that day they heard an aircraft passing overhead, but these were the only incidents before they sighted land again; in the early hours of 9 July the four ships ran into a fiord, in the northern half of Novaya Zemlya, and here they were once again able to conceal themselves against the background of a sparkling glacier. While *Ayrshire* took this opportunity to coal and water from the freighter *Troubadour*, Gradwell called a conference of the three ships' Masters aboard his trawler to discuss their further plan of action.

He had tried in vain to contact Archangel, so he had directed his wireless operator to try to pick up any German broadcast about the convoy. As the four ships lay at anchor in this fiord, the latest communiqué from Germany was picked up: this announced that in a series of air and submarine attacks, 'only three ships escaped destruction so far, which however are still being pursued'. This was discomfiting news, but Lieutenant Gradwell had the message sheet posted on his ship's bulletin board, with the hopeful postscript that perhaps the German facts should be 'taken with a pinch of salt'.*

The three merchant ships' Masters were not encouraged to learn that apparently only their ships had survived this far; it was clear that their morale was very low indeed. Lieutenant Gradwell learned that they had decided on an almost certain way of bringing their three crews safely to Archangel. They planned to scuttle their three ships in that very fiord, transfer their crews and food supplies to the trawler and travel the rest of the way as inconspicuous passengers aboard her. A pained Lieutenant Gradwell pointed out to them that this was not the object of convoy operations.

---

* The despatch appears to have been a telegraphic communiqué transmitted for foreign newspapers. Gradwell headed it: 'German version of Russian Convoy. Intercepted Enemy Press Report.'

Having completed coaling and watering, he sent his First Lieutenant, Elsden, aboard *Ironclad* to defuse the shell that had been put through her bows by another freighter on 4 July, and he announced that he intended to lead them to Matochkin Strait and arrange for the radio station at its western end to apprise Archangel of their presence. There was but one obstacle to this plan: he was convinced that the Germans were masters of the Barents Sea, which meant that there would be a German occupation force to be silenced in the strait before his three charges could safely anchor there.

As the four ships moved out of the bay, and headed south towards the well-concealed entrance to Matochkin Strait, Dick Elsden assembled a raiding party of sailors and American Armed Guard personnel from the merchantmen. They were armed with a remarkable collection of tommy-guns (broken out of the M-3 tanks in the deck cargo),pistols and rifles, ready to invade Novaya Zemlya from *Ayrshire*'s whaler. With total silence ordered on all ships, the little armada crept round the mole at the entrance to the strait. They were not challenged, but with a loud screech the *Ironclad* went aground on a submerged rock formation. As Gradwell hastened to screen the merchantman, believing that she had been torpedoed, *Ayrshire* also ran aground, crushing her Asdic anti-submarine dome.

Relations with the American officers were strained at this time in any case, in consequence of Gradwell's rejection of their Master-plan for scuttling the freighters. *Ironclad*'s Master, a former tugboat captain from New England, met Gradwell as he came aboard and in a drawl which the British officer found rather offensive said, 'All right, Lootenant, if you're so smart—you get her off.' The Master descended to his own quarters to have lunch, leaving Gradwell in command.

With the Americans refloated, the invasion began afresh. At six o'clock that evening, the ships anchored and swung their sterns round in the tide just sufficiently to bring the entire weight of ship and tank armament to bear on the unsuspecting radio station. While *Ayrshire*'s whaler was lowered, Gradwell ordered his 4-inch gun to be laid off with shrapnel for use if the Germans should prove tougher than expected. But as the Naval party advanced across the strait, a civilian came out to meet them in a

punt—very evidently a Russian. At the same time, they saw a
Soviet flag being hastily run up the radio-station's flagpole. Never
can machine-guns and pistols have been harder to conceal in
Naval clothing.

Half an hour later, Elsden was back aboard the trawler. He had
a scrap of paper given him by the Russians, showing the cruising
order of the little convoy that had left the strait three days before.
Apparently there were still five other merchantmen afloat at that
time, and several escort vessels.

The Russians had also told him that to the south of the strait
there were three lifeboats full of shipwrecked seamen. *Ayrshire*
proceeded at once to the spot, and found that they were seamen
from the American *Fairfield City*; there were thirty-four of them,
all delirious and in a very bad way except for the German-
American Third Officer and the Chief Engineer, who was as fearful
as his comrades were ill. As soon as he boarded the trawler, this
officer unbuckled a large automatic pistol and presented it to
Gradwell, crying that he did not want to be found armed in any
way if the Germans should capture the trawler. He kept asking,
'Do you think we are going to get through? Do you think we'll
be mined? Do you think we'll be torpedoed?' Gradwell accepted
the gun, and coldly told him that he had no doubt whatsoever
that they would be sunk; there was not the smallest chance of
getting anywhere near Archangel.

Lieutenant Elsden had been advised by the Russians that the
best anchorage was some nine miles up the strait, and a Russian
motor launch piloted them to it; Gradwell had no chart of Novaya
Zemlya, and had been relying only on a *Times Handy Atlas* for
his navigation. According to the manuals, the eastern part of the
strait was habitually cold, and it was indeed bitterly so. The strait
was deep, and the cliffs were high; to find bottom at all, the
freighters had to anchor close to these mountainous cliffs. But by
their new anchorage was a Russian hospital, and Gradwell had
three seriously ill survivors from *Fairfield City* transferred ashore.
Here too they found a fourth merchant ship, the American
Liberty ship *Benjamin Harrison* which had put out with *Zamalek*'s
little convoy some days before, and lost contact in the fog.
Benjamin Harrison's Master, Captain E. J. Christensen, told
Gradwell that his men wanted fresh milk, now that they were in

harbour; the British Lieutenant was unable to humour his request. Uncertain whether or not the wireless station had reported the ships' arrival to Archangel, because of the language difficulty, Lieutenant Gradwell waited for further instructions.*

✳   2   ✳

Lieutenant Gradwell's private convoy was not alone in Novaya Zemlya. After seeing *Alcoa Ranger* torpedoed before his eyes some days earlier, the *Empire Tide*'s Master had turned his ship round and run for shelter into Moller Bay on Novaya Zemlya's south-western coast. There was a little wireless station and a settlement there, and by this means Captain Harvey had sent a message to Archangel asking for medical aid for one of his gunners, who had been shot through the thigh by a machine-gun bullet during the air battle on the 4th. He had also asked the Russians to inform British Naval Control of *Empire Tide*'s presence there.[4]

Several rafts and lifeboats had also reached the shores of the huge, barren island, and the seamen were now eking out an uncomfortable 'Robinson Crusoe' existence.

Through the morning mists of 8 July, nine survivors of the sinking of *Olopana* had seen the phantom shapes of *Zamalek*'s convoy flit by, as they crouched on a raft with the ship's Master, Captain Stone.[5] They had lit flares and shouted, but 'no assistance was rendered, probably because vigilance could not be relaxed,' as Captain Stone reported later in Archangel. In fact, none of the ships or their escorts seems to have seen the flares. During the night, it began to rain lightly, but Captain Stone kept all the men manning his raft's oars to maintain their blood circulation and make some progress to land, which he thought should be only ten miles away. During the early hours, two corvettes were seen through the mist, 'hunting around like bloodhounds', but efforts to attract their attention were again disappointing. At about eight

---

* Later, the Americans joined in the universal praise of Gradwell and his 'mighty little ship'. In Archangel, the Master of *Silver Sword* wrote on 8 August to Captain Maund, the SBNO, drawing attention to the Lieutenant's 'high courage' and adding 'I do not know how we could ever have reached Archangel without his aid.'

o'clock in the morning, the fog had lifted, and they sighted North Gusini Light on Novaya Zemlya; then they sighted land itself.

After two days' continuous rowing, they beached their heavy raft at 4.30 a.m. on 10 July, on a stretch of beach seven miles south of the Light, and free of outlying reefs—a circumstance which undoubtedly saved many lives, for to the north were the high, rocky cliffs and to the south were reefs extending for several miles offshore. The exhausted American seamen tumbled on to dry land, and after a short spell for them to relax and for 'everyone in his own way to meditate on his survival', the rafts were broken up and used to build a windbreak, while driftwood was collected to start a fire. Two officers set off towards the Light, to see if there was any means of communication there. The others drifted off into a deep sleep before a blazing fire.

As the two *Olopana* officers approached the Light, they found that three miles beyond it a large merchant ship had evidently run aground. Captain Stone and a number of men set off on a forced march towards this ship, leaving the Second Officer in charge of their makeshift 'camp'. Stone was afraid that the stranded ship might manage to refloat herself and sail away before he could get his men safely aboard her. Upon reaching the Light, he lashed a yellow flag to its top, some four hundred feet up, and he started a fire to attract the strange ship's attention.

After a time, one of the ship's lifeboats was seen to put out, and after a long pull against the current it beached below the lighthouse. The lifeboat was manned by an Armed Guard officer of the US Naval Reserve. He brought some provisions for the shipwrecked seamen. The American officer told the astonished Captain Stone that the Master of his ship, *Winston-Salem*, was 'preparing to abandon her'. Stone requested to be taken to see the Master, and within an hour he was talking to him, together with the injured Captain Stephenson of the British *Hartlebury*. It was decided to build a camp ashore capable of housing about a hundred seamen. For legal reasons, *Winston-Salem*'s seamen would ferry the large quantities of stores carried by the ship ashore, while *Hartlebury*'s survivors assisted in handling them on the beach and erecting a tarpaulin covering for them. The three Masters also agreed that should *Winston-Salem* be attacked, a radio message would be broadcast covering all three ships. During the afternoon, they had their first alarm when a flying-boat arrived and circled the ship, drawing closer each time. As *Winston-Salem*'s guns had been 'rendered useless in preparation for abandonment of ship'*—as Stone reported in Archangel—the seamen were all more than anxious about their position. But then they saw its Red Star emblem, and realized that it was a Russian-manned Catalina. The plane headed off southwards, while the seamen resumed their round-the-clock work of unloading the ship's cargo.

The Russian Catalina, piloted by a famous Arctic flyer, Captain I. P. Mazuruk, brought medical aid for the injured gunner aboard *Empire Tide*, about thirty miles to the north. Russian officials aboard the aircraft instructed Captain Harvey to remain at anchor where he was. A woman doctor examined the injured gunner and decided that an immediate operation was necessary. He was transferred on a stretcher to the Catalina by motor-boat; Mazuruk took off, and transferred the gunner to a hospital elsewhere on the island. Harvey logged, 'His effects and wages due—amounting to £1 12s 6d—are to be handed over to HM Consul at Archangel.'⁶ Before he left, Mazuruk told Harvey that a Russian coaster had been sent to pick up further survivors stranded along the coast; he had seen some of them already making their way towards the settlement.

Captain Harvey sent a party ashore to forage for eggs and birds, and to erect signs and beacons along the shore to guide the other shipwrecked seamen to *Empire Tide*'s anchorage. In the meantime he would not sail without a full naval escort.

---

* The Sailing Orders issued to Masters of US merchant ships specifically prohibited this kind of action: 'There shall be no surrender and no abandoning ship so long as the guns can be fought. The Navy Department considers that so long as there remains a chance to save the ship the Armed Guard should remain thereon.' Equally, the Master's order to abandon ship did not apply to the Armed Guard, who were to stay until their officer so instructed them (Chapter IV, Section 1, Paragraph 413). Captain Frankel, the US naval attaché at Archangel, subsequently (13 August 1942) reported to Washington that he considered the *Winston-Salem* Armed Guard Officer's decision to render his armament inoperative 'justified in view of the factors involved'.

Captain Mazuruk made several flights up the Novaya Zemlya coast locating and picking up scattered groups of shipwrecked seamen. In the early hours of 13 July, he landed in Matochkin Strait, and discussed the position with Lieutenant Gradwell. Only now did Gradwell learn that there had been no great surface battle in the Barents Sea. He had been thinking in terms of breaking through into the Kara Sea, and heading for Siberia or even for Canada to restart the war from there. Now he began to re-examine the prospect of heading for the White Sea and Archangel.

He still refused to put out to sea without a proper escort. Before Mazuruk returned to Murmansk, Gradwell wrote a hurried report on the position for the naval authorities in north Russia:

> The situation at present is that there are four ships here in Matochkin Strait. My Asdic is out of action, and the Masters of the ships are showing unmistakable signs of strain. I much doubt if I could persuade them to make a dash for Archangel without a considerably increased escort and a promise of fighter protection in the entrance to the White Sea. Indeed, there has already been talk of scuttling ships while near shore rather than go to what they, with their present escort, consider certain sinking.
>
> In these circumstances, I submit that increased escort might be provided, and that I may be informed as to how to obtain air protection. I shall remain in the Matochkin Strait until I receive a reply.[7]

Having despatched this note, Lieutenant Gradwell took his convoy some twenty miles farther eastwards along the strait as the Russian officer had warned him that his ships were still visible from seaward.* They did make some attempt to set off for Archangel, but *Ironclad* and *Troubadour* 'went aground' almost at

---

* Gradwell's letter was the first news of *Ayrshire* and several other ships that had been received by Admiral Bevan, the SBNO North Russia. 'It was a great adventure,' he wrote to ex-barrister Gradwell on 15 July. 'I believe that *Ayrshire* is very legally minded. All I can say is that if this is the case, the more law that comes to sea the better, and let litigation look after itself, until there are no more PQ convoys!' Even the Russian Admiral Golovko felt compelled to write to Bevan on 16 July praising Gradwell for saving three ships, and for refloating *Ironclad* when she had run aground.

once and more time was wasted in towing them off. On the following afternoon, the heavily armed Russian trawler *Kirov* arrived, with news that a search party was being organized to take them in. Communicating by means of the International Code, Gradwell learned that Archangel was sending out corvettes to meet him and bring him in, and that a Russian ice-breaker was also coming. Four days later, the ice-breaker *Murman* arrived, with the Russian tanker *Azerbaijan* from the convoy; the tanker had gaping holes in her sides and her decks were buckled from the blast of the torpedo that had struck her a week before. But still there was no sign of a naval escort proper.

On 13 July, Mazuruk's Catalina landed about a thousand yards offshore, opposite a camp set up by nine of the *Olopana*'s survivors; the seamen had found *Hartlebury*'s empty jollyboat washed ashore several miles to the south, and used it now to put out to the flying-boat. Mazuruk told them to come aboard, and he flew them to a small mining town on the Soviet mainland. They reached Archangel some days later. The Soviet officer also made a detailed report to Vice-Admiral Golovko, the Admiral Commanding, Northern Fleet, on the strange affair of *Winston-Salem*, still aground in a bay on the south-western coast of Novaya Zemlya. As he reported to Golovko, he had landed his Catalina and boarded the ship, which was completely deserted although unharmed. On inspecting the ship's armament he had found that all her guns had been rendered useless. Her crew had set up camp on shore, and her Master refused to take them back on board. He told Mazuruk that he had turned his vessel into the first bay he had come to—no doubt an action which had saved her from the fate which had met the *Hartlebury* and *Olopana* and many other ships off this very stretch of coast—but had then less prudently run his ship deliberately aground, and ordered the guns to be wrecked. Of Mazuruk as a 'representative of the Soviet Government' he demanded to be provided with a seat on the first available plane to the United States. He had lost all further interest in his ship and her cargo, which were, he said, 'now in a harbour of the Soviet Union'.

Admiral Golovko must have choked to hear this latter claim. 'By harbour,' he wrote in his diary, 'this shameless entrepreneur meant a deserted bay on an Arctic island, thousands of miles from the nearest railway line. And these are our Allies!'⁸

From midnight of 10–11 July, the German submarines were returning to base, covering as much of the convoy's route as possible as they did so. Admiral Schmundt recorded a hope that his U-boats might still be able to set about rescue ships searching for shipwrecked seamen. One by one, the U-boats ran low in fuel, and broke off the sweep to return to base. *U-355* and *U-88* returned to Narvik on 12 July and reported fully on this extraordinary convoy to Admiral Schmundt. Finally, early on 13 July, Commander Reinhard Reche radioed that he had found a deserted and drifting freighter about six hundred miles north of Murmansk —the Dutch *Paulus Potter*, still afloat eight days after being bombed and brought to a stop. Reche's signal added, 'Papers salvaged'. He had cautiously approached the merchantman, on the very edge of the ice-field, and put a three-man boarding party aboard her, including the U-boat's Chief Engineer, to see whether the ship's engines could be restarted. The latter reported that the engine-room was awash with water. As in *Marie Celeste*, the lunch-tables were fully laid. The pantry was raided, and the tables were stripped bare. The ship had oviously been abandoned in a hurry, for the boarding party found a box of secret papers on the bridge: it had been holed and staved in, but nobody had actually thrown it overboard. The papers showed the ship to be of 7,169 tons, and owned by the Dutch Government in London. Her cargo was of aeroplanes.⁹ According to Reche, the box contained 'exact details of the composition of PQ.17, the new signals codebook for convoys and other welcome papers'.¹⁰ The papers showed that the major part of the convoy had been bound for Archangel, with a minor section bound for Murmansk.

To the melancholy trill of the boatswain's pipe the Dutch flag was hauled down. While his chief officer filmed the scene from *U-255*'s conning tower, Commander Reche put his U-boat's last torpedo into the ship, and within two minutes she had sunk, on fire.¹¹ The ice-floes closed over her.

'Thus,' commented the German Naval Staff that evening, 'the last victory has been scored in the battle of PQ.17. This brings the U-boats' score up to sixteen ships totalling 113,963 tons, of which twelve ships have been identified by name. The cross-checked Air Force score is 20 ships, totalling some 131,000 tons sunk. By this reckoning, only one or two units of PQ.17 can have reached harbour at most.'[12] A study of the U-boat records shows that during the entire operation, from 2 to 10 July, the 'Ice-Devil' submarines expended seventy-two torpedoes on the convoy's ships and escorts, of which twenty-seven hit their targets and exploded.[13] On 15 July, Timm, Reche, von Hymmen, Bielfeld and Marks all brought their submarines into Narvik, followed by Brandenburg next day.

✳ 3 ✳

Shipwrecked seamen, very inadequately clad for these latitudes, were still struggling into sight of land. The raft of the *Olopana*'s Chief Engineer had finally landed thirty miles south of the Captain's raft on the coast of Novaya Zemlya. The twelve shipwrecked seaman found some oil in a can that drifted ashore, and with this they lit a driftwood fire. The smoke attracted the attention of a small Russian coaster, which took seven who were seriously ill to a hospital in Byelushya Bay. Proceeding along the coast, this little ship picked up forty-one more castaways from *Alcoa Ranger* and *Olopana*, and ferried them to *Empire Tide* in Moller Bay.

The newcomers were a considerable embarrassment to Captain Harvey and his officers, as the ship's accommodation was already strained; they were unaware that worse was to follow. Suffering badly from hunger and exposure, the crews of the *Washington* (forty-three men) and *Paulus Potter* (twenty-eight men) had also made land about forty miles north of Moller Bay after battling through floating ice and two days of snowstorms. They brewed duck soup in the lifeboats' balers, and after resting overnight followed the coastline southwards in their lifeboats until 15 July, when they were picked up by the Russian coaster and, together with fifteen more *Hartlebury* and two *Olopana* survivors, placed aboard the crowded *Empire Tide*, at anchor in the bay. Both the indigenous crew and their 129 guests were put on short rations, and fresh water was at a very high premium indeed.[14] Almost all these new survivors were in a pitiful condition, having crossed

[279]

several hundred miles of open sea in their lifeboats. Fifty of them were unable even to walk, and were suffering from severe frostbite. A British Catalina seaplane landed in the bay, and Captain Harvey went out in *Empire Tide*'s motor-launch to ask the pilot to report the critical situation to the Archangel naval authorities. He could already sense very grave trouble brewing between the crews.

The Russian coaster had also brought a small stock of foodstuffs salvaged from *Winston-Salem*, aground farther down the coast, including tins of pork, corned beef, some bags of beans and one bag of flour; these were held in reserve. With great foresight the Russian vessel had also towed along six of the shipwrecked seamen's lifeboats, for use should the British vessel be attacked when she made her final dash for Archangel. It was a voyage to which nobody was looking forward with enthusiasm.

The motor-launch was used to ferry many of the worst frostbite cases, their fingers and toes black from exposure to the Arctic elements, to the settlement ashore. The others crept into every corner of the ship seeking warmth and sleep: 'Wherever you look you see poor chaps sleeping heavily in a state of exhaustion.'[15]

Once ashore, the task of carrying the sick up to the huts of the settlement was a nightmare. The groaning seamen had to be manhandled over sharp-edged rocks buried beneath the snow 'like huge tiles set up on edge'. The ship had only two stretchers, so most had to be carried bodily up the slope on the backs of their more fortunate comrades, while the local population of snarling husky dogs snapped around their heels. 'This insignificant little hill grew to be a mountain, with a fairly hefty man on your back,' Harvey recorded.

The nine worst frostbite cases were put aboard Captain Mazuruk's Catalina when he next called, on the 17th, to be flown to base hospital for immediate amputation of their feet. When Mazuruk left, he took Captain Stone to report personally to the Naval authorities, as there was distressingly little news from them.

It was two days before he reached Archangel. He reported to the US Assistant Naval Attaché, Captain S. B. Frankel, and to Captain Maund. He told Frankel that *Winston-Salem*'s Master was demanding to be fetched by an American destroyer and flown back to the United States with his crew; Frankel's reaction was to 'let them stew in their own juice'.[16] Captain Maund learned that *Winston-Salem*'s crew had removed a 'hell of a lot' of foodstuffs from their ship.[17] As a result of Stone's reports, steps were taken to send food and blankets up to Moller Bay, and to find some way of refloating *Winston-Salem*. 'The fly in the ointment in North Russia,' reported Stone, 'is apparent lack of close liaison between Russian and Allied forces.'

The condition of several of the survivors worsened after Mazuruk's plane left, and the Russian settlement's medical officer was brought aboard *Empire Tide* on the 17th to attend to them. While he was ministering to them that evening, a single Junkers 88 bomber appeared overhead, and circled the ship at great height. Captain Harvey prepared to catapult his Hurricane from the foredeck, but the sight of the fighter's whirring propeller appears to have sufficed, for the enemy aircraft sheered off at once. The half-forgotten sound of alarm bells ringing 'action stations' was the last straw for the survivors, however. All had been sunk once by the Germans, and none wanted a second dose. After a heated 'council of war', forty-six of them decided to abandon ship and set up camp ashore. If the ship was sunk, at least they would not have to swim for it. 'This decision was made entirely on their own accord, and they received no suggestion or order from me of any description,' stressed Captain Harvey.[18]

The foodstuffs 'salvaged' from *Winston-Salem* were divided equally among three of the lifeboats, and Harvey gave each boat a bag of flour from his own stores. The seamen were warned that they could not 'make a restaurant' of the merchant ship. At 11.15 p.m. the three boats left, crowded with the survivors of *Washington, Olopana* and *Hartlebury*. They set up two camps ashore in sight of the ship, leaving some officers and ratings, and all the ships' Masters, aboard *Empire Tide,* which they clearly considered doomed.

The ships' Masters (*Olopana*'s chief officer deputising for Captain Stone, now in Archangel) signed a declaration rejecting all liability for the deserters:

Empire Tide
This is to Certify: that the men who decided to land ashore from the above ship were given an equal proportion of the stores which had

been brought up for them, and that they left the ship of their own free will and responsibility, having had no orders or suggestions from us to do so, and that we, the undersigned, accept no responsibility whatsoever for their actions.[19]

Captain Harvey had, in any case, problems of his own, of which the freshwater shortage was the most critical.

British inventiveness in desperate plights came to his aid. Originally, they had tried filling the ship's American steel lifeboats with snow and towing them back to the ship; but this brought very little water indeed. Harvey's seamen found a freshwater river some way inland, but how could they get the water to the ship? Working parties were organized to dig a small canal down to the sea shore; driftwood was collected and the canal was lined with rocks and wood to keep the water flowing clean; sluices were built to control the flow. The ship's Chief Engineer constructed a funnel and nozzle from several tins. The trench was extended by means of an aqueduct across the beach, so that it was above the level of the lifeboats' gunwales. The river water was then led along the canal and aqueduct into the funnel, and poured through one of the ship's firehoses into the steel lifeboat. When it was half-full, the sluices were closed and the lifeboat was towed to the ship and pumped out into the ship's water tanks. In this way, *twenty tons* of fresh water were gathered as boiler feed, to economize on the drinking water; and the shipwrecked seamen had something to wash down their diet of snared birds and beans.[15]

In Archangel, the first steps to organize the rescue of these last frightened merchant ships were being taken. Chaos after a military defeat always seems more complete than at other times, and in Archangel the chaos was absolute. News was beginning to filter through about the reasons for the disaster, but the truth was hard to come by, and it seemed to become lodged at the higher levels without permeating down to levels where the mood was already ugly, without the truth to make things worse. Lieutenant Caradus and several officers searched out Captain Maund's headquarters at Norway House, hoping to hear some details of what had happened to ships of the convoy, and what had happened to the 'German destroyers' which had put such fear into them.

'Reluctance on part of staff to discuss the subject. Not unwelcome, but not welcome.'[20]

On the 16th, Lieutenant Rankin's corvette *Dianella* returned from her lone nine-day search for survivors with sixty-one of the crew of the British *Empire Byron* aboard, the first ship to go down after the convoy was scattered. To the American authorities, he reported that he had sighted much wreckage in the Barents Sea, including a ship's bell marked with the name SS *Edmore*. According to Lloyd's Register, this was the former name of one of the convoy's missing freighters, *Honomu*: so she had been sunk as well.*[21]

At midnight that night, Commodore Dowding sailed for Novaya Zemlya again in the corvette *Poppy*, with her sister-ships *Lotus* and *La Malouine*, on a search for further ships and survivors that would last about eight days. The indomitable Dowding was wearing a borrowed Army battledress and a junior naval officer's cap. Big green Russian charts of these unfamiliar waters had been issued to them, but they treated them with caution. There was still no food other than rice to eat, and cigarettes were strictly rationed. It was raining in torrents as the three ships sailed up the Gorlo, and blowing very hard as they thrust out into the Barents Sea. The big ice-barrier of ten days before had vanished.

Next day, the seas were still very rough and it was growing bitterly cold. *Lotus* came abeam of *La Malouine* and signalled: 'Will swap two USSR officers for fifty survivors or one packet Woodbines—won't have part open.' And of her own goods she added, 'Very seasick and reek of perfume and other non-British smells.' *La Malouine* answered shortly, 'Will keep our Woodbines.'[22]

Early on the afternoon of 19 July, they entered Byelushya Bay, where they found an anonymous raft, well stocked with biscuits, pemmican, Horlicks tablets and chocolate; upon these the hungry sailors feasted. As they sailed farther north, they sighted two Russian trawlers trying to pull *Winston-Salem* off her stretch of beach. *Lotus* 'interrogated' *Winston-Salem*, while *Poppy* approached

---

* On 17 July, the SBNO Archangel signalled *Dianella*: 'The Commander-in-Chief of the White Sea Flotilla has asked me to convey to you, your officers and ship's company his warm appreciation of your good work in rescuing sixty-one survivors under difficult conditions.'

the lighthouse nearby: here Dowding found a party of nineteen of the American ship's crew still camped, 'with two lifeboats and ample stores.'* *Poppy* lost her Asdic dome on an uncharted rock in the bay, which left only *Lotus*'s in working order. In the early hours of the 20th, the corvette *La Malouine* entered Moller Bay and found the quiet reaches where the *Empire Tide* lay at anchor— in a famous bird sanctuary, sheltering some queer feathered creatures which required a hundred yards take-off room before they could get airborne. Lieutenant Bidwell steered his corvette through squawking flocks of thousands of these birds, and brought her alongside the towering British merchantman; what seemed like hundreds of seamen were lining the latter's rails, and cheering wildly. Bidwell laconically signalled Captain Harvey: 'Greetings. Will tow you round and out of bay later.' He told Harvey to be ready to sail the following day.

Amidst great activity nineteen of the sick men were carried back aboard *Empire Tide* from the settlement hospital ashore, after the corvette had left, and the 'campers' were re-embarked before breakfast on the 20th. The officers' smoke-room was converted into a sick-bay for the seriously ill: 'Most of them cannot help themselves,' wrote Harvey in his diary that day. 'Don't know what will happen if we get an attack on the way down. Still, must not think about that!'[15] The six extra lifeboats were hoisted on to the ship's decks, or hung over the side on derricks. All her crew and survivors were allocated boat stations, and lifeboat drill was held; then they settled back to await the return of the corvette that night.

Some hours later, the three corvettes entered Matochkin Strait. The sun shone brilliantly on *Ayrshire* and her several charges, all

---

* On 22 July the US naval authorities in London cabled Washington: 'SBNO Archangel reports *Winston-Salem* not heavily aground off North Gusino and inner bottom not pierced. Crew have abandoned ship and now living in lighthouse. They have taken machine-guns and have thrown overboard breechblocks of guns and refuse assistance to Russian surveying vessel which is attempting to refloat ship. Frankel proceeded by air to take charge and now reports *Winston-Salem* crew refuse to return and navigate ship. Therefore C-in-C Northern Fleet will provide Russian crew if necessary.'

unnaturally white as though they had been through some ghastly and unnerving experience. Lieutenant Bidwell broadcast to his ship's company that Gradwell's trawler had been found alive and well, and 'great cheers' were heard from the corvette's mess decks. After a brief Masters' conference held by Dowding, to plan courses, speeds and dispositions, all the ships sailed out of the strait that evening. The corvette *La Malouine* went on ahead to collect *Empire Tide*. She passed an officer with medical knowledge to the merchantman, and brought a small quantity of foodstuffs. Eight of the worst frostbite cases from *Paulus Potter* and ten from *Hartlebury* were transferred to the corvette for the passage, then the hour-long struggle began for the 950-ton corvette to tow the 10,000-ton freighter round to face the open sea. At 2 a.m. on the morning of the 21st, in the pale light of the midnight sun, Lieutenant Bidwell shouted 'Please follow me' over his loud-hailer, and proudly led the ship out of Moller Bay. With useless Asdic, the corvette none the less zigzagged impressively ahead of *Empire Tide* as they set a perfect course to join Commodore Dowding's convoy, already some way to the south-east of them.

Two days out, and with two days to go, *Pozarica*, *Leda*, *Hazard*, *Dianella* and two Russian destroyers joined the convoy to afford extra protection, but the Germans left these ships alone. In *La Malouine* somebody was playing an 'Ink Spots' gramophone record of '*Someone's Rocking My Dream-Boat*', over and over again in his cabin. Her Captain was fast asleep in his wooden chair on the bridge. To the Germans, these ships didn't even exist.

9

INQUEST

Buzz this day that PQ.18 did not sail. Means one thing: we'll be here much longer than we hoped.—Private diary of Naval officer at Archangel, 29 July 1942

AFTER THE PQ.17 DISASTER, the British Admiralty advised suspending the Arctic convoys altogether until the autumn was drawing in. Mr Churchill proposed a rudimentary plan, whereby two battleships would accompany the next convoy to Russia, keeping well to the south and not hugging the ice; but the Admiralty could fortunately not be persuaded, and the Prime Minister had to telegraph Marshal Stalin on 17 July that 'with the greatest respect' the Western Allies had concluded that to attempt to run PQ.18 now would bring the Russians no benefit and involve a dead loss to the common cause; as he told Stalin, the final results of PQ.17 were not yet known. Only four ships had arrived at Archangel, he said, while six others were in 'harbours' in Novaya Zemlya, and these latter stood to be attacked at any time. He proposed that a senior Air Force officer be sent to Russia to discuss air protection of the convoys.[1]

He found Marshal Stalin's answer to this a 'rough and surly' one. Unimpressed by Churchill's summary history of the PQ convoys, and their perils and anxieties, the Russian leader focused his wrath on the British Admiralty's signals ordering the convoy's Naval escorts to withdraw while the merchant vessels were expected to reach Soviet ports singly and unprotected.[2] (It might here be recalled that the British was not the only Admiralty to have taken recourse to such desperate measures in an emergency; one year before, in August 1941, the Russians had abandoned sixty-seven merchant ships carrying thousands of Soviet troops from Tallinn to Leningrad to the mercy of German aircraft, and half the ships were sunk. This was not known in England at the time.)

The scale of PQ.17's material losses, when they finally became known, was indeed staggering. On Captain Frankel's orders,

[286]

Winston-Salem was refloated and finally brought into Molotovsk on 28 July, partially crewed by survivors from other ships, but she was the last to arrive. Of the thirty-five merchant vessels that had sailed with PQ.17 from Iceland, only eleven had reached Russian ports, and three of these had been saved from scuttling only through the intervention of Lieutenant Gradwell, RNVR. His little trawler *Ayrshire* suffered her final indignity—which she ill-deserved, having been the only escort to stay with her charges throughout the operation—when on traversing the last stretch of the River Dvina into Archangel she ran out of coal and had to be towed the last few miles by Commodore Dowding's corvette. But twenty-two freighters, one rescue ship and the fleet oiler had been sunk, a total of 142,518 tons of shipping. Of the eleven British ships in the convoy, only two would ever see British shores again; three more of PQ.17's surviving ships went down on the return convoy—*Silver Sword, Bellingham* and *Gray Ranger*. Nor was the loss of shipping space the only consideration, for 3,350 motor vehicles, 430 tanks, 210 bomber aircraft, 99,316 tons of general cargo including crated vehicles, radar sets, foodstuffs, steelplate and ammunition were also lost in the disaster. One-third as many tanks as in the gigantic Battle of Kursk, three times as many bombers as in the catastrophic American attack on Schweinfurt were lost in this convoy operation. In addition, the Soviet tanker *Azerbaijan* had been holed and lost her cargo of linseed oil, and much of *Winston-Salem*'s cargo had been jettisoned in Novaya Zemlya. 'Apparently PQ.18 did not sail,' Hitler was told late in August.[3]

For Disaster Convoy PQ.17 this was almost the end of the story. In Archangel, rumour had it that seven of the eight seamen who had deserted *Azerbaijan* had already been executed by their fellow-countrymen; certainly, the eighth was clamouring to the Master of one of the rescue ships to be taken back to England before the police caught him.[4] A British seaman had been shot by a Russian sentry during an air-raid, and *Troubadour*'s mutinous crew were being rounded up in the streets of the city and confined in chains below decks after a riot over women.[5] The story of how the *Carlton* had 'defected', apparently lured by the promise of a substantial reward, into German hands, was the talk of the survivors.[6] In *Silver Sword*, they were just discovering that somebody had attempted to sabotage the engines by putting emery powder in the engine-oil somewhere between Iceland and Archangel.[7] The Master of the beached *Winston-Salem* was seriously ill and being readied for immediate return to America.[8] One of the AA ships was driven aground by her Russian pilot, and had to be floated free. Lieutenant Caradus observed in his diary, 'Nobody is very concerned, and no ship has volunteered to pull her off.' In fact, the crews of the two anti-aircraft ships were hardly on speaking terms. Mr Godfrey Winn was touring the wardrooms of the escort vessels, organizing party games. In *La Malouine* he was asked how he had liked being guest of *Pozarica*'s captain; he replied, 'Captains are heavenly, but Admirals make me shy.'* On the quayside, the tanks were being unloaded, greased, run around the dockyard a bit, and then loaded on to flat-cars for their journey to the front; and Russian labourers were carefully painting out the inscriptions like 'Gift from the people of Plymouth' on the sides of the scores of Red Cross ambulances, as soon as they were swung out of the holds of one of the ships. Even *Norfolk*'s battered Walrus, which had been towed all the way by the *Palomares*, had been loaded aboard a flat-car in Archangel docks as the Russians refused to believe that it was not part of the Allied supply programme.

In face of the Allied unwillingness to mount an early Second Front in the West, the Russians were also taking reprisals against such Allied personnel as were in their hands, and this was a double misfortune for the survivors of PQ.17 in Archangel. The ships' crews were subjected to every indignity. The crews of the merchant ships were at first not allowed to visit other ships, and armed guards were placed on their gangways; ships' mail was deliberately withheld by the dockyard authorities, and the ships had to go on plundering expeditions to secure the food they needed, as the Russians refused to supply any. *Ayrshire* at last had her 'invasion' when she raided a dockyard coal dump—'very

---

* Lieutenant Caradus of *La Malouine* added that Winn was a tough character beneath the surface. '*Pozarica* gunnery officer on board— relates several incidents of voyage out.' A couple of verses were written about *Pozarica*, to a popular tune, but they were not very complimentary.[9]

poor quality' commented Elsden. Much of the Royal Navy's ammunition reserves had been lost with the convoy, and four destroyers had to be rushed through to Archangel before the end of the month, laden with ammunition and foodstuffs.* Admiral Tovey, who had heard 'disquieting reports' from Admiral Miles about the conditions under which the maimed and sick PQ.17 survivors were being treated by the Russians, arranged for a British medical unit to transfer to Archangel. The Russians refused permission for them to land from the destroyers.[10] Eventually Admiral Miles travelled personally to Archangel, where there were now 1,200 survivors in very unattractive mood. Over lunch, Captain Maund told him that the Russians were doing what they could, and had turned all the children out of their schools and turned them into hospitals. Miles saw the most ghastly cases, including two young British seamen who had lost all their limbs from frostbite. †[11]

Worst of all for the authorities was the fear that there were still some lifeboats unaccounted for; there was an awkward discrepancy between the numbers of lifeboats seen to have got away from the sinking ships and the number so far accounted for. Gradually the gap diminished. Two of *Alcoa Ranger*'s lifeboats had made Novaya Zemlya, and the third had reached the mainland at Cape Kanin Nos. Thirty-seven survivors of the *Honomu* had drifted for thirteen days before being picked up by a British minesweeper hundreds of miles off Murmansk. *Peter Kerr*'s

---

* There were numerous instances of extreme lack of co-operation from the Russians. On one occasion the cruiser *Norfolk* carried two hundred RAF personnel to Murmansk, where they were to establish a Coastal Command unit in support of the convoys. This had been agreed with Moscow in advance, yet the Russians refused to allow them to land and *Norfolk* had to take them home again.

† Several of the ships' reports made complaints about the conditions the officers and men were subjected to in Archangel. Captain Stone's (*Olopana*) was the exception. He found no cause for complaint about the food and medical treatment: the food was 'more than Russian people on rations received'; and the authorities placed a 'practically new' hospital at the survivors' disposal. The real problem was that this was the first time that such a survivor problem had been encountered there, and the Russians were not equal to the task.

survivors had made landfall a short distance east of Murmansk, where they had been met a mile offshore by a highly suspicious and heavily armed Russian torpedo-boat, after rowing 360 miles from the spot where their ship went down.

The two *Bolton Castle* lifeboats had drifted apart soon after their ship sank, as one had a sail and the other an engine. As the days had turned into weeks, and the water and food ran out, knife-fights broke out between the Arabs and the white seamen in the Captain's lifeboat, and Pascoe despaired of ever surviving to see land again. Then a seaman in the bows had shouted that they were approaching an empty lifeboat. Across its stern was painted SS *El Capitán, Panama*.

There was every sign that its occupants had abandoned it in haste. On its bottom boards were discarded clothes and a half-eaten biscuit. But that was not all, for in the provision-lockers the incredulous Pascoe found large stocks of food, liquor and drums of fresh water. There were even compasses, charts, a gun, fishing nets, lines and reels. Marvelling at the munificence of the Panamanian Mercantile Marine, Pascoe transferred the stores to his own lifeboat, and increased the water ration to one cupful per day. Some days later, both *Bolton Castle*'s lifeboats independently reached the north Russian coast.

One of *Earlston*'s lifeboats with twenty-eight survivors had been picked up by a British escort vessel seven days after the freighter had been sunk. The other had rowed for ten days and nights towards Russia, on rations badly diminished by the fact that Clydeside dock-workers had broken open the lifeboat's lockers and stolen most of their contents. After ten days' rowing, sustained only by half a cupful of water in the morning, and half a cupful mixed with condensed milk at midday, the British seamen had come ashore, delirious from hunger and thirst, only to find themselves in German-occupied Norway, ten miles to the east of North Cape. Too weak to weep, the twenty-six angry seamen had been hauled off to spend the rest of the war in a German prison camp.[12]

By 24 July, almost a month after the convoy set out from Iceland, all the survivors of PQ.17 were on dry land or aboard rescue vessels, with the exception of one hapless craft—the lifeboat of the American freighter *Carlton*. This was still tossing and heaving

eutenant James Caradus,
Malouine

Captain F. W. Harvey, *Empire Tide*

Pozarica and *Poppy*, seen from *La Malouine*, find refuge
in Matochkin Strait with *Palomares* and her group *(see page 204)*

Pan Atlantic, hit by a bomb from a Ju.88 *(see page 210)*

Olopana breaks in two as the American ship's Captain Mervyn C. Stone's lifeboat pulls away *(see page 236)*. A frame from a cine-film taken from *U-255* by Chief Officer Hugo Deiring

The anti-submarine minesweeper HMS *Britomart* and the first ship
to reach Archangel, the corvette HMS *Dianella,*
which promptly put to sea again on a lone search for survivors

Commander Friedrich-Karl Marks of *U-376*
watches his torpedoes give the *coup de grâce*
to the abandoned *Hoosier* (see page 262)

Ironclad aground in Matochkin Strait, from *Troubador (see page 271)*.
A photograph by Ensign H. E. Carraway

The sinking of the abandoned *Paulus Potter* with the last torpedo
held by Commander Reche's *U-255 (see page 278)*

Rewards. Colonel-General Stumpff awards decorations to his pilots,
and the crew of Commander Siemon's *U-334* muster on deck
at their base at Kirkenes to receive their commendations

out in the Barents Sea, numbering among its seventeen passengers a modern Jonah without parallel, who brought calamity with him wherever he set foot. James Akins has related how their voyage ended:

Every day was about the same. We saw plenty of birds, which made us think that we must be near land. Now, it's very hard to get comfortable with seventeen men in a boat 32 feet long. We didn't mind it for a few days, but after five days' sitting up, one's back begins to feel like it's broken. Lieutenant Harris and C. Blockstone, it seems, were always leaning on me. I would push them off, but a minute later they would come back.

We rationed our food and water after the first day. Hurley who was in charge said we were within a hundred miles or so from Russia one day. I stood six hours lookout that day to see if I could be the first one to sight land. Kelly and Gonzales offered a case of whisky to the first one to see land. Malchy came up and relieved me. I told him to keep a sharp lookout, as we should see land any minute. He said the wind had changed, and we were going away from Russia. I felt like jumping overboard I was so mad.

On the ninth day we saw something we thought was a destroyer. As it came closer, we changed our mind about twenty times. It finally turned out to be a German submarine. They came alongside and asked a lot of questions. They gave us a compass, blankets, water, biscuits, cigarettes and a course to steer for the U.S.S.R. They wished us Good Luck, said they were sorry but it was nothing personal: they had no room to take us on board. (And this is *war* . . . ?)*

---

* The U-boat was *U-376*, commanded by Lieutenant-Commander Friedrich-Karl Marks. He sighted the lifeboat at 2.30 p.m. on 13 July, at which time, from the pinpoint he gave for it in his signal to Admiral Schmundt, it was 350 miles from North Cape. The summary of statements by *Carlton*'s survivors described how the U-boat's commanding officer regretted that he could not take them on board as he was 'still outbound on patrol', and offered medical aid, which was refused: 'He gave them a compass, charts, position, time and course and the distance to the nearest Norwegian coast, also biscuits, cigarettes, water and blankets. Most of this gear was of US manufacture. The German stated that he had torpedoed the SS *Hoosier* a few days before and later boarded her after the crew had been removed.'

The same day, the first assistant engineer became sick. His feet began to swell and get purple. Three days later he froze to death. He had his wife's name on his lips. Hurley read a sermon, and we tossed him overboard.

The seas were running high, between fifteen- and thirty-foot waves; we all began to argue and quarrel with each other. We caught Benny—a Philippino mess-boy—stealing water. We made him do without water for the rest of the day.

On the morning of 24th July, I was on lookout forward and sighted land. For a while, nobody would believe me. From the time I first saw land, it took us about eight hours to reach it. We started up a small fiord. The current was rather strong and pulling was tough. We fell to arguing again about nothing in the world. Finally, everybody was threatening to beat everybody up when they got ashore.

A man and a boy came out in a small boat, and they took us in tow. We were surprised to see how easily they pulled us. We didn't realize how weak we were. We came alongside a dock, and Dooley climbed out with Hurley; they staggered all over the place. I didn't know what was wrong with them. I was the third man out and fell flat on my face. I just could not get used to my legs after nineteen days in the boat.

All the women brought food, milk, coffee, fish, etc., and we had a good meal. We all had four months' beard and I guess we looked a pretty tough bunch.

Our propaganda messed us up again, as we had heard how the Germans killed anyone they caught.[13]

Carlton's lifeboat had landed—like *Earlston*'s—in Norway. Three days before, the German propaganda service had again broadcast the lie that *Carlton*'s crew had brought her to a German-held port, and this time they had named names.

Among the survivors were three officers of the US merchant fleet: officer Vernon Frank, from New York; officer Joseph Eshwode of Rhode Island; and Captain Frederick A. Strand.* Captain Strand said that his transport had been one of the last to be sunk, and they had already abandoned all hope of rescue when German Red Cross planes appeared and searched for survivors. Despite the rough weather, a German Red Cross plane

---

* Vernon Frank was *Carlton*'s Third Officer, but Strand was Captain of *Honomu*, rescued by submarine.

came down and picked them up. He did not think anyone who had escaped this hell would ever volunteer for a convoy through the Arctic Ocean again. . . .'¹³

Carlton's survivors were brought down to Tromsö, where those who were not suffering from frostbite left for Bergen and Oslo on 7 August.

Soon after, they discovered that their 'Jonah' was still with them. At 4 a.m. on 16 August, the American seamen were taken to an Oslo dock where a thousand German troops were embarking on the large troop-transport *Wuri*. The American prisoners embarked with them on the last leg of their long voyage, this time bound for Denmark and Germany. 'We kept the guards busy all night,' recorded James Akins unabashed, 'as our kidneys were on the bum.' At 8.30 a.m. the following morning, the ship entered Aalborg channel and everybody handed in his life-jacket. As the troop transport edged towards the quay, still hundreds of yards off-shore, it hit a mine and began to sink:

Boom, we had got it again.

Everyone ran to the ladder leading to the upper deck. The soldiers were afraid of the sea anyhow, so they just went crazy. Charles Dooley and I grabbed life-jackets and handed them out— in fact we made them put the jackets on.

We stayed below until all were out, and then we went on deck.¹⁴

The American seamen calmly organized the Germans' rescue. By this time, the sinking transport had a twenty-degree list to starboard. A lot of the rafts were already in the water, and some of the troops were jumping into the sea, where they were in some danger of the rest of the rafts hitting them; the Americans shouted to warn them of the danger. Hurley found a first-aid kit under his bed, and some of the Americans set to work bandaging the wounded and showing them how to get away from the ship when it went down. *Carlton*'s seamen themselves clustered on top of the No. 4 hatch, planning to use this when the ship sank; the ship listed several more degrees, and the German troops in their hobnailed boots found it difficult to keep their balance on the deck. 'By this time, a large wooden platform was in danger of sliding off the hatch and crushing a lot of men lining up along the rail.' They called the attention of the German officer-in-charge to this, and he moved the Germans aside while the Americans toppled the platform over.

I looked over the side and saw a large wooden raft with Dooley and Mulchey on it. Hurley, Gonzales and myself jumped overboard and swam to the raft. Between the five of us, we managed to pick up a dozen or so soldiers. By that time, a large number of small boats were around the ship, picking up the men. We were taken aboard a small trawler, where we found one of the guards.

Carlton's survivors found themselves the heroes of the hour. The captain gave them schnapps, and everyone handed them cigarettes. Next morning, the German officer-in-charge came personally to see them, and thanked them for saving the lives of hundreds of his troops. (German records do in fact show that of the 1,000 soldiers on board, only six were lost.) The officer promised to write personally to the Führer about their bravery, recommending the award of a decoration to them.

The American seamen entrained for Germany, followed at every station and junction—or so it seemed to them—by Allied air raids, and sabotage attempts by the Danish Resistance. On 27 August, the saga of the *Carlton* ended, with the last of her crew under lock and key in Marlag-Milag Nord on Lüneburg Heath, braving the contempt of their countrymen for having 'surrendered their ship to the Germans' in Norway. Nor did they hear any more of the Führer's medal that had been promised them.

✳   2   ✳

On 28 July, four days after *Carlton*'s lifeboat brought the last survivors of PQ.17 to land, the joint Anglo-Soviet inquiry into the disaster finally took place, as ordered by Mr Churchill. The scene was Eden's room in the House of Commons. Anthony Eden himself, A. V. Alexander the First Lord, and Admiral Pound the First Sea Lord were present to state the British case.* Eden invited Pound to speak, but before the Admiral could do so Ambassador Maisky interrupted that he wanted to know when

---

* At the meeting, according to Maisky, were Eden, Alexander, Pound, Maisky himself, Admiral Harlamov and his assistant H. G. Morozov.[15]

the next PQ convoy was to sail. Pound countered that Marshal Stalin had not so far replied to Churchill's proposal that a senior Air Force officer should go to Russia to arrange air cover for the convoys. To the Russians, this remark seemed to be just a means of gaining time. According to Maisky's version, Harlamov criticized the Admiralty's orders that the cruisers were to withdraw and the convoy was to scatter, whereupon Pound, 'his face growing redder and redder', retorted: 'That order was given by me! Me! What else should have been done?' A. V. Alexander intervened to apologize for the Admiralty's and Pound's actions, and Maisky commented ingratiatingly that 'even British admirals make mistakes'. At this, Pound grew even more furious and said, 'Tomorrow I shall ask the Prime Minister to appoint you First Sea Lord instead of myself!'[15]

There was a brief exchange in the House of Commons next day on the armament of merchant ships.[16] Several Members were evidently extremely disquieted by facts that had been revealed to them in Secret Session two weeks before, and Mr Emanuel Shinwell asked the Financial Secretary to the Admiralty:

> Is my right hon. Friend aware that a recent convoy proceeding in a very important direction was denuded of Admiralty protection almost at the last minute and that a large number of vessels were lost?

There was mounting uproar as Members chanted, 'Answer, answer!' but the Minister concerned, Mr George Hall, remained resolutely seated and refused to reply. No news of this extraordinary convoy operation reached either the British or the American publics before 1945. When Mr Vernon Frank, *Carlton*'s Third Officer, wrote a brief account of the disaster to his wife in America, his letter—which had been forwarded by the Red Cross out of Germany—was censored, and his description of how 'the naval escort left the convoy and we were told to split up and make port the best we could alone', and of how 'the entire convoy was defenceless and sunk by bombers' as a result, was excised by the US censorship authorities.[17]

Since then, an uncomfortable silence has descended on the history of PQ.17. Occasionally, like a ghost from the past, the designation PQ.17 has been mentioned, but as quickly glossed

THE COST OF CONVOY PQ.17

Alcoa Ranger	5,116 tons	1919	US	Sunk	
Aldersdale (oiler)	8,402	1937	UK	Sunk	
Azerbaijan (tanker)	6,114	1932	USSR		
Bellingham	5,345	1920	US		
Benjamin Harrison	7,191	1942	US		
Bolton Castle	5,203	1939	UK	Sunk	
Carlton	5,127	1920	US	Sunk	4 killed
Christopher Newport	7,197	1942	US	Sunk	3 killed
Daniel Morgan	7,177	1942	US	Sunk	3 killed
Donbass	7,925	1931	USSR		
Earlston	7,494	1941	UK	Sunk	
El Capitán	5,255	1917	Pan.		
Empire Byron	6,645	1941	UK	Sunk	18 killed
Empire Tide (CAM ship)	6,978	1941	UK		
Fairfield City	5,686	1921	US	Sunk	6 killed
Hartlebury	5,082	1937	UK	Sunk	37 killed
Honomu	6,977	1919	US	Sunk	19 killed
Hoosier	5,060	1920	US	Sunk	
Ironclad	5,685	1919	US		
John Witherspoon	7,180	1942	US	Sunk	1 killed
Navarino	4,841	1937	UK	Sunk	1 killed
Ocean Freedom	7,173	1942	UK		
Olopana	6,069	1920	US	Sunk	6 killed
Pan Atlantic	5,411	1919	US	Sunk	26 killed
Pankraft	5,644	1919	US	Sunk	2 killed
Paulus Potter	7,169	1942	Dutch	Sunk	
Peter Kerr	6,476	1920	US	Sunk	
Rathlin (rescue ship)	1,600	1936	UK		
River Afton (Commodore)	5,423	1937	UK	Sunk	23 killed
Samuel Chase	7,191	1942	US		
Silver Sword	4,937	1919	US		
Troubadour	5,808	1920	Norw.		
Washington	5,564	1919	US	Sunk	
William Hooper	7,177	1942	US	Sunk	3 killed
Winston-Salem	6,223	1920	US		
Zaafaran (rescue ship)	1,559	1921	UK	Sunk	1 killed
Zamalek (rescue ship)	1,567	1921	UK		

Sources: *Lloyd's Register 1941–2, Lloyd's Register 1942–3,* and their *Supplements.* Ships' logs, C & D lists, and articles held by Registrar General of Shipping and Seamen, Cardiff. Armed Guard and voyage reports, and private papers.

over and put away. Stung by Soviet allegations in 1946, the Admiralty issued a formal statement about its actions during the PQ.17 affair, but it was dishonest and untruthful to say the least of it.[18] As recently as 1962 the Admiralty has repeated its denial of Russian accusations that British escort vessels deserted the convoy after the 4 July attacks, and asserted in turn that the German battle fleet broke off its attack because the British fleet was moving to engage it. This is just not true. As we have seen, the Home Fleet was withdrawing at the time of the *Tirpitz* group's advance; and the German operation was broken off in spite of this British movement, not because of it.[19]

Even the version of the convoy operation reproduced in the otherwise excellent Official History, *The War at Sea*, is incomplete in its depiction of the naval operations, while its account of the fate of the merchant vessels themselves is perhaps necessarily less than summary. The passage of merchant vessels and their cargoes was, on the other hand, what convoys and the naval operations surrounding them were about.

PQ.17 was not the only costly convoy operation of the war— only five of the fourteen big merchant ships survived in the '*Pedestal*' convoy to Malta in the following month, and in March 1943 the combined North Atlantic convoys SC.122 and HX.229 lost twenty-one ships totalling 141,000 tons. What was exceptional about PQ.17 was the manner in which the disaster was brought about, and the feelings it left in the Merchant Navy's ranks. A first privileged group of survivors was brought back to England in the USS *Tuscaloosa*, and the remainder returned as passengers in QP.14. They sailed up the Clyde on 28 September 1942, but instead of being allowed to proceed home immediately the 1,500 seamen were marched into St. Andrews Hall in Glasgow for a civic welcome, and they were addressed by the Under-Secretary to the Minister of War Transport, Mr Philip Noel-Baker. 'We know what this convoy cost us,' said Noel-Baker. 'But I want to tell you that whatever the cost, it was well worth it.' His speech was howled down by the weary and embittered seamen. 'At times,' said one who was there, 'the noise in Saint Andrew's Hall was as bad as it had been on Saturday 4th July in the Barents Sea.'[20]

The convoy cost the lives of 153 Allied seamen, all of them in the merchant ships. Of these deaths, only seven occurred before the convoy was scattered. In view of the catastrophe's magnitude, the casualties seem in fact remarkably low, and this inevitably invites comparisons. During the whole war, 829 officers and men were lost in the north Russian convoys, in ninety merchant ships —an average of just over nine men killed per ship lost. The casualties during PQ.17 were just over six men per ship lost. Even taking into account the mild season of year and the prolonged hours of daylight, this does seem to indicate that there was a greater tendency for crews to abandon their ships during PQ.17.

Indeed, as we have seen, never were so many ships abandoned while still seaworthy as during this convoy. Counting *Winston-Salem*, no fewer than nine ships (of which one was British) were deserted by their crews after being attacked by German aircraft or submarines although they were still nominally seaworthy. Had there been a German surface attack on the convoy, many of these might well have been captured by prize crews and removed to German ports, for such was their intention as we know.

Convoy PQ.17 was born not of sound strategy and reasoning, but of pressure and despair; it had been launched by the British only after the most strenuous appeals had been made by the Americans and Russians for the convoy to be run. But while it was the Americans and Russians who had called the tune, it was the British Merchant Navy who had had to pay the eternal 'price of Admiralty' in blood. Of the 153 seamen who lost their lives, no less than half came from ships under the British flag, which was out of all proportion to the number of British ships in the convoy. The Allies achieved nothing by the tragedy. Admiral Hamilton's only private comment at this time was in a letter to his mother, when he wrote: 'I have just returned from running the Russian convoy, where we lost a lot of good merchant ships without doing any damage to the *Tirpitz*. However, that is all in the game and we have got to face up to it.' He urged her not to worry about the war, as he was sure that Hitler was finding it very much more unpleasant than the Allies were.[21] Broome was subsequently promoted to Captain, but Hamilton was posted to shore command for the rest of his career. Hamilton was in no doubt about where the real blame lay.

Mr Churchill had also reached conclusions about this, which in no way would reflect upon the integrity of the First Sea Lord. He chose to have no doubts as to who was to blame for the fate of the merchantmen after their scattering, and was out for his blood: 'I was not aware until this morning', he minuted A. V. Alexander and Admiral Pound on 15 July, 'that it was the Admiral of the cruisers, Hamilton, who ordered the destroyers to quit the convoy.' This was just not true, of course. Churchill asked ominously: 'What did you think of this decision at the time? What do you think of it now?'[22] Mr Churchill awaited the results of an inquiry into the conduct of those concerned. Not surprisingly, the inquiry assigned the blame to no one. On 1 August, Admiral Pound described to the Cabinet the reasons for the scattering of the convoy. In particular, he stated that during the night of 3/4 July the Admiralty had learned that *Tirpitz* had eluded the submarines patrolling off North Cape. Although information given to the author by the then First Lord supports Pound's contention, we learn from the Official Historian that 'the existence of such precise Intelligence has not been confirmed by post-war research', and this statement must be respected.[23]

It was unfortunate for Hamilton that it was one of the recipients of Mr Churchill's peremptory minute who was himself most to blame for the disaster, even if Mr Churchill himself could disclaim responsibility for the actual decision to sail the convoy. Despite Hamilton's insistence that the fuel situation of Broome's escort destroyers was quite critical, Churchill subsequently expressed the view that their withdrawal was a 'mistake', and he thundered in his War Memoirs: 'All risks should have been taken in defence of the merchant ships.'[24] Was this the same pen that had in 1942 privately stated that a convoy was 'justified' even if half the merchant ships were lost (page 14)? It was sad that 'Turtle' Hamilton should have been made the butt of this unattractive campaign.

In his report on the operation, Hamilton stressed again the vital importance of air cover, and in particular of shooting down the persistent shadowing aircraft. It seemed 'not unreasonable' to expect a much more effective means of dealing with them than the one catapult Hurricane mounted on a merchant ship. He believed the provision of an auxiliary aircraft-carrier in the close escort presented the obvious solution.[25] In a personal letter to Admiral

Tovey on 10 September, he reiterated that Britain would pay for the Government's unsound strategy of starving the Navy of aircraft: 'We have taken a chance with our communications,' he wrote, 'and concentrated on killing women and children in Germany as a quick road to victory.'

A few days later he wrote to another admiral a letter which those who knew the mild 'Turtle' Hamilton would find hard to believe he had composed:

All the public wants is to be told the facts, and they will see that Winston & Co toe the line. We all know the R.A.F. have behaved like shits as far as naval air is concerned: the Old School tie means nothing to them. The First Lord and Winston hate the sight of Tovey and are trying their best to lever him out of his job and get a 'yes-man' in as C-in-C who will sit down calmly under this unsound Bombing Policy and allow the Navy to go on fighting with last war's weapons.

I have only been a ruddy admiral eighteen months, but during that time I have nearly got the sack three times and in addition been called a funk by the Prime Minister. The Russian convoy is and always has been an unsound operation of war.[26]

Hamilton himself went into hospital for an appendicitis operation, and another admiral took his place when PQ.18 was eventually sailed in the middle of September. This time it had an auxiliary carrier in the escort, as Hamilton had asked. By the time the convoy ran into the White Sea on 21 September, ten of its forty merchant vessels had been sunk by torpedo-bombers, and three more by submarines. The German fleet did not come out on this occasion, but the lessons had already been learned. As Tovey wrote to Hamilton soon after, 'On this occasion I was able to prevent unnecessary signals emanating from the All Highest.' In fact, Admiral Tovey had also learned a lesson, for he had remained at Scapa Flow and run the operation from there, which effectively cut out what Hamilton termed 'Admiralty interference'.[27]

By destroying PQ.17, the Germans had achieved strategically more than was at first apparent. They had deprived the Russians of the cargoes not only of the vessels that went down, but of several entire convoys in the months remaining before winter closed in again. The exemplary PQ.18 was run, but only as a showpiece to abate Marshal Stalin's anger; after that, all convoy sailings ceased until the winter, when they became once more a feasible operation of war. The German operation *The Knight's Move* had touched the lines of Anglo-Soviet communication at their tenderest joint, and at just the moment to create maximum discord between Germany's Allied enemies. There was one consolation for the Allies: when the convoys were finally resumed, with the ominous 'PQ' cypher dropped, in December, the German fleet again intervened, and again fumbled and ran. With the German battle fleet's cringing attitude during its brief *Knight's Move* sortie six months earlier uppermost in his mind Hitler summoned Raeder and delivered a diatribe on the failure of the German Navy in all wars since 1866. He announced that he was scrapping the battleships. Raeder resigned, and Admiral Dönitz, the submarine admiral, succeeded him.[28]

APPENDIXES

APPENDIX I

THE ADMIRALTY'S INSTRUCTIONS OF 27 JUNE 1942*

Naval Message to Commander-in-Chief, Home Fleet.
From Admiralty.   Secret. Immediate.

Hush. Your 1355 22nd and 1727 25th and my 0221 25th [June 1942]

(*a*) After consideration of above telegrams and as Admiralty may be in possession of fuller and earlier information of movements of enemy surface forces than our forces will be and as you may not wish to break W/T silence it appears necessary for Admiralty to control movements of convoy as far as this may be influenced by movements of enemy surface forces.

(*b*) Paragraph (*a*) will not prevent either C-in-C H.F., C.S. One [Hamilton], Senior Officer of Escort [Broome] or Commodore of Convoy [Dowding] giving such orders regarding movements of convoy as local conditions may necessitate.

(*c*) Should Admiralty consider it necessary to reverse course of convoy, the time on which reverse course is to be held will be specified and it is to be understood that it is a temporary measure unless Admiralty give the order for convoy to return to Iceland.

(*d*) Admiralty may be unaware of weather conditions in the vicinity of the convoy and even though Admiralty may give the order for course of convoy to be reversed it is at the discretion of Senior Officer present with convoy to ignore the Admiralty order should the weather be thick.

(*e*) As Admiralty will be exercising control, it is essential that they should be kept informed not only of positions and movements of forces but also of any damage incurred. It is not intended above should be carried out when ships by breaking W/T

---

* From an original on *Wichita*'s file in Washington.

silence would give away their position, but only when position of forces must be known to the enemy.

(*f*) Generally speaking the safety of the convoy from attack of surface ships must be met by our covering forces to westwards of meridian of Bear Island and be dependent on our submarine dispositions to eastwards of that meridian

(*g*) The Admiralty will keep all forces as fully informed as possible of enemy movements.

(*h*) The movements of the Battle Fleet covering force will be at the discretion of C-in-C H.F., but it is not expected that this covering force will be placed in a position where it will be subject to heavy air attack unless there is a good chance of bringing *Admiral von Tirpitz* to action.

(*j*) The movements of cruiser covering force will be at the discretion of C.S. One subject to instructions from Admiralty or C-in-C H.F. It is not intended that cruiser covering force should proceed to eastwards of Bear Island unless convoy is threatened by the presence of surface forces which cruiser covering force can fight. In any case it is not intended that cruiser covering force should proceed eastwards of meridian of *25° East*.

(*k*) Our primary object is to get as much of the convoy through as possible and the best way to do this is to keep it moving to the eastwards even though it is suffering damage.

(*l*) Should the passage of the convoy be barred by a force including *Admiral von Tirpitz* in weather of good visibility and to eastwards of meridian of Bear Island there will be no alternative but to reverse course of convoy, anyhow for a time. This action may be taken by Admiralty, but if necessary C-in-C H.F. or Senior Officer of cruiser force or Senior Officer with convoy may give this order.

(*m*) Once convoy is to eastwards of meridian of Bear Island circumstances may arise in which best thing would be for convoy to be dispersed with orders to proceed to Russian ports. It is at the discretion of either C-in-C H.F., Senior Officer of cruiser force or Senior Officer of escort or convoy to give this order.

(*n*) C.S. One pass [this signal] to *Keppel* and destroyers of escort and Commodore of convoy.

Time of origin: 0157B 27 June 1942

APPENDIX II

THE DESTROYER WITHDRAWAL

The issue of the withdrawal of the escort's destroyers by Commander J. E. Broome, RN, is not as complicated as it has been made since the war. Captain S. W. Roskill, for example, writing in the *Sunday Telegraph* on 11 February 1962 commented that the Admiralty's decision to scatter the convoy was

> aggravated by the action of the admiral in command of the escorting cruisers (Rear-Admiral L. H. K. Hamilton) who withdrew the destroyers of the escort with his own ships. The C-in-C was astonished and dismayed on finding that this had been done, and left his junior in no doubt of his views. But Churchill has written that 'this decision was at the time accepted as right in the circumstances'.

Captain Roskill wondered what grounds existed for such a view.

Admiral Tovey, the C-in-C, certainly did not think Broome's action culpable. He advised the Admiralty that he did not consider Broome in any way to blame for PQ.17's heavy losses. Tovey may well have concluded that from the signals which Broome received, he was justified in deducing that surface action was imminent and in deciding therefore to concentrate his destroyers and rejoin Hamilton. It is clear that Broome was unaware that the cruiser force had been ordered to withdraw from the area, and that he expected to be ordered back to the convoy once the threat from surface forces had subsided. This reading places responsibility for Broome's withdrawal squarely on Rear-Admiral Hamilton, so Hamilton has a right to be heard. It is at once apparent that there was the soundest possible reason for the destroyers not to be sent back. As Hamilton described, once he found (pages 135–6) that Commander Broome had had no *instructions* to withdraw his destroyers and attach them to his cruiser force, he was fully aware that it was out of the question to order them to return to the scattered merchant ships, and he made this quite clear to Tovey in a letter soon after: 'I visualized their fuel situations becoming acute by the time they could have found scattered ships of the convoy, let alone the increased distance to Russian ports,' wrote Hamilton. 'The possibility of finding the convoy oiler was problematic.' It would indeed have been more than problematic, for within one hour of Hamilton's learning that Broome had been acting on his own initiative, the oiler *Aldersdale* had been bombed and abandoned, and all possibility of refuelling the destroyers had vanished.

At the time that the convoy scattered (position 75° 55′ North, 27° 52′ East) over 1,300 miles of sea journey lay ahead of the surviving ships; for some ships the journey was even longer. The destroyers could not have completed the journey on their existing fuel, and they would very likely have met the same fate as their one-time charges. The issue could hardly be simpler.

Had Commander Broome *not* withdrawn his six destroyers in the first place, one can assume that the fleet oiler would have had a greater chance of survival and the problem would not have arisen. That Admiral Tovey had tacitly accepted Hamilton's argument on the fuel position, while publicly castigating him for not returning the destroyers on the afternoon of the 5th, was implicit in his arrangements for the next convoy, PQ.18: for this convoy, *two* fleet oilers were provided, with *two more* standing by in case either was sunk. In short, the point of no return was at Commander J. E. Broome's withdrawal of his escort destroyers, on his own initiative, and not in Hamilton's refusal to send them back to what would have been almost certain destruction.

SOURCE NOTES

Chapter 1: The Regular Millstone—pages 1–23

1. House of Commons, *Official Report* (Hansard), vol. 381, cols 423–4, 1 July 1942.
2. This early narrative is based except where otherwise stated on the *Despatch* submitted by Admiral Sir John C. Tovey to the Lords Commissioner of the Admiralty, 20 May 1942 (published with his later *Despatches* as a supplement to the *London Gazette*, 17 October 1950). See also Admiralty monograph BR. 1736, 'Battle Summary No. 22: Russian Convoys 1942'.
3. Hamilton to C-in-C Eastern Fleet, 30 September 1942. See also p. 300.
4. Interview with Vice-Admiral Sir John Eccles, April 1963 (since deceased).
5. Except where otherwise stated the following paragraphs are generally based on the study, *Die Lage im Nordmeer im Winter 1941/42* prepared by the German Admiralty's Historical Branch and circulated in *Operation und Taktik (Heft 13)* in August 1944. A copy of this is in file K 10—2/74 *OKM—Seekriegsleitung* in the German Federal Archives, Koblenz.
6. *OKW*'s assessment of the situation in Norway, dated 25 December 1941; copy in War Diary of German Army of Norway.
7. Report of the C-in-C Navy to the Führer on the evening of 29 December 1941 at the Wolfsschanze. These conferences will be cited uniformly as Führer Naval Conferences. Abbreviated English translations were published in *Brassey's Naval Annual*, 1948. The German originals of these documents were held by the British Admiralty in London, and given PG-serial numbers; they were subsequently microfilmed, each film being given a T-number. As these micro-

films of German documents are shortly to become generally available through the National Archives, Washington, I am giving the file and film number where applicable. This conference is in file PG/32186 (Film T-14-B).
8. Führer Naval Conference, 13 November 1941. File PG/32186 (Film T-14-B).
9. Interview with Vice-Admiral Sir Norman Denning, April 1963.
10. Churchill, *The Second World War*, vol. IV, *The Hinge of Fate* (Cassell, 1951).
11. Cf. Captain S. W. Roskill, *The War at Sea*, vol. II (HMSO, 1956), pp. 119–20.
12. *Vorstoss Tirpitz (BdS) mit 5. Z. Fl. nach der Bäreninsel 6. bis 9. März 1942*, a study by German Admiralty Historical Branch issued in *Operation und Taktik (Heft 13)*, August 1944. Also, German Naval Staff War Diary. See note 5.
13. Memorandum by Hamilton, 12 March 1942.
14. Cf. Roskill, op. cit., p. 124.
15. German Naval Staff War Diary. There is also a version of this appreciation in Führer Naval Conference, 12 March 1942. File PG/32187 (Film T-14-B).
16. Führer Naval Conferences, 13 April and 14 May 1942. File PG/32187 (Film T-14-B).
17. Führer's order issued through naval operations branch of *OKW*'s operations staff, dated 14 March 1942, number 55493/42. *OKW* file 119.
18. AI (K) Report 196/1942.
19. Roskill, op. cit., p. 127; and Tovey *Despatch*, 2 August 1942.
20. Churchill, op. cit., p. 231. Telegram Roosevelt to Churchill, 27 April 1942.

21. Führer Naval Conference, 13 April 1942. File PG/32186 (Film T-14-B).
22. *Operationen von Flottenstreitkräften im Nordpolarmeer im Jahre 1942*, published in *Operation und Taktik (Heft 13)*, August 1944. See note 5.
23. Quoted by Roskill, op. cit., p. 130. Cf. Tovey *Despatch*, 2 August 1942.
24. Churchill, op. cit., pp. 233–4. Minute, Prime Minister to General Ismay for COS Committee, 17 May.
25. Quoted by Roskill, op. cit., pp. 115 and 130.
26. See note 22.
27. German Naval Staff War Diary, and AI (K) Report 196/1942.
28. This narrative was made available to me by Mr Akins in December 1962. It was written during captivity in German prison camp.
29. For an authentic account of PQ.16, written from private records, see Graeme Ogden's *My Sea Lady—the Story of HMS Lady Magdeleine* (Hutchinson, 1963).
30. German Naval Staff War Diary, 27 May 1942.
31. For details of the German air units' training, tactics and equipment, see Air Ministry pamphlet No. 248, *The Rise and Fall of the German Air Force (1933–1945)*, issued by Air Ministry, A.C.A.S.(I), 1948, Cf. *Die Kampfführung der Luftflotte 5 in Norwegen 1942*, by Major-General von Rohden. According to a document dated 18 September 1942 in file PG/31793 (Film T-576-B), the Blohm & Voss 138 had an operating radius of 450 miles and an endurance of about 14 hours; the Heinkel 115 torpedo plane an operating radius of 280 miles and the Junkers 88 an operating radius of about 650 miles as a bomber with 2000 kilograms of bombs.
32. Information from Lieutenant-Colonel Karl-Otto Hoffmann, director of the Air Signals Troops archives in Germany, given the author in 1962. Frequent results of the cryptographic work will be found in the German Naval Staff War Diary.

33. *Vorstoss Tirpitz (Flottenchef), Scheer (BdK), Hipper, 5. und 8. Z. Fl. (FdZ) in die Barentssee, Unternehmung Rösselsprung, 2. bis 7. Juli 1942*, published in *Operation und Taktik (Heft 13)* August 1944, which will be cited hereafter as *Tirpitz* Sortie. See note 5.
34. General-Admiral Carls, *Final Report on The Knight's Move*, dated 12 July 1942. Cited hereafter as Carls's Final Report. This is in file PG/32508, and there is a British Admiralty translation under reference NID/X.106/47. Also, German Naval Staff War Diary, 1 June 1942. File PG/32054 (Film T-14 Part I).
35. Admiral Schniewind's appreciation of the naval situation is entitled '*Operative Verwendung der Flottenstreitkräfte im Nordraum*', 30 May 1942. File PG/32586 (Film T-41-B).
36. German Naval Staff War Diary, 1 June 1942.
37. Naval Group North's operational directive, 4 June 1942, is in file PG/36795 (Film T-60-D): '*Operative Weisung für Einsatz der Drontheim-und Narvik-Gruppe gegen einen PQ-Geleitzug. (Deckname: Rösselsprung)*'. As an appendix it contains an appreciation of the situation. Cf. also *Tirpitz* Sortie.
38. German Naval Staff War Diary, 6 June.
39. German Naval Staff War Diary, 9 June.
40. German Naval Staff War Diary, 9 June. The 'detailed scheme' is contained in a *Vortragsnotiz* (conference note) prepared by the Naval Staff, and dated 9 June 1942. It is reproduced in file PG/31747 (Film T-353-B), and appears in translation as the appendix of Führer Naval Conference, 15 June 1942, *Brassey's Naval Annual*, 1948, pp. 286–7.
41. Details on German Intelligence about PQ.17 are in *Tirpitz* Sortie. The ordering to sea of the nine U-boats is reported in German Naval Staff War Diary, 10 June, 17 June, and 23 June 1942. Admiral Schmundt's signals to the U-boats,

ordering them to sail, are in the German Admiralty's special *Knight's Move* file PG/32586 (Film T-41-B).

42. Admiral Schniewind's Operation

Order. *'Operationsbefehl. Einsatz der Flottenstreitkräfte im Nordraum gegen einen PQ-Geleitzug'*, 14 June 1942, is an Appendix to *Tirpitz* Sortie.

Chapter 2: 'The Knight's Move'—pages 24–51

1. Diary of Martin Bormann as Secretary of the Führer, 11 June 1942.
2. Führer Naval Conference, 15 June 1942. File PG/31762 (Film T-413-B). Cf. diary of Captain Assmann, translated in *Report on the German Naval War Effort*, Admiralty document NID.24/T.65/45, 15 June 1942: 'Proposed attack on PQ.17. H[itler] sees grave danger to heavy ships through enemy carriers. . . . Planning of attack on PQ.17: there must be extensive reconnaissance and attack only to be carried out if enemy naval forces are proved to be not superior in strength.' For additional general German material on north Russian convoys, see Assmann's *The German Conduct of the War Against the Anglo-Russian Convoy Traffic in Northern Waters, 1941–1945*—a general study, summarizing German records.
3. Schniewind's Operation Order, 14 June. Fifth Air Force War Diary, with its complete summary of operations against PQ.17.
4. Admiral Schmundt's War Diary, *passim*.
5. Cf. *The German Northern Theatre of Operations* (US Department of the Army pamphlet No. 20–271), p. 216.
6. The signals ordering the U-boats to sea are in file PG/32586 (Film T-41-B), and the despatching of the U-boats is also recorded in German Naval Staff War Diary, 17 and 23 June. Cf. Herbert Zeissler, *U-Boots-Liste* (Hamburg, 1956).
7. German Naval Staff War Diary, 19 June.
8. German Naval Staff War Diary, 29 June.
9. German Naval Staff War Diary, 30 June.

10. Action Report on Voyage of *Troubadour*, by Ensign Howard E. Carraway, USNR, 25 July 1942; and recorded statement by Carraway in US Naval Archives.
11. Cables from Assistant US Naval Attaché, London, to Chief of Naval Operations, Washington, 4, 11 and 20 June 1942.
12. Information from Captain I. J. Anderson, *Bellingham*'s Second Officer, July 1962.
13. Tovey *Despatch*, 3 January 1943. Cf. Roskill, *The War at Sea,* vol. II, p. 135.
14. Signal from C-in-C Home Fleet, originating at 10.41 p.m. GMT, 22 June 1942. Paraphrased also in *Wichita*'s War Diary, 23 June.
15. Signal from C-in-C Home Fleet to Admiralty and Rear-Admiral Hamilton, originating at 11.55 a.m. GMT, 22 June.
16. Hamilton's letters home, 15 February, 26 March, 26 November, 22 February 1942.
17. Ibid., Easter Sunday, 26 March, 11 April 1942.
18. Cf. Roskill, op. cit., p. 124. Hamilton wrote a memorandum on the subject of tackling *Tirpitz* and the failure of the *Victorious* operation, dated 12 March 1942. The latter quotations are from his letters home dated 14 March and Easter Sunday 1942.
19. Rear-Admiral Commanding, First Cruiser Squadron: 'Report of the Proceedings of the Cruiser Force Covering Convoy PQ.17', dated 11 July 1942. (Secret, W.09/8/148.) Cited hereafter as Hamilton's Final Report.
20. Lieutenant Douglas E. Fairbanks, Jr., USNR: 'Cruiser Covering Force,

June 25 to July 8, 1942' (94 pages). My copy came from Vice-Admiral Howard E. Orem's personal files. Cited hereafter as Fairbanks Diary.

21. Fairbanks Diary, 25 June. Also a file of *Wichita*'s signals in US naval archives; signals between *Wichita, Tuscaloosa,* ComDesRon 8 and Com-TaskForce 99 (Admiral Giffen) between 4.30 p.m. and 5.01 p.m. 25 June.

22. Rear-Admiral Commanding, First Cruiser Squadron: 'Operation Orders', dated 25 June 1942 (Secret, W.09/8/604). Copies of this, of Commander Jack E. Broome's 'Instructions for Close Escorts, PQ.17' dated 28 June 1942, and of the improvised '*Keppelcode*' devised by Broome for his force's signalling are in *Wichita*'s file at US naval archives.

23. Admiralty signal to C-in-C Home Fleet, repeated to C.S. One, to be passed to *Keppel,* originating at 1.57 a.m., 27 June. Reproduced as Appendix I, pp. 303–4.

24. Fairbanks Diary, 27 June.

25. Rear-Admiral Hamilton's pencilled 'Notes for PQ.17 Masters' Conference at Hvalfiord', 27 June 1942. Cf. Hamilton's Final Report. The

description of the conference is also based on information from Mr Leo Gradwell, March 1963, and on several of the ships' Voyage Reports.

26. Log kept by Captain O. C. Morris (*Zamalek*). Also *Zamalek*'s Voyage Report, dated 11 July 1942.

27. Captain Mervyn Stone: *Olopana*'s Voyage Report.

28. Fairbanks Diary, 27 June.

29. US Naval Institute *Proceedings,* January 1946. War Diary of Iceland Naval Operating Base, 27 June 1942.

30. PQ.17 Convoy Orders. Roskill, op. cit., p. 137, writes: 'All the merchant-men were bound for Archangel.' Not so.

31. *Troubadour*'s Armed Guard Report.

32. Diary of Lieutenant James Caradus, *La Malouine*'s Asdic officer, cited hereafter as Caradus Diary. Cf. *Zamalek*'s Master's Log, Hamilton's Final Report, and information from Mr Leo Gradwell, March 1963.

33. Roskill, op. cit., pp. 135–6.

34. Tovey's Final Report, and Tovey *Despatch.* For the movements of the Home Fleet, the War Diaries of USS *Mayrant* and USS *Rhind* were also consulted.

35. Fairbanks Diary, 30 June.

Chapter 3: 'The Victim Is PQ.17'—pages 52–89

1. *Tirpitz* Sortie. Carls's Final Report. Summary of Operation in Schmundt's War Diary, and summary in Fifth Air Force War Diary.

2. Schmundt's War Diary, 1 July. German Naval Staff War Diary, 1 and 2 July. (File PG/32055; Film T-14 Part II, 1–14 July; Film T-15, 14–31 July 1942).

3. Godfrey Winn, *PQ.17, the Story of a Ship* (Hutchinson, 1947), p. 70.

4. Fairbanks Diary, 1 July.

5. *La Malouine*'s signal log.

6. Schmundt's War Diary.

7. Ibid., 1 July.

8. *Wichita*'s War Diary, 1 July.

9. Tovey's Final Report.

10. *Eingegangene Meldungen Generalstab Luftwaffe,* printed as daily appendices in War Diary of German High Command Operations Staff (*OKW/WFSt*), 1 July 1942. Cited hereafter as German Air Staff Brief Report. The text of the signal is in Schmundt's War Diary.

11. Carls's Final Report.

12. Appreciation in German Naval Staff War Diary, 2 July.

13. War Diary of Fifth Air Force.

14. *Tirpitz* Sortie. German Naval Staff War Diary, 2 July. Schmundt's War Diary.

15. *La Malouine*'s signal log. *Bellingham*'s Armed Guard Report.

16. German Air Staff Brief Report, 4 July.
17. Hamilton's Final Report. USS *Wichita*'s War Diary. USS *Rowan*'s War Diary. USS *Tuscaloosa*'s Report, 'Operations of Cruiser Covering Force with PQ.17', 9 July 1942. Fairbanks Diary, 2 July.
18. Fifth Air Force War Diary. Air Ministry pamphlet, *The Rise and Fall of the German Air Force*, pp. 111–13.
19. Notes by Lieutenant-Commander Higgens, gunnery observer in *Wilton*.
20. *El Capitán*'s, *Troubadour*'s and *William Hooper*'s Armed Guard Reports.
21. *Zaafaran*'s Voyage Report.
22. *Zamalek*'s Log, Master's Log, Ship's Articles, and interviews with Captain Owen C. Morris and Surgeon-Lieutenant N. McCallum.
23. *John Witherspoon*'s Armed Guard Report.
24. *Tirpitz* Sortie. German Naval Staff War Diary, 3 July.
25. Schmundt's War Diary, 3 July.
26. Picker, *Hitler's Tischgespräche* (Seewald Verlag, Stuttgart, 1963), pp. 433–4.
27. Report by the Chief of Naval Operations in German Naval Staff War Diary, 3 July.
28. Schmundt's War Diary, 2 July. Brief Reports of *U-88* and *U-355* contained as an Appendix.
29. Harald Busch, *So War der U-Bootkrieg* (Deutscher Heimat-Verlag, Bielefeld, 1957), p. 307.
30. Hamilton's Final Report. Also, Rear-Admiral L. H. K. Hamilton, 'Report on the Operation of the Cruiser Force Covering PQ.17', 6 July 1942. (Secret. W.09/8/141.) Cited hereafter as Hamilton's Preliminary Report.
31. *Wichita*'s War Diary, 3 July.
32. Hamilton's Final Report.
33. *Zamalek*'s Master's Log, 3 July.
34. Tovey *Despatch*; Roskill, *The War at Sea*, vol. II, p. 137.
35. Fairbanks Diary, 3–4 July.
36. Tovey's Report. *Tirpitz* Sortie. German Naval Staff War Diary, 3 July.
37. Schmundt's War Diary, 3 July.
38. Schmundt's War Diary, 3 July.
39. *Tirpitz* Sortie. Bormann Diary, 3 July.
40. Information from Mr (now Lord) Justice Winn, April 1963. The then Commander Rodger Winn, RNVR, was CO of the Admiralty's submarine-tracking room at the time.
41. *Tirpitz* Sortie. Schmundt's War Diary, 3 July.
42. Diary of *Bellingham*'s Second Officer.
43. Notes of gunnery observer in *Wilton*. Hamilton's Final Report. *Zamalek*'s Master's Log. Information from Flight-Officer H. H. Edwards, the pilot, and Mr W. C. Taylor, the Walrus's catapult officer in *London*.
44. German Naval Staff War Diary. Schmundt's War Diary.
45. Diary of *Bellingham*'s Second Officer.
46. *Tirpitz* Sortie. German Naval Staff War Diary, 3 July.
47. Information from Vice-Admiral Denning.
48. Appreciation timed soon after midnight, 3–4 July, in German Naval Staff War Diary.
49. *Samuel Chase*'s Armed Guard Report.
50. Statement by Armed Guard officer, Ensign Howard E. Carraway, USNR, in US Naval Archives. Quoted in S. E. Morison, *History of United States Naval Operations in World War II*, Vol. II, p. 182.
51. Based on information from the Voyage Reports of *Olopana*, *John Witherspoon* and *Christopher Newport*; and from Mr James E. Akins (seaman) T. J. Mooney (Chief Engineer), and Mr W. Feldheim (seaman) of *Carlton*. Also, letter of commendation of *Christopher Newport*'s gunner Hugh P. Wright, written by Armed Guard officer Lieutenant F. M. Coy, USNR, 11 September 1942.
52. *Zamalek*'s Master's Log and ship's log. Information from Captain O. C.

Morris, her Second Officer Captain T. G. Lennard and Surgeon-Lieutenant N. McCallum.

53. Information from Leiutenant-Commander J. Rankin (*Dianella*). Apropos the way in which the freighter had

been abandoned, he commented: 'I have never seen a ship abandoned as fast as she was; within 30 seconds of the torpedo's striking home, the lifeboats were being lowered away over the side.'

Chapter 4: Decisions and Disaster—pages 90–138

1. German Naval Staff War Diary, 3 July. In general, during this and successive chapters extensive use has been made of a file of 800 memoranda prepared by the Office of Naval Intelligence, the summaries of statements by survivors of US merchant vessels torpedoed during World War II. Those relating to PQ.17 are from the crews of *William Hooper, Carlton, Daniel Morgan, Honomu, Pankraft, Washington, John Witherspoon, Alcoa Ranger* and *El Capitán*.
2. Schmundt's War Diary.
3. Hamilton's Final Report.
4. Caradus Diary, 4 July.
5. The cable quoted is a naval message from Commander, US Naval Forces Europe, to Commander-in-Chief US Fleet, Washington, 4 July 1942 (US Naval Archives). Information on subsequent developments in London is from Captain G. R. G. Allen, Admiral E. L. S. King, who was ACNS (Trade), the late Rear-Admiral E. J. P. Brind who was ACNS (Home) and Sir Henry Moore who was Vice-Chief of Naval Staff. Rear-Admiral H. B. Rawlings was ACNS (Foreign).
6. Signals Appendix to Hamilton's Preliminary Report, 6 July.
7. Hamilton's Preliminary Report; and letter, Hamilton to Tovey, 9 July 1942.
8. Tovey, *Despatch*; cf. Tovey's Report and *London*'s Signal Log.
9. Letter, Hamilton to Tovey, 9 July.
10. German Naval Staff War Diary, 4 July.
11. Naval Group North's War Diary, 4 July, quoted in PG/31747 (Film T-353-B) and in *Tirpitz* Sortie.
12. Fifth Air Force War Diary, 4 July.

13. A.I.(K) Reports Nos. 175/1942 and 196/1942, July 1942.
14. German Naval Staff War Diary, 4 July; German Air Staff Brief Report, 4 July. ComDesRon 8's report. Hamilton's Final Report. Notes by Lieutenant-Commander Higgens. *La Malouine*'s signal log. *Keppel* Diary, 4 July.
15. Schmundt's War Diary, 4 July.
16. *U-88*'s Brief Report, 12 July; *U-88*'s torpedo log.
17. *Britomart*'s Report. Caradus Diary.
18. Signal C.S. One to *Keppel* originating at 8.11 p.m., 4 July.
19. *Zamalek*'s logs and reports. Interview with Surgeon-Lieutenant N. McCallum. Notes by Lieutenant-Commander Higgens. *Wainwright*'s Report. *La Malouine*'s signal log.
20. Commodore Dowding's Report.
21. *William Hooper*'s Armed Guard Report, and summary of statements by her survivors.
22. *Bellingham*'s Armed Guard Report and *El Capitán*'s Armed Guard Report; also diary of *Bellingham*'s Second Officer. Commodore Dowding stated: 'The concentrated fire on him was terrific and he must have been riddled with every kind of projectile —a very brave man.'
23. Interviews with Captain John Evans (*Navarino*'s Second Officer) and with Mr Iain Laing.
24. Diary of *Bellingham*'s Second Officer.
25. *The Sundial*, USS *Wichita*'s newspaper 5 July.
26. Letter, Hamilton to Tovey, 6 July.
27. Interview with Captain Rupert Hull, Second Officer of *El Capitán*, January 1963.

28. *Olopana*'s Report.
29. Notes by Lieutenant-Commander Higgens.
30. *Wainwright*'s Report.
31. Signal, Hamilton to *Keppel*, originating at 8.40 p.m. 4 July.
32. *Life* magazine, 3 August 1942; Caradus Diary, 4 July.
33. Fairbanks Diary, 4 July.
34. From an article by Broome in *TV-Times* in the summer of 1960 in connection with an episode of the television series *Sea War* for which he wrote the script.
35. Hamilton's Preliminary Report.
36. Caradus Diary.
37. Information from Mr Nathaniel E. Platt, second assistant engineer, *John Witherspoon*.
38. Narrative by Ensign Howard E. Carraway, *Troubadour*'s Armed Guard officer, 26 March 1945, in US Naval Archives. Some waggish reviewing officer wrote, 'Damn polite torpedo!' beside this passage of Carraway's report.
39. Other information from Mr James Bruce (*Zaafaran*) and from Captain C. T. R. Lennard, Surgeon-Lieutenant N. McCallum and Captain Owen C. Morris (*Zamalek*).
40. *Britomart*'s Report, and signals appendix.
41. Information from Captain John Evans, Second Officer of *Navarino*. The sinking of *Navarino* and other British ships in this convoy is formally recorded in Admiralty monograph BR. 1337, *British and Foreign Merchant Vessels Lost or Damaged by Enemy Action during Second World War*. Time, tonnage and location are given.
42. Interview with Captain John Litchfield, MP, executive officer of *Norfolk* at the time, January 1963.
43. Schmundt's War Diary; German Naval Staff War Diary, 4 July. Schmundt's 'Order for the Transfer of the *Lützow* Group . . . from Narvik to Trondheim' is in his War Diary, and also in *Tirpitz*'s files, PG/48556 (Film T-74-E).

44. Interview with Vice-Admiral Sir Norman Denning, April 1963.
45. Interview with Mr Justice Winn, April 1963.
46. Interview with Admiral Sir Patrick Brind, April 1963 (since deceased).
47. Interview with Admiral E. L. S. King, April 1963.
48. Interview with Admiral Sir Henry Moore, March 1963.
49. Interview with Admiral Sir John Eccles, April 1963 (since deceased).
50. *La Malouine*'s signal log.
51. Interviews with Commander J. Rankin (*Dianella*) and Commander P. L. Newstead, January 1963.
52. Roskill, op. cit., p. 141*n*. Cf. J. E. Broome, *Make a Signal* (Putnam, 1955), p. 214.
53. Information from Mr E. C. Miller (Chief Engineer, *River Afton*), November 1962.
54. Rear-Admiral S. E. Morison, *History of United States Naval Operations in World War II*, Vol. II, p. 185*n*.
55. Information from Vice-Admiral R. M. Servaes, October 1966.
56. Hamilton's Final Report. *Wichita*'s War Diary. Interview with Captain John Litchfield, February 1963. USS *Tuscaloosa*'s War Diary records that the six destroyers of Broome's force joined the cruiser squadron at 11.05 p.m., 4 July.
57. Notes by Lieutenant-Commander Higgens (*Wilton*), 4 July.
58. Interview with Mr W. G. Taylor, January 1963. G. Winn, op. cit., p. 92.
59. Signal, ComDesRon 8 to DesRon 8, Captain (D) 6, C.S. One, originating at 5.20 a.m., 5 July. In Hamilton's Final Report, *London*'s signal log and *Wainwright*'s War Diary.
60. Interview with Mr D. D. Summers (*Keppel*), March 1963.
61. Interview with Captain Archibald Hobson (*Aldersdale*), November 1962.
62. Interview with Mr Leo Gradwell, March 1963; cf. *My Sea Lady*, p. 171.
63. Information from Mr F. N. Lewin, May 1962.

64. Interview with Captain G. R. G. Allen, April 1963.
65. Churchill, op. cit., p. 236. The Admiralty strongly regretted that this passage had been published, as it contradicted the etiquette that orders were issued by the 'Admiralty' rather than by individuals.
66. Memorandum, Tovey to Secretary of the Admiralty, 11 July: 'Most Secret. Reports of the Operations of the Forces Covering Convoys PQ.17 and QP.13 (919/HF.01325/4/98).' This will be cited as Tovey's Report.
67. Letter, Captain J. E. Broome to *Daily Telegraph*, 30 October 1950.
68. Diary of Nathaniel E. Platt, 4 July.
69. Interview with Lieutenant-Commander J. G. Rankin, January 1963.
70. *Britomart*'s Report and signals appendix.
71. Interview with Commander S. S. Stammwitz, March 1963.
72. Interview with Mr Leo Gradwell, March 1963. Cf. the account by Mr Richard Elsden, *Ayrshire*'s First Lieutenant, in *My Sea Lady*, pp. 171–4.
73. *Ayrshire*'s Report. Letter, Gradwell to Admiral Commanding, Iceland Command, and SBNO North Russia, 26 July.
74. List of PQ.17 signals maintained by Lieutenant Caradus of *La Malouine*.
75. Narrative by Ensign Howard E. Carraway, 26 March 1945. Also *Ayrshire*'s Preliminary Report: letter, Gradwell to SBNO North Russia, 13 July 1942. Cf. *My Sea Lady* and various official accounts.
76. Interview with Vice-Admiral R. M. Servaes, March 1963. Mr J. M. Waterhouse described in November 1962 the mood in the Chief Petty Officers' mess of *London* after the text of the Admiralty's signals became known.
77. Signal, C.S. One (Hamilton) to: General, originating at 1.15 a.m., 5 July, on *London*'s signal log. There is a copy in *Wichita*'s Report, and in USS *Tuscaloosa*'s 'Report of Operations with British Cruiser Squadron One in Covering Voyage of Convoy PQ.17 to Murmansk, Russia'.
78. *Wichita*'s War Diary, 5 July.
79. Signal *Keppel* to C.S. One, originating at 5.25 a.m., 5 July.
80. Signal, C.S. One to *Keppel*, originating at 2.39 p.m., 5 July.
81. Signal, *Keppel* to C.S. One, originating at 4.04 p.m., 5 July.
82. Private Diary of Vice-Admiral Sir Geoffrey Miles, July 1942; amplified in an interview, February 1963.

Chapter 5: The Better Part of Valour—pages 139–69

1. Schmundt's War Diary, 5 July 1942. For operational charts and U-boat overlays showing the progress of the submarine attack on PQ.17, use was made of files PG/71900b to PG/71900d (Film T-375-B). These originate from General-Admiral Carls's office, Marinegruppenkommando Nord.
2. *U-334*'s torpedo logs.
3. Interview with Captain J. Wharton, October 1962.
4. *U-703*'s torpedo logs.
5. *Peter Kerr*'s and *Bellingham*'s Armed Guard Reports.
6. Further information from interview with Mr Ed Soliman, the former chief cook of *Empire Byron*, June 1963. It would have been of interest to hear Rimington's account of these events, but I finally traced him only just after a severe road accident in which he lost his speech and memory. The military hospital provided me with his passport and papers which were themselves of some assistance. Herr J. Plambeck, one of the Germans who interrogated Rimington in Norway, has told me that they were able to gain no Intelligence of value from him.
7. Signal, *U-703* to Schmundt, originating at 10.15 a.m., 5 July.

8. Signal, C.S. One (Hamilton) to *Wichita*, originating at 11.30 a.m., 5 July.

9. *U-88*'s torpedo log.

10. The description of *Carlton*'s sinking is based on information from Mr T. J. Mooney, the chief engineer, in October 1962; from Mr James E. Akins, a seaman, in December 1962; and on the summary of statements by *Carlton*'s survivors, March 1945. Times in my narrative are given two hours later than GMT, of course—hence the American ship's apparently unorthodox watch-keeping hours.

11. *U-88*'s Brief Report, 12 July. Schmundt's War Diary.

12. *Tirpitz* Sortie. German Naval Staff War Diary, 5 July.

13. Signal, Naval Group North to Schmundt and others, received at 7.02 a.m., 5 July.

14. Tovey's Report.

15. German Naval Staff War Diary, 5 July.

16. Schmundt's War Diary. The usual delays held up the codeword's transmission. It is not clear at what time the signal reached *Tirpitz*, but it took thirty minutes to reach Schmundt by teleprinter in Narvik. The text of the codeword as quoted in the footnote was obtained from a signal in file PG/32586 (Film T-41-B).

17. Preliminary Report of Fleet Commander [Schniewind] on *The Knight's Move*, reproduced in German Naval Staff War Diary, 12 July. Carls's Final Report.

18. German Air Staff Brief Report, 5 July. Summary in German Naval Staff War Diary, 5 July. German Fifth Air Force War Diary, 5 July. Schmundt's War Diary, 5 July.

19. Caradus Diary, 5 July.

20. Diary of *Bellingham*'s Second Officer.

21. *John Witherspoon*'s Armed Guard Report.

22. *Daniel Morgan*'s Armed Guard Report.

23. *Benjamin Harrison*'s Armed Guard Report.

24. *U-88*'s Brief Report, 12 July.

25. Interview with Mr T. D. Nield, British gunner in *Fairfield City*, June 1963.

26. *La Malouine*'s signal log.

27. *U-88*'s torpedo logs; *U-88*'s Brief Report.

28. Statements from *Daniel Morgan*'s survivors, November 1962.

29. *Honomu*'s Armed Guard Report; information from Matson Navigation Company; summary of statements by *Honomu*'s survivors. Information from Mr Alan L. Harvie, *Honomu*'s second assistant engineer, September 1962. Many *Honomu* survivors were again sunk when *Silver Sword* was lost on the return convoy.

30. *U-334*'s torpedo log. Also interviews with *U-334*'s wireless operator Herr Otto Bork, and her torpedo mechanic Herr Günther Döschner, in September and October 1962, and Döschner's diary notes.

31. Summary of statements by *Honomu*'s survivors.

32. *U-456*'s torpedo logs.

33. Signal, *U-456* to Schmundt, received at 5 p.m., 5 July.

34. G. Winn, op. cit., pp. 97–98.

35. Letter from the Secretary of the Navy to Masters of US Merchant Ships, subject: 'Instructions for Scuttling Merchant Ships', 30 March 1942. The copy cited was in *Fairfield City*'s file, dated 17 April 1942 (US Naval Archives).

36. *Alcoa Ranger*'s Report.

37. Interview with Mr Hawtry Benson (the Chief Officer), December 1962.

38. Interview with Mr Thomas Goodwin (*Earlston* fireman), November 1962.

39. *La Malouine* signal log. *Bellingham*'s Armed Guard Report. The German monitoring services also picked up this entire range of distress signals, and they are reproduced in file PG/32586 (Film T-41-B).

40. Information from Mr James E. Akins. Summary of statements of *Carlton*'s survivors, 10 March 1945.

41. Letter from Mr Walter Feldheim to his wife from a German prison camp, 1944.
42. Information from Mr T. J. Mooney.
43. *Signal,* second September issue, 1942. This feature carried a series of photographs taken by the German war reporter Benno Wundshammer, who flew with one Ju. 88 squadron attacking the scattered freighters on 5 July. There are lengthy reports on the German Air Force interrogations of fourteen *Carlton* survivors in the German Admiralty's *Knight's Move* file, PG/32586 (Film T-41-B).
44. *Völkischer Beobachter,* Berlin Edition, 2 August 1942.
45. German Radio in Danish for Denmark, 11.40 p.m., 8 July.
46. Zeesen transmitter in Spanish for Latin-America, 3.15 a.m., 4 August.
47. Station Debunk (Axis Origin), in English for America, 4.30 a.m., 20 July.
48. These signals are recorded in several War Diaries. My text is taken from *La Malouine*'s signal log.
49. Admiral Giffen's War Diary, 5 July.
50. German Naval Staff War Diary, 5 July. According to *Tirpitz* Sortie, a shore station was overheard acknowledging the first transmission. This is at variance with the version in other German records. According to contemporary war diaries, the first signal was believed by the Germans to be from a British submarine.
51. Carls's Final Report. A chart of the German battle fleet's track and their

Intelligence on the PQ.17 convoy's movements was reproduced at the end of *Tirpitz* Sortie. The original of this chart is in file PG/71923 (Film T-342).
52. Report by German Naval Staff's Chief of Naval Signals, reproduced in Naval Staff War Diary, 6 July.
53. German Naval Staff War Diary. Carls's Final Report. In the German Admiralty's *Knight's Move* file PG/32586 (Film T-41-B) there is a note in Captain Assmann's handwriting describing the various arguments raised for and against breaking off the sortie, written on 5 July.
54. Schniewind's War Diary, quoted in *Tirpitz* Sortie. Also, Schniewind's Preliminary Report, 12 July 1942.
55. *Tirpitz* Sortie.
56. Commentary by Naval Group North on Schniewind's Preliminary Report, summarized in German Naval Staff War Diary, 12 July.
57. Schniewind's War Diary.
58. German Naval Staff War Diary, 7 July.
59. German Naval Staff War Diary, 8 July.
60. This was at a war conference on 6 July. German Naval Staff War Diary.
61. *German Northern Theatre of Operations,* p. 238. See also Chapter 9's Source Note 28.
62. Schmundt's Summary of Operation, in his War Diary; and Raeder's comments at 6 July war conference.
63. *Tirpitz* Sortie. Schniewind's Preliminary Report, 12 July.

Chapter 6: A Duty to Avoid Destruction—pages 170–202

1. Summary of Statements by *Peter Kerr*'s survivors. Information from Mr William P. Connolly, *Peter Kerr*'s Second Officer.
2. *Völkischer Beobachter,* 22 August.
3. Fifth Air Force Intelligence Report to German High Command.

4. *Hoosier*'s Armed Guard Report. Each Captain had been issued by the Naval Control Service Officer, Iceland, with a secret sealed list of points through which the convoy would pass and with a one-page 'Stragglers' Route' to take him either back to Iceland or on

to the White Sea. A copy is in US Naval Archives. See also footnote on p. 215.

5. *Washington*'s Armed Guard Report. Summary of statements by *Washington*'s survivors, 9 November 1942.
6. Interview with Captain John Pascoe, January 1963.
7. Information from Captain J. R. G. Findlay, who was at the time a British cadet in *Paulus Potter*; and from Directoraat Generaal van Scheepvaart, 's-Gravenhage, Holland.
8. Interview with Mr William Arnell-Smith (*Bolton Castle*'s carpenter) January 1963. Also *Washington*'s Armed Guard Report, which added: 'We were sure they would machine-gun us, but they didn't.' Summary of statements by *Washington*'s survivors. Interview with Herr Benno Wundshammer, April 1967.
9. *Olopana*'s Voyage Report.
10. *Zamalek*'s reports and logs. Interview with Captain O. Morris, February 1963, and with other *Zamalek* officers.
11. *Aldersdale*'s Official Log.
12. Information from Mr James Bruce, July 1962.
13. Interview with Captain Archibald Hobson, November 1962.
14. Interviews with Mr Hawtry Benson, Chief Officer; Mr R. F. Crossley, gunner; Mr T. F. Goodwin, fireman; and Mr J. J. Collins, Second Engineer, in November and December 1962.
15. *U-334*'s torpedo log.
16. Information from Otto Bork (*U-334*'s wireless operator) June 1962, and with Günther Döschner (torpedo mechanic) October 1962.
17. Schmundt's War Diary.
18. Naval Staff War Diary, 5 July. Signal, Schmundt to Naval Commandant Kirkenes and AOC North-East Air Command, 5 July. How the Fifth Air Force was able to escape the blame is something of a mystery, for in a signal to Naval Staff in Berlin on 5 July they themselves claimed to have

strafed a diving U-boat with machine-gun fire. The original signal is in file PG/32586 (Film T-41-B).
19. German Naval Staff War Diary, 13 July.
20. Interview with Mr Hawtry Benson (*Earlston*'s Chief Officer), who also met the two American seamen concerned at Marlag-Milag Nord.
21. *Signal*, September 1942.
22. Schmundt's War Diary.
23. Caradus Diary.
24. Diary of Captain I. J. Anderson (*Bellingham*'s Second Officer).
25. *La Malouine*'s signal log.
26. *Pankraft*'s Armed Guard Report.
27. *La Malouine*'s signal log. *Bellingham*'s Armed Guard officer logged the signal at 7.46 p.m.
28. Summary of statements by *Pankraft*'s survivors, 2 November 1942. On 27 July, Commander Roullard, Assistant US Naval Attaché at Archangel, cabled the Chief of Naval Operations in Washington: 'American ship *Pankraft* bombed and sunk on 5 July. All crew now Archangel and healthy except David Stockton, 2nd Mate, last seen floating in water killed by machine-gun bullet. John L. Carley died from injuries in lifeboat, buried at sea.'
29. G. Winn, op. cit., p. 103. Substantially the same signals are in *Samuel Chase*'s Armed Guard Report.
30. *Samuel Chase*'s Armed Guard Report.
31. *Pankraft*'s Armed Guard Report.
32. Interview with Mr F. A. Leycock (pom-pom gun officer in *Lotus*), November 1962.
33. Letter, Gradwell (*Ayrshire*) to SBNO North Russia, 26 July.
34. *U-703*'s torpedo logs.
35. Information from Captain Harold Charlton, November 1962. *River Afton*'s report.
36. Information from Mr E. C. Miller, November 1962.
37. Interview with Commodore J. C. K. Dowding, November 1962 (since deceased).
38. Broadcast by Mr William Joyce,

'Views on the News', at 10.30 p.m. from Breslau in English, 5 July. Among the papers of the late Lieutenant-General Sir N. M. Mason-Macfarlane, who was Head of the British Military Mission in Moscow, is his description of Russian comments on the material they received: 'The Russian reactions were only what was to be expected. No word of appreciation for the ghastly losses sustained by our northern convoys. On the contrary, the material we provided was severely criticized and at a Press Luncheon one day the notorious Ilya Ehrenburg said that he wished that we would send less stuff but of a better quality. . . . It didn't help matters when the first batch of Valentine and Matilda tanks which were sent by the northern sea route to Archangel arrived with burst cylinder blocks as the radiators had never been emptied before the start of their Arctic trip. Neither did it help that the compressors of the Matildas all failed at low temperatures. The Russian comments on the power/weight ratios of our tanks, the narrowness of their tracks and the utter inadequacy of their two-pounder guns were difficult to counter.' Mason-Macfarlane held the view that firmer political commitments should have been exacted from the Russians in return for the aid they received from the West.
39. Tovey's Report.
40. Hamilton's Final Report.
41. G. Winn, op. cit., p. 99.
42. German Naval Staff War Diary.
43. Hamilton's Final Report. USS *Washington*'s Report of Proceedings, and War Diary of Commander, Task Force 99, Admiral Giffen, 6 July.

44. Signal, DOD(H) for First Sea Lord, to SBNO North Russia, SBNO Archangel, Admiral Miles and C-in-C Home Fleet, originating at 2.31 a.m., 6 July. A similar signal is quoted by G. Winn, op. cit., p. 106.
45. Signal, Most Immediate, Most Secret, from DOD(H) for First Sea Lord to Escorts of PQ.17, repeated to SBNO North Russia, SBNO Archangel, C-in-C Home Fleet, originating at 2.30 a.m., 6 July, Cf. G. Winn, op. cit., p. 102.
46. Tovey's Report. Hamilton's Final Report.
47. Interview with Mr Leo Gradwell (*Ayrshire*), March 1963. He learned of the signals only when shown them in Archangel.
48. Summary of signals kept by Lieutenant Caradus (*La Malouine*).
49. Caradus Diary, 5–6 July.
50. Interview with Mr E. A. Leycock, November 1962. Commodore Dowding's Report. *Pankraft*'s Armed Guard Report.
51. Schmundt's War Diary. German Naval Staff War Diary.
52. Signal, C.S. One (Hamilton) to *Norfolk, Wichita* and *Tuscaloosa*, originating at 9.47 p.m., 6 July. Also Appendix to letter, Hamilton to Tovey, 6 July. Also reproduced in *Wichita*'s War Diary.
53. Signal, *Norfolk* to C.S. One, received at 10.36 p.m., 6 July.
54. Signal, *Wichita* to C.S. One, received at 10.40 p.m., 6 July.
55. Signal, C.S. One to *Norfolk*, despatched at 10.40 p.m., 6 July.
56. Signal, C.S. One to *Wichita, Tuscaloosa*, C.D.S.8 (Captain Moon), *Wainwright, Rowan*, despatched at 10.44 p.m., 6 July.

Chapter 7: The New Land—pages 203–68

1. *The Arctic Pilot* (HMSO), Volume I, p. 165.
2. *Britomart*'s Report.

3. Interview with Commander S. S. Stammwitz, March 1963. Information from Mr W. A. Dunk, June 1962.

4. Caradus Diary.
5. G. Winn, op. cit., p. 108.
6. *Hoosier*'s Armed Guard Report.
7. *El Capitán*'s Armed Guard Report, and interview with Captain Rupert Hull, January 1963. *Benjamin Harrison*'s Armed Guard Report.
8. Interview with Surgeon-Lieutenant N. McCallum, January 1963.
9. *Zamalek*'s Master's log.
10. *Olopana*'s Report.
11. German Naval Staff War Diary, 6 July. Schmundt's War Diary, 6 July. German Air Staff Brief Report, 6 July.
12. *Daniel Morgan*'s Armed Guard Report.
13. *John Witherspoon*'s Armed Guard Report.
14. *U-255*'s torpedo log.
15. Diary of Mr Nathaniel E. Platt, 6 July.
16. *U-88*'s Brief Report, 12 July.
17. *Pan Atlantic*'s Armed Guard Report.
18. *U-703*'s torpedo logs. Schmundt's War Diary.
19. Schmundt's War Diary, 6 July.
20. Summary of Operations against PQ.17, in Fifth Air Force War Diary.
21. German Naval Staff War Diary, 6 July.
22. Schmundt's War Diary, 7 July.
23. Diary of *Bellingham*'s Second Officer, 7 July. *Bellingham*'s Armed Guard Report. Information from Mr George Bissilf, July 1962.
24. *Alcoa Ranger*'s Armed Guard Report.
25. Captain F. W. Harvey's Diary. *Empire Tide*'s Voyage Report. *Olopana*'s Voyage Report. Cf. Royal Mail Line's official history, *Eight Bells*, by T. A. Bushell.
26. Interview with Lieutenant-Commander J. G. Rankin, January 1963. Information from Rear-Admiral J. H. F. Crombie, April 1963. Interview with Captain Guy O. Maund, April 1963.
27. Interview with Rear-Admiral Sir R. H. L. Bevan.
28. BBC Monitoring Report No. 1085.

Broadcast from Luxemburg in German for Germany, 2 p.m., 7 July.
29. *OKW Sondermeldung*.
30. *Wichita*'s signal log.
31. Caradus Diary, 7 July.
32. *Zamalek*'s Master's Log. *Britomart*'s Report.
33. Information from Mr W. A. Dunk, April 1962.
34. *U-355*'s Brief Report, 12 July.
35. *U-355*'s torpedo log.
36. Diary of Mr Needham Forth, 7 July.
37. Interview with Captain S. J. Gordon, December 1962.
38. Interview with Mr R. B. Fearnside, December 1962.
39. Interview with Mr Needham Forth, December 1962.
40. Other documents used were Fearnside's Diary; *Olopana*'s and *Empire Tide*'s Voyage Reports, and the latter's Official Log, and *Hartlebury*'s C & D List.
41. William Joyce, speaking in English, broadcast from Breslau in English at 10.30 p.m., 7 July.
42. Wilhelmstrasse comment, quoted in broadcast from Calais in English, 7.30 p.m., 7 July.
43. German Naval Staff War Diary. Schmundt's War Diary.
44. Summary of statements by *Olopana*'s survivors.
45. Diary of *Bellingham*'s Second Officer, I. J. Anderson, 8 July.
46. *Bellingham*'s Armed Guard Report.
47. Bormann's notes on Hitler's lunchtime conversation, 8 July. Reproduced in *Hitlers Tischgespräche*.
48. Fairbanks Diary, 7 July. Under 5 July, 1942, the War Diary of Iceland Naval Operating Base records: 'At 2040, QP.13 and British escorts struck the minefield off the North-West tip of Iceland. O-in-C unable to determine exact location of safe channel. Due to 'thick' weather for past 48 hours and faulty instruments convoy entered minefield. Ships sunk were: *Hybert* (US), *Massmar* (US), *Heffron* (US), *John Randolph* (US), *Rodina* (Rus.), and *Niger* (Bf.). Ships

damaged were: *Richard H. Lee* (US), *Exterminator* (Pan.), and *Capira* (Pan.). All damaged ships were brought to port and repaired. Forward portion of *John Randolph* (US) from 15′ abaft No. 2 hold towed to Onundafjordur and beached. Survivors landed and hospitalized where necessary.'
49. Letter, Hamilton to Tovey, 6 July (not delivered until the 7th).
50. Letter, Captain Bellars to Hamilton, 8 July.
51. Letter, Hamilton to Tovey, 9 July.
52. Interview with Vice-Admiral R. M. Servaes, March 1963.
53. Interview with Mr J. Waterhouse, November 1962.
54. William Joyce, 'Views of the News', Breslau in English, 10.30 p.m., 8 July.
55. New British Broadcasting Station, broadcasting at 8.30, 9.30 and 10.30 p.m., 8 July.
56. Tovey *Despatch.*
57. Hansard, House of Commons, *Official Report*, vol. 381, columns 951–4, 9 July. The shipping Debate was held in Secret Session on 16 July, after which the only published statement was, 'The House considered the shipping situation and heard a statement from the Government.' *Official Report*, vol. 381, column 1376; see also columns 1361 and 1363. The BBC's confidential Monitoring Report warned the Government that during 9 July 'full propaganda use was made of the fact that the Commons Debate on the Shipping Situation was now to be held in Secret Session. (German Home Stations, 8 p.m., Italian Home Stations, 10.45 p.m., Calais in English, 9.45 p.m.)
58. Schmundt's War Diary, Signals Appendix.
59. Schmundt's War Diary, 9 July.
60. German Naval Staff War Diary.
61. Interview with Captain Rupert Hull, First Officer of *El Capitán*, January 1963.
62. Moscow Radio in Russian, 8 a.m., 9 July.
63. Schmundt's War Diary, and its Signals Appendix.

64. *Zamalek*'s Voyage Reports and Master's Log. Interview with Captain Owen C. Morris, February 1963.
65. Fifth Air Force War Diary.
66. German Air Staff Brief Report, 9 July. Fifth Air Force War Diary. German Naval Staff War Diary.
67. *Hoosier*'s Armed Guard Report.
68. Information from Lieutenant John F. Geisse (*Tuscaloosa*), April 1962.
69. *El Capitán*'s Armed Guard Report. Cf. James Caradus' article, 'Convoy Will Scatter', in the Auckland *Weekly News*, 22 August 1962.
70. Schmundt's War Diary, 10 July.
71. *Zamalek*'s Master's Log and Official Logbook. *Zamalek*'s Report. Interviews with Captain O. C. Morris, February 1963, Captain T. G. Lennard (Second Officer) and Surgeon-Lieutenant N. McCallum, February 1963.
72. Caradus Diary. The bombing is reported in *El Capitán*'s and *John Witherspoon*'s Armed Guard Reports.
73. Letter, Captain John Thevik to Captain Rupert Hull, 7 December 1955.
74. *Britomart*'s Report. German Air Staff Brief Report, 10 July. Summary in Fifth Air Force War Diary.
75. Caradus Diary, 10 July. Also, manuscript by James Caradus.
76. *Samuel Chase*'s Armed Guard Report.
77. *Ocean Freedom*'s Official Log.
78. German Naval Staff War Diary, 10 July.
79. BBC Monitoring Report No. 1089, issued 11 July.
80. *Daniel Morgan*'s Armed Guard Report.
81. Commodore J. C. K. Dowding's Report, 13 July. Quoted in Roskill, op. cit., p. 143.
82. Information from Mr James E. Akins, December 1962. Summary of statements by *Carlton*'s survivors.
83. Signal, Stumpff to Göring, 12 July, in Fifth Air Force War Diary.
84. Fifth Air Force War Diary, 10 July. Complete Report on the Operations against PQ.17.
85. Private Diary of Admiral Sir

Geoffrey Miles, 11 July 1942. Interview with Admiral Miles, February 1963.

86. The Earl of Avon: *The Eden Memoirs*, vol. II: *The Reckoning* (Cassell, 1965), pp. 376–7. Eden was evidently writing from *aides-mémoires* written at the time. Cf. Sir Llewellyn Woodward, *British Foreign Policy in the Second World War* (HMSO), p. 198.

87. 'From the Ambassador's Notes', by Ivan M. Maisky, published in *Novye Mir*, Moscow, No. 7, July 1965. A version of these has been published (1967) by Hutchinson, London, but I have preferred my own translation.

Chapter 8: First Back from Hell—pages 269–85

1. Based also on interviews with Mr Leo Gradwell, February and March 1963.
2. Cf. chapter on convoying in ice and ice-navigation in *Arctic Pilot*, vol. I, p. 33 *passim* (1959 edition).
3. Letters, Gradwell to SBNO North Russia and others, 13 and 26 July.
4. *Empire Tide*'s Voyage Report. T. A. Bushell, *Eight Bells*.
5. *Olopana*'s Voyage Report.
6. *Empire Tide*'s Voyage Report. *Empire Tide*'s Official Log.
7. Letter, Gradwell to British naval authorities in north Russia, 13 July.
8. Diary of Admiral Golovko, Russian text published in Moscow in 1960: *Vmeste s'Flotom*, by Admiral A. G. Golovko. See especially pp. 99–115, the chapter entitled, 'Istoriya PQ.17', where he recounts in lurid detail the Russian submarine's torpedo-attack on *Tirpitz*. An English edition has since been published under the title *With the Red Fleet* (Putnam, 1965).
9. Schmundt's War Diary, 13 July. Schmundt's summary of U-boat operations, and his appreciation of future convoy operations (appendix to his War Diary). Information from Commander R. Reche and Herr Hugo Deiring.
10. Reche wrote an account of *U-255*'s operations in Harald Busch's *So War der U-Bootkrieg* (Bielefeld, 1957). The above incident is described in part on pp. 311–12. Detailed descriptions of the secret Allied papers captured in *Paulus Potter* were given in a telegram from Schmundt to Berlin at 7.10 p.m.

on 19 July (in the German Admiralty's *Knight's Move* file, PG/32586, Film T-41-B). They included the convoy disposition and Sailing Orders issued by the Naval Control Service Officer, Iceland, which listed the minefields and the correct approach routes to Archangel; the ship's log; a volume entitled, 'Confidential Admiralty Merchant Shipping Instructions'; two volumes of 'Merchant Ships Signal Books 1941'; the 'Merchant Ships Code' in use for radio signals since 1 July 1942; 'Signal Codes for Use with Aircraft', and many similar documents. These were forwarded by courier to the German naval radio monitoring service for immediate exploitation.

11. *U-255*'s torpedo log.
12. German Naval Staff War Diary, 13 July.
13. Summary from torpedo logs of all submarines present.
14. *Olopana*'s Voyage Report. *Empire Tide*'s Voyage Report. *Empire Tide*'s Official Logbook. T. A. Bushell, *Eight Bells*.
15. Diary of Captain F. W. Harvey, Master of *Empire Tide*.
16. Interview with Commander S. S. Stammwitz (to whom Frankel related this), March 1963.
17. Interview with Captain Guy O. Maund, April 1963.
18. Captain Harvey's Report to Royal Mail Lines.
19. Copy of 'Certificate' supplied to me by Captain Mervyn Stone (*Olopana*).
20. Caradus Diary, 15 July.

21. Interview with Lieutenant-Commander J. G. Rankin, January 1963. Signal, Captain Frankel, Archangel, to Chief of Naval Operations, Washington, 18 July.
22. Caradus Diary.

Chapter 9: Inquest—pages 286–301

1. Telegram, Churchill to Stalin, 17 July (published in Churchill: *Second World War*, vol. IV, pp. 239–41).
2. Telegram, Stalin to Churchill, 23 July (Churchill: op. cit., pp. 241–2).
3. Führer Naval Conference, 26 August; in file PG/31762 (Film T-413-B). Captain Frankel reported the arrival of *Winston-Salem* in a cable to Washington on 30 July. He added: 'Crew co-operated fully.'
4. Interview with Surgeon-Lieutenant N. McCallum, January 1963.
5. Statement by *Troubadour*'s Armed Guard officer, 26 March 1945.
6. Interview with Captain Rupert F. Hull, January 1963.
7. Summary of statements by *Silver Sword*'s survivors, 2 November 1942.
8. Cable from Captain Frankel to Washington, 16 September.
9. Caradus Diary, 29 July.
10. Tovey *Despatch*.
11. Diary of Vice-Admiral Sir Godfrey Miles, 5–8 July 1942. Also interview with him, February 1963. On 27 July 1942, the Assistant US Naval Attaché, Archangel, cabled to Washington: 'There are now 1,200 survivors here of all nationalities, 500 of which are American.'
12. Interview with Mr Thomas Goodwin, November 1962, and other *Earlston* survivors.
13. English-language propaganda broadcast from Breslau at 11.30 p.m., 21 July.
14. Information from Mr James E. Akins, December 1962. The first definite news to reach the US authorities of the fate of *Carlton* was a postcard received from Captain Hansen by his former trade union officials in Galveston: 'The s/s *Carlton* was torpedoed and sank south of Spitzbergen on July 5, 1942. I lost four men and all my records including my Skipper's Certificate. Please keep one on ice for my return. All is well here.' Confirmatory data on the loss of the troop transport *Wuri*, and its casualties, were obtained from the German Naval Staff War Diary, 17 and 20 August 1942. File PG/32056 (Film T-15).
15. Maisky's memoirs published in *Novye Mir*, Moscow, No. 7, 1965.
16. House of Commons *Official Report*, vol. 382, col. 489.
17. Letter from Vernon L. Frank to Mrs Sarah A. Frank, Philadelphia, postmarked 14 December 1942; uncensored original in US naval archives.
18. The statement was published in House of Commons *Official Report*, vol. 431, cols. 1777–1781. Cf. *The Times*, 16 December 1946.
19. The Russian accusations were made in an article by Pavel Barvinchenko published in *Vodny Transport*, Moscow. The Admiralty *démenti* was quoted by the *Daily Telegraph*, 26 December 1962.
20. Information from Mr James Bruce, 1962. *Olopana*'s Voyage Report. *The Times*, 29 September 1942.
21. Hamilton, letter home, 14 July.
22. Published in Churchill, op. cit., pp. 237–8. Churchill would by then probably have read Tovey's Report, which was no more judiciously worded.
23. Roskill, op. cit., p. 144.
24. Churchill, op. cit., p. 238.
25. Hamilton's Final Report.
26. Letter, Hamilton to Admiral Sir James Somerville, C-in-C Eastern Fleet, 30 September 1942 (pencil draft).

27. Letter, Tovey to Hamilton, 20 September 1942.
28. After Grand-Admiral Raeder's resignation, Hitler continued to fulminate about the orders issued by the Naval Staff and their 'over cautious leadership'. These criticisms reached the Naval Staff, who drew up a memorandum, on 13 February 1943, in which they sought to assess how far the orders and directives they had issued had been in accordance with Hitler's often repeated comments like, 'we cannot afford any loss of prestige at this moment' and 'the loss of our ships must be avoided at all costs'. The memorandum contained a number of quotations from the War Diary of Naval Group North about *The Knight's Move*—around which operation the whole Raeder-Hitler controversy centred. It cited the principles which the Führer had laid down at his conferences with Raeder on 12 March and 15 June 1942, urging extreme caution and the elimination of any possibility of surprise air attack on the German heavy warships; but in the end, the memorandum concluded that the documents in the Naval Staff's files were not alone sufficient to remove responsibility for the battle fleet's behaviour from Raeder's shoulders. The memorandum (which is in file PG/31747, Film T-353-B) ended with the words: 'These comments are herewith placed on record to preserve them for History.'

INDEX

Aalborg, 162

Aasfiord, 70

Admiral Hipper (heavy cruiser; Captain Meisel), 21, 26, 28, 39–40, 59, 77, 92, 243; leaves for Norway, 10; at Trondheim, 19; leaves Trondheim, 66–7, 70, 72; at Altenfiord, 95; at sea, 149, 163

Admiral Scheer (heavy cruiser), 5, 31, 40, 58–9, 77, 92, 114–15, 129; at Narvik, 19, 26, 38; Admiral Kummetz's flag transferred to, 67; at Altenfiord, 95; at sea, 149, 163

Admiralty, 2, 3, 6, 8, 32, 71, 82, 88, 91, 101, 147, 217, 299; intervenes in Home Fleet operations, 8; given an impossible task by the Cabinet, 33; instructions to Tovey and Hamilton, 41–2, Appendix I (pp. 303–4); and close cruiser support, 49; informs Hamilton that convoy has been sighted by U-boat, 57–8; sends 'Home Fleet Operational' signal, 68; sends order to sail north of Bear Island, 72; informs convoy escort of shadowing units, 76; signals that German aircraft are using beacon procedure, 80–1; uncertain of position of German heavy ships, 91–2; orders Hamilton to proceed eastward at discretion, 93, 94; and patrols along Norwegian coast, 95; orders cruiser force westward, 113, 116; orders convoy to scatter, 114–15, 135, 138; informs Hamilton that German battleships are at Altenfiord, 135; suggests that Home Fleet engage *Tirpitz*, 165; signal to Tovey regarding his southwesterly course, 194; signal to Tovey on *Victorious* engaging *Tirpitz*, 195; warns of possible surface attack on scattered convoy, 197; temporarily suspends convoys, 268, 286; formal statement in reply to Soviet allegations, 297

Admiralty Peninsula, Novaya Zemlya, 152, 187

Akins, James E. (of the *Carlton*), 16–18, 143–5, 159, 291–3

Alafusov, Admiral (Deputy Chief of Russian Naval Staff), 137–8, 268

Albacore aircraft, 6, 7, 195

Alcoa Ranger (American merchantman; Lieut.-Commander Hjalmar Christophsen), 157–8, 207, 245, 273, 279; torpedoed and sunk, 216–17, 223; survivors, 289

Aldersdale (British oiler; Captain Archibald Hobson), 47–8, 55, 61, 71, 87, 99, 108, 126, 170, 179; immobilized, 179–81; sunk, 223

Alexander, A. V. (First Lord of the Admiralty), 294, 295, 299

Alexandria, 1, 221

Allen, Captain G. R. G., 92, 95

Allied Intelligence, 115; appreciates German plans for attacking PQ.17, 33

Altenfiord, 21, 26, 96; German battle fleet at, 66, 73, 75*n*., 77–9, 90, 95, 115, 135, 147; battle fleet leaves, 148, 149; battle fleet returns, 169

American Task Force 99, 34

Archangel, 32*n*., 39, 41, 47, 54, 88, 95, 131, 143, 161, 204, 221–2, 238, 240, 246, 265, 269–70, 278, 280, 282; Naval Control in, 177; first convoy vessel arrives at, 217; the *Zamalek* convoy enters, 265–6; convoy survivors in, 287–9

Atlantik (German tug), 30

Ayrshire (Asdic trawler; Lieutenant Leo Gradwell), 45, 109, 126, 131, 207, 222, 269–73, 287, 288–9

Azerbaijan (Russian tanker), 63, 109–11, 277, 287; torpedoed, 107, 108*n*.

Banak airfield, 11*n*., 71; squadron of *KG.26*, 62, 149; *KG.30*, 175, 253–4, 256–7, 264

Index

Matshar radio station, Novaya Zemlya, 203
Matson Navigation Company, 236
Maund, Captain G. O. (SBNO at Archangel), 197, 217–18, 266, 273n., 280–2, 289
Mazuruk, Captain I. P., 275–7, 280
Meisel, Captain, 169
Melville, USS (depot ship), 47
MERSIGS code books, 49
Miles, Rear-Admiral Sir Geoffrey (head of British naval mission in Moscow), 137–8, 197, 268, 289
Miller, Edward (Chief Engineer, River Afton), 191–2, 194n.
Moller Bay (Mali Karmakulski), Novaya Zemlya, 206, 214–16, 223, 273, 281, 284–5
Molotovosk, 266
Moon, Captain D. P., USN, 34, 99, 101–2, 126
Mooney, Chief Engineer T. J. (Carlton), 160, 163
Moore, Vice-Admiral Sir H. R. (Vice-Chief of Naval Staff), 92, 117, 120
Morris, Captain Owen, 43, 86–7, 112, 178–80, 252–3, 256–9, 261, 265; awarded the DSO, 180n., 264n.
Mortensen, Captain S., 238
Mottram, Lieut.-Commander W. R., 180
Murman (ice-breaker), 277
Murmansk, 3, 9, 13, 15, 16, 50, 161, 254, 264, 276, 278, 289n.; air raid damage, 53

Näröy Sound, 66
Narvik, German naval base at, 15, 19, 25–6, 30, 38, 55–6, 66, 69, 114, 135, 169, 278, 279
Nash, Captain C. E., 86, 87
Navarino (British merchantman), 107, 109, 110, 131; torpedoed, 105–6, 139; abandoned and sunk, 111–12
Newstead, Lieutenant P. E., 121
Noel-Baker, Philip, 297
Nordkyn, 164
Norfolk, HMS (cruiser; Captain E. G. H. Bellars), 34–6, 89, 113, 123, 134, 196–7, 202, 219, 241, 288, 289n.
North Atlantic convoys, 297
North Cape, 10, 19, 21, 71, 96, 163, 184
North Gusini Light, Novaya Zemlya, 274

Northern Gem (trawler; Lieutenant W. G. Mullender), 101, 206, 247
Northern Spray (trawler), 17
Northey, Lieutenant Adrian, 65
Norway: Germans strengthen coastal defences, 4; transfer of heavy warships to, 4; submarines stationed along coast of, 14–15; German air force in, 15, 19
Novaya Zemlya, 152–3, 168, 171, 176, 180–1, 187, 193, 201–2, 203ff., 271, 279, 283, 289

Obsiedya Bay, Novaya Zemlya, 237
Ocean Freedom (British merchantman; Captain Walker), 179–81, 203, 245, 247, 253; bombed and crippled, 261, 263
OKW. See German High Command
Olopana (American freighter; Captain Mervyn C. Stone), 174, 176–7, 185, 189, 207–8, 214, 216, 273; torpedoed and sunk, 236–7; survivors on a raft reach Novaya Zemlya, 273–4, 277, 279, 281; survivors in Archangel, 289n.
Operational Intelligence Centre (O.I.C.), Admiralty, 115–17, 120–1
Orem, Commander (Wichita's Executive Officer), 38, 45
Oslo, 162, 293; German Fifth Air Force base on, 26

P-614 (HM submarine; Lieutenant D. J. Beckley), 41, 108, 121
P-615 (HM submarine; Lieutenant P. E. Newstead), 41, 121
Palomares (anti-aircraft ship; Captain J. H. Jauncey), 54, 127, 130–1, 150–1, 179–80, 201, 203–5, 208, 219, 222, 247, 258, 288
Pan Atlantic (American merchantman; Captain J. O. Sieber), bombed and sunk, 210
Pankraft (American merchantman; Captain Jacob Jacobson), 200, 207, 270; bombed and abandoned, 185–9
Pascoe, Captain John, 171, 174–7, 290
Paulus Potter (Dutch merchantman; Captain Sissingh), 171, 176–7, 236; abandoned, 175; sunk, 278; survivors, 279, 285

Index

'*Pedestal*' convoy to Malta, 297

Pelt, Fireman W. (*Carlton*), 145

Pelworm (German tug), 30

Peter Kerr (Liberty ship; Captain William H. Butler), 142, 181; bombed and abandoned, 170–1; survivors, 289–90

Petsamo, German air base at, 151, 263

Petter, Lieutenant Frank (of *La Malouine*), 124

Polar Geophysical Laboratory, Novaya Zemlya, 203

Polyarnoe, Russian naval base at, 122*n*.

Pomorska Bay, Novaya Zemlya, 205, 207

Poppy, HMS (corvette; Lieutenant N. K. Boyd), 86, 130, 150, 204, 248, 255, 283–4

Pound, Admiral Sir Dudley (First Sea Lord), 96, 138, 217–18, 268; warns Cabinet Defence Committee of possible severe losses to convoys, 11; on convoys as a 'regular millstone', 14; and possibility of scattering the convoy, 49, 92–3; and close cruiser support, 49; interviews Captain Allen, 92; seeks information on *Tirpitz*, 115; decides to move cruiser force westward, 116; decides to disperse convoy, 117, 120–1; Churchill's excuses for, 127; and the inquiry into the disaster, 294–5; his explanation to the Cabinet, 299

Pozarica (anti-aircraft ship; Captain E. D. W. Lawford), 121, 131, 150–1, 156, 184, 187–8, 198–9, 204–5, 248*n*., 261, 288

PQ.8, 2

PQ.13, 10

PQ.15, 12, 15

PQ.16, 15–18, 22, 25, 70, 143, 243

PQ.17, 15, 19, 20, 21; the American crews, 31–2; mutiny on the *Troubadour*, 32; awaits sailing orders, 32–3; expectation of surface attack, 33–4; distant covering force, 34, 39; cruiser covering force, 34–5, 37–9, 41–2, 50; close escort, 35, 41, 48; the operation as a trap for the *Tirpitz*, 39–40; wireless silence imposed, 40–1; main convoy conference, 42–5; leaves Hvalfiord, 46–7; individual ships

poorly armed, 47–8; final escort conference, 48–9; last conference, 50–1; German air reconnaissance, 54–5; Broome's wireless signals reveal convoy to Germans, 55; sighted by aircraft and U-boats, 55–61, 67–9; attacked by torpedo-bombers, and *Christopher Newport* lost, 62–3, 65–6, 83, 85–9, 93–4; U-boats close in, 79–81, 83, 85; layout of ships (diagram), 84; torpedo-bombers strike three more ships, 97–113, 153; Admiralty orders convoy to scatter, 113–15, 123, 135, 138; cruiser and close escort withdrawn, 123–30, 135–6, 241; the RN vessels left with convoy, 130–1; Gradwell steers N.-W. with *Ayrshire* and three other ships, 131–3, 269–70; U-boat attacks, and loss of the *Carlton*, 140–5; *Daniel Morgan* and *Honomu* sunk, 152–6; plight of the solitary ships and survivors, 156–63; attacked by dive-bombers, 170–1, 174; position after the scatter (map), 172–3; loss of *Washington*, *Bolton Castle* and *Paulus Potter*, 174–6; 150 seamen drift for weeks in open boats, 176–7; rescue ships under attack, and loss of the *Aldersdale*, 177–81; U-boats sink the *Earlston*, 181–3; Germans bomb their own submarine, 183–4; loss of *Pankraft* and *River Afton*, 184–94; Admiralty warning of possible surface attack, 197, 199; anti-aircraft ships expect imminent destruction, 198–200; *River Afton*'s survivors picked up, 200–1; RN vessels reach Matochkin Strait, 203–7; ships in the Strait spotted by a Focke-Wulf, 207–8; loss of the *John Witherspoon*, 208–10; *Pan Atlantic* sunk, 210; U-boat patrols and sightings, 211, 213, 215–16; the stragglers make for Novaya Zemlya, 214–15; loss of the *Alcoa Ranger*, 216–17; first ship to reach north Russia, 217; the search for survivors, 217–18; special broadcast on German radio, 218–19; conference in the Strait, 219, 221; the convoy leaves for Archangel, 221–3; Dowding requests fighter protection,